INSURRECTION

ROAD TO THE BREAKING
BOOK 5

CHRIS BENNETT

Insurrection is a work of historical fiction. Apart from well-documented actual people, events, and places that figure in the narrative, all names, characters, places, and incidents are the products of the author's imagination, or are used fictitiously. Any resemblance to current events, places, or living persons, is entirely coincidental.

Insurrection

Copyright © Christopher A. Bennett – 2021

ISBN: 978-1-955100-01-4 (Trade Paperback)
ISBN: 978-1-955100-02-1 (eBook)

Cover Image Photo:

"Union Soldier Kneeling, Firing Rifle"
Copyright © Philip Halling

Publisher's Cataloging-In-Publication Data
(Prepared by The Donohue Group, Inc.)

Names: Bennett, Chris (Chris Arthur), 1959- author.
Title: Insurrection / Chris Bennett.
Description: [North Bend, Washington] : [CPB Publishing, LLC], [2021] I Series: Road to the breaking ; book 5
Identifiers: ISBN 9781955100014 (trade paperback) I ISBN 9781955100021 (ebook)
Subjects: LCSH: United States. Army--Officers--History--19th century--Fiction. I United States--History--Civil War, 1861-1865--Fiction. I Revolutions--Virginia--Fiction. I Enemies--Virginia--Fiction. I Statehood (American politics)--Fiction. I LCGFT: Historical fiction.
Classification: LCC PS3602.E66446 I57 2021 (print) I LCC PS3602.E66446 (ebook) I DDC 813/.6--dc23

To sign up for a
no-spam newsletter
about
ROAD TO THE BREAKING
and
exclusive free bonus material
visit my website:

http://www.ChrisABennett.com

Insurrection [in-suh-**rek**-shuhn] noun:
A violent uprising against the
government or other authority; a
mutiny; a rebellion.

DEDICATION

To my mother
Marilyn (Pember) Bennett;
my most dedicated reader
and
most avid promoter of my series!
I love you, Mom.

Contents

"Mr. Wiggins ...
I want it bloody;
the bloodier the better.
Teach these oath-breakers
what happens to
traitors and thieves."

– Nathan Chambers

Chapter I. Battle of Rich Mountain

"We heard no noise from our front,
and had no time to think the reason why."
– Brigadier General William S. Rosecrans, U.S. Army,
(on Major General George McClellan's failure
to support his flanking attack as promised)

Thursday July 11, 1861 – Randolph County, Virginia:

"Well, Billy?"

"Enemy pickets, two dozen or more, Captain. Spread in a line a few hundred yards below us just in front of a low fence line. Hiding behind rocks, trees, and fallen logs. Not dug in. No fortifications."

"So ... not been here long. Anything else?"

"We saw the Hart farmhouse further down the hill but couldn't see if there are men inside. Through the rain I could see another group of ... hmm ... twenty or so gathered in a group a few hundred yards back across a road. Not sure what they were doing—too much rain to see."

"I assume the enemy's aware of us?"

"Pickets alert and watchful, bayonets fixed, rifles pointed our direction. So yes, they expect to entertain guests today, Captain," Billy smiled at his own attempted humor, but Nathan wasn't in the mood for it.

"*Damn it!* Untrained, inexperienced, over-eager officers ... puffed up with their own importance! Blowing bugles and lighting fires to start a covert flanking march! *Idiots!* Likely half the countryside knows we're here!"

"Yes, Captain, it was ... *foolish.*"

"Well, nothing to be done for it, now," Nathan sighed.

He pulled the collar of his overcoat tighter in a vain attempt to staunch the flow of cold rainwater streaming down the back of his neck. Though it was now midafternoon, dark rainclouds and a

1

heavy downpour made for a cold, miserable day, adding to his ill humor.

And to make matters worse, Harry the Dog chose that moment to shake the accumulated rainwater from his prodigious coat. It splattered whatever part of his master might have still been dry, along with everyone else within a five-foot radius. Nathan spit a knot of wet fur from his mouth and scowled at Harry. Harry seemed unconcerned; his tongue lolled out to the side as he gazed back at his master.

"Mr. Hart, anything to add?" he eyed the young civilian standing next to Billy. David Hart was lean and fair haired; Nathan figured him for not yet twenty years old. But he'd proved vigorous and resourceful leading them up the back trails on their long, difficult hike up the mountain.

"Me and your Indian scout ..." Hart began.

"*Mr. Creek,*" Nathan corrected him.

"Uh, sorry ... *Mr. Creek* ... I'm not so good with names ..." he said, looking at Billy apologetically. Billy just smiled and shrugged.

"Anyways, me and *Mr. Creek* crept to within a few dozen yards of the enemy, like he says. I reckon there's more of 'em up inside the house, though we never saw any. Papa built her sturdy with solid log walls, so if they's in there I expect they'll be hell to root out."

"Hmm. What about your folks?"

"Long gone by now, I'm sure. They've no love for rebs ... they'd not stick around with them bastards roaming all about the farm and a battle likely brewing. Figure they've headed off to town until the whole thing blows over."

"Let's hope so. We'd not like to see good loyal Unionists hurt in the crossfire."

"I'll say *amen* to that, Mr. Chambers."

"What's the terrain like between here and your folks' farmhouse?"

"It's fairly steep, sir, for about the next ... oh, two hundred yards or so. Thick woods mostly, like this-here," he gestured toward the large trees surrounding their current position,

2

huddled behind a small rock outcropping at the crest of a rise. From here they would have had a good view of the valley below if it weren't for all the trees blocking the view.

"Heavy underbrush most of the way with a few scattered openings," he continued, "Then there's a four-foot-high split-rail fence where it levels off into a pasture. The farmhouse is maybe ... fifty yards from the fence. A couple hundred yards beyond the house there's the road, running east-west. On the other side of the road it rises again, though not as steeply. There's less trees and it's more open on that far side. That's where the other group of men Mr. Creek mentioned was huddled together."

Nathan nodded and said, "And a couple miles or so past that to the northwest is their main fort made of logs, I understand, from what General McClellan said yesterday."

He was thoughtful for a moment. Then looked over at Tom and Jim where they huddled a few feet away to his right, rainwater streaming off the brims of their hats, "Gentlemen, let's give these rebels what they've been asking for, shall we?"

But it was young Lieutenant Brantley who answered, "I will remind you, Mr. Chambers, I'm in command here. You are simply a civilian advisor."

Nathan turned to face Brantley. The young man, more than ten years Nathan's junior, stood shivering, arms clasped tightly to his chest. The pristine officer's uniform he'd donned at the start of their march, in the dark pre-dawn more than twelve hours ago, was now soaked through and badly soiled from the long scramble up the mountain and through the underbrush. Brantley had said little up until now, leaving Nathan as de facto commander of the scouting and skirmishing party ever since they'd split off from the main column just after daybreak.

"Certainly, Lieutenant, I stand corrected. What are *your* orders for the men, may I ask ... *sir?*" he resisted the urge to infuse the question with heavy sarcasm.

"Our orders were to scout the enemy and report back on their position. We were *not* instructed to engage them, Mr. Chambers. I intend to carry out my orders."

3

"You mean to only *report* their position, Mr. Brantley? Those orders assumed we still held the element of surprise. Clearly that's no longer the case."

"Those are still my orders, sir."

"So you don't mean to fight them?" Nathan growled, "Mr. Brantley, these *secess* bastards stole my home and murdered a number of my men. I mean to pay them back ... *with interest!*"

"I hear you sir, but—"

"But what, Lieutenant?"

"They ... they haven't fired on us yet, Mr. Chambers. Nobody's been hurt so far. They're Americans too, like us ... *aren't they?* Perhaps if they see we've got 'em outnumbered they'll think better of it and just ... give it up. Go home peaceful-like, maybe. Don't you think, sir?"

Nathan nodded his head noncommittally but didn't immediately answer. He reached inside his coat and pulled out a cigar, and then a match.

After he lit the cigar, and blew several puffs up through the downpour, he said, "Mr. Brantley ... in my experience nobody ever won a war without hard fighting. Me and my men are here to do just that. If I'm your 'advisor,' then I *advise* you to join us. How will it look if us 'civilians' rout the pickets and take the house from the enemy while you and your men are back reporting their position to the general—a position they will no longer hold, I might add?"

Brantley stared back at him, open-mouthed.

"Lieutenant ... nobody ever got a medal pinned on him for following orders. He got it for taking the battle to the enemy. These *secess* rebels have stolen our property, broken our laws, and killed our people. Their officers have broken a solemn vow to defend our country—they'd rather tear it apart. They must be fought where found and killed when necessary. In war there must be no hesitation, Lieutenant."

Nathan and Brantley locked eyes for a long moment. Finally, Brantley nodded.

"Good. Send a couple of your men back, if you would, to report the enemy's troop disposition and our *present* position to

4

the general. Have them tell him we are preparing to engage the enemy's pickets on this side, after which we'll press the assault across the road and on the farmhouse."

Then Tom added, "And ... do just ask him to kindly come along and join the party with the rest of his brigade. At the general's leisure and convenience, of course."

Brantley nodded, then called over two of his privates to carry out the mission.

"Mr. Wiggins ... organize our assault."

"Yes, sir!"

"And Jim ..."

"Sir?"

"I want it bloody ... the bloodier the better. Teach these oath-breakers what happens to traitors and thieves, and show these young recruits what it means to fight a *real* battle."

"With pleasure, sir!" Jim snapped a salute and smiled broadly for the first time that afternoon, despite being soaked to the bone, and shivering with cold. Big Stan, who'd crouched next to Jim so he could listen in on the discussion, broke into a grin, and nodded his head at the Captain, but said nothing.

"And don't worry, Mr. Brantley; I know General Rosecrans ... he's a West-Pointer like me. He'll appreciate you taking the initiative."

"If you say so, sir."

Nathan smiled and slapped him on the back, "Good man."

Brantley rolled his eyes and looked up at the sky, which he immediately regretted, receiving a face full of cold rain. He ducked back down again and shook the rainwater from his face, wondering what he'd just gotten himself into.

ᛥᏬᏬᏬᏬᛥᏬᏬᏬᏬᛥᏬᏬᏬᏬ

Three days earlier, when Nathan and his men first arrived at the Union camp at the base of Rich Mountain, he was immediately brought before Major General George B. McClellan, commander of all Union forces in the western Virginia theatre.

Nathaniel Chambers and George McClellan were well-acquainted, members of the fifty-nine-man graduating class of

West Point in 1846; after which they'd both served in the Mexican-American War. But their four years together as cadets had not been especially amicable.

One incident in particular had caused a rift that had never totally mended. The two had come to blows after an especially rough sporting contest. Nathan, standing several inches taller and possessing much greater strength along with a quick, brutal temper, had gotten the best of McClellan, who'd suffered a severe beating.

Nathan had willingly confessed his part in the altercation to the commandant, and stoically suffered the consequences, which included an aspect of painful corporal punishment. But McClellan had denied any wrongdoing, and with Nathan refusing to speak against him, he'd been entirely exonerated. As a result, Nathan received a black mark on his record that contributed to him finishing well down in the graduating class rankings, while McClellan finished second in the class.

But Nathan's service in the war had been exemplary, even heroic, for which he was later awarded a gold medal by his commanding general.

McClellan, on the other hand, had served competently and bravely by all accounts, but had not especially distinguished himself in battle. However, because of his father's friendship with commanding General Winfield Scott, he'd received a field promotion to Captain, a rank which, at the time, Nathan wouldn't receive for several more years—years of hard service in Texas.

And McClellan was keenly aware of how his fellow West Point classmates had performed, and any recognition they'd received; Nathan Chambers' medal had rankled.

When Nathan entered the command tent, McClellan sat behind a makeshift desk, poring over a stack of papers. He looked up but didn't bother to rise or extend a hand, and didn't offer Nathan a chair, despite the lack of respect and decorum that implied. When he'd first learned McClellan commanded the Union effort in western Virginia, Nathan had hoped his old classmate might have matured with age, that they might put the past behind them. But based on this reception, it was looking like that would *not* be the case.

Nathan hadn't seen McClellan in years, not since the war had ended. He looked well, vigorous and energized. With his dark intense eyes and handsome visage—dark mustache and hair, neatly groomed—it occurred to Nathan the two of them looked very much alike. Enough so someone who didn't know them might think them brothers. But ... McClellan would definitely be the *little* brother—a good half foot shorter, Nathan considered, and smiled.

The other difference was McClellan acted the part, vainly proud of his looks, while Nathan gave such matters little mind. He'd done nothing to earn whatever gifts God had seen fit to bless him with, so he figured he had no reason to take pride in them.

So Nathan stood in front of the general's desk, waiting to be acknowledged. Harry the Dog, however, not standing on formality, went ahead and sat next to Nathan, who could tell by Harry's body language he was suspicious of McClellan; his hackles were up, doubtless picking up cues from his master.

When McClellan paused in his writing, Nathan said, "General; good to see you again, sir. It has been ... fifteen years, five months and ... hmm ... eight days since we last saw each other in Mexico City."

"Hmm ... yes, that seems about right. You always were the one for remembering insignificant details, as I recall. I suppose welcomes are in order, Chambers. Though as you can imagine I am quite busy just at the moment; I have a battle to plan. What is it I can do for you, sir?"

Not exactly a warm welcome for an old classmate, but Nathan decided to let that pass. "Thank you for seeing me, general. I'm here at the behest of the Governor of Virginia."

"Letcher? I thought I'd heard you were on the *Union* side, Chambers," he scowled. Nathan half expected him to call for his guards.

"No, sir. John Letcher is no longer the Governor of Virginia; he's a traitor and the illegitimate head of a false government that has vacated its authority over the state. I come here representing his honor Francis Pierpont, the *true* governor of Virginia."

"Ah ... the new Wheeling Government?"

"I'd prefer to call it the *'Restored'* Government of Virginia, if it's all the same to you, sir."

"As you wish. At any rate, that sounds more hopeful. And what is it his honor the governor wishes you to speak with me about?"

"Nothing specific, sir. He has asked me to join your command as his military representative while he continues organizing the state's contribution to the Union forces — a civilian observer and advisor to the Union forces currently deployed in his state, I suppose you might say."

McClellan set down his pen, and sat back in his chair, giving Nathan a stern look.

"Let us speak plainly to each other, Chambers."

"Certainly, general, such has always been my preference."

"Chambers, I'm familiar with your record after being decorated for valor in Mexico. Served on the frontier, most recently in command of a fort in Texas conducting operations against the hostiles in that region. Resigned your commission shortly before the current crisis came to a head.

"What I'm having a hard time understanding, is why you aren't back in uniform, sir. To be blunt, why on God's earth are you still a 'civilian,' Chambers? There's a damned war on now, or haven't you heard?

"And for God's sake, man, why have you brought that ... *creature* ... into my tent?"

Nathan felt the heat rising and his face reddening. He didn't care for the man's tone or what he was implying. Though it hadn't been spoken, the implication of cowardice was clear.

But he decided to ignore it for the moment. Too much was at stake to take offence and come to blows with this man, no matter how rude and arrogant he might be. He instead determined the safest course was to address the last question first.

"The hound serves as my personal guard, sir. And he has proven his worth; twice now he has saved my life from almost certain death. I no longer go anywhere without him."

McClellan gazed at the dog for a moment, then said, "Ah ... I've heard of such animals serving as bodyguards for officers. Very good. Glad to hear he's a well-trained military animal, not just some mangy mongrel tagging along after you."

Nathan nodded, not bothering to correct the general—that Harry was in fact a mangy mongrel, and as far as he knew had never once received *any* training, military or otherwise!

"And as for the other, sir ... I can understand your *confusion* about my lack of a uniform. Believe me, there is *nothing* I would rather do than lead men into battle on behalf of Mr. Lincoln," he locked eyes with McClellan, giving him a stern look that brooked no argument or further discussion.

"But I am currently duty-bound to help stabilize the new Virginia government and bring a new state into the Union."

"Ah ... the new *West Virginia* state that's being bandied about. I'm a bit skeptical that'll ever come to pass. Well, I suppose one must do what one thinks is best. But, be that as it may, I can't help but think it's a waste of a valuable military asset, Chambers."

"I have a hard time arguing with you there, general."

"To be perfectly honest, Chambers, I am not feeling especially enamored of your decision to remain a civilian, and it makes me less than enthusiastic about having you here in my camp. And I certainly have no interest in any 'advice' given to me by a civilian—regardless of his theoretical expertise—of that you can be certain."

Nathan fought down a growing urge to snap back at McClellan. He'd remembered now why he'd never liked the man—arrogant and full of himself, but not nearly as competent as he tried to make others believe. But for some reason at that moment, he thought of his old neighbor and adversary, Walters, and his unnerving bland expression. He decided to use the same tactic on McClellan and not give him the satisfaction of a heated response.

It seemed to have the desired effect; after a few moments McClellan looked back down at his stack of papers, and no longer made eye contact.

"Well, Chambers ... far be it from me to give the *officially recognized* Governor of Virginia reason to take offense. So I suppose I must accept you into my command, like it or no.

"But I'll not have you underfoot. Please report to General Rosecrans. Perhaps he will find some use for you. At least that will make you and Governor Pierpont *his* problem, and no longer mine. Good day to you, sir."

"General."

But before he ducked through the tent flap, Nathan, remembering their West Point days together, couldn't resist one last retort. He turned back and gave McClellan a hard look, "Oh ... and never fear, general; I may now be *just a civilian*, but ... I haven't forgotten how to *fight*, sir!"

He smiled and stuck an unlit cigar in his mouth before turning on his heels. McClellan scowled but refrained from responding; both knew full well who'd gotten the better of their one physical altercation back at West Point.

But if McClellan's reception had been cold, General Rosecrans' was entirely the opposite. "Welcome, welcome, Chambers!" He grinned broadly, stepping out from behind the crude table serving as a desk and shaking hands firmly while ushering Nathan to a chair in his command tent.

"A pleasure to welcome a fellow West-Pointer, sir; and may I say your reputation has preceded you."

"Thank you, general. It's a pleasure to be here and to meet you at last."

"The pleasure is all mine, Chambers. And please call me William."

"Nathan, then."

"Nathan ... what an amazing animal you have there! I've never seen the like. What kind is he?"

"My scholar William Jenkins says he's an English Mastiff / Irish Wolfhound mix. But an overly large specimen for either."

"I should say so! When you run short of horses you could just throw a saddle on him!"

Nathan laughed. "I'd not want to be the one who tried it. He's killed men for less!"

Rosecrans smiled, and shook his head, continuing to gaze at the dog.

Harry for his part seemed much more relaxed around General Rosecrans than he'd been around McClellan. It occurred to Nathan that Harry was a good judge of character.

"I heard you visited with General McClellan earlier. How did you fare with our esteemed commander?"

Nathan grimaced, "None too well, I'm afraid. We already had an unfriendly history going back to our Academy days. The general expressed doubts about my manhood due to the lack of a blue uniform. He ... hmm ... tested my good humor and self-restraint, shall we say."

Rosecrans chuckled, "Oh, he *will* do that! George B. McClellan will treat the lowliest private with the utmost dignity and respect—the very picture of caring kindness and civility. The rankers love him and would do anything for him.

"But woe be unto you if you're one of his subordinate officers, especially if you're a general, God forbid! Almost every time I meet with the man, I feel a very strong urge to plant my fist firmly against his nose."

Nathan laughed, "Well, since you're still here, it appears you've manfully resisted that impulse."

"So far, Chambers ... so far."

ജ്യോ൝ඥ౫ഇ൝ඥ౫ഇ൝ඥ౫

The next morning Nathan was sitting in his tent talking with Tom and Jim when a lieutenant poked his head inside.

"Excuse me, sirs, and please pardon the interruption. Mr. Chambers, General Rosecrans sends his compliments and asks if you would be so kind as to join him in General McClellan's command tent at once, for a meeting with the Commanding General."

A few minutes later he and Rosecrans were seated opposite General McClellan in the command tent. McClellan's chief of staff, an older officer, Colonel Randolph Marcy, stood behind the general. Harry the Dog, as always, sat to the side and slightly behind Nathan's chair. Nathan surreptitiously reached down and scratched Harry's head between the ears.

Standing next to the general's desk was a fair-haired man, looking to be about twenty and dressed as a civilian, nervously crushing a felt hat in his hands.

"Gentlemen, this is Mr. David Hart," McClellan began. "He entered our camp last night and was brought to me by the sentries. He has a very interesting tale I wish to share with you, General Rosecrans. And, of course, you are most welcome as well, Mr. Chambers, since the general has seen fit to bring you along.

"It seems young Mr. Hart and his family are loyal Unionists who own a farm just up the pass on Rich Mountain. And he has graciously volunteered to serve as a *civilian advisor*," McClellan gave Nathan a look, but then continued, "and assist our efforts in whatever capacity we may require. The question for this meeting is how to best use his valuable local knowledge to our advantage."

McClellan, Rosecrans, and Nathan spent the next hour quizzing the young man on every detail of the farm, its location on the Rich Mountain pass, the various approaches to the pass, the terrain surrounding it, and on and on. General McClellan called for a map of the area, and one of his aides provided one, which he spread out on the desk. They spent another half-hour laying out the position of the farm, the position of the rebel fort, hastily built from logs harvested on the hillside, and any details Hart could provide about the lay of the land around the house and fort.

When they'd finished quizzing the young farmer, McClellan dismissed him.

Then the commanding general looked at Rosecrans, "So what are you thinking, Rosecrans?"

"I'm thinking Mr. Hart's knowledge of the back trails provides us a rare opportunity to sneak a force up the mountainside to the farmhouse. From there we can launch a flanking attack against the fort from above. I'd be more than happy to lead such an expedition general, if it pleases you."

"Hmm ... to be honest, I'm not much enamored of the idea, Rosecrans. Dividing our forces when we're already likely outnumbered by a well-fortified enemy, seems unwise."

Nathan was surprised by this statement. From what he'd seen and heard it was obvious to him the Union forces in the area were vastly superior to the rebels in numbers. Not to mention equipment and provisions.

"Outnumbered, general? What makes you think so?" Nathan couldn't help asking.

"Chambers ... you may believe you have some knowledge in these matters, but I am the commanding general. I have intelligence resources you aren't privy to in your position as a ... *civilian advisor*," he accompanied the last part with a sneer, as if it were a curse.

"I have it on good authority the enemy before us numbers between eight and ten thousand. With several dozen cannon at their disposal. While we number just under seven, with less than a dozen artillery pieces. To divide our forces and further deplete our numbers in this camp seems ... highly suspect. It might leave us vulnerable to a rebel counter-attack."

Nathan glanced over at Rosecrans to gauge his reaction to this statement. But Rosecrans was keeping his feelings veiled.

"I can't speak to any specific ... *intelligence*, general," Nathan responded, "but I do have a certain amount of ... *experience* in the field ... to draw upon. And I've been out to have a look at the enemy's fort through my spyglass. It appears to me the log fortress before us isn't large enough to comfortably hold such a sizable force."

"Chambers, if you are going to question my every statement, you can depart and leave the military men to decide this matter. I too have *'experience in the field,'* I will have you remember!" McClellan was turning red in the face, clearly becoming agitated.

Nathan knew he was on shaky ground; it was well within the general's rights to have him dismissed from the meeting, or even from the entire operation.

"Yes, certainly, general ... I am very familiar with the extent of your experience; I clearly recall seeing you in the field down in Mexico on several occasions. My apologies if I've overstepped my bounds. I am only trying to offer any assistance I may for the benefit of the present discussion."

"Hmm ... apology accepted," McClellan answered, though he seemed far from mollified. Nathan knew he'd have to step lightly from here on.

But Rosecrans came to his rescue by diving back into the conversation, "I hear what you're saying, general. It *is* a concern ... but perhaps taking advantage of a flanking maneuver plus the element of surprise will offset the risk. And give us the opportunity to overcome the enemy's superior numbers. The alternatives of sitting in camp awaiting reinforcements, or launching a full-frontal assault seem less than appealing."

"I'll agree with you there, Rosecrans," the general answered. "A frontal assault against such a well-defended position would cost us more in blood than I'm comfortable with."

He was quiet and thoughtful for a long time. Though Nathan had never had any great love for McClellan back at West Point, he'd never seen *this* side of his old classmate: the hand-wringing hesitation. The fear of making a decision that might be wrong.

"I'm sure the prudent plan would be to call for reinforcements before launching any kind of assault, whether it be flanking or frontal," McClellan finally said.

"Agreed, general," Rosecrans said, "but ... there's always the risk the enemy may also receive reinforcements while we wait ..."

"True ..." McClellan answered. But he seemed distracted, as if lost in thought.

"General ... if you will indulge me ... can we break it down in detail and discuss how the flanking maneuver might be carried out ... while minimizing the risk?" Rosecrans asked.

"Very well, general. Do proceed ..."

ဆဝ၆ဥ၈၁ဆဝ၆ဥ၈၁ဆဝ၆ဥ၈၁

In the end it had taken another three hours of detailed discussions for Rosecrans to lay out his strategy.

The plan was relatively simple: Rosecrans would lead a brigade-sized force up the mountain, guided by young Mr. Hart. Then they'd attack the fort from behind and uphill. As soon as Rosecrans engaged the enemy, and the sounds of battle echoed down the mountainside, McClellan would launch a frontal assault with the main force. If all went according to plan, the enemy would be caught in a pincer that would crack their fortress like an egg.

But despite Rosecrans' best efforts, McClellan remained skeptical until Colonel Marcy, who'd said but little during the entire meeting, leaned in close and in low tones, said, "General ... I believe this plan may just work. And I can see no other plausible alternative."

Nathan was surprised when McClellan looked up at Colonel Marcy, nodded, and said, "Agreed. General Rosecrans, you may proceed with your plan, but let me make myself clear; if this operation fails, it will be on your head."

After the meeting Nathan and Rosecrans walked back to the general's tent together, and Nathan couldn't resist asking the question that'd been burning in his mind since the conclusion of the meeting, "William ... what in the devil happened in there at the end? You'd argued most persuasively for hours, but McClellan remained unmoved until Colonel Marcy simply told him to proceed with it. That was ... *odd*, to say the least."

Rosecrans snorted a laugh, "Ah ... yes, I'm sure it would seem so, Nathan. Would it help to know Colonel Marcy is McClellan's father-in-law, and that Marcy had intervened on George's behalf when his daughter wished to marry another officer?"

Nathan's eyes widened, "Ah ... that would explain it. A bit of nepotism, perhaps?"

Rosecrans grinned, "You never heard that from me."

Nathan nodded, then slowly shook his head, a sour expression on his face.

After a short pause the general changed the subject, "Nathan, do I understand correctly the men you brought with you to this camp are experienced Army veterans and Indian fighters from Texas?"

"You are correct, sir. Blooded veterans all. And some of the best men I've ever had the privilege to command. I'm still baffled as to why such men would accompany me back east to help run my farm in Virginia. But such is the case, and my present good fortune. Why do you ask?"

"Because the day after tomorrow I'll be leading a covert flanking attack against a well-fortified enemy position. My brigade will contain nearly two thousand officers and men, most of whom have never fired a gun in anger. The prospect is daunting ... *frightening* might not be too strong a term, I suppose."

Nathan smiled, and said, "To be honest, general, we didn't come here to just *observe and advise*. We are soldiers, sir, despite our lack of uniform. We'd much rather be out in the field slaughtering our enemies, than sitting back safely in camp, scratching our backsides. You may assume we are entirely at your service, sir."

"I was hoping you'd say that, Chambers. Thank you most kindly, sir."

ᘓᘔᘕᘖᘓᘔᘕᘖᘓᘔᘕᘖᘓᘔᘕᘖ

Nathan stood in front of the Union troops on the thickly wooded hillside. Most of the nervous looking young men staring back at him were barely old enough to shave, preparing for their first action, though his group of veterans was also among them. All were sodden, dripping rainwater, and shivering from the cold—both new recruits and veterans alike.

Steamy puffs of breath came from Nathan's mouth as he addressed them.

"Gentlemen ... I would be remiss if I didn't call upon divine providence in our hour of need. In Joshua chapter one, verse nine the Lord says, '*Have not I commanded thee? Be strong and of a good courage; be not afraid, neither be thou dismayed: for the Lord thy God is with thee whithersoever thou goest.*'"

Nathan's own men smiled and nodded, appreciating the long-standing tradition before battle. But Brantley's recruits were wide-eyed: Nathan's strong baritone voice reciting the Bible was a perfect complement to the tension of the moment, and the damp,

16

dreary weather. With rain streaming down on a day nearly as dark as night, and their first ever life or death battle in the offing, it was a thoroughly surreal experience for the young men. Several made the sign of the cross over their chests. Others turned away, discreetly emptying their stomachs onto the ground.

Nathan signaled his two sergeants to move out. He'd dispersed his veterans amongst the green soldiers to give them more confidence and keep them moving in the right direction.

And he'd politely asked Lieutenant Brantley to stay next to him during the fighting—ostensibly so they could confer as needed during the battle. In reality, he wanted to ensure the young man didn't do anything stupid to contradict his own orders.

Billy led the way down a winding trail through the trees and underbrush, until they were within firing distance of the rebel pickets. As they dispersed in a line parallel to the enemy, they could now make out the split rail fence and farmhouse beyond. The pickets themselves were more difficult to spot, doing their best to hide behind cover. But Nathan's men were used to fighting Indians out West; by contrast these green rebel soldiers were practically standing in the open.

"Mr. Wiggins … as we discussed. Commence firing, if you please."

"Companies A, C, and E will fire on my command! … Companies present! … Aim! … FIRE!"

A thunderous noise temporarily drowned out the noise of the raging downpour, and gun smoke fought to rise up through the damp, but could only manage to swirl around the shooters, temporarily obscuring their view.

Tom Clark's voice then called out, "Companies B and D will fire on my command! … Present arms! … Aim! … FIRE!" Another thunderous volley rang out.

Nathan looked out through the mist and smoke with his brass spy glass. He could just make out two enemy soldiers leaping the split rail fence, clearly in full retreat.

"Mr. Wiggins … give the men time to reload, then fix bayonets."

"Aye, Captain." Jim stood and looked up and down the line to make sure the reloading was progressing timely. After a half-minute or so he called out, "Companies will fix bayonets ... FIX ... BAYONETS!"

The clattering sound of metal on metal could be heard down the line. Jim looked up at Nathan for the signal. Nathan held up his hand, wanting to give the new soldiers a few more moments to prepare.

After another half-minute Nathan looked back at Jim Wiggins and snapped his hand down.

"CHARGE!"

Fifty men, one officer, and eight civilian "advisors" leapt up and charged downhill through the bushes toward the enemy position. The "advisors" among them gave out a great shout which quickly spread among the green troops.

There was a smattering of gun fire from the enemy line, but to no effect, being ill-aimed. Before they'd covered half the distance a dozen or so enemy soldiers abandoned their posts and ran for the fence. Several had dropped their rifles in their haste. The Union civilians paused in their charge, took careful aim, and fired, immediately cutting down half those attempting to retreat. After Nathan's men had fired their rifles, they set them aside and unholstered pistols, downing several more.

When the Union soldiers reached the picket line, they found the position entirely vacated aside from five dead rebels and three wounded. They stripped the arms from the wounded, but otherwise left them where they lay—as such things went, the injured men would have to wait for a lull in the battle to hope for any aid from either side.

Nathan's veterans knew what to do with little guidance from him; soon the entire Union force was aligned behind the split rail fence, looking out toward the farmhouse and the roadway beyond. The retreating enemy pickets who'd abandoned their line had now nearly reached the relative safety of the farmhouse, about forty yards back and to the right of the fence. Nathan's men continued to reload and fire at them, but most of the remaining pickets made it to safety behind the house.

Straight in front of them Nathan could see the knot of enemy soldiers Billy had described previously; they were about two-hundred yards away, on the far side of the road up a small rise. He reconnoitered their position through his spy glass. He saw they were crouched behind bushes. Several began returning fire.

They also started taking incoming fire from the second story windows of the farmhouse, so Nathan ordered another group of men to return fire on those windows.

He turned to Brantley, "Lieutenant, I suggest we concentrate on taking out the enemy to our front across the roadway first, then worry about the house. Otherwise those on the roadway will target us from behind while we're trying to breach the doors. Let's have a few of our rifles continue peppering the house windows to keep them from giving us too much trouble."

Brantley looked at him and nodded. He was wide-eyed but didn't appear panicked to Nathan's eye.

"Tom, Jim … keep a few rifles on those windows, and then prepare the men to attack the enemy out across the roadway. Let's split into three groups, with those on the left and right going wide to try flanking them. And make sure those on the right look out for anything coming from that house. Let's move at a good trot. The center group will pull up about halfway and give them half the rifles. Then a full bayonet charge. The flanking groups will move as exigencies allow."

"Sir!" they both answered and began relaying his instructions to the others.

A few minutes later all three groups moved out. Jim led the flanking group on the left, and Stan the group to the right. By unspoken agreement Tom stayed in the center group next to Nathan. Lieutenant Brantley was there also, as was Harry the Dog, as usual.

They made good progress at first, moving quickly across the pasture. Nathan never believed in marching toward the enemy, rifles on shoulders—it was just asking for high casualties. So they trotted, rifles held in front and ready, bayonets already fixed.

Strangely, the enemy had left off firing, so they met no resistance as they moved forward. But the enemy had not retreated. Nathan could still see them moving about behind the bushes on the slope. But in the dim light and continued downpour he was unable to discern what they were about.

He felt a sudden familiar rush of air followed by a resounding *BOOM!* A large plume of smoke rose from the bushes across the roadway where the enemy had been positioned. Men to both sides of him stopped still in midstride. Brantley looked at him, "What ...?"

"Cannon, Mr. Brantley! Six-pounder—round shot from the sound and feel of it."

Rifle fire now came from the enemy in earnest, and several Union men were hit. Clearly the enemy had hidden more men across the roadway than Billy had initially seen. And now the mystery made sense; the group of soldiers he'd reported were artillery men gathered around a cannon.

Nathan's flanking units had also stopped. To the left Jim Wiggins yelled at his men, red faced. Though he couldn't make out the words, Nathan could imagine the string of expletives coming from the sergeant, trying to get his frightened green soldiers moving again. To the right Stan was likewise struggling to keep his command intact. On Stan's side they were also taking fire from farmhouse windows, and many of his men had ducked to the ground and refused to move further.

Nathan cupped his hands around his mouth, turned and shouted at Sergeant Wiggins. Jim looked up and Nathan signed him to retreat. Then he looked over and saw Stan already looking his way, so he gave him the same sign. Stan nodded and began giving the order to his men.

"Mr. Brantley let's pull back to the trees and regroup. I fear your young men are not yet prepared to face cannon fire."

"Yes, sir," Brantley answered, finding his voice again. "FALL BACK ... FALL BACK! Keep in good order now! No running! Show the enemy we're still men!"

Nathan was gratified the young officer had remembered his training despite the terror of their situation. It spoke well of him.

BOOM! Another cannon ball zipped overhead, crashing well back into the woods.

The Union troops moved quickly back to the fence line and then continued beyond. To their credit the young men had taken time to drag and carry their dead and wounded with them as they'd withdrawn. William examined the casualties and took charge of the wounded, ordering the soldiers to lay them out behind cover in any place they could find a little flat open ground. He then had them carry over the wounded enemy pickets so he could tend to them as well.

As they'd crossed the fence in retreat, they'd heard the rebel soldiers give a great cheer; they'd faced the dreaded Union Army and had sent them running!

Nathan scowled. *It's not over yet, boys ... you'll not celebrate long, I promise you that ...*

ಐ೫ಐೞ೦ಿ೪ಐ೫ಐೞ೦ಿ೪ಐ೫ಐೞ೦ಿ೪

Not receiving any news from General Rosecrans' flanking force since early morning, General McClellan had sent out scouts to climb the face of the hill and reconnoiter the enemy position to see if Rosecrans had proceeded as ordered.

One of these scouts was sent around to the right to see if he could observe Rosecrans' activities. He was within a quarter mile of Nathan's position when he heard the first cannon shot fired, soon followed by another. Then he heard a loud, enthusiastic cheer, which was certainly coming from the rebels as Rosecrans had been unable to bring any cannon with him on the steep climb up the mountain.

The scout quickly returned to camp and reported directly to General McClellan that General Rosecrans had already been defeated by the rebels using artillery. Likely the enemy was even now preparing a counterattack against McClellan's position.

ಐ೫ಐೞ೦ಿ೪ಐ೫ಐೞ೦ಿ೪ಐ೫ಐೞ೦ಿ೪

Nathan called the men together, back within cover of the trees.

"Men ... they think we're beaten. But let me assure you we are *not!* We're going to move up to the edge of the tree line and give them God's good holy hell with our rifles. It's not much more than two hundred yards, so we'll make it very uncomfortable for those

21

rebels back of the roadway. And don't worry about that cannon, these rebs are amateurs. They couldn't hit a barn door from five feet away!"

This last statement had the desired effect: breaking the tension. He heard snickers and laughter down the line.

"General Rosecrans will be here shortly with the main column, then we'll have another go at crossing that field. Let's move."

He called Jim Wiggins over, "Jim, take a dozen or so men and see if you can't work your way along the back side of those brambles over there along the left side of the field. It'd be good to give them a little crossfire to worry about."

"It'll be done, sir! Corporal Tucker! You and the rest of Company A with me!"

The rebs continued to fire their one cannon as quickly as they could reload it. They kept adjusting their aim, but it had become obvious they were firing blindly into the woods, aiming for the puffs of gun smoke but not knowing the exact location of their enemies.

Nathan had just crouched down next to Lieutenant Brantley to get a read on the young man's morale, when someone tapped him on the shoulder. He turned and was surprised to see a serious-looking man about his same age, crouched down behind him. The man wore a broad-brimmed hat with gold braiding and a brass bugle insignia on the front, water dripping from the edges of the brim.

Harry the Dog stood just a pace away, eyeing the newcomer with suspicion, his fur bristled up on his back. But he relented and relaxed when he saw Nathan's reaction and caught a good whiff of the man.

"General! Good to see you, sir."

"Chambers."

Lieutenant Brantley spun around, and started to rise to attention, but Nathan grabbed the back of his coat and held him down. He sheepishly snapped a salute from his enforced crouch.

"General Rosecrans, sir!"

"Lieutenant. As you were."

They could see another Union officer, Rosecrans' executive Colonel Lander, crouched just behind the general, but no sign of other Union troops. Rosecrans looked over at Nathan, "What's the situation?"

But Nathan didn't answer, instead motioning with his eyes toward Brantley. Rosecrans nodded and turned to the Lieutenant. "Lieutenant ... report, if you please."

Lieutenant Brantley proceeded to describe their initial attack, driving off the enemy pickets, then the assault across the field and subsequent withdrawal after taking incoming artillery fire. Nathan was pleased to see him gain confidence and composure as he spoke.

The general looked out across the field, "Well done, Lieutenant. I like it when my officers take the initiative and press the enemy. Too many Goddamned nervous nellies — won't take a piss without orders ..."

Brantley glanced over at Nathan, and they shared a grin.

"Lieutenant ... *uh* ..."

"Brantley, sir. Tenth Indiana, under Colonel Hanson."

"Lieutenant Brantley ... continue to hold this position and keep the enemy pinned down. I've got the remainder of the brigade just back in the woods. We'll get them organized and ready for the assault."

BOOM! Another cannon ball passed just over their heads, ripping through the trees beyond. The general turned and looked to see where it had landed.

"*Damn!* If they're not careful they'll hit my men back in the woods by pure accident. We need to silence that cannon first thing!"

ಬಿಜಿಬಿಜಿಬಿಜಿಬಿಜಿಬಿಜಿ

Like a grown-up version of Nathan's earlier assault plan, Rosecrans ordered his men divided into three groups: flanking maneuvers to the right and left and a main assault group in the center. But having twenty times more men at his disposal, he ordered the right flanking group to assault and secure the farmhouse, and the left group to work their way up and beyond the brambly hedgerow to turn the enemy line. The largest group in the center would assault the main group of rebels and take out their artillery piece.

Rosecrans placed Colonel Lander from his own staff in overall command of the right flank, but as a "reward" for his aggressive action earlier, he gave Brantley the honor of leading the group charged with taking the farmhouse, within Colonel Hanson's overall command in that sector. With a wink he asked Nathan to accompany Brantley, since they were now "such fast friends."

He gave Colonel Sullivan, Thirteenth Indiana, command of the left flank, and the general requested Jim Wiggins accompany the colonel as his "advisor." Privately to the side he strongly suggested the colonel heed whatever *advice* Mr. Wiggins might feel inclined to give, Wiggins being a battle-hardened Indian fighter from out West. The nervous-looking colonel readily agreed.

General Rosecrans himself would lead the large center group.

Tom Clark and Big Stan joined Nathan's group while William stayed behind, tending to the wounded and organizing the other surgeons in preparation for likely additional casualties. He planned to move the wounded into the farmhouse once it was cleared of the enemy.

The rest of Nathan's original soldiers from Texas—Jamie, Georgie, and Billy Creek—went with Jim on the left. All the civilians, including Nathan, wore normal clothing, but had been given blue army hats so they'd not be mistaken for the enemy, most of whom had no military uniforms.

Nathan wore his wide-brimmed Army Captain's hat, the same he'd worn on many patrols out in Texas, however, he'd removed the bugle insignia in front to indicate his non-military status.

Bugles sounded and the entire Union forced moved forward as one. In addition to his original force of fifty, Brantley now commanded another fifty men he'd been assigned. He ordered the windows targeted as the men quickly closed on the farmhouse.

Though the snipers in the upstairs windows were kept pinned down by incoming fire, the enemy had made chinks in the logs in various places along the walls of the house and in the thick shutters of the closed-up downstairs windows. The rebels used these loopholes to good effect, inflicting casualties on the Union troops. Soon Brantley's men were pressed up against the outside walls of the house, preventing the rebels inside from targeting them.

Nathan and Brantley, both armed with pistols, worked their way along the left-side wall toward the front door which faced toward the road and away from the direction of the assault. When they reached it, they saw the enemy had notched several loopholes in the door and were firing out from them. One Union soldier had been hit when he'd approached the door; his lifeless body lay sprawled on the wooden stoep, a stream of blood dripping down the stairs.

Brantley looked over at two soldiers on the opposite side of the door and whistled to get their attention. He mimed battering down the door with their rifle butts. The two nodded, and rushed up the stairs and to the door, leaping over the body of their fallen comrade. They slammed against the door, narrowly avoiding being hit by enemy fire from the loopholes. Then they stood back, clear of the holes, and began hammering on the door with their rifle butts.

But Mr. Hart had built the door to last, and it's solid, thick timbers stubbornly resisted the soldiers' best efforts.

Nathan felt someone tug on his sleeve and looked back to see what Tom wanted. With the noise of yelling, screaming, hammering and hundreds of rifles going off all around them, verbal communication was nearly impossible. Tom pointed behind him at Big Stan. Stan looked at Nathan, grinned and raised an eyebrow. Nathan nodded, turned back toward Brantley and motioned him to stand aside.

Stan slipped past them and stood at the edge of the stoep. Brantley looked puzzled but Nathan grinned and pulled out his other pistol, so he now held one in each fist. Tom did likewise.

In a great rush Stan leapt up the stairs and crashed into the door, right between the two startled Union soldiers. The door burst inward off its hinges, falling to the floor with Stan on top. A rebel soldier standing too close was crushed underneath.

The two Union soldiers who'd been battering the door stared open-mouthed for a moment, then recovered their wits and reversed their rifles, firing at enemy soldiers inside.

In the next instant Nathan hurled himself through the opening, leaping over Stan where he lay on top of the door. Tom and Harry the Dog followed fast on his heels. Nathan fired both pistols, dropping two enemy soldiers moving down the hallway. A motion above caught Tom's eye, he raised his pistol and shot another coming down the stairs. The dead man's momentum sent him tumbling, sprawling to a stop halfway down.

Stan was back on his feet, pistols in hand as Brantley and a knot of Union soldiers poured in the open doorway. Nathan motioned Brantley to take the upstairs, and Stan to come with him and Tom.

They rushed down the hallway toward the other side of the house where they could hear rifle fire, likely coming from the kitchen area.

As Nathan passed a small closet door on his right, the point of a bayonet thrust out. Only lightning-quick reflexes saved him from being skewered, deflecting the thrust with his right pistol. The steel blade passed inches from his belly. His attacker pushed forward into the hallway. Nathan's feet tangled with a body on the floor, and his back slammed against the far wall. The enemy pressed his rifle across Nathan's neck forcing him to drop both pistols to protect his throat. Bent backward and pressed against the wall, he'd lost all leverage.

Harry lunged forward, jaws agape. But Tom put a pistol to the rebel's temple and fired. *BOOM!* Blood splattered the wall. The body crumpled to the floor and gun smoke swirled thickly in the narrow hallway.

Stan grabbed the front of Nathan's shirt and yanked him to his feet.

Tom handed Nathan his dropped pistols and they continued down the hall. Harry paused to sniff the rebel's body, teeth bared. Apparently satisfied, he followed the men.

They reached the end of the hall where it opened into a large room. Nathan had correctly guessed it was the kitchen. Gun smoke wafted out from the room and the near-deafening cacophony of battle echoed off the walls inside. He stood at the edge of the opening and ducked his head in for a quick look. He turned back toward Tom and Stan, pointed to his right and held up three fingers, then pointed at them. They nodded. Then he pointed the other direction, held up two fingers and pointed at his own chest. Again, they nodded understanding.

Nathan mouthed, "Now," pivoted to his right, and stepped into the room. Tom and Stan rushed in after him, facing the opposite direction. Multiple pistol shots rang out in quick succession; then a sudden, near silence. As the gun smoke cleared, five rebel soldiers lay dead in the room, rifles no longer effective in lifeless hands.

The silence was only relative, however; battle still raged further down another hallway leading off to the left of the direction they'd come.

But before Nathan could take the lead again, Stan leapt in front of him and raced down the hall. Nathan, Harry, and Tom followed. This section of the house featured several bedrooms off a main hallway. Stan paused briefly at each doorway, firing several shots from his pistols before moving to the next. When Nathan and Tom passed these same doorways and looked in, they saw only bodies sprawled on the floor.

They reached the end of the hallway and realized they'd cleared all the rooms. This section of the house was suddenly quiet except for the sounds of gunfire from the outside.

"Damn it Volkov! You've killed them all," Tom said with a scowl.

"What? You weren't wanting me killing these rebel *bezobraznik?*"

"It's not I didn't want them killed, but you didn't leave any for us!"

Stan laughed. "Sorry, Sergeant Clark. You know me, once the joy of battle is on me, I am thinking of nothing else. Next time I step back and let you shoot all the rebel bastards you want."

"Thanks, I appreciate that; it'll begin to make amends ..."

But their moment of comradery was interrupted by gunfire coming from upstairs.

"Come, we must aid young Brantley!" Nathan shouted. They ran back down the hallway toward the front door, then up the stairs, hurdling bodies as they went.

But when they arrived, it was already over. In a large room at the top of the stairs six rebel soldiers stood, backs against the wall, their hands held in the air and rifles on the floor. Brantley and his men held them at bayonet point. A quick glance around the gun smoke filled room showed three rebels and one Union soldier down.

Though the brief battle for the house was over, the room was far from safe; Union soldiers outside continued to pound the house with rifle fire, targeting any open window or loophole. Brantley and his men were forced to keep against the walls avoiding the windows as bullets ricocheted off the window frames and deadly splinters flew across the room.

Nathan noticed a sergeant carrying the colors of the Tenth Indiana Regiment on a pike in addition to his rifle. "Color Sergeant, slip up next to that open window, poke the colors out and wave them. Let 'em know the house is ours before we're all shot by our own troops."

"Yessir!" he said, and quickly obeyed. In a few minutes the incoming fire ceased, and they heard shouts and cheering from outside.

"Mr. Brantley, this is *your* moment. Do step up and acknowledge your men's appreciation and adulation."

Brantley looked shocked, but did as advised, moving to the open window where the colors had been waved. He poked his head out, removed his hat, and waved it. The men below gave another loud cheer. When Brantley ducked back in, his face beamed, and he shook his head in wonder.

The smile didn't fade until they stepped back into the kitchen downstairs. Brantley's eyes widened when he saw the devastation wreaked by Nathan and his two men armed only with pistols. "I guess you weren't bluffing before, Mr. Chambers, when you said you and your men would take the farmhouse without any help from us soldiers."

Nathan smiled. "No bluff, Mr. Brantley. We *would've* done it on our own. But ... we *do* appreciate your help."

Stan, who'd been listening in, snorted a laugh, and walked away chuckling to himself.

ᏚᎤᏚᏬᎡᏅᎡᏅᎡᏚᎤᏚᏬᎡᏅᎡᏅᎡᏚᎤᏚᏬᎡᏅᎡᏅ

General McClellan sat on his horse, staring out in the direction of the enemy fort, just five hundred yards away up the heavily wooded hillside. Through his spyglass he could make out rebel sentries pacing the ramparts. He saw no indication the fort was under attack, despite the sounds of battle echoing down from above—the occasional cannon shot mixed with hundreds of rifle shots.

The noise had continued off and on for nearly two hours now. He had to assume Rosecrans' attack had stalled well short of the fort. Likely the continuing sounds of battle were the general's brigade in retreat, attempting to extract themselves from the mountain pass.

He turned to Captain Winston, officer in command of the forward pickets. "Winston ... any word from Lieutenant Poe?"

"Yes, sir. Last word came an hour ago. He'd still been unable to reach the knoll with the artillery due to the steep terrain and heavy woods, despite working at it all last night and throughout the morning. He reports it may take the remainder of the day to clear a proper road, sir."

McClellan nodded, and turned back toward the enemy fort, dubbed "Fort Garnett" after the enemy commanding general, though he'd positioned himself twenty-some miles further north.

"What're your orders, general? Shall I move the pickets forward into a skirmish line for the assault, sir?"

McClellan didn't immediately answer, again staring out toward the enemy fort through his spyglass. This time he saw an enemy officer standing atop the ramparts. He appeared to be speaking to his troops, gesturing broadly. They responded positively with shouts and shaking of rifles—not a good sign.

29

"No ... I think not, Captain. I have it on good authority the rebel force in the fort stands at eight to nine thousand men. Without Rosecrans' flanking attack a frontal assault would be extremely costly in Union blood. Likely it would fail utterly. In fact, I anticipate an enemy counterattack shortly now that they've repulsed Rosecrans' assault. Damn! Without his brigade we are clearly outnumbered. Pull back to your previous position guarding the camp."

"Yes, sir."

"Lieutenant Billingsley ..."

"Sir?" McClellan's fair-haired young aide snapped a salute from atop his horse a few feet back of the general.

"Ride back and relay my orders; the Ninth Ohio will stay and guard Lieutenant Poe's efforts to get the artillery onto that knoll. Tell them we've got to have that artillery in place by first light tomorrow so we may begin bombarding the enemy's fort should he fail to attack our position today. Should our camp be attacked, the artillery on the knoll may serve to support our defense.

"The rest of the force will withdraw to camp at Roaring Creek and dig in for an expected assault by the enemy. With us so shorthanded, I'll have even the cooks and teamsters armed."

"Sir!" the lieutenant saluted again, turned his horse, and trotted back toward the Union forces gathered below in preparation for the assault. They'd been in place for nearly three hours now, awaiting the general's order to attack.

While Rosecrans' brigade continued their assault of the Confederate forces across from the Hart farmhouse, General McClellan withdrew his 5,000-strong Union force to a defensive position back at camp, in fear of an imminent counterattack by the enemy. Unknown to him, the entire enemy force in Camp Garnett numbered only 1,300 men, most of whom were presently engaging Rosecrans.

ഇൗൟരൟരൟഇൗൟരൟരൟഇൗൟരൟരൟ

"Hello, general. How goes the battle?"

"Chambers. It was a bit dicey for a while there, mostly due to the greenness of the officers and men, not to mention all the

30

reinforcements the enemy kept bringing up. But we've finally managed to drive them from their position above the roadway opposite the farmhouse."

"And captured that bothersome cannon, I understand."

"*Two* actually."

"Oh? I was sure I'd heard only one firing."

"You heard correctly. And we had the devil's own time capturing it, too."

"And the *second* cannon?"

"Oh, that was a *gift* from our Southern friends. They sent it up to reinforce the other, but it arrived too late. Our attack was well under way when they brought it up the road. Apparently, the noise and commotion spooked the horses and it ended up sideways down a ravine. My men have thrown ropes around it and pulled it out. So now it's mine, along with its powder and ammunition."

"Well, I'm sure you'll find *something* useful to do with it."

"Yes, indeed I shall, Mr. Chambers," he grinned brightly, a cigar clenched between his teeth. "Oh, and I understand congratulations are in order for a very efficient liberation of the farmhouse. I hear you and your men acquitted yourselves handsomely."

Nathan didn't immediately answer but gave the general a meaningful look. "I believe I will give the lion's share of the credit to young Lieutenant Brantley. He has once again shown aggressiveness in the face of the enemy and courage under fire."

Rosecrans nodded, "I see. Well, then I believe a field promotion may well be in order ... to *Captain*, say? I want the other officers to witness how initiative is rewarded under my command."

"I whole-heartedly agree, general," Nathan answered, though the thought of rewarding the young man with a promotion to Captain on the strength of one battle seemed ironic to him. He remembered the long years he'd labored in Texas fighting Indians after the Mexican war before receiving his Captain's bars — despite his West Point credentials and war medal. He shook his head — the exigencies of war!

31

"And what of the enemy's fort, general? Now you've secured the road, do you mean to launch your attack?"

Rosecrans frowned. "I dare not. We are nearly out of daylight and I have no idea how many men the enemy still has defending the fort, nor if they're still capable of mounting a counterattack against this position. Besides ..."

"Yes?"

"Do you hear that tremendous sound of battle raging below us down the hill, Union forces storming the enemy fort from below?"

Nathan was quiet for a moment, listening. "No ... I don't hear a thing."

Rosecrans scowled. "Neither do I. As you well know, General McClellan promised to attack their front as soon as he heard our guns engaging the enemy from *this* side."

"That's odd. He certainly would have heard the noise ... what do you suppose went wrong?"

"I have no idea, Mr. Chambers. None at all."

→←→←→←→←→←→←

The following morning, several hours before daybreak Nathan sat in the kitchen of the Hart farmhouse drinking hot coffee with General Rosecrans and Tom Clark, an oil lamp burned brightly between them on the table. Tom sat next to Nathan, respectfully keeping out of the conversation unless specifically addressed. Harry the Dog lay curled up underneath, occasionally twitching and growling in his sleep.

The general had set up his cot in the kitchen and was using the kitchen table for a desk. The cot had mostly gone unused, as the general had suffered a restless night; nervous Union pickets had fired their rifles multiple times during the night, though no enemy sightings were confirmed.

William Jenkins had filled all the other rooms and even the front stoep with the Union wounded, and Rosecrans refused to displace any of these that he might have his own room. The enemy wounded had been cared for as well, but these they'd relegated to the barn and other outbuildings. William had been up all night along with the other surgeons and was now getting some well-deserved rest on the general's cot over in one corner of the kitchen.

"I can't thank you enough for the use of your physician, Nathan," Rosecrans said, nodding toward the cot in the corner. "The man's a Godsend. I can't imagine how many men will still be alive tomorrow thanks to the timely application of his knowledge and skills today. Our regular Army surgeons ... well, let's just say they're even less experienced and competent than our soldiers."

"Yes, William's a blessing, there can be no doubt. One of the smartest men I've ever met. But don't be fooled by his appearance, the man's as tough a fighter as any of my Texas men."

"You don't say? A fighter and a healer. Will wonders never cease!"

The general's aide, a young lieutenant named Waverly poked his head in at the door, knocking politely on the doorframe.

"Sir, we have a prisoner out in the hallway. He gave himself up to our pickets this morning. Says he was sent from the fort to speak with you, sir. He's ... well, one would have to consider him 'walking wounded,' sir."

Rosecrans raised an eyebrow at this and shared a look with Nathan.

"Well ... bring him in, then, and let's hear what he has to say."

"Yes, sir."

Waverly motioned down the hall, and a Union private came in escorting the prisoner. Waverly dismissed the private and ushered the prisoner over to stand in front of the general.

The prisoner saluted the general with his left hand; his right being held in a sling that was partially soaked through with blood. "Private Sam Pendleton, general, sir!" he said, gazing around the room nervously, especially after Harry yawned, displaying a large, fearsome looking set of sharp teeth.

"At ease, private. I understand you've come from the rebel fort?" Rosecrans asked.

"Yes, sir. As you can see, I am among the wounded who were left behind. As I was better able to walk than most, I volunteered to come speak with you, sir."

"Left behind? What do you mean? Speak plainly, if you please."

"Sorry, sir. I am come to tell you our commanding officer, Lieutenant Colonel John Pegram, has abandoned the fort as of late last evening. Those of us remaining in the fort were them as was too wounded to make the withdrawal afoot. Though as you can see, I have since recovered enough to make the hike to here."

"He has abandoned his fort?"

"Yes, sir. Your assault of yesterday afternoon has completely decimated our garrison, leaving the colonel insufficient men to hold it. If you will approach the stronghold this morning, you will see we have raised the white flag in surrender, sir. We will offer no further resistance."

☙ℭℰ☙ℭℰ☙ℭℰ☙ℭℰ

"Are the artillery pieces in place now, Lieutenant Poe?" McClellan asked.

"Yes, general. We are even now getting them properly aimed after which we shall commence loading, preparing to fire on your orders, sir."

"Excellent, Poe. I'll give the command when you're ready."

"Sir!"

McClellan sat his horse a few yards behind the row of three six-pounder guns, along with Colonel Marcy and several other of his immediate staff. He raised the spyglass to his eye and looked across at the enemy's log fort, five-hundred yards away and now slightly below their present position at the top of the knoll. Poe and his men had worked through the night to clear a suitable road to the summit, and then had spent several hours leveling a site for the big guns.

Though the sun was now up, it was once again a gloomy, overcast day; apparently the previous day's foul weather intended to continue its reign of misery. McClellan could see no movement along the fort's ramparts and wondered what that might mean.

After a few moments, Poe turned to McClellan, stood to attention and saluted. "The artillery is aimed and prepared to fire on your command, sir."

McClellan didn't immediately respond but took one more look through the spyglass. Still no movement nor sign of the enemy.

"Very well, Lieutenant. You may open fire — "

But even before the general completed his command, a hard-charging horse rushed past him on his right and circled in front of the cannons before jerking to a rearing stop.

"Belay that order!" the rider shouted, waving his hat at Poe to make sure he had young officer's attention. A dark-haired man with a full beard, in his mid-thirties, the rider wore the uniform of a Union cavalry officer. His horse was lathered and breathing hard, nearly at the end of its strength.

"Major! Explain yourself, sir!" McClellan barked. He was not used to having his orders countermanded; the man had better have a damned good answer!

The major turned his mount and walked up to stand in front of the general's horse. He snapped a salute, but McClellan returned it with a glare.

"My apologies for *that*, general, sir, but I assure you it was entirely necessary."

"Necessary to what end, Major?"

"To prevent us firing upon our own men, sir! I am sent by General Rosecrans to give you his compliments, sir. And I am to inform you he has seized control of Fort Garnett as of first light this morning. He stands even now within its walls with members of his staff, the surrendered enemy in hand."

"*Oh!*" was all McClellan could think to say.

இல்தைக்தை அல்தைக்தை அல்தைக்தை

Thursday July 25, 1861 – Randolph County, Virginia:

"Listen to this, Chambers, it's a telegram from General McClellan to the war department in the wake of our victory at Rich Mountain and the panicked withdrawal of General Garnett's

35

entire army thereafter. A friend of mine in the War Department relayed it to me:

> *Garnett's forces routed—his army demoralized—Garnett killed. We have annihilated the enemy in western Virginia. Our success is complete & secession is killed in this country.*

Rosecrans shook his head, but Nathan scowled. "It galls me how he takes credit for *your* victory at Rich Mountain, while he dithered back in camp."

"Yes, but he is right about one thing, it was an unmitigated disaster for the secessionists. Ought to make your job of putting together a new state a whole lot easier without the fear of imminent rebel action."

"True ... but still, *you* ought to be the one returning to Washington the hero, not him. They have rewarded his lackluster performance with command of the Army of the Potomac, effectively giving him control over all Union forces in the East!" Nathan shook his head in disbelief.

"Well, after the disaster at Bull Run, they're in need of a hero to rally the troops and keep up the morale. And George looks—and *acts*—the part better than I could. The newspapers are proclaiming him the next Napoleon, if you can believe it."

"Idiots!"

"Yes, most certainly. But look on the bright side, Chambers; at least we've gotten rid of him here in western Virginia. Now he's Washington's problem."

"Well, I suppose there is *that* silver lining on the dark cloud. Oh ... speaking of ... belated congratulations on your promotion. I understand now that McClellan's gone you've been given command over all his forces here in western Virginia."

"Thank you, though it's a bit of a backhanded compliment, I'm afraid. From what I understand Washington told him to '*just give over command to someone who won't mess it up too badly, perhaps that Rosecrans fellow or someone.*'"

Nathan shared a rueful smile with him, and once again shook his head.

"So ... what's next for you, Nathan?"

"Back to Wheeling, I suppose. See if we can't build that new state for Mr. Lincoln now that the immediate rebel threat has been dealt with."

"Sure you won't reconsider my offer? I have received authority to grant you a brigadier general's commission—brevet, of course. Though it's far less than you deserve. If anyone should have had that job back East it ought to have been you, and *not* McClellan. It goes without saying, I would be delighted and honored to have you on my staff."

"Thank you, William. You shamelessly tempt me. There's nothing I'd rather do than suit up and join the fight, as you well know. But as I've said, my duty right now is back in Wheeling. Fear not, I'm confident we'll see each other out in the field one day soon. Only next time I won't be just a *'Goddamned civilian'!*"

They shared a smile.

"Well, in the meantime," Rosecrans said, still holding onto his grin, "we can at least make a pact to stick together in our fight against the common enemy, Nathan."

"The rebels?"

"No ... an enemy much more treacherous: *Major General George B. McClellan!*"

Chapter 2. Restoration and Separation

"The loyal citizens of Virginia …
are but recurring to the
great fundamental principle of our fathers,
that to the loyal people of a State belong
the law-making power of that State.
The loyal people are entitled to the government
and governmental authority of the State."
– Governor Francis H. Pierpont,
Restored Government of Virginia
(Inaugural Address)

Sunday August 18, 1861 – Wheeling, Virginia:

"Captain, sir … you asked to see me?" Henry poked his head in the door of the farmhouse "library" where the Captain was seated next to a small, rough table that served for a desk. Henry nervously clasped his straw hat in his hands. He felt a bead of sweat run down the side of his face and resisted the urge to wipe it away. The day was already hot outside, though it was not yet noon. But he wasn't sure that was the cause of his sweating; he'd never been called in to speak with the Captain before. Fortunately, it was the Sabbath, so he'd not have to work in the fields and could spend the rest of the day in the shade once this meeting was over. Unless the Captain was finally sending him away.

The Captain sipped a whiskey as he leafed through a stack of papers on the desk, "Hello, Henry. Yes, please … come in. Have a seat."

"Thank you, Captain, sir," Henry seated himself in an old, worn wooden chair a few feet from the desk. He'd been told this house was simple and shabby compared to the Big House back at Mountain Meadows. But to Henry, who'd never set foot inside a white man's house before, it seemed large and grand. He couldn't help gazing around at the brightly painted walls, with their fine woodwork around the doors, windows, floor, and ceiling.

The Captain turned away from the stack of papers and looked Henry in the eye, "How have you been getting along here on Belle Meade Farm since our arrival?"

"Getting along, sir?"

"Yes ... you know, with the others. You joined our party on the road not knowing anyone, other than Miss Margaret. So I was wondering if you've gotten to know some of the folks by now and are feeling more ... *comfortable.*"

Henry wondered where this was leading. It had been several months since he and Margaret had met up with the Captain's caravan and he now, for the most part, thought of himself as one of the "Mountain Meadows" men. But there was always a difference hanging over him, a nagging doubt and fear; they were all freemen and he was still just a runaway slave.

But what he answered was, "Oh, yes, sir! I been most happy here. I've grown mighty fond of talking with Big George, fo' instance. From what I understand, he and I are among the few that's lived on farms other'n your old farm of Mountain Meadows. And I've not yet had my fill o' hearing about them battles y'all done fought in order to get to this-here place. Some o' the young men, like Tony and Ned seem like old hands at fightin' and are happy to tell me all their tales. And ... hmm ... I've talked with Rosa a bit."

"Rosa?" Nathan raised an eyebrow at this. He was surprised by his own reaction—a sudden protective instinct. "But ... what about your wife back east?"

"Oh, *no*, sir! It ain't nothing like *that!*" he shook his head emphatically, and grinned. "Why, I's old enough to be her daddy, sir. Though ... I ain't."

"Ah ... then, what is it you've been talking with her about, if you don't mind my asking?"

"Oh ... we just found we had a ... certain matter in common we could discuss. It's nothing important to *you*, sir."

"Oh. I see." He was tempted to inquire further but decided that would be heavy-handed, using his presumed authority just to satisfy his curiosity. He reminded himself his "people" were now freemen, and it was important to give them the respect that entitled. So he let the matter drop.

But Henry was not yet one of his people, and was *not* a freeman, but rather a runaway slave from Walters Farm. Nathan had thought and prayed over what to do with Henry and had discussed it at length with Tom, Miss Abbey, and Margaret. He'd even met with Reverend Holing, their Methodist pastor—the very same pastor who had officiated at the 'Big Wedding' of Mountain Meadows slave couples the previous summer, and who had been overjoyed to see Nathan and Miss Abbey when they showed up in his congregation, surprising him on their first Sunday in Wheeling. Though everyone's ideas and opinions had been helpful, in the end he had to make up his own mind about Henry, as he'd known from the start.

"Henry, I asked you here today because I wanted to thank you again for helping Miss Margaret escape to safety. Since we first met, she has told me the whole story in detail. From what I understand, you behaved with great courage, determination, and honor throughout the whole ordeal. That was most admirably done, and I want you to know how much I appreciate it."

"Thank you, sir. It was ... a *hard* thing. Difficult to think on, even after all this time. Had to kill a man with my own two hands. Ain't never done a thing like that before." Henry's face betrayed the pain the memory caused him.

Nathan was sympathetic, remembering the first time he'd killed men in battle—the odd mixed feelings of elation and remorse that haunted him for a long time after.

"Yes ... it's not an easy thing ... the first time. But ... you *do* get used to it after a while."

"Oh, I hope to never have to do such a thing again, sir!"

"Amen to that, Henry," Nathan said. But he was skeptical; with the war on he suspected that men like Henry would probably, at some point, be on the very front lines.

"Anyway, sir, Miss Margaret likely helped me as much as I helped her. She's mighty clever and tough for such a slight young lady."

"True enough. But, be that as it may, I wish to thank you with more than just words. Miss Margaret means a great deal to me and it's likely without your help she'd not be alive today. That's something I will *never* forget.

"Henry ... I've thought long and hard about this and am feeling good about my decision. I've decided to give you *this* ..."

He handed Henry a large piece of heavy, yellowish-colored paper. It was filled with writing on just one side, written in a strong, bold hand. But Henry had never learned to read, so he looked up at the Captain, "What is *this*, sir?"

"This, Henry, is your deed of manumission."

Henry's mouth dropped open, "But ... how? Surely Walters ain't agreed to free me."

"No, even if I *could* ask him, he'd certainly never do *that*—not even with a gun to his head! No, this was written and signed by me."

"*You*, sir? But you ain't never been my real master. I's just a runaway and weren't never sold to you proper like."

Nathan stood and walked over to the side of the room where a small wooden box sat on a shelf. He opened the lid and took out a cigar, then stuck it unlit in his mouth. He turned back toward Henry.

"Henry, you now have the dubious honor of being one of the few men I've ever intentionally lied for. If anyone ever asks, I shall shamelessly lie and say the family has owned you for dozens of years. That paper in front of you says as much. With the present upheaval, which forced us to leave most of our old records behind, it'll be almost impossible to prove one way or the other. If it ever comes to it, it'll be my word against Walters'. And if I know him, he's likely never even *looked* at your face. And even if he had, he'd never have cared enough to remember it."

"That's true enough, sir. I ain't never seen him face to face—thank the Lord!"

"Yes ... if you had, it might've been your last sight on Earth. Anyway, I don't lie easily or lightly. I've agonized over it and have lost a bit of sleep. But finally, I decided it was justified; you deserve to be free, and if that costs me a little guilt or shame, so be it. It's a small enough price to pay.

"So ... once again I say, most sincerely, thank you very kindly Henry, for saving my *sister*, Miss Margaret. And congratulations ... you are now a free man."

"I ... I ... don't know what to say, sir."

"A simple 'thank you' will suffice," Nathan answered, and grinned brightly.

"Oh, yes ... thank you, thank you, *thank you*, sir! Oh, my good gracious Lord ... I only wish my wife could see this!"

"Well, we must trust in God that someday she will. Where did you say she was?"

"On a big farm ... outside a little town called Lynchburg, sir."

"Oh! I've been to Lynchburg very recently, when I escaped from Richmond. And I have some unfinished business there, as a matter of fact. But unfortunately, the war has intervened. Guess we all now have one more reason to visit Lynchburg."

He thought of Rosa's mother, Lilly, and the mystery of the girl's father. And how Tom had accidentally come face to face with her at a farm outside Lynchburg without realizing it at the time.

Then Nathan smiled remembering his promise to return and pay for the chickens they'd stolen from that farm during their desperate escape. He still meant to do it, though now with the world in upheaval he wondered if he'd ever get the chance.

ᏚᎷᏋᎰᏣᎧᎫᏚᎷᎰᏣᎧᎫᏚᎷᎰᏣᎧᎫ

Henry was still shaking his head in wonder, staring at the precious piece of paper as he left the house and walked across the porch toward the stairs.

"Henry ..." he heard the Captain's voice behind him. He stopped and turned to look. He hadn't known the Captain was following. He was surprised to see Miss Abbey standing there as well, just outside the doorway. And though he'd only ever spoken with her once before, and that very briefly just after his arrival, she smiled so brightly he couldn't help but smile back.

"Yes, Captain, sir?"

"Henry ... as important as it is, I think you should lower that paper now and look out toward the lawn."

At first, he didn't understand what the Captain meant. He had an odd, amused look on his face that Henry couldn't quite read. So he did as he was bid, and looked out toward the lawn.

The first thing he saw was Miss Margaret standing on the gravel path at the bottom of the stairs. Like Miss Abbey, she was beaming. But he could see her eyes sparkling with tears.

"Miss Margaret, what—" then he noticed something more. Across the drive, on the grassy pasture beyond was a gathering of people. A whole lot of people. All the people of the farm, both white and black, who'd earlier gathered for the Captain's sermon. They should have been dispersed about the farm by now, but here they all were to witness ... *this*. Henry's mouth dropped open.

"Henry," Margaret began, projecting her voice even as she wiped tears from her face, "like the Israelites of old, you have lived your entire life in the land of Egypt ... held in a cruel and unjust bondage. But this driveway is the River Jordan. And across it, on the other side are your brethren, freemen both black and white. They stand ready to welcome you to the land of freedom.

"Since you and I escaped our recent captivity together, it seems fitting we should also cross *this river* together. Will you do me the honor, sir, of walking with me over to freedom?"

Henry looked at all the people gathered on the grass: welcoming smiles and gestures awaited him. He looked back at Margaret, but she'd become blurry and indistinct, and he had to wipe his eyes. "Yes ..." was all he could manage to say.

He walked down the steps and she took his arm. Together, arm in arm, they strode boldly into the promised land.

ॐঔৎঙৰঔৎঙৰঔৎঙৰঔৎঙ

Tuesday August 20, 1861 – Wheeling, Virginia:

"Thank you again for doing *that*, Nathan. It was ... just *wonderful!* Truly! Next to jumping the broom with his wife, I'm sure it was the happiest moment of Henry's life. It makes me cry whenever I think about it." Margaret sighed and wiped back a tear.

"And ... I know it cost you ... *some pain* ... to falsify those papers, Nathan. It hurts me too, whenever I must lie, though it seems I've had to do a great deal of it lately to escape Walters. I'm so very grateful to you for making that sacrifice on Henry's behalf."

Nathan smiled, "Think nothing of it, my dear. It was the *right* thing to do. I've accepted the necessity and righteousness of it, and that helps lessen the sting. Even as you were forced to do distasteful things to save your own life."

"Yes," she answered and gazed out the window of the carriage at the passing countryside, currently a wide field of beans. Harry trotted along next to the carriage, keeping a close eye on his master, his tongue hanging out to one side. They were headed toward Wheeling for another meeting of the Convention, which was starting back up after a two-week recess.

She also appreciated taking the carriage and not bouncing along on the back of a horse. And likely Cobb appreciated getting off the farm for the day to hobnob with the other drivers waiting outside the Customs House. She knew Nathan would rather have ridden his horse out front with Tom and William—and Harry—and that he was in the carriage to keep her company out of pure kindness. He really was the most thoughtful and gentlemanly man she'd ever met.

And though he was a good man, and admirable in every way, she'd never felt anything other than warm, familial feelings toward him. Besides, she knew his heart belonged to another woman. Though he never mentioned her, plenty of others on the farm did: *Evelyn.* From what they said she was exceptionally beautiful, outgoing, witty, intelligent, and charming, and yet could ride a horse better than most men! A woman good at anything and everything she undertook. And everyone at Mountain Meadows had loved her, especially Nathan.

But Margaret had come to entirely despise this woman, Evelyn. Not out of some petty jealousy—she knew herself well enough to know that was *not* the case. She could picture being very happy for Nathan if he were to marry the *right* woman. And she could picture being as a sister to his future wife as well.

No, she detested Evelyn because of what she'd done to Nathan. By all accounts, just as it was looking like a betrothal was imminent, she'd suddenly left Mountain Meadows with no explanation. Nathan was devastated. And it was clear he'd still not gotten over her. Though he never discussed it, Margaret was inquisitive enough to have discovered he was still exchanging regular letters with her. Though it was not her usual way, she often fantasized about coming face-to-face with the woman one day and giving her piece of her mind. And *not* in a nice way!

But she shook off these wicked thoughts and tried to focus on the positive things that had recently come into her life. *Be grateful for what you have, Margaret! It's a thing more wonderful than you deserve or ever expected. Be thankful for the best brother a woman ever had! And the best momma*, she added, thinking fondly of Miss Abbey. Her warmth and love were something Margaret had never experienced in her life—her own parents rarely showed her any affection.

She forced her mind from its reverie back to the present and asked, "Do you think they'll approve holding a referendum on the new state today?"

"I would think so. The federal government has now officially recognized the 'Restored Government' as the legitimate government of the entire state and has seated its senators and representatives in congress in Washington. And the Restored Government has approved the creation of West Virginia. So I can see no reason not to put it before the people for a vote. I doubt there'll be much if any dissent today at the convention, but of course, you never know what men will decide to do when it comes right down to it."

"True. But which people do you think should be allowed to vote on it? Only the counties currently held by the Union? That doesn't seem quite fair somehow, since several counties we intend to include in the new state wouldn't be able to vote at all."

Nathan scowled, "I think we're past the point of caring about such niceties. If I described to you all the boorish, lawless behavior in Richmond to ensure the secession, it would make your skin crawl."

"But ... does that justify *us* behaving dishonorably?"

Nathan thought about that a moment, and absentmindedly reached in his pocket for a cigar and stuck it in his mouth. But then, remembering the lady's presence, he resisted the urge to light it.

"Just because the enemy controls those counties at present with force of arms doesn't mean they *own* them. Nor the people in them. I think if we're going to create a new state it must be done based on such boundaries as logic and geography dictate, not based on current military exigencies."

"Agreed. I suppose we could say those counties are *eligible* to vote but may not be *able to*, due to present military circumstances."

"Yes ... I think something of the kind makes sense. That includes my own county, Greenbrier, by the way. There is some reluctance to include it as it's seen as loyal to Richmond. But it's on the west side of the Alleghanies—I will insist on its inclusion," then he grinned, "even if I have to threaten violence in the convention hall."

She returned the smile and rolled her eyes. She knew he was a true gentleman and would do nothing of the sort. But ... it did have a certain appeal, she had to admit. And Nathan was certainly a man capable of doing so, if he chose to.

"I have to congratulate you again, Margaret. If this whole thing succeeds it will be in no small part because of you. If not for your brilliant suggestion—creating the 'Restored' Virginia government in Wheeling—this new state would never have made it past the U.S. Congress nor the president, regardless of how badly we'd wanted it to."

"Thank you for saying so, Nathan. When I thought about the creation of a new state and read back through every word of the Constitution concerning the matter, it became crystal clear; a new state can never be created from within an existing state without the consent of the legislature of the *original* state. Clearly the government in Richmond would *never* grant permission. And there are no exceptions, no way around it without amending the Constitution."

"So ... the only solution was to declare the government of the whole state vacated, due to the secession?" Nathan prompted.

"Yes, exactly. If you think about it, it makes perfect sense; by declaring secession and disavowing the United States Constitution, the government of Virginia has given up its right to be considered legitimate under that same Constitution. That has left the door open for loyal citizens living within the state—mostly those of us on the western side—to 'restore' the legitimate state government under the Constitution."

"And ... then that new, *Restored* Government could grant permission for the West to split off into its own new state?" he asked.

"Precisely."

"Like I said, Margaret: brilliant! Once again, I must praise God for His prescience—He instilled in you the desire to study Constitutional law at a young age, helped you escape, and guided your steps directly to us on the road to Wheeling. In doing so, He has provided the expertise Wheeling needs to successfully navigate this complex legal process at precisely the moment in time when it is needed.

"I think John Carlile was flabbergasted when you suggested your idea. He also thought it inspired, though I think he was a little miffed he hadn't thought of it himself."

"Well ... perhaps it's the sort of indirect, subtle thinking a woman is better equipped for than a man. Men are much more ... *straightforward* in their thinking. Which is not *always* for the best."

"You mean like riding in, guns blazing, and kicking in the door? Only to find out the person you've come to rescue has already escaped on her own?"

She smiled warmly at him, "Yes, *exactly* like that. Though the rescue *attempt* was greatly appreciated, dear one, late or not."

He returned the smile and tipped his hat to her, sticking the unlit cigar back in his mouth.

"In any case, Mr. Carlile needn't worry for his reputation. I have assured him he may take all the credit—I shall not claim otherwise. If the other delegates had known the idea came from a *woman* ... who knows what might've happened!"

"Yes ... I hate to admit it, but there's some truth in what you're saying. But it was your idea, *your* brilliance that made it possible—it galls me you will receive no credit."

She nodded thoughtfully, then said, "I have read some accounts that suggest Miss Abbey's namesake, Abigail Adams, wife of the second president, was as influential as any man in the founding of our country, but has never received any credit." She shrugged, and continued, "But such is the world we now live in. Perhaps it will not always be that way, even as you have spoken of a day when the black men may be treated more equally. For now I shall be content if I am allowed to participate, albeit behind the scenes, and feel like I'm having my say.

"And as for Mr. Carlile, he has been most magnanimous in private. Even when we met with the new governor, Mr. Pierpont, he gave me credit for giving him the suggestion. And he glowingly praised my knowledge of Constitutional law. His honor agreed to include me in future discussions concerning the new state constitution!"

"Well, that sounds more promising. And if you'll help write the new constitution, it makes me feel much better about the future of the new state," Nathan grinned, with the cigar between his teeth.

☙☙☙☙☙☙☙☙

"Oh, Miss Abbey ... I just don't think I can say it *that way*. Not after all these years!"

"Come now, Megs ... I'm honoring your wishes by continuing to call you *'Megs'* even though your *real* free name is now *Magdalena*. The least you can do is honor my wishes and call me *Abbey*. Or at least *Abigail*, if that makes you feel any better."

Megs continued to frown at Abbey and shake her head. They sat side by side on Abbey's bed in her tiny upstairs bedroom. The bed was presently stripped of bedding, and a freshly ironed and folded set of sheets sat in a neat pile next to Megs.

"Megs ... you're no longer my ... *servant* ... so now, finally, we can just be friends. No ... *closer* than friends; we've been together so long we're more like sisters."

"Well ... I agree with *that* part, it's the *so long* part of it I'm having trouble with. I been calling you *Miss Abbey* almost my whole life and I'm over fifty now! How you expect me to change after all this time?"

"Because you're *free* now, dear. The world has changed ... so maybe it's time *you* did, too."

Megs continued to shake her head, but the frown had been replaced by a twisted grin. "All right ... if you'll agree to stop pestering me, I'll agree to ... *think* about it."

Abbey rolled her eyes, "Well, one thing's for sure, you're upholding the family name in one regard: you're just as stubborn as the rest of the Chambers!"

Megs chuckled, "Oh, I'm stubborn all right. But not *that* stubborn!"

Abbey giggled and patted her affectionately on the arm.

"Well, now that's settled, we may as well get on with it. Come on."

"You sure about this ... *Abbey?*"

"*Oh! There* ... you did it!"

"Did what?"

"Called me just *Abbey.*"

"No, I didn't."

Abbey scowled, and they both shared a laugh.

"I'm serious now, Abbey ... after all this time, why you want to learn how to do all these household chores anyway?"

"I *told* you ... until we can get back to Mountain Meadows the money's going to be very tight. Dear Nathan doesn't like to worry me about such things, but I know for a fact most of Jacob's money was in the farm itself—the land and all its buildings and equipment."

"And us slaves," Megs added, becoming more serious.

"Yes ... that's true. More proof our Nathan is a *truly* good man, in case we had any doubts. There's likely never been another master who's voluntarily given up such a large fortune just so his people could be free."

"No ... I reckon not. You must be very proud to have such a man for a son."

Abbey smiled and said, "So must *you.*"

Megs looked away and wiped at her eyes, "Oh ... *stop* that."

Abbey continued to smile, but said, "Anyway ... Mountain Meadows made most of its money each year from the cotton harvest. This farm, Belle Meade, is a fine piece of land, but it's just too far North to grow cotton. And though the corn is looking lovely, with all the attention Toby's been giving it, my understanding is it's not nearly as valuable. Tom says we *may* be able to cover our expenses, if prices are good. But if not ... well, let's just say after buying this land and keeping us all fed, there's little money left.

"So the point I'm getting at is ... no longer having free labor, if I'm not able to afford to pay for it, I can't expect to be served by others. I must learn how to ... fend for myself, as they say."

"So ... if the money runs out ... you gonna just throw me outta here?"

"Oh! *No*, dear! Certainly not! I'd *never* do that. Never in life!"

"Then what're we worrying over? As long as I'm here I'll take care of you, Abbey. Even if I have to do it all by myself with my own two hands. I ... need something to do, or I'll go batty."

"But my dear; what if you want to go somewhere else? You're *free* now ... you could go somewhere they might pay you good money to run a large household like you've been doing. And ... maybe you could ... I don't know ... find a husband."

"Oh my goodness, Abbey! Why on Earth would I want one of *those?!* I seen all the trouble yours caused you! And since I'm too old now for children, what would be the point of it anyway?"

"Well it wasn't *all* bad," Abbey got a wicked grin. "Sometimes ... up in the bedroom ... when Jacob and I were alone, we'd ..."

"*Abigail!* You *stop* that right now! That is *way* more'n I want to know, or to ever think about!"

50

Abbey started laughing and couldn't stop. Soon Megs had joined her. They laughed until they were choked for breath and wiping their eyes.

"Oh ... you are so ... *bad* ... Abbey!"

Abbey giggled, "Yes ... just please don't tell Nathan, he'd be horrified!"

Megs continued to smile and shake her head.

Once they'd recovered sufficiently to do what they'd come to do, Megs said, "All right ... if you're determined, we may as well get on with it."

They stood up from the bed.

"So ... here's how I go about making a bed ..."

ಬಿ8ುದ8ುಜ8ುಬಿ8ುದ8ುಜ8ುಬಿ8ುದ8ುಜ8ು

Rosa reached over and yanked a weed out from between two bean plants and tossed it out onto the bare dirt between the rows. She sat up, tipped back her straw hat and wiped the sweat from her forehead. She looked back where she had been, at the trail of pulled weeds, now withering after their uprooting. She'd go back through and scoop them up into a basket later when she needed a break from crawling in the dirt on hands and knees. She looked up at the sun, noting it now stood almost directly overhead — midday. It would be a long, hot afternoon before she could quit for the day, just as the sun was setting.

She was determined to do her bit and not shirk her duties. But she missed being a maid in the house — cool shade and no dirt! But they said the house was too small for so many maids, and even some that had been doing it for years were turned out to do farm work.

But mostly she missed ... being near *him*, the Captain. Just thinking about him still gave her an odd empty feeling in the pit of her stomach. Like something in her was missing or incomplete.

And not for the first time she wondered what good it had done her to be freed. The work was harder, the food was worse, the housing not as nice — even the cabins had been better than tents — and there was still no money to buy things one might want. And worst of all, she rarely saw the Captain, except from a distance.

She remembered the excitement and joy when she'd first learned he was going to free them. It would be a new life, a new *world!* And he would no longer be her master, she no longer his slave. But would that really change anything? Could he ever love her as he had Evelyn?

And what if he did? Then what? A white man would never marry a black woman ... the world just wasn't ready for such a thing. So what did that leave? Being his mistress? How would *that* feel, knowing all the other women, both black and white, despised you? And the men thought you no better than a whore?

She had no answers to these questions. But it didn't stop her thinking about him and what it might be like to be with him. To gaze lovingly into those deep, dark eyes! To softly kiss his lips ... it was ... almost beyond her imagining. She got an odd, tingling feeling all over whenever she thought about it.

But ever since the day of their freedom he'd been too busy to give her any time, and barely any notice. First fighting off the slavers, then the long trek north in the wagons, and now off doing ... whatever it was he was doing for the governor. She had no idea what that might be.

On the rare occasions she had seen him, he'd smiled and treated her kindly. But ... she could sense something was amiss with him. Something had changed. Did he no longer care about her? Was his earlier care and concern only an act? She didn't think so, but she couldn't shake the feeling he was now trying to avoid her, and she had to admit it hurt to think on.

But fortunately, she had other thoughts to distract her. And she'd even felt some new feelings, *good* feelings that had nothing to do with the Captain.

It was while they were still traveling north in the wagons that a miraculous thing happened in her life — a thing she had never dreamed possible. It started when the runaway slave Henry had joined the caravan. After they met, they had come to realize he had married her long-lost mother, Lilly, on a farm somewhere over to the east.

At first it was too shocking and upsetting to comprehend. But her curiosity eventually drove her to seek Henry out time and again. He always took time for her, and patiently answered her every question about her momma. And when she wasn't asking specific questions, he was telling everything he could remember about her—the things she said and did, the way she smiled and laughed. Songs she liked to sing, the foods she liked best, her favorite color and flower, and on and on. Most important, he told Rosa anything he could remember Lilly'd ever said about her young daughter. For the first time in her life, Rosa felt like she knew something about her momma. For the first time, her momma felt *real*, part of the waking world and not just a dream to help her sleep well at night.

And after a time, she realized she was seeking Henry out not just to hear stories of her momma, she was starting to have warm feelings toward *him*. Not romantic feelings, but familial feelings. She knew he wasn't her *real* daddy, but ... he was kindly, and gentle. He treated her with such care and warmth she found it easy to imagine him being her daddy. And why not? He was married to her momma, after all. And if Miss Abbey could adopt Miss Margaret for a daughter, why couldn't Henry make her *his* daughter? The thought of it was a comfort to her.

And Henry spoke of Lilly in such glowing terms it was clear to Rosa how much he still loved her, despite their long separation. It gave her new things to consider that she'd never thought about before. If even slaves could be happily married despite having nothing to call their own, how much better would it be for freemen? And for some reason when she thought these thoughts, she always saw Tony in her mind.

He'd expressed his feelings for her back at Mountain Meadows, but she'd turned him down cold and hurt him. She cringed every time she thought of it; he'd not deserved such treatment, and she felt ashamed of her actions.

And hadn't he proven himself to be a *real* man? Smart, tough, brave ... heroic even? She also had to admit these thoughts helped lessen the sting of her forced separation from the Captain.

෩෨෬෪෩෨෬෪෩෨෬෪

July 23, 1861
Manassas Junction, Virginia

Dear Evelyn,

*I hope and pray these words find you happy and in good
health.*

*It is difficult to find the words to express all I have
experienced and felt these last few days. Excitement, fear,
elation. And also, great sorrow. All these feelings and
more I have known in quick succession.*

*By now you must have heard the glorious, good news of
our victory over the Northerners at Manassas. Our
regiment had been assigned to a brigade of fellow
Virginians under a commanding officer also from the
Commonwealth, Brigadier General Thomas Jackson.
General Jackson is a pious and serious man, a war veteran,
and an instructor at the Virginia Military Institute. He
has made sure every man under his command has been
properly trained and equipped for battle.*

*Sadly, that has not been the case for other units of the
army, and such was well demonstrated yesterday during
the battle.*

*Our brigade arrived late to the battlefield, and
immediately witnessed a scene of smoke, noise, death, and
chaos such as one can hardly imagine without being there.
Though we could see but little, it appeared all our
Southern forces were in full retreat after unsuccessfully
engaging the enemy.*

*I looked over at Captain Bob Hill, my immediate superior,
to see if we ought to join the retreat. But General Jackson
rode out in front of the brigade and ordered us to stand-to
right where we were and prepare to fight. So we stood,
shoulder to shoulder, a great force of two thousand brave
men, never knowing if we were staring at the approach of*

our own deaths in the form of the Northern army. Even writing these words later, I swell with pride at the very thought of it.

And when we fired our guns it was a thunderous noise and choking thick smoke. We reloaded and fired, over and over again, standing firm, our general steadfastly refusing to retreat even a single step.

And though our own men fell to the enemy's guns all around us, still we fought on. Soon we noticed other companies of our army, but not of our brigade, were rallying around us, no longer running away. The approaching enemy faltered, paused, and began to fall back. Our brave stand was the turning point of the battle, which eventually drove the Northerners from the field in defeat.

Today at camp a story has been going around—one of the retreating Southern generals said to his men, "Look, men; there stands General Jackson, immovable as a stone wall. Rally around the Virginians!" And now people have started calling our general "Stonewall" Jackson, and our brigade "The Stonewall Brigade"! Isn't that something?

But even so, there is also a great sadness. Nearly half the men in the brigade are either killed or wounded, though I never suffered so much as a scratch, thank the Lord. Many fine young men are gone, several of whom I have gotten to know well in the past few weeks. Surely this must be the worst and hardest aspect of war, much more so than any sort of hardship or deprivation.

I must finish this letter so it will go out with today's post. I think of you often and pray you will find it in your heart to answer this letter, whenever most convenient. I would be most appreciative to hear any mundane detail of the "normal" life back in Richmond.

Your sincere friend,

Jubal Collins

Second Lieutenant, 27th Virginia Volunteer Regiment

"Hey, Captain Hill, I'm heading over to the quartermaster's to mail off this letter. You want me to send yours too?"

"Thank you, Jubal, but *no*. I ... I don't know where to send it."

"You don't know the person's address, sir? I'm sure if you just put their name and the town on the envelope the postal service will get it to them."

"It's ... more complicated than that, I'm afraid. You see ... the young lady was ... she ... well, to be honest, I don't even know what town or even which state she may be in by now."

"Oh ... sorry, sir. What with the war on, I'm sure there's gonna be a lot more of that type of thing going on. But ... maybe she'll write to *you* instead."

"Not likely, Lieutenant. Last time I saw her I hadn't yet enlisted. She'll not know which unit I'm in, nor where I'm deployed."

"Oh. Sorry, sir. Ain't none o' my business, but just curious; if you don't know how to get the letter to her, why'd you take the time to write it, anyway?"

Bob was quiet for a moment, thinking of how to answer. Though it really was no one else's business, he liked the young man and knew he was just trying to be helpful and friendly. "I guess it ... well, it makes me feel like I'm talking to her, even if she never reads it. Does that make any sense?"

"Oh, yes, sir. I understand completely. I feel the same when I'm writing to *my* friend—like she's sitting next to me and I'm talking directly to her. Well, I'd best be running so I don't miss the mail. I hope you locate your lady friend sometime soon."

"Thank you, Jubal."

Bob leaned back against a stump where he sat on the grass. The brigade would be moving out soon, and he was taking a few moments to catch a little rest. He gazed up at the sky, watching a puffy white cloud sail by, wishing for the thousandth time there was some way to know if Margaret had made good her escape. And if she was still alive. And if so, where she was.

And for the thousandth time he chastised himself for a fool and a coward for not taking her away with him, Walters be damned. After the battle he'd just survived he no longer felt intimidated by his old boss. Why hadn't he just killed the man as he'd so richly deserved?

He sighed. At the time he'd thought helping to arrange her escape would be enough to ease his guilty conscience and put him on a solid path toward redemption. But now if anything he felt even more guilt than before. In the end he had abandoned her to her fate; he had failed her.

ೞೞ಄಄ೞೞ಄಄ೞೞ಄಄

Evelyn finished reading Jubal's letter for the second time, folded it and put it in her handbag before knocking at the Hughes' door. She'd never spoken with Jonathan or Angeline about her agreement to exchange letters with Jubal. She didn't want to feel any pressure to betray him; she'd promised herself never to use any information he provided in a way that might harm him.

She already felt guilty about him resigning as a police officer and joining the army because of his conflicted feelings about her. The letter describing his part in the battle had been terrifying; she prayed he might somehow stay safe in the midst of the terrible carnage the war now seemed to promise.

Though she had no intention to share the letter, she wanted to discuss the battle with the Hughes. It was all the talk in town, and she was eager to get their opinion on its meaning, though it was clearly a disaster from the Union perspective.

But she was pleasantly surprised to find Angeline in an upbeat humor as they sat down to tea.

"I must say, Angeline, I'd expected a longer face. You're not upset about the Manassas Junction battle?"

"Well, of course one never wants to hear of their side losing a battle. And the terrible human toll and suffering ..." she shook her head. "But one battle does not a war make, my dear. And losing the first major battle may be a blessing in disguise."

"Oh? How so?"

"Because it may give the South an exaggerated opinion of their own capabilities versus the North, so they'll be slow to make the improvements necessary for the greater war effort.

"While just the opposite will be the case in the North; they now know they must get their house in order if they wish to win this conflict. From what Jonathan has heard from his cousins, losing the battle, which is called the 'Battle of Bull Run' in the North, has fired them up like no victory ever could have. Volunteers are flooding into the army recruitment posts.

"And President Lincoln now knows he'll have no easy victory and will need to get the right general officers in place if he expects to win."

"Well, when you explain it like that it sounds a whole lot more hopeful!"

"Of *course* it's hopeful, my dear! This is only the opening prelude; the symphony is far from over. We are still confident in the final victory. This defeat has, ironically, moved that one step closer.

"And ... we've had better military success out west ... Confederate forces have been all but driven out of northwestern Virginia by General McClellan, from what we understand. It seems at least one Union general knows how to fight."

"Oh! Nathan must be so pleased."

"Yes ... it'll make securing the new state in the west much easier, I should think."

"That *is* good news! Thank you, Angeline, you've made me feel so much better. Now I can feel lighthearted and not resentful as the city celebrates."

"Yes, you may celebrate as well, though you will celebrate for a different reason and no one will be the wiser!"

"Oh! Speaking of celebrations, I meant to ask if you would be attending my friend Belinda's wedding on Saturday? I am to serve as her maid of honor."

"Oh, truly? Congratulations on that. It speaks to a true friendship between the two of you. But sadly, no, I will not be in attendance. Jonathan and I will be ... otherwise engaged that day."

"Oh, I see. I will miss seeing you there."

"Likewise, my dear. I understand the groom, Oliver Boyd has accepted a commission as a Major in the Confederate Army and is deploying immediately after?"

Evelyn looked down at her feet. It was another heavy weight on the guilt side of her scales. "Yes ... though in Ollie's case I think it is *very* reluctantly," she answered. "He is really such a gentle soul. I doubt he could kill a fly. I'm sure his parents expected it of him to uphold the family's honor. His father is quite stern by contrast. I pray Ollie stays safe in the conflict."

"I will say amen to that, Evelyn. It is another sad story in this great sad tale. But you mustn't make what happens to him your responsibility. Even though it feels like he is being forced, he is *not*. He is an adult, a grown man. He makes his own decisions and suffers his own consequences. If something bad happens to him, you mustn't take ownership of that."

"Not even if the information I provide the Union side gets him killed?"

Angeline paused and looked her hard in the eyes, "Not even then."

Chapter 3. High Hopes and Ambitions

*"In this world you've just got to
hope for the best and prepare for the worst
and take whatever God sends."*

- Lucy Maud Montgomery

Saturday August 24, 1861 – Wheeling, Virginia:

Nathan and Tom brought their horses to a stop in front of the U.S. Customs House in Wheeling and dismounted, looping their reigns over a hitching post. The street was mostly empty, it being a Saturday.

In addition to Customs, the building, which also housed the U.S. Post Office, currently served double duty as the Capitol Building for the *Restored* Government of Virginia. The three-story, rectangular masonry building had been a true godsend to the new government; it had been completed at the expense of the federal government less than two years before the secession. It featured a stylish exterior in the Renaissance Revival style with decorative sill courses between each floor, round-arch window and door openings, and an arcaded set of five fancifully arched doors at the entrance. These were reached by a set of seven broad stones steps.

The interior featured similar design elements, including a large, elegantly decorated court room, which currently served as the legislative house. Both "Wheeling Conventions" took place in this room.

As they entered the building, Tom headed down the hall to the post office to see if they'd received any mail, while Nathan climbed the stairs to the second floor for his meeting with Governor Francis H. Pierpont. Harry bounded gamely up the stairway behind him, though he'd still not grown overly fond of stairs—he was still not used to being *inside* buildings.

When they reached the governor's office midway down the hall, Nathan peeked in and saw his honor seated behind a desk, gazing at a stack of papers in front of him. Nathan knocked on the door sill.

"Ah ... Chambers! Come in, come in. Thank you for coming in on a Saturday," Pierpont said, rising from his chair and extending his hand to Nathan.

"Governor. Never mention it, your honor ... I am entirely at your service."

Pierpont smiled, "Well ... for the moment, anyway."

Nathan smiled and shrugged noncommittally.

"Please ... have a seat, Nathan," he chuckled when he glanced down at Nathan's large, furry companion, "and you too, Harry."

"Thank you, Francis," Nathan answered, removing his hat and sitting in the single, bare wooden chair directly in front of the governor's desk.

The desk was small and simple, in keeping with the office itself. "Spartan" wouldn't have been too strong a term, Nathan decided. The small office featured a single large, multi-pane window—arched on top, of course, like all the others—and a few modest pieces of furniture. About the only attempt at luxury in the room was a small fireplace to one side, though of course that was currently unlit, it being high summer. Nathan had to smile as he recalled Governor Letcher's massive, ornate office inside the elegant Capitol Building back in Richmond.

Governor Pierpont himself was anything *but* Spartan, Nathan thought. He was a tall, burly man with a thick, unruly head of dark hair and beard that rendered him seemingly larger than life. His typically jolly demeanor and warm smile tended to put men at ease and win over new acquaintances easily. But Nathan knew he had a strong, serious side as well, which he'd displayed on the rare occasions it had been needed.

"I trust all is well at your new farm, sir? With your mother, the impeccable Miss Abbey? And your delightful sister, Margaret?"

"Yes, your honor, all is well with them, thank you kindly for asking. We've managed to settle into our new residence. It's *comfortable* ... though not quite what we're used to. But it will certainly suffice for the foreseeable future ... and for that we are *most* thankful."

61

"Yes, I would think so. I can scarcely imagine the heart-rending ordeal you've recently experienced, having to virtually fight your way out of your own home, and then leaving everything you owned behind. How terrible!"

Nathan shrugged. He had no interest in dwelling on things he couldn't change, at least not any time soon.

"Anyway, Nathan, I asked you here to discuss the military situation in the state. With everything that's been happening concerning the West Virginia referendum, we've not had a chance to meet one-on-one, and I very much wish to discuss in detail the ramifications of the most-gratifying Union victory at Rich Mountain."

"Certainly, your honor. I'll be happy to relate anything I know. And, of course, spew forth *pontifical opinions* about anything I don't," he grinned at Pierpont, who returned the gesture, appreciating the humor. The governor knew plenty of men who would happily do just *that*, but Nathan Chambers definitely was *not* one of them!

"First, let me say how delighted I was to read your dispatches after the wonderful victory at Rich Mountain!" Pierpont continued. "I only wish I'd been there to see it! No ... never mind *that* ... I speak casually of matters of which I have no knowledge. I'm sure the ... *carnage* of war ... must be most upsetting and unpleasant."

"Yes ... it's not a thing to be taken lightly. Even in victory there is always heart-rending suffering, injury, and death. On both sides."

"Most certainly ... most certainly. Be that as it may, I couldn't be more pleased with General McClellan and his conduct of the war. From what I understand, the Confederate forces that weren't defeated outright have fled back over the mountains to the east in great haste and complete disarray. I'm sure you heard I presented a resolution to the legislature praising General McClellan's heroic efforts, a resolution that passed unanimously."

"Yes ... I heard about it. But I wish you'd have waited for my full, detailed report, before you'd presented your resolution."

"Oh? What is it I'm missing?"

Nathan reached into his pocket for a cigar. He stuck it in his mouth and chewed on it a moment before responding.

"Let's just say I am less than enamored of my old classmate George B. McClellan. His performance in command of the Union armies was ... *lackluster* at best."

"Oh, come now, Nathan! Surely you can't argue with success, despite whatever shortcomings he may have had. No operation is perfect, but the results of this one are indisputable."

"True ... it *ended* well. Probably as well as could be expected with so many green troops and officers. Still, it galls me McClellan is feted as a hero. I can assure you sir, he was anything *but!*"

"Oh, I see ..."

"I'm also not pleased about his pronouncements concerning slavery—that he would use the Union Army to forcefully suppress any slave uprisings and help return runaway slaves. What was he thinking?! Makes people wonder why we're bothering to fight this war at all!"

"Yes, it certainly sends mixed messages, if nothing else. But, to his credit, I think he was just trying to convince slave-owning Virginians on *this* side of the mountains that he is *not* their enemy."

"Yes, well ... maybe he *should* be ..."

"Well, you and I may believe so, but ... the issue of slavery— or not—is certain to be a sticking point for the new state. It's already causing some friction in preliminary discussions. Fortunately, the final decision on it can wait until later. It won't have to be resolved until we draft the new constitution."

"True ... but I can't see the point of creating a new state for the Union, and then bringing it in as a *slave* state! And I can't envision Mr. Lincoln agreeing to it."

"I can't either. Hopefully it will be resolved to our satisfaction when the time comes." Then he smiled, "Perhaps your very impressive and persuasive sister will be able to convince the others."

Nathan returned the smile, "Well, if anyone can, she can," he shook his head, thinking on all the ways in which she continued to amaze him. "She is ... really quite extraordinary, I must say."

"Very true, very true," Pierpont agreed, nodding his head. "Getting back to McClellan's handling of the military operations, I was just thinking ... perhaps you set too high a standard, Nathan. Whenever I've mentioned your name in military circles, I've heard effusive and enthusiastic praise. By all accounts you are an exceptional and highly admired officer, with a stellar, even heroic service record. Could it be other men ... can't quite measure up to your expectations?"

"I don't think my standards are too high, Francis. I just expect officers to do their duty, not *shirk* it. For instance, I can tell you in no uncertain terms, General Rosecrans performed admirably in the campaign—no man could've done better. If you ask me, he's the *real* hero of Rich Mountain."

"Oh! Well, then I shall have to keep that in mind, thank you for the information. And that bodes well for us in the short term, since Rosecrans is now the commanding officer over western Virginia."

"True, and I couldn't be happier about *that*. I expect he'll continue to drive hard against any remaining enemy forces in the North, likely turning south and routing them out of the Kanawha Valley next. Then there'll be no rebel armies west of the mountains, and we can focus all our attention on putting the new state together and raising more armies."

"That's something to look forward to."

"Agreed. And since things seem to be going so well militarily here in the West, I wanted to start discussing with you when you might be able to part with me. As you know, my men and I are most eager to don the blue and take the fight to the enemy in earnest."

"Yes of course, Nathan, of course. No one expects you to stay here indefinitely and forego your rightful destiny as one of the Union's foremost general officers. And I agree with you, things are now looking very positive indeed for the new state, from the military perspective.

"But ... I do still have critical need of you and your men in the short term. Until we can re-organize the county governments and ensure they are run by loyalists, I'm afraid local law enforcement is spotty at best—in places entirely non-existent. Add to that the fact many of our loyal law officers have already enlisted with the army—their knowledge and expertise in handling arms being invaluable to the regiments. As I mentioned briefly in our previous meeting, I would ask you to help maintain law and order while we're getting our feet under us, so to speak.

"And of course, I would appreciate it if you would help me finish organizing the recruitment and training of western Virginia troops—recommending the proper officers, defining appropriate training regimens, procuring necessary arms and equipment, and what not.

"And, finally, continuing to be our official liaison with the Union Army operating within Virginia, making sure our best interests are represented in all plans and contingencies.

"If you can stay long enough to do that, then it should be sufficient. Just enough to get us started on the right foot, so to speak. Only another month or so more, I would think. No ... let's call it *two* months. That will get us past the election on October 24th. Then you'll have seen the new state through to its initial budding, if not the final fruition."

Nathan thought about that a moment, then nodded, "That should work, governor."

"Splendid! That's settled then. Now, if you would be so kind as to indulge me, I would be delighted to hear a detailed account of the battle ..."

ဆဲၥဆၟၶၠၶဆၠၥၶၟၠၶၠၶ

As he and Tom walked back toward the house from the stables that evening, it occurred to Nathan he hadn't checked in on the special project he'd assigned to Jim. So he parted with Tom and changed directions, moving toward the collection of outbuildings.

He approached a large, single-story building with wide doors, clearly a building for storing wagons and such—a barn would be taller, and a toolshed not so wide.

When he stepped up to the open doors, he could see all the wagons and large farm implements had either been taken outside or pushed to one side. A wall at one end appeared to have recently been painted with a very dark colored paint. And the men were industriously sawing and hammering boards.

"Looks like everything's coming along nicely," he said, as he stepped into the room.

"Very good of you to say, sir," Sergeant Jim responded, looking up from his hammering. "We'll be ready in time, don't you worry. Even if'n I have to lose a thumb doing it! Just putting the finishing touches on, so to speak. We'll be ready by tomorrow first light ... right on schedule, sir!"

"Excellent, excellent! Thank you very much, Jim! Georgie, Jamie ... Stan. Thank you."

"You are quite welcome, sir. It has been our great pleasure ... except for perhaps my small disagreement with the hammer ..." Jim said and stuck his sore thumb in his mouth for emphasis.

"I am greatly looking forward to seeing it finished. Good evening, gentlemen."

ཥ༠ฝ༠ด༠ฌ༠ฝ༠ด༠ฌ༠ฝ༠ด༠

The next morning was the Sabbath, but Nathan was having trouble focusing on what he planned to say. He was feeling distracted this morning because of the little surprise he had planned for the freemen. After the sermon they would unveil the thing he'd had Jim and company working on for several weeks now.

The idea for it had started shortly after they returned home from the Rich Mountain campaign. Nathan and Tom were sitting on the veranda, enjoying their evening ritual of whiskey and cigars. They'd managed to acquire a Richmond newspaper, several weeks old, from among the goods left behind by the rebels when they'd abandoned the fort. Tom had been reading aloud from it an account of a slaveholder in southern Virginia who had been brought before a judge after being accused of beating one of his slaves to death with a club. The man did not deny doing it, but argued the slave had been his property, had been disobedient and disrespectful, and the law did not preclude him from dealing out whatever punishment he saw fit. The judge agreed with him and

66

ordered him set free. The newspaper appeared to side with the slave owner.

The story made Nathan think of Walters, and it made his blood boil. Especially when he considered, "Restored" Government or no, he was still subject to the laws on the books for the state of Virginia—at least until the new state was created with its own constitution.

After stewing on it a few moments, he suddenly sat up straight, and pounded his fist on the table. "Dammit, Tom! If I were to take a book in my hand, walk down to the tents, pick out one of the freemen and start teaching them to read and write, I'd be breaking the laws of Virginia, and would be subject to imprisonment! But if they were still slaves and I were to take a knife or a club instead, and murder that same person for no good reason, like Walters does, the law would happily look the other way! Damn it!" his mood had suddenly turned sour. "You know ... if I were *half a man*, I would say 'to hell with the law' and go ahead and teach them anyway."

Tom looked up. He set down his whiskey glass, and said, "But, sir ... you *are* very much *more* than half a man ... does that mean ...?"

"Yes, dammit, Tom! I *am* fixing to teach these people to read and write, and they can throw me in jail if they want to!"

Tom leaned back and whistled, clenching a cigar between his teeth. Then he smiled, and said, "Yes, Captain, but before they can throw you in jail, they will have to *catch* you at it! And out here on the farm, who's going to know anyway?"

"True, Tom. Very true," Nathan agreed, "besides which, the new Restored Government doesn't yet have any courts or law officers!" Then he held out his glass to Tom, and they clinked them together, to finalize the decision.

Shortly after, he'd enlisted Jim to start working on an appropriate classroom and recruited William and Margaret to be the teachers, them being the two obvious scholars of the group. The rest of the men would help in whatever capacity was needed.

They had decided to hold school in a large, barn-like shed used to store wagons, the formal carriage, and any number of large farm implements, such as plows, rakes, and harrows. With the help of Stan, Georgie, and Jamie, Jim had it swept it out and dusted it off, making it into a respectable classroom, despite the dirt floor underneath.

The larger items, such as the carriage and wagons, would be pulled outside during class time, with the other items strategically moved to the sides or back so as not to interfere with the students' view of the teacher. They had also built rows of benches for the students to sit on, which Jim had cleverly designed using hinges so they could be folded up and stored out of the way after class. They had constructed a "chalkboard" of sorts on one end of the room by sanding down the boards on one wall until they were relatively smooth, and then painting the wall black. William had obtained plenty of chalk, and a wide variety of reading materials on his last trip to Wheeling; everything from used children's elementary reading books, to old newspapers—anything to be had reasonably cheaply.

They figured their "classroom" could hold roughly fifty students, more if some stood in the back, or sat around the edges, or up front by the teachers. In good weather any overflow could stand in the doorway of the large barn doors opening on one side of the room. Since they didn't know what the interest would be, they had no idea if they had over- or under-planned it.

Now, if only they could get the students to show up. Nathan was determined at least all the young children should be there, and he hoped the younger men and women as well. Back at Mountain Meadows he might have been tempted to use his authority to compel them if they were hesitant. But now that they were freemen he'd just have to do his best to persuade them it was in their best interests.

And so today, at the end of his Sabbath sermon, he announced the existence of the new classroom and then gave a rousing speech on the need for freemen to be able to read and write, especially the young children just starting out in the world.

As it turned out, he needn't have worried. As soon as he dismissed them, the entire congregation immediately moved, en masse, to the new schoolroom. The work on the building had not, of course, gone unnoticed, and rumors of its purpose had been swirling around the farm ever since work on it had begun. Now it seemed everyone wanted to see it for themselves, to at least have their curiosity satisfied, if not to participate in the lesson.

It was another sunny day, so William and Margaret decided to leave the large barn doors on the sides open. This would let in more light, and allow anyone who was curious, but not yet committed, to observe without feeling pressured to participate. This turned out to be fortuitous, as otherwise there would have been no way to accommodate the entire population of the farm, as had proven to be the case.

Realizing what was happening, and wanting to seize the initiative, William immediately took charge and started instructing people on where to sit—youngest children in front, teenaged and young adults in the middle, and adults in the back and on the sides. Margaret saw what he was doing and jumped to the fore, directing anyone who just wanted to observe to stand in the doorway. Their new students were well used to following instructions, of course, so it was easily managed. It occurred to William he'd never seen a classroom this large organized so easily in any school he'd ever attended through all his years of education!

There was much excitement and chattering, especially amongst the young children, so William raised his arms and asked for quiet. A hush quickly fell over the crowd. "Good morning," he said.

There was a silence as everyone stared at their new teacher, waiting to see what would come next.

William smiled, and said, "In a schoolroom, when the teacher says, 'good morning' to the class, the class responds back with a hearty 'good morning' of their own to the teacher. Now, let's try it again. Good morning."

This time there was a rousing *"Good morning!"* from all in attendance, with some of the younger children feeling compelled to shout.

"Thank you, that was much better. That was the first lesson of the day, and you all passed," he said with another smile. There was a smattering of giggles at this, especially from the front rows.

"Now, the second lesson, especially for you younger children seated up front, is ... in a classroom we don't shout. We speak clearly, and loudly enough to be heard throughout the classroom, but we never, ever shout. So let's try once again. Good morning."

This was answered by another "good morning" from the class, this time the young children using more normal voices.

"Excellent, thank you!" William responded. "For any of you who don't yet know, my name is Mr. William, and this is Miss Margaret. We will be your teachers for this class. Class, please say 'good morning' to Miss Margaret."

This time there was no hesitation, and an enthusiastic "Good Morning, Miss Margaret" was soon echoing off the walls of the room.

Margaret smiled brightly, and responded, "And good morning to all of you."

William continued, "In this class you are going to learn the most wonderful and useful thing there is to know in all the world. The greatest thing ever taught in all the long history of the world, and that is ... *how to read and write*. It will take a little while for you to learn it well, and at first it may seem difficult, and you may become confused or frustrated. But let me assure you, each and every one of you within the sound of my voice *can* learn to do this, and you *will* learn it, if you try."

He knew the young children, and even the young adults would have no trouble accepting this statement, but he wondered about some of the older adults. He looked around to see if he could gauge their reaction. He noticed a few whispering amongst themselves, and he wondered how many of these would return after this first day. Then something the Captain had said in one of his sermons suddenly came to him—the Captain had said some of them already knew how to read and write. If William could take advantage of those ...

"Before we begin, I have a question for all of you. How many of you already know how to read and write? Please raise your hand and hold it up if you do."

At first there were shy looks, and he could see some whispers and some nudgings with elbows, but soon there were four people holding up their hands.

"Excellent, excellent! Thank you. If you are willing, we would be very honored, and would appreciate it very much if you would be our assistant teachers for this class. Would you be willing to do it?" he asked, of the people holding up their hands.

They looked from one to the other, and after some shrugging of shoulders, Megs, who was, of course, one of those who had raised her hand, took charge and said, "Yes, of course we will help, Mr. William. It would be our honor and pleasure. Ain't that right?" she asked, turning to look at the others.

"Yes, Megs," an old man responded meekly, and the others soon followed with their own, "Yes, Megs," and "Yes, Mr. William."

"Thank you very kindly," William responded. "I won't make you stand up here the whole time, and in fact I would like it if you would place yourselves around the room so you can assist the others, once we get started with the lesson. But will you come up here by me for just a moment, please?"

The small group obediently made their way forward to stand in the front of the class between William and Margaret. "Now, I know you all know one another, so it may seem kind of silly, but it is traditional for the teachers to introduce themselves to the class. Also, if you would be so kind, I would like each of you to tell me how it is you learned to read and write, how difficult it was, and whether or not you think the others in this room can learn it as well."

Megs smiled at this. *Very clever, Mr. William Jenkins, very clever*, she decided, nodding her head appreciatively. *Show them examples of their own kind who have already learned it, and they will see it can be done, even those having their doubts.*

To set the example, Megs immediately stepped forward and faced the class. "Good morning," she said. When there was no response, she raised her hands and gestured to the class in a *come-here* motion, which immediately provoked a hearty "good morning," back at her, followed by a smattering of laughter.

"You are quick learners," William said with a smile, which was followed by more laughter from the class.

"My name is Megs," she said, to which there were a few good-natured responses such as "Hello Megs," "nice to meet you," and so on from the audience, which prompted a scowl from Megs, and a "Please, do be respectful," from William.

"When I was a very young girl, I was moved from the fields into the Big House to be a maid. Then just before the Captain was born, Miss Abbey came to me and said she thought I would make a good nanny for the child, but I would need to be able to read and write so I could help teach him when the time come. One of the older maids learned when she was a young'n like me and so Miss Abbey had her teach me. I remember it was hard at first, but one day it just ... well, I don't know how to describe it but ... it just sort of became easy-like. Now, those of you who know me well know I am stubborn, and determined, which helped. But I am *not* the smartest person alive, so if I can learn it, y'all can too." Then she stepped back and motioned the next person in line to step up.

William smiled at her performance. Megs was something special, as he'd already known, and he felt grateful for her timely intervention in helping his plan come together.

One by one the others stepped forward, and said, "Good morning." This was now immediately met by an enthusiastic "good morning" in response, with much smiling and laughter, the class now keenly aware of their expected role.

Each told a story of how they had learned to read. Each story was slightly different. The old man had been taught as a young boy by his grandfather, who said it would be a good thing to know one day, though he never said why.

A woman had been taught by her mother who was very pious and believed it was important that her young daughter be able to read the holy book, which she now did every day—having inherited her mother's old Bible, though she didn't know how her mother had come by it.

The last woman told a similar story — an older relative who had taken her under her wing. Megs was the only one who had learned because the white masters had compelled it.

William thanked them kindly, and asked them to disperse themselves throughout the classroom, so they could assist anyone who had questions.

"Today, Miss Margaret and I will teach this class together. However, in the future it may be one or the other of us will need to be away on other business, and you will only have one teacher. So it will be especially helpful to have you assistants in the class."

William was delighted to have this new, unexpected set of helpers. In his mind, it couldn't have possibly worked out better if he had planned the whole thing that way from the beginning.

"Miss Margaret will begin our lesson for today," he gestured toward her, and she stepped up the chalkboard and wrote a single letter.

"Okay, class. The first thing we are going to learn, is the English alphabet, starting with the letter 'A,'" she began.

೮Ƿ๑๏೮Ƿ๑๏೮Ƿ๑๏೮Ƿ๑๏

Evelyn dabbed at the sides of her eyes with a handkerchief, careful not to smudge her makeup, as she watched Belinda and Ollie join hands for the final part of the wedding ceremony. It was the first time she'd worn any makeup since she'd been unceremoniously banished from her mother's house, now more than three months ago. Surprisingly, it was once again her mother, Harriet, who had applied her makeup for her.

When she had first heard the news from Belinda that Belinda's mother had insisted on inviting Harriet — them being old friends — Evelyn had felt a wave of apprehension. She anxiously envisioned the awkwardness of meeting her mother for the first time in months on the day of the wedding. They'd had no contact at all since the day Harriet had caught Evelyn meeting with two men working for the Underground Railroad and, after a brief, stormy argument, had expelled her rebellious daughter from her house.

But Evelyn had been surprised when a letter arrived two days later by courier. It had been addressed to "Evelyn Hanson, care of Belinda Evers" at Belinda's address, as Harriet still didn't know where Evelyn now lived.

> *My dear Evelyn,*
>
> *I wished to reach out to you to see if we might rekindle our relationship on an adult basis. Though it may no longer be practical for us to live under the same roof, it has greatly pained my heart for us to be so distant from each other.*
>
> *I realize now you are a woman and no longer a child, and as such must make your own choices in life. And though I may disagree with those choices, and wish not to participate in their consequences, I have resolved myself to allow you to handle your own affairs. My only desire at this point is to still be your mother, and you my (adult) child.*
>
> *Toward that end I would be honored if you would come to my house early on the day of Belinda's wedding that I might assist you in your preparations, as is befitting of your station.*
>
> *Best regards,*
> *Your Momma*

Not much of an apology, and not exactly warm and loving, Evelyn thought with a sigh, *but maybe it's a start.*

So she'd reluctantly agreed, and happily it hadn't been as awkward as she'd feared. By the end of her readying, including Harriet's now masterful use of the French makeup, they were chatting amiably as if nothing had ever come between them. It warmed Evelyn's heart, but she feared it wouldn't last; that Harriet might not be able to resist the urge to reinsert herself in Evelyn's life in her old, domineering way.

Evelyn refocused her attention to the festivities at hand, the pastor droning on in a prayer that was overly-long, in Evelyn's opinion. She stood up front with the other bridesmaids, next to the pastor. From here she had a good view of the venue, the vast back yard at Belinda's parents' home. It'd been decorated with all manner of flowers, ribbons, and banners mostly in yellow hues, Belinda's favorite. And dozens of rows of seats were filled with several hundred well-dressed guests. Evelyn had been determined to remember as many of the details as she could, to include in her next letter to Jubal. It was just the sort of thing he had been asking for, and would help with her typical dilemma of what to say to him in her regular correspondence.

But then when she looked back at the bride and groom she noted Ollie's light gray officer's uniform, elegantly trimmed in gold, and she felt the familiar twinge of guilt; that her spying activities could very well put his life in jeopardy once he deployed with the Confederate Army. Despite Angeline's words to the contrary, it was hard for Evelyn to reconcile her conflicted feelings about it.

And then she noted the sword hanging down from Ollie's left hip — an elegant, enameled scabbard with intricately carved brass handguard protruding from the top. She suppressed a quick chuckle as it reminded her of her disappointment when she'd noticed Nathan wasn't wearing his sword at the "Big Wedding" of the slave couples back at Mountain Meadows, opting for the more practical pistol instead.

But thoughts of *that* wedding brought back painful memories of what happened after, and her bright humor suddenly dimmed. She gazed around the venue once again, this time imagining her own wedding that never was ... with Nathan standing there, handsome, tall, and strong, smiling down at her lovingly.

And when the pastor said, "I pronounce you man and wife. You may now kiss the bride," Evelyn's tears were already flowing in earnest, but only she knew the *real* cause.

ༀༀༀༀༀༀༀༀༀ

"Hey Jesse, you hear them two darkies talking over at the General Store this morning?"

"What? Why would I care what a couple o' damned jungle savages was saying, Levi?"

"Well, normally you wouldn't. But I couldn't help overhearing these'ns saying they was learning to read and write! In a real classroom! And they wasn't just any ol' darkies—these was *women* to boot!"

"*No!* Levi, you gone daft? Ain't no one gonna bother teaching a bunch o' dumb darkie women. Prob'ly a waste of time I expect—too stupid to learn anyhow."

"These're some o' them freemen living out at the old Patterson place bought up by that abolitionist, Chambers."

"Chambers? That fella done freed his hundred-some slaves and brought 'em here from down south and pitched a whole field o' tents for 'em?"

"Yep, the same."

"*Damn* ... that don't seem right. I don't care if they's free, mind. Don't care nothing 'bout slaves one way or the other. Never could afford one myself. I just wish they'd go on and be free somewheres else."

"I say amen to that, brother."

"Next thing you know, they's wanting to be in the same schools with our kin. And in our churches. Sittin' right next to good, honest, God-fearing white folks! It ain't right I tell you, Levi."

They were quiet for several minutes, taking turns sipping from a ceramic bottle of homemade whiskey they were passing back and forth. They sat on the floorboards in the shade on Levi's porch, on a small farm only a few miles southeast of Wheeling, gazing out across his pasture, where a milk cow grazed contentedly. Levi idly swatted at a fly that had settled on the side of his neck, attracted by the steady stream of sweat running down it.

"Hey, you know what else I heard them darkies say, Jesse?"

"What now?"

"I heard them say *exactly* when the next lesson would be held out at the Chambers' farm."

"*Oh?* Hmm ... you thinkin' what I'm thinkin', Levi?"

"Yep. Maybe we round up a few of the boys and go teach them abolitionists they can't just turn Virginia over to a bunch o' black savages just 'cause they got a whole passel o' blue-coat Northerners marching around acting all high-and-mighty important."

"I say amen to that, Levi. Amen to that."

ഇഇഇഇഇഇഇഇഇഇ

"It ain't *right*, is all I'm sayin', George!"

"Why you so all-fired anxious to go'n get yourself shot at again anyway, Ned?"

"I ain't lookin' to get shot at—just lookin' to give them slavers more payback, is all. So why they lettin' all them white boys go fight, and we can't? We already been trained ... by the Captain *hisself!* I bet the Captain knows more about fightin' than any of them officers that's marching out there now. And Sergeant Jim, and Mr. Tom ... and all the soldier men of the Captain's."

"That's true," Tony agreed.

"And we already done fought *real* battles—with guns and bayonets. And plenty o' blood. We done killed rebels already, lots of 'em. I bet most o' them white boys marching out now don't even know which is the pointy end of a stick!"

They all chuckled at this.

"Well, I reckon they'll find out soon enough, like we did," George said, trying to be the voice of reason in the group.

"Maybe we should just go ask the Captain about it," Henry said. "I know he done said 'no' when you asked him before, but maybe if we was to ask it again ... tell him how *important* it is to us ... he'll change his mind on it."

"It ain't the Captain's choice, Henry," Tony answered.

"How you know?"

"'Cause he done told me so himself," Tony answered. "Said if it was up to him, we *could* fight."

"*You* asked him, too?" Ned asked.

Tony was quiet for a moment, looking down at his feet. "You ain't the only one wants to fight, Ned."

"Well, if it ain't up to the Captain, then who?" Henry asked.

"I dunno. Mr. Lincoln, I reckon," Tony answered.

They were quiet again for a while, each lost in his own thoughts.

George stood up, "C'mon. No sense sittin' around here wasting our breath on it. Truth is, ain't none of us knows nothing. Let's at least go ask the Captain again. Ask him all our questions so we know. So we finally know what's going on."

Nobody could think of an argument to this, so they rose and followed George out the door of the tent.

ᔛᔤᦂᦆᔛᔤᦂᦆᔛᔤᦂᦆ

"Gentlemen, I've asked y'all to come here tonight because I know y'all are good, loyal Virginians. Virginians who can't just sit idly by while these Godless Northerners take over our state.

"Now I know most of you don't care a whit about slavery, one way or the other. That goes for me as well. This ain't about slavery. It's about having a say in our own state, not letting foreigners from up North come here and lord it over us, telling us what we can and can't do.

"If you believe, deep down in your heart, like I believe, then I'm asking you to join me to support this most noble cause. If we truly believe in what Virginia stands for, then we must be willing to fight for her."

"But Zach, the Confederate army's been all but whupped in this part of Virginia. Only over in Shenandoah or further east are there any of our troops still fighting at all. Maybe some down south in Kanawha—though I heard those ain't faring too well neither. How we gonna fight if we got no army here? You want us all to leave our homes and hike over to Richmond? With Union troops marching around everywhere like they own the place?"

There were several nods of agreement, and affirmative mutterings in the small crowd of twenty or so local men. They were gathered in Zach Cochran's small barn in the little town of Boothsville, several miles outside Grafton.

"No, Jeremiah. I ain't saying to march to Richmond. I'm saying to fight *right here*. Fight for our own homes and our own way of life. My cousin, 'Grumble' Jones, is an officer in the Confederate Army. He sent me a message sayin' to fight any way we could until the regular army can regroup and come back. Says they've had great success back East and have the Yankees on the run over there. So it's only a matter of time before our boys are back here in force. Until then, we gotta do our part."

"But how?"

"Well, I'm still sheriff here, despite what them traitors over to Wheeling say about it. Which means I can still collect taxes for use in our purpose, especially from them pro-Union traitors. And I can enforce the law — that of Richmond, not Wheeling. And y'all have guns. Y'all have stout hearts. That's all it takes. Oh ... and one more thing you'll need, brains! We got to be smart about this. We're badly outnumbered and outgunned by the Union soldiers. But we know the terrain, it's our home, our territory. We know how to get from place to place without being seen. We can sneak into a Union army depot, destroy or take their supplies, and be gone before they know what's happened. We can break their wagons, kill their horses, cut their telegraph lines, and any dozens of other things to disrupt their fighting."

Then he paused, and gazed about the room, making eye contact with each man there.

"And then ... we can hide along the road, up in the woods. And when a Union convoy comes along, we can attack and ... kill them."

ಬಿಎನಿ೦ಚಿಬಿಎನಿ೦ಚಿಬಿಎನಿ೦ಚಿ

Wednesday August 28, 1861 – Wheeling, Virginia:

"What do you make of it, Billy?" Nathan asked, between puffs on his cigar. Nathan and his men stood in the middle of a burned-out supply house, with no roof, and only charred timbers for walls. It had been used to store supplies for Union army troops expected to pass through Cameron, in Marshall County, on their way south. Fortunately, there'd been no gunpowder present, or half the town might've been destroyed in the resulting blast.

Governor Pierpont had asked Nathan to ride out and investigate after receiving a telegram earlier that morning reporting the incident.

He'd brought his original Texas soldiers with him plus Zeke, his favorite farmhand, who was now treated as just another of the troops. Nathan didn't really think there'd be any need for them, not expecting any *real* trouble. But he figured it would give them something to do. He feared boredom worse than any action by the enemy at this point. He wished to hold the men together long enough for him to properly complete his duties with the governor. Then they could all enlist and serve together as they'd done in Texas. If the men started enlisting now, before he and Tom did, they'd soon be scattered to the four winds. So far, the men had chosen to stay with him. But how long that would continue was anyone's guess. The outside pressures on the men to join up continued to mount.

Only William hadn't accompanied them this time. He and Margaret had begged Nathan to allow the reading class twice a week so the students would be less likely to forget the previous lesson. They'd discussed it at length and agreed to hold a second class on Wednesday afternoons. That way the participants could work half a day but wouldn't be too exhausted to learn anything, as they might with an evening class.

Billy looked up at Nathan, "Not an accident, Captain. Someone has poured kerosene on the floor and on the supplies. Set it afire with a torch," he held up the charred remains of a two-foot-long stick as evidence. "They also stole items before the blaze, sacks of flour at least. Maybe other things."

"*Damn it!*" the proprietor swore, grabbing a handful of his hair in both hands and grimacing in despair. "Damned rebel scum! *May they rot in hell!* Burning down my warehouse just to deprive Union troops of a few supplies! What's the world coming to?" he asked, looking at Nathan and shaking his head.

"Nothing good, apparently," Nathan answered, taking another puff on his cigar. "Come, men. There's nothing more we can do here. Let's head over to the inn and get settled for the night and have a meal. Then I'll send a telegram to the governor reporting our findings. Tomorrow we can ask around, see if anyone saw anything, and if they're willing to talk about it."

ऴ૭ऴ௸ऴ௸ऴ૭ऴ௸ऴ௸ऴ૭ऴ௸ऴ௸

"When you put the letters 'T' and 'H' together it makes the sound, *thhhh*," William said, pointing to the two letters he'd written on the chalk board. "As in the word *THINK*." He wrote the word out in chalk next to the letters he'd previously drawn.

But before he could turn back toward the class, he heard a gasp from Margaret standing next to him, and a short squeal from the back of the class—a sound of surprise ... or fear.

He turned. Strange men had entered the room. Eight white men of varying ages, mostly early twenties or thirties, though one appeared older, with graying hair. They were dressed in the rough garb of common laborers or farmers, and had a generally unkempt, ragged, and dirty look about them.

But the thing that immediately captured William's attention was what they carried. One held a hunting rifle and three carried revolvers. Two men carried torches, burning brightly in the shade of the classroom. William felt a chill run down his spine when he noticed one of the men held a metal can; he recognized it as the type used to carry kerosene.

"What is the meaning of this?" he demanded, stepping forward. He instinctively reached for his pistol, before remembering he wasn't wearing a holster. He rarely wore one around the farm, and certainly *not* when teaching class.

"The meaning is ... we come to stop to this blasphemy, teachin' no-good darkies on readin' and writin'. Such ain't allowed in these parts, and we mean to put a stop to it," the one in front said. With his lean face and scraggly beard, he reminded William of the outlaw Gold-tooth back in Texas. He stepped toward William as he spoke. The others spread themselves around the room. The freemen sat still, wide-eyed. Children fearfully leaned in toward their parents.

"You'll do no such thing!" William answered. "Leave this place at once. Or—"

"Or what, *Mr. Fancy Pants?* We seen Chambers and his other men ride off this morning, all packed up like they wasn't comin' back any time soon.

"Ain't nobody here but you and a bunch o' darkies. And *you* sure don't look like much ..." the man sneered at William and stepped up toward the front of the class.

But in that instant William realized he was no longer the shy, mild-mannered, studious bookworm he once was. He'd become a battle-hardened veteran soldier, and he no longer felt inclined to take orders or insults from villains like this one.

William took a step forward. His right fist shot up. The blow caught the man under the chin. He staggered backward, banging against the wall.

But three others jumped forward. The armed men menaced the class, preventing any of the black men from coming to William's aid.

William swung at the first man to approach him, but the assailant threw up his arms and blocked the blow. Then two men had William pinned back against the wall by the arms. The man he'd punched staggered up and hit William hard in the stomach.

Margaret screamed, "Stop that this instant!" but it was to no avail. She tried to rush forward to William's aid, thinking to jump on the man's back and squeeze his throat as she'd once seen Henry do. But another man reached out and caught her by the arm. He held her back easily, laughing at her ineffectual struggles, and harmless punches, easily deflecting them with his free hand.

But William wasn't finished yet. Though his arms were firmly pinned to the wall, his feet were still free. As the man in front stepped forward to throw another punch, William lifted both feet from the floor and kicked out, catching his assailant mid-chest with both boots. For a second time the same man was knocked, staggering, across the room.

But the men who'd been holding William turned and proceeded to punch and kick him until he was balled up on the floor in a vain attempt to protect himself from the blows. Margaret winced with each blow, tears of fear and frustration streaming down her face.

Then she heard a strong, deep voice, loud and clear from the back of the classroom, "Y'all stand still where y'are! Or y'all's gonna *die!*"

The man punching William paused, fist drawn back, and looked to the door. Big George stood there, a rifle in his hands, and a dark scowl on his face. He pointed the weapon directly at the white man with the rifle. Five other freemen stood beside him: Tony, Ned, Henry, Cobb, and Phinney. Cobb and Phinney held revolvers, the rest rifles.

"Drop them guns or we open fire. *NOW!*" George ordered. The armed men did as they were told. All eight men raised their hands in surrender.

"Shit ..." the leader said, breaking the silence that had fallen over the room. "Where'd you damned blacks get all them guns, anyhow?"

But George pointed his rifle at the man's crotch, "It ain't for y'all to be askin' no questions, lest you figure on bein' done fatherin' children."

The man got the point, and clamped his mouth shut.

George resisted the strong urge to glance over to where his wife Babs, and his two young daughters, Annie and Lucy, sat on the far side of the class. He was determined not to have his attention distracted from the intruders—plenty of time for family later.

Tony, on the other hand, couldn't help but glance over at Rosa near the back of the class. Looking for her in any given situation had become almost an unconscious habit. But when he looked at her, she surprised him by gazing back. Their eyes met, and she smiled. It caught him off guard, and he didn't know how to react. So he just nodded, and turned back toward the prisoners. Despite his continued strong feelings for her, they'd barely talked since coming north. Generally, he tried to avoid her, though he could never help himself from looking. Now he couldn't stop wondering what that smile had meant ... *if anything.*

Henry noticed the look between them and smiled. He'd come to think of Rosa in a fatherly way, him being married to her mother, though he wasn't her *real* daddy. He thought highly of Tony and reckoned it would be a good match.

Margaret rushed over and helped William to his feet. "Oh, *dear!* William ... are you all right? Oh, what have they done to you?"

He was bloodied and battered, but still managed to smile, "I'm ... all right, Miss Margaret. Believe it or not, I've had worse."

She reached down and retrieved his glasses from the floor where they'd been knocked. The frames were slightly bent, but luckily the lenses were still intact. She handed them back to him and he nodded his thanks, immediately wiping them down and straightening them before putting them back on.

William turned toward the freemen at the door, "Thank you George, Tony ... the rest of you. That was ... most timely and handsomely done. Please ... search these men for any more weapons, then put out those torches and escort them from the property."

George nodded, then gestured the white men to move over toward the door.

Then William had another thought, "Oh ... and George ..."

"Yes, Mr. William?"

"Kindly resist the urge to shoot any of them along the way. I don't believe the Captain would approve."

George grinned, "All right, Mr. William, if you say so. We'll only shoot 'em if they tries somethin' *stupid*. Come on you scoundrels, move it out. And don't give me no lip, now; the man ain't never said I couldn't give y'all a well-deserved beatin' if I had a mind!"

After the men departed, Margaret dismissed the class. She and William now sat alone on one of the classroom benches. She gently dabbed blood from his battered face with a damp cloth.

"Does it hurt much, William?"

"*Ow!* Uh ... only a little."

"That was courageously done, William. It was ... *oh, my!*" she shook her head in amazement. "It was one of the bravest things I've *ever* seen, taking on those men all by yourself!"

William smiled, "*Foolish* is probably a better word for it. But I thank you for the kind words, Miss Margaret."

She nodded in acknowledgment, continuing to dab at his face. But then she paused to have a look and their eyes met. Neither seemed inclined to break the contact for several seconds.

Finally, Margaret looked away and smiled. William shook his head slowly, trying to decide what had just happened ... *if anything.*

છ૭ઈ૭ભ૩છ૩ળ૭ઈ૭ભ૩છ૩ળ૭ઈ૭ભ૩છ૩

After the fury of his initial reaction cooled, Nathan decided to take a more measured approach to the unwanted incursion.

Two black women who'd been in the reading class identified one man, and possibly another, as men they'd seen buying goods down at the General Store. A quick reconnoitering by Tom, including a none-too-gentle interrogation of the store's proprietor, soon uncovered the identities of the perpetrators. They were close neighbors of Belle Meade Farm; the ringleader of the group, Jesse Ward, lived only a few miles down the road.

But the last thing Nathan wanted was to start another long-running feud with a neighbor in his new locale. The deadly Chambers-Walters feud had given him more than a bellyful of that.

So on the Saturday following the classroom incident, Nathan and his men rode out to meet with the neighbor. Nathan meant to keep his temper in check and bury the hatchet if at all possible. But his men went fully armed, just in case.

When they stopped their horses in front of the house, no one was in sight. Nathan wasn't surprised the place looked shabby and rundown, obviously in need of a fresh coat of paint at a minimum. Weeds sprung up in random locations around the house and even out in the gravel of the drive. A milk cow cropped grass out in an equally weedy pasture across the driveway from the house. A few dozen yards off to one side sat a well-worn barn with a sagging roofline. A decrepit-looking pig pen ran up against one wall. They saw several large hogs lounging inside.

Nathan debated whether to shout or get down from his horse and knock on the door. But his dilemma was solved before he had to decide. A lean, scruffy-looking man with a scowl on his face came out of the house, followed immediately by several others — six in all. They appeared to be unarmed. The significance of their number wasn't lost on Nathan — it was the same count as the men who'd disrupted the Belle Meade classroom.

He glanced over at William, who gave him a meaningful nod, confirming these were the same men.

"This is *my* property, mister. You're not welcome here," the first man said. Nathan thought he had a disreputable look. And his immediate, instinctive reaction was the same as he'd had many times out West when confronting outlaws.

"I'm well aware who's property this is, *Mr. Ward*. But since you and your fellows saw fit to visit *my* property — *uninvited* — earlier this week, I felt obliged to return the favor."

The man continued to scowl but couldn't disagree with Nathan's point. And if he was surprised Nathan knew his name, he didn't betray it.

"What is it you want, *Chambers?*"

Nathan pulled on his cigar, slowly releasing the smoke.

"Believe it or not, Mr. Ward, I come here in peace. I've no interest in starting a feud with you and would like to see if we can ... come to an *understanding* of sorts."

The man exchanged a look with his fellows, then turned back toward Nathan. "An *understanding*? Like ... y'all is gonna stop teaching school class to a bunch o' darkies? That y'alls gonna send all them all packin' — up North somewhere they's actually *wanted* now they's no longer slaves?"

Nathan fought to suppress his ire and stay calm. He could see Tom's eyes on him in his peripheral vision at his left side. He was determined to maintain his composure.

"No ... that's not *exactly* what I had in mind ..."

"Then what's the point of y'all ridin' out here? We got no use for no black abolitionists in these parts! We're good, honest, God-fearing white folks. Working to scratch out a simple living on our own lands. Ain't never had hundreds of black men doin' our work for us, so's we could lord it over others."

The other men on the patio nodded their agreement, one saying, "You tell 'em, Jesse."

Nathan closed his eyes for a moment, fighting to remain calm. He took another long drag on the cigar, letting it out slowly. He looked back up at the man.

"Clearly we have our disagreements. But can we not at least agree to leave each other alone? Allow each to his own, and not instigate any further violence?"

"Depends."

"On?"

"Whether or not y'all are willing to leave off your illegal and blasphemous actions over at y'all's place. As I said before, we ain't just standing by allowin' such doin's in our own *back yard*, so to speak. Bad enough all them foreign, Yankee Northern blue coats marching around everywhere, pokin' their noses into everyone's business. Now you want us livin' next to a whole passel o' darkies—treatin' 'em like they was kin! What next, you want us sittin' next to 'em in church? Or maybe just kissin' their backsides?"

He had a sneer on his face and was clearly enjoying himself, warming up his audience, who snickered and nodded encouragingly.

"Look, Ward ... I'm not asking you to become *best friends* with the freemen, just to leave them alone, in peace. They've done nothing to harm you or yours. I see no reason why their *mere existence* should cause you such consternation."

"I'll tell you why, since y'all are too muddled by abolitionist talk ... or maybe too dense ... to understand. 'Cause next thing you know the damned Yankee government over to Washington's gonna decide them poor blacks needs land o' their own and then ups and buys every farm in sight and gives it to 'em. Next thing a man can't make a decent living on his own farm on account o' all them that's been given it for nothing. And likely seed crops, equipment, and whatnot they ain't never had to earn the money for."

Nathan chose to ignore the insults for the moment, focusing on the man's arguments instead. "Though I disagree that they haven't 'earned' anything, given they've worked their whole lives for no pay, still, what makes you think that would happen? I've never heard any such notion discussed at any level of government."

"'Cause that damned Yankee Lincoln is a black-kissing abolitionist, that's why. He won't stop 'til the blacks are in charge and all us whites are slaves."

Nathan snorted derisively, "Now you're just being ridiculous. Surely no one can believe such drivel!"

"Here's what's 'drivel,' *Mr. High-And-Mighty, move-in-here-and-Lord-it-over-all-us-as-has-lived-here-our-whole-lives*; every fucking word of horse shit coming out of your ass-backwards mouth, Chambers!" Ward's audience continued to encourage his rant with nods and utterances of encouragement.

Nathan frowned, and stuck his cigar back in his mouth. He looked over at Tom and let out a deep sigh. Tom returned the look, shook his head, and shrugged his shoulders. Nathan took two more deep pulls on the cigar, slowly releasing the smoke, which drifted away lazily in the hot, still air.

He leaned forward, glaring at his counterpart, his face now as dark and dangerous as a storm cloud—his temper held back by the barest thread.

"Y'all are clearly unrepentant of your trespass. And remain unashamedly belligerent, despite my honest attempt at neighborly reconciliation."

He sat up straight on Millie, "Such being the case, allow me to speak plainly, that there may be no *misunderstanding* between us ..."

He broke eye contact with Ward and turned to Jim.

"Mr. Wiggins ..."

"Sir!"

"Take a good look at these men's faces. If any one of these sorry *sons of bitches* ever shows his ugly, ass-wiping face on my property again ... *shoot him.*

"If he survives the gunshot, give him a bayonet or knife to the guts. And if that doesn't finish the job, hang him twitching from a tree until he expires. Bury the ... *refuse* ... back in the woods, hidden so his kin may never consecrate the grave. Leave him there to rot in hell for eternity."

This pronouncement had the desired effect, wiping the sneering looks from their faces, replaced by frowns of consternation and even a few expressions of wide-eyed fear.

"Do I make myself clear, Mr. Wiggins?"

"Yes, sir! Perfectly clear ... though ... I was thinking, sir; once we've gutted them, why not just let your hound *eat* 'em?" he gestured toward Harry, who stood stiff-legged next to Nathan's horse, the fur on his back bristled up and his teeth bared in a silent snarl. "Saves us the trouble of stringing 'em up and digging a grave after."

Nathan was quiet a moment, puffing on his cigar, as if contemplating the suggestion. "No ... I think *not*, Mr. Wiggins; these fellows are so foul and disagreeable they'd likely give the beast indigestion."

Jim resisted the urge to chuckle, instead snapping the Captain a salute, "Very good, sir!" He turned and graced the residents with an evil leer as he pointedly gazed from face to face around the group. Nathan's other men likewise took a careful look at all the faces before them, so they'd not forget. He noticed several of Ward's men had trouble making eye contact with his men. Some turned away as if not wishing to be recognized later.

"Gentlemen ... a good day to you," Nathan said, tipping his hat and poking the cigar back in his mouth. He turned Millie's reins and walked her back toward the road. Tom and the others followed.

Stan and Jim were the last to go, taking the rear-guard position. Before they followed, Jim pulled out his revolver, spun the chamber, deliberately making sure all cylinders were loaded.

Then he returned the weapon to its holster in a single, neat spin, a move only possible from long years of experience.

Stan pulled out his wicked, foot-long Bowie knife and made a point of testing the razor-sharp edge, cutting his thumb and sticking it in his mouth to suck away the blood. Then he smiled wickedly, blood showing on his teeth. The men standing on the porch stared wide-eyed as the terrifying giant slid his blade slowly back into its sheath.

Jim grinned and tipped his hat, then he and Stan turned their horses and trotted away.

CHAPTER 4. A BOILING CAULDRON

"The nations slithered over the brink
into the boiling cauldron of war
without any trace of apprehension or dismay.
The nations backed their machines
over the precipice.
Not one of them wanted war,
certainly not on this scale."
– David Lloyd George, Prime Minister of England
(in reference to the start of World War I)

Thursday September 5, 1861 – Wheeling, Virginia:

The following Thursday, Nathan, Tom, Jim, and William sat around a table in an oversized office on the second floor of the Customs House, just two doors down from the governor's office. This room was every bit as austere as the governor's simple office, containing only the bare minimum furniture and fixtures. But despite its simplicity the room had become, at least temporarily, the de facto command center for the armed forces of the Restored State of Virginia. They'd been working in this room all week, from early morning until well into the evening. Nathan drove them hard, eager to finish the task that they might get out in the field with the Army where they belonged as quickly as possible.

Nathan had a stack of papers in front of him describing potential officers for the new regiments of West Virginia, starting with the Seventh Infantry.

The state's first six pro-Union regiments, the First through the Sixth "Virginia Volunteer Infantry Regiments" were already in the field. Their formation had begun shortly after the secession, even before the conclusion of the Second Wheeling Convention or the creation of the Restored Government. And they were only unofficially called "*West* Virginia" regiments, since that state didn't yet exist. They were also referred to as "Loyal Virginia

Regiment" or "Union Virginia Regiment" so as not to be confused with their Confederate counterparts from Virginia.

But neither Governor Pierpont nor Nathan was especially pleased with the results to date. For the most part these regiments had been recruited a single company at a time by private citizens, mostly in Ohio, Pennsylvania, or Kentucky.

Many of the companies had been turned away by their own state governments, either because they had already met their federal government prescribed quotas, or because they were skeptical of the quality of the recruits and their officers. So the new recruits had crossed over into western Virginia where they were desperately needed. Most of these units had voted on their officers, which usually meant they elected the people who'd done the recruiting—no actual military experience or competence was necessary!

The result was not surprising: poor training, inexperienced officers, and inconsistent equipment leading to questionable effectiveness and unnecessarily high casualties. And since it was no secret the vast majority of these regiments were made up of non-Virginians, the federal government continued to pressure the Restored Government to supply troops, unwilling to give the state credit for their contribution to date.

Nathan was determined not only to include more Virginians, but to improve the quality of the regiments sent out by the Wheeling government going forward. He intended to make the Seventh Infantry Regiment the model for those to come. Of course, the Eighth, Ninth, and so on would follow in short order; in fact, their recruitment and training would have to overlap the Seventh to meet the aggressive schedule they had laid out. Things would move quickly, and there would be little or no time to test the effectiveness of their plans before applying them to the next group. Nathan intended to closely follow the actions of the Seventh once they were in the field. Their success, or lack thereof, would tell him what they might do to improve their efforts.

At this point, there were very few qualified officers sitting idly by waiting to be called up. Most such men from Virginia were already assigned to other units in the Union army. But Nathan assumed they could be lured away from other regiments by offer of an instant promotion to the next rank up—a lieutenant to a captain, a captain to a major, and so forth, all the way up to colonel, the highest rank they'd be allowed to assign without going through Washington for permission.

Governor Pierpont had made several suggestions; "upstanding gentlemen of good character and leadership skills" he'd called them. Nathan had scowled and named them what they were, "political appointees", with no military training or experience. He had heatedly refused to put such men in charge of "his" regiments, pointing out men's lives were at stake, along with the safety and reputation of the Wheeling government. The governor had relented, but Nathan knew if his efforts to bring in "real" officers faltered, the pressure would build to accept the men Pierpont recommended.

Jim sat to his right, and though he'd never learned to read or write with much skill or speed, he was a keen judge of character and ability—especially concerning all things military. So Nathan read aloud the record, letters of recommendation, etc. of any officers who sounded interesting. Nathan leaned on Jim for advice and opinions as the officers all tended to sound very similar on paper, making it difficult to judge. They'd requested the War Department in Washington send them a copy of the record of every officer from Virginia currently commissioned in the Army. Based on the stack of papers Nathan had piled on the floor behind him, it appeared they'd happily complied!

Though Nathan planned on staffing the officers of the Seventh this way, he didn't yet share with the men his intention to personally take command of the next one and bring them all along as his officers.

Further down the table, William worked on writing up plans for efficient, regimented training of the troops they'd eventually recruit, starting with the duties required at the lowest level of the individual soldier—rifleman, cavalryman, artilleryman, teamster, etc.—and working up from there. From a rifle *squad* of six to ten men, to a *platoon* of three to four *squads*, to a *company* of three or four *platoons*, and so forth. All the way up to a *regiment* of around

800 men. They'd decided not to try going beyond that, there being no need to worry about larger units. Large formations, such as brigades and divisions, would only be put together by Washington from multiple, disparate regiments as needed.

William knew many of the details off the top of his head, having recently been through the Captain's rigorous training himself out in Texas. He also had a stack of books on military training and tactics he'd borrowed from the local library. Nathan recognized a few of them from his studies back at West Point. What William didn't know or couldn't find in one of the books he asked Tom or Nathan.

Meanwhile, Tom worked on what he did best, logistics. He drew up detailed plans for every piece of equipment and sundry item that would be needed, using the same grouping levels as William. When he was finished, these would constitute the planning documents and training materials required for quartermasters at each level. They would also give the governor the details he needed to develop the budgets and acquire the goods from the myriad sources required to get military units into the field.

At mid-morning, Governor Pierpont surprised them by sticking his head in at the doorway. He normally sent one of his aids if he had a question or had some information to pass along.

They all rose immediately to their feet.

"Oh … no, gentlemen, please! As you were, as you were. I'm sorry to disturb you at your important, nay, *critical* labors. But …"

"Sir?" Nathan asked. He saw the governor clutched a small piece of paper in his fist.

"Mr. Chambers … I just received this message and thought you ought to have a look."

He handed the paper across to Nathan. He unfolded it and read aloud:

Thursday September 5, 1861

To whom it may concern,

One of my farmhands seen vultures circling out over past one of our hayfields this mornin so went to have a look, fearful a cattle may of expired untimely.

When he got over to the edge of my fields he seen said buzzards was farther off, over to the neighboring farm. He bein of a curious nature, done walked over to have a looksee.

I am heavily hearted to tell you he has found a most upsetin scene. Of which appears to be homicidal murders. He found the whole family of my neighbors, a very nice and polite young black freeman couple and youngens, was kilt dead with copious amounts of blood all hither and yon.

I have writ this note in haste and sent my man to deliver it unto the proper authorities at Wheeling. Whom we trust will timely catch hold o said foul perpetrators at the earliest possible hour that justis mite be served.

Sincerest regards,

Wilford M. Campbell

At my farm, approx. 5 miles Southeast from Wheeling town.

Nathan scowled, and reached for his hat, "Come on, men." He headed for the door, the three men and Harry the Dog following in his wake.

⁀⁁⁂⁀⁁⁂⁀⁁⁂

On their way out of the Customs House they collected the young farmhand who'd delivered the note and brought him along so he could guide them. He was clearly shaken by the experience, and had a hard time describing what he'd seen without choking up, other than to repeat how horrible it had been.

Since Belle Meade Farm was on the way to Mr. Campbell's farm, they stopped off and gathered the rest of the men. Mostly, Nathan wanted Billy, but the others would also prove useful of course, if they ran into any trouble.

After a brief look around, they now gathered at the edge of a pasture a few yards away from the house and its outbuildings, while Billy investigated the scene in detail.

They'd seen enough to know it was certainly "homicidal murder," as Mr. Campbell had stated in his letter, and had confirmed the young farmhand's assessment of absolute horror. Both Campbell and the farmhand had declined to accompany them, neither having any desire to be anywhere near the place.

Nathan couldn't blame them. It was a truly shocking scene. Even the hardened veterans from out west were having a hard time digesting it, and Nathan could feel the bile threatening to rise in his own throat. As the neighbor had stated in his letter, the victims were a young black freeman couple with two children. A crime having nothing to do with secession, Union, or the new state—a purely evil crime of hatred and convenience, taking advantage of the chaos and lack of local law enforcement.

The young black man had been shot outside in front of the house but had apparently continued to struggle, a blood trail showed where he had dragged himself before being shot again multiple times, apparently with pistols. The young mother had been murdered in the bedroom after being stripped naked and presumably raped. She'd been stabbed multiple times with knives.

But the worst were the children, a girl and a boy. The little boy was found out in a pasture. They hadn't seen him at first, but Harry caught a scent and trotted over to where the body lay in a knee-high field of pasture grass, scattering a buzzard and several crows. The boy had been shot by two rifle bullets. From the tracks, Billy speculated he'd been turned loose to run and been used as target practice. The first bullet had shattered his arm, but he'd kept running. The second had hit him mid-back, killing him instantly.

The little girl was found in the same room as the mother, her throat had been slashed so violently it had nearly decapitated her. Billy couldn't tell which had died first, the daughter or the mother. Nathan prayed the child had gone first and been spared the sight of what they'd done to her mother.

The family had only been dead for a day, according to Billy, so they hadn't yet ripened enough for the vultures to show anything more than mild curiosity. Besides, the carrion birds were much more interested in the milk cow. She'd been shot and left dead in the middle of a pasture a short distance from the house. Between the vultures and other earth-bound scavengers, there'd have been little left of the two bodies lying outside, save bones, in a few more days, with the midsummer sun beating down like a hammer.

Nathan smoked a cigar and paced about, staring at his boots. He recollected all the horrific, bloody scenes he'd seen in his violent army life, many of which he'd had a direct hand in instigating. The bodies of young soldiers torn apart by artillery or shattered by rifle fire were sobering, but at least they'd had a fighting chance. They'd died with weapons in hand.

The worst were unarmed civilians — men, women, and children brutalized in their own homes. The fear and helplessness of having no way to fight back ...

He'd seen the aftermath of a few such incidents over the years; soldiers retaliating against civilians they'd accused of aiding the other side; Comanche Indian raids against settlers they believed were encroaching on their traditional hunting grounds, and so on. It was something he never got used to, never accepted as "normal" or routine.

But few measured up to the beastly, dreadful, senselessness of this scene. Whoever had done this wasn't even human in his book. They'd given up the right to claim that title. Though when he considered it, few non-human animals were capable of such mindless evil.

Adding to the surreal malevolence of the scene was the setting itself. Nathan couldn't help comparing this well-kept, neatly trimmed farm to the shabby overgrown property of his neighbor Ward. The house and outbuildings were freshly painted, the fence around the farmhouse new and straight. There were no weeds poking up through the drive or anywhere around the house. A field of corn just past the barn glistened in the sun, its crops lined up in perfectly straight rows. These people had taken great pride in their homestead. And now ...

He looked up and was surprised to see Stan staring off into the distance with tears in his eyes. He'd never seen Stan cry before. It was nearly as shocking as the rest of the scene. Then, perhaps sensing the Captain gazing at him, Stan looked over and their eyes met.

Stan's face twisted with pain and anger and turned a dark red, "I will ... tear them apart ... piece by piece ... this I swear, Captain! *AHHHHHH!*" he shouted out at the world, closing his eyes and holding his huge, clenched fists high in the air as the sound echoed across the valley. And though the men turned to stare, the world didn't seem to care, continuing to go about it's business as usual.

Nathan stepped over and put a hand on Stan's back, "We'll get them, my friend. And when we do ... I *will* let you rip them apart piece by piece. This *I* swear!"

Stan gazed at him for a long moment, then nodded and turned away. He walked off into the field and sat down by himself, facing away from the farmhouse. There he sat until it was time to leave, face buried in his hands.

₦₧ℛ₧ℜℛ₦₧ℜℛ₦₧ℜℛ

Despite his best efforts, Billy could discover very little of use. Four men had arrived on horseback. There were no distinguishing marks among the horses' hooves; all were neatly shod, no bent nails nor cracked hooves, and none of the horses appeared to have been lame in any way.

There were also no distinguishing features among the men's boots. All were of a similar size and all the men seemed to be of medium build and weight.

They'd killed the man with at least two pistols—he had both .44 caliber wounds and those of the smaller .36 caliber. Likewise, the son had been shot by more than one rifle; a .54

caliber round ball from a smoothbore musket, and a .58 caliber Minni ball from a rifled gun.

The mother's stab wounds also showed at least two different knives were used, and Billy confirmed the woman had been raped, likely by multiple men. Possibly by all four.

After they'd buried the family and left the scene, they visited all the neighboring farms, but no one had seen anything. And the sounds of gunfire in the distance were so commonplace they were generally ignored, hunting being a favorite pastime of many rural residents.

Nathan was frustrated they'd drawn a complete blank. He'd even ridden out to confront his incorrigible neighbor Jesse Ward again, to see if he may have been involved or knew who was. But he'd gained nothing there, either. Ward would neither confirm nor deny involvement in the incident, simply refusing to answer any questions whatsoever from "any damned abolitionist," as he called Nathan.

This time he threatened to shoot Nathan and his men if they ever returned. Nathan smirked, and said, "That would end badly for you, sir, I can promise you that. My men are all experienced Indian fighters from Texas. They'd make short work of you and your disreputable friends."

But Ward was unimpressed and refused to be intimidated this time, "Maybe so, Chambers, but I'd be in the right and you know it. Though I'd be deceased, you'd swing from the gallows for ridin' onto a man's own property and shootin' him dead."

As much as it galled him to admit it, the man was right about that. So he'd been forced to leave balked and disappointed, learning nothing useful.

There being little else they could do, they returned to the Customs House and resumed their work. But Nathan swore to never rest and never forget until the foul perpetrators were brought down.

꒰꒱꒰꒱꒰꒱꒰꒱꒰꒱꒰꒱

A few days later another report came in about an incident down in Marion County. This time a white family had been attacked. Though no one had been killed, the pro-Union farmer had been beaten, his livestock stolen or driven off, and his barn torched. Governor Pierpont begged Nathan to continue his work, that he'd asked the Army to investigate since there were no serious casualties. Nathan grudgingly agreed.

The next day another pro-Union farm was targeted in the same area. Though the farmer escaped with a minor wound, one of his farmhands was killed in a gunfight that ensued after masked horseman rode onto his property.

And the next day there was another incident, just miles away from the one on the previous day. This time an unabashedly pro-*Confederate* farmer and his wife had been shot dead on their front porch, and their house set ablaze.

After reading the latest report Nathan locked eyes with the governor and frowned. Pierpont winced. Both men knew if this wasn't stopped soon, everything they'd been working toward could come unraveled very quickly.

And to make matters worse, Pierpont reluctantly confessed all three recent incidents had taken place in his own hometown, Fairmont, where his family still owned property. Nathan grabbed his hat and said, "I'll see you back here in a week or so, your honor. But don't worry, I intend to start training the Seventh shortly after our return."

This time the governor only nodded, slowly sinking back into his chair. He knew better than to try to talk Nathan out of it. The new West Virginia army units would just have to wait for his return.

ဆၣၢၣၣၢၣၣၢၣၣၢၣၣၢၣ

Fortunately for Nathan in his current role as ... *whatever he was* ... for the governor, he could get to locations across the northern half of western Virginia and points to the East very quickly; the B&O Railroad had its western terminus in downtown Wheeling.

For the time being it went no farther west than Wheeling as the planned railroad bridge over the Ohio River had not yet been started. Goods going into Ohio had to be transferred to a ship for transport across the river or loaded on wagons and driven over the suspension highway bridge that had been completed a little over a decade earlier.

Heading back to the East, the B&O first headed southeast out of the Wheeling panhandle into western Virginia proper until it reached Grafton. There it intersected with the Northwestern Virginia Railroad, which ran almost due west to Parkersburg, also on the Ohio River, about ninety miles southwest of Wheeling.

The B&O main line then turned due east from Grafton, running all the way to Baltimore. And from Baltimore a branch line ran straight to Washington, only forty miles away.

For most civilians, riding the train had become very problematic ever since the war broke out. The line was regularly disrupted by rebels, destroying bridges and tearing up tracks. And the Union army had commandeered the B&O for military and essential freight purposes only.

So even when it was running, the trains no longer stopped at unscheduled whistle stops, and passengers were only welcomed if seats were available after accommodating military personnel — and only then if the train wasn't in a particular hurry, which they usually *were,* and if the military conductor was in an accommodating mood, which he usually *wasn't!*

But Pierpont had solved the military-only problem for Nathan; he'd written out and signed a special pass that allowed Nathan and his men — with horses — to ride on any military train as special representatives of his honor. And he'd specifically mentioned Nathan's dog, knowing he couldn't be left behind. The pass from the governor and Nathan's stern scowl were usually sufficient to get them on board, as long as there was any room at all.

And so what would have taken a day and a half on horseback to reach the town of Fairmont in Marion County took only three and a half hours on the train. An hour after unloading their horses, they arrived at the site of the most recent incident.

And once again Nathan and his men looked over a gruesome scene of civilians murdered at a farmstead. The farmer and his wife, appearing to be in their late forties or early fifties, had been shot by rifle fire at close range — a single bullet each to the chest.

And although a fire had destroyed the farmhouse, the bodies were unburned. It appeared someone had dragged the bodies off the porch and out onto the open driveway where the fire hadn't touched them. They'd even been laid out respectfully, face up, side by side, with their arms folded across their chests, as for a funeral viewing.

Though it was another unpleasant scene, at least this time there were no children, and the deaths had been quick and relatively painless. And Nathan had to admit he felt less affected by it for another reason: these people had been adamantly and actively pro-secession, and pro-slavery, according to the governor's brother, Zacquill Pierpont.

Zac had awaited Nathan and company at the train station already mounted on his horse, having been told to expect their arrival in a telegram received from his brother, the governor. The family home was located here in Fairmont, as was the family tanning business, now run by Zac. Francis had also recently sponsored a coal mining business somewhere on the family property.

Zac had guided Nathan and his men to the scene and now stood with them, gazing about while Billy conducted his usual detailed inspection.

"Mr. Pierpont, do you have a theory on what happened here, who's responsible, and whether it is connected to the other recent ... *incidents?*"

"I'll answer the second question first, Mr. Chambers. It is almost certainly related, and likely a direct result. The Calvins' only son was killed in the recent fighting up at Rich Mountain— fighting for the *rebel* side. I expect that's what set off John Calvin.

"Before the outbreak of hostilities, he was an avowed and unashamed secessionist. But rumor has it since his son's death he's been advocating and participating in armed resistance against Union soldiers, the pro-Union government in Wheeling, and anyone who supports it. Needless to say, that hasn't set well with me."

"No ... I should imagine *not!* And ... concerning my *first* question?"

"Mr. Chambers ... there's a war on, as you well know. And like it or not, it's not all being fought by soldiers marching in neat rows on the field of battle. Some of it is playing out in our own back yards, unfortunately.

"So let me ask *you* a question before I answer yours. I know you're charged by the governor to put down such lawlessness. But ... what would you say to those who might be breaking the law, but are doing so to put a stop to those who would attack our legitimate government, soldiers, and private citizens? Men who are loyal to the Union, but feel forced to take matters into their own hands for lack of soldiers or law enforcement to do it for them?"

Nathan looked Zac hard in the eye and said, "I'd say ... there's a war on, even as you say. And likely we need all the help we can get to keep the rebel side from getting a foothold in this country, armies or no. But ... I would need to be sure that's what's *really* going on here, and not just some personal vendetta being played out, with the war for a cover."

"I agree wholeheartedly, Mr. Chambers. And from what I've heard ... Calvin here was responsible for the attacks on pro-Union farmers, and so this reprisal was justified. A shame about Mrs. Calvin, though. I'm sure that wasn't in the plan and was likely someone's mistake ... or bad judgment."

"Hmm ... I'm not sure murder could ever be shrugged off as merely *bad judgment*. But let's assume for a moment the wife's death was some sort of unfortunate *accident* ... I would still like to know who's responsible. I've no intention of arresting them if they are *truly* acting in the broader definition of self-defense, and for the good of the country.

"But if that's the case, let's have a reckoning with those who choose to side with the enemy and raise arms against us, and put an end to the matter here in Fairmont. I've no stomach for this back-and-forth, action-and-reaction business—killing, burning, and then payback for same. If the pro-Union side will meet with me and help identify those on the *other* side, my men and I will deal with them and put an end to this business."

"That would be excellent, Mr. Chambers! And I have to say, your men look more than up to the task!" He nodded his head in the direction of Stan, who stood a few yards off, chatting quietly with William. "But ... I must warn you, we may well know who's on the enemy's side, but we may not be able to prove it."

Nathan gazed at Pierpont a moment before answering, "Mr. Pierpont, because of this war, President Lincoln has suspended the *writ of habeas corpus* in places up North where there isn't even any actual fighting going on. I'd say if he can do it *there*, we should be able to do the same *here*."

"*Writ of habea ... what?* Sorry, Mr. Chambers, I'm not a lawyer like my baby brother, Frankie—oh, sorry! Uh ... *Governor Francis Pierpont*, I should say ... I just run the family tanning business."

"Oh, sorry. It's Latin. It literally means, 'produce the body.' In legal terms it means the government's law officers must show just cause for imprisoning someone. In a nutshell, there must be an *actual crime* before there can be any punishment.

"But Mr. Lincoln has suspended the rule so the federal government can arrest people who are actively promoting the rebel cause—advocating secession and sedition, or raising arms against the government—but haven't yet committed an actual crime."

"Ah ... that makes sense."

"Yes, I believe so, given the present circumstances. And all the more so here in western Virginia, especially considering our new Restored Government doesn't even have a judicial branch—no official judges, courts, or lawmen. We're ... just ... trying to use common sense and hold as few actual trials as possible. I've no desire to arrest anyone who's pro-Union if I can help it, though I'll not countenance red murder disguised as warfare."

"Agreed. That being the case ... I believe I can arrange a meeting between you and the local ... *loyalists.*"

"Excellent. Thank you kindly."

A sudden movement caught Nathan's eye, and he turned to look over at Billy. He'd apparently completed his examination of the burned-out farmhouse and patio and had worked his way over to where the body of the farmer and his wife lay side by side in the driveway. He now moved quickly in the direction of one of the farm's outbuildings.

Billy strode up to the door of a medium-sized shed—the type used to store large farm equipment like wagons or plows. But instead of entering, he turned and looked toward his Captain. He gave a "come here" signal, and Nathan immediately headed in his direction, followed by the others, who'd also seen Billy's gesture.

"What is it, Billy?"

"Captain ... the bodies weren't moved to the drive by those who killed them."

"Oh? Then by who?"

"Other men came after the killers left. These men dragged the bodies away from the burning house. They laid them out neatly on the drive, then walked back to ... here," he pointed at the door.

Nathan gazed at the door and drew his pistol. The rest of his men followed suit. Harry the Dog stood next to him, the fur on his back bristled up. Zac Pierpont held back several yards; he was unarmed, and suddenly looked very nervous.

"One more thing, Captain ... these men were barefoot. Like—"

"Slaves." Nathan finished the sentence for him and let out a sigh. He holstered his pistol and stepped up to the door. He pulled back one side of the wide double doors to reveal darkness within. The building had the usual musty smell of old hay and axle grease.

"Whoever is in here, come out slowly and no harm will come to you. We are with ... Mr. Lincoln's government," Nathan said, choosing the most straightforward and simple explanation as to their loyalties.

He was answered by silence.

"Come on now ... I expect y'all are hungry and thirsty. We have food and water for you, but you'll have to come out and get it. Come on."

There was another moment of silence, but then a soft shuffling sound came from within, and Nathan detected movement across the room in the darkness. Soon four black men came slowly out, squinting their eyes in the bright daylight, and gazing around at the men gathered there.

"Gentlemen, please ... have a seat," Nathan said, gesturing toward four cut log sections that had been set on end in a row out on the driveway opposite the burned-out farmhouse, each log spaced a foot or so from the others. The four slaves did as they were bid and sat on the chunks of wood. Nathan sat opposite them on an identical seat and Harry plopped down beside him, his tongue hanging out dripping a steady stream in the hot afternoon sun.

Around them stood Nathan's men, and Zac Pierpont. Zac looked curious, but Nathan's men appeared more amused, having a pretty good notion where this was headed.

The slaves, all men in their twenties by their appearance, were clearly frightened, and wouldn't make eye contact with Nathan.

"Firstly, I would like to know your names. You first, sir," he said, pointing to the man on his far left.

"Ben, master."

Nathan gazed at him a moment and scowled.

"I would very much appreciate if you men would look me in the eye when you speak to me. And ... I am *not* your master, nor is anyone else at this point, your old master now being deceased. You may address me as Mr. Chambers, or Captain as my men do ... or just 'sir,' if that pleases you. At any rate, please don't refer to me or anyone else here as *master*. Now, Ben ... if you will, look me in the eye, and say your name again."

Nathan's men were now openly grinning. It was almost a repeat of what the Captain had said to the slaves when he'd first arrived at Mountain Meadows, now more than a year ago. Zac looked surprised but offered no comment.

Ben looked up at Nathan and met eyes with him. He still seemed hesitant, but perhaps not as afraid. "My name's Ben, sir."

"Very good to meet you, Ben. And you?" he said, gesturing toward the next man.

The man began to speak, still looking at his feet.

But Nathan immediately interrupted, "Uh ... uh ..." and waggled his finger at the man, though he appeared more amused than angry. The man looked up at Nathan's face and grinned.

"Sorry, sir ... old habits is hard to break. My name is Jeffry, Mr. Chambers, sir."

"Pleasure to meet you, Jeffry."

The next man looked up and spoke without prompting, "I'm called Al, sir."

And finally, the last man took his turn, "Abraham, Mr. Captain, sir. Same as the President, Mr. Lincoln." He managed a hesitant grin, which was returned by Nathan.

"Yes indeed, Abraham, the very same name as our beloved leader, Mr. Lincoln."

The other slaves nodded their agreement to that.

"Gentlemen, were you out in the fields when this attack happened?"

The men nodded, and Abraham spoke up, "Yes, mast ... er, *Captain*, sir. We was out on far side of yonder field hoeing weeds with Master White—oh, he was Mr. Calvin's hired man and overseer.

"First, we heard gunshots, but thought little enough of it. We reckoned Master had just caught old skunk or fox gettin' after his chickens again.

"But then we seen the smoke, thick and black as tar. We come at the run and found the house already afire and the Master and Missus layin' there on the steps to the patio, dead as stone. We ain't never seen no one else about.

"Master White, he tells us to pull the bodies away from the house, though we'd have done it anyways, it not seeming right they not get a proper Christian burial and all. But then Master White runs and saddles a horse and rides out. We asks him what we ought to do, and he says whatever we likes, and rides off. We been talkin' 'bout what to do, but ain't yet figured it out. Then today we seen y'all riding up the road and decides to hide, not knowin' if you was more o' them as done the murders, or else lawmen who might blame us all for the killin'."

"Well, men, I want to make it clear we aren't blaming you, and know you've done nothing wrong. In fact, pulling the deceased away from the burning house was highly admirable and brave."

At this statement all four seemed to relax, Ben looking over at Al and cracking a slight smile for the first time.

Nathan and Tom exchanged a meaningful look. They'd previously discussed what they would do when faced with this situation, so weren't caught flatfooted by it.

"And as for what you ought to do next," Nathan continued, "I believe I have an answer for that as well."

All four now gazed at him intently as if he were about to pronounce their fate, which in fact he was.

"Though it may be a ... *loose* ... interpretation of the law, I intend to enforce the new 'Confiscation Act' signed into law by Mr. Lincoln only last month. Under the law, Union forces may confiscate property of those in open rebellion to and taking up arms against the federal government. And according to Mr. Pierpont here, such was the state of affairs with Mr. Calvin, your late master.

"That being the case, by the power vested in me by his honor, Governor Francis Pierpont of the State of Virginia, I hereby declare Mr. Calvin's property forfeit under the law. And as such, it shall be immediately appropriated by the military authority of the State of Virginia, which at this point is ... *me*.

"And given the governor's avowed opposition to slavery, I am going to take the liberty of representing his honor in this matter and on his behalf grant y'all manumission, effective immediately. Mr. Clark here will draw up the necessary papers as soon as practical, which will make it all legal and binding."

The four men stared at him, mouths agape, but said nothing.

"Congratulations, gentlemen ... y'all are now freemen."

They continued to stare, then looked at each other and began smiling and shaking their heads.

"Do you mean ... we's *truly* free, Mr. Captain, sir? Just like that? It don't seem ... *possible*," Abraham said, continuing to shake his head.

"It's true. From this day forward, you men and all your future descendants, shall be forever free."

The men looked from one to the other, patting each other's backs, and smiling brightly, eyes becoming watery. Nathan's men shared smiles and handshakes among themselves, also enjoying the happy moment. Zac Pierpont was now smiling brightly as well.

"Now ... as for what to do next ... the border of Pennsylvania is only twenty miles or so to the north — only a good day's walk." He looked over at Zac, "What's the nearest town across the border, Mr. Pierpont?"

"Um ... well, the easiest to get to would be a little town called Brave. About twenty-five miles by the road. But it's not much of a town. In fact there's nothing but very small towns in the southwest corner of Pennsylvania nearest us. To get to a larger city, you're talking Pittsburg. That's ... oh, a good hundred miles, I reckon."

"All right ... so let's say twenty-five miles, then, to the nearest town. We'll give you plenty of food and water skins to carry on your journey. Once you're there, you'll be in a free Northern state with no fear of being re-enslaved."

"Thank you, sir. But ... where will we go ... what will we do in Pennsylvania? We don't know no one there, o' course, sir."

"Well, I would think with all the young white men marching off to war there'll be plenty of need for strong, hard-working men like you. I think you'll have no problem getting jobs. Only this time they will *pay* you to do it. *Do* make sure they pay you, mind. If someone tries to tell you to work for free, just walk away. You ought to make ... hmm ... at least a dollar a day for hard labor — don't take less. And don't put up with any abuse: beatings or lashings. No one has a right to treat freemen that way. Understood?"

"Yes, sir," Abraham answered. But his look betrayed fear and reluctance. The others likewise seemed unenthusiastic about Nathan's suggestion.

"You are ... not convinced of what I'm saying?" Nathan asked.

"Oh, *no*, sir! It ain't that. You seem like a most sincere sort of gentleman," Abraham answered. "We just … well, with all the fightin' and whatnot going on … and we's heard rumors of free blacks being attacked by them as don't think any o' us kind *ought* to be free. We fear being alone out on the road, even for a day. And with we not knowing the way …"

The others nodded their heads.

Nathan looked from one to the next. He was touched by the earnestness in their eyes. He reached into his pocket, pulled out a cigar and lit it. He sat up and blew several puffs into the air, before letting out a heavy sigh and turning back toward Tom.

"Tom … do we have any sailcloth left?"

Tom answered with a grin, "Oh, yes sir! At least enough for … two or three more tents."

❧❦☙☙❧❦❧☙☙❧❦❧☙☙❧❦❧

Lieutenant James Hawkins wiped away the stream of sweat running down the side of his neck with a handkerchief. He sat on his horse off to the side of the road as his caravan of supply wagons passed. As each wagon rolled by, the drivers tipped their hats to him by way of a salute, which he returned in like manner. Things were a bit less formal out here on the road, which Hawkins preferred. He enjoyed the feeling of having his own command, away from the prying, judgmental eyes of senior officers, even if his command only consisted of six covered supply wagons—each with four mules and two drivers—and twelve mounted privates as guards, six in the front of the caravan and six in the back.

One must start somewhere, he thought and shrugged. He'd been riding up front with the forward guard and had a mind to check on the rear guard, to make sure they were all wide-awake and attentive. There'd been no rebel activity in some time, and by all reports there were no longer any rebel soldiers on the west side of the mountains—not since the Rich Mountain battle. But still, it was good to maintain discipline among the troops. Then when the enemy *was* at hand, they'd be well practiced and ready.

He'd taken advantage of a wide spot in the road to wait, having noticed the road just ahead narrowed into a steep-sided

110

ravine, not wanting to wait until they passed through to the other side. As the last wagon passed, he saw the six mounted rear guards riding their horses behind, two abreast. And as expected, the privates were chatting and joking, paying little attention to their surroundings.

When they spotted the lieutenant, they suddenly straightened and snapped salutes. The two in the back even turned and looked back along their trail, as if they'd been doing so the whole time.

"Gentlemen ... having a pleasant outing?" Hawkins asked, scowling and infusing the question with heavy sarcasm. No one answered, but the embarrassed looks were sufficient to know he'd gotten his point across.

"There's a reason y'all are called *guards* ... you're supposed to be *guarding* these wagons, not having a tea party. Am I understood, gentlemen?"

"Sir!" they answered.

"See that it's so," he snapped. He turned his horse and trotted back along the side of the caravan toward the front. He wondered if his latest attempt at discipline would have any lasting effect, or if they'd just roll their eyes and go back to what they were doing once he left. He realized it probably didn't help he was younger than any of them and had a pathetic growth of hair on his face that didn't yet need regular shaving.

Well, one can only do what one can do, he answered himself as he trotted alongside the wagons of the caravan.

He'd intended to rejoin the front guard—no sense in eating dust if one didn't have to; there had to be *some* perks to being the commander, after all. But when he'd passed the third wagon, he realized the ravine had narrowed so much he'd not be able to squeeze by the next wagon on horseback. So he raised his hand for the third wagon to slow so he could slip his horse in front, behind the second.

He rode between the wagons for several minutes and started wondering how long this ravine would last. He'd studied the map, of course, but it hadn't been a very good one, and certainly hadn't mentioned this canyon. Fortunately, the tiny creek that ran through it, and presumably had carved it over the eons, was nearly dry this time of year, no more than a trickle down the right side of the roadway. He could imagine the road might become impassable in the early spring when the stream had a heavy flow.

Though it was unpleasant being wedged in line between the two wagons, he could at least enjoy the relative coolness of the shade in the deep gorge. And in a few minutes the rhythmic movement of the horse, combined with the monotonous view of the back of the supply wagon, and the cool shade made him feel drowsy. He fought to keep his eyes open, but they seemed uncooperative. He shook his head, but that only helped for a few moments ...

A heart-stopping explosion rang in his ears and snapped him wide awake. The noise was immediately followed by several others. *Gunshots!*

He turned his head to look at the drivers seated in the wagon behind him and saw they were wide-eyed, scrambling to extract their rifles from behind their seat.

The gunshots came from in front and above, and in a flash, he realized he'd blindly ridden his caravan into the perfect place for an ambush. He unholstered his revolver and gazed up the hillside, fearing to see a rifle barrel aimed at his face. But he saw only thick trees and bushes. Then the wagon in front lurched to a stop. Hawkins' own horse had no choice but to do likewise. It was the worst possible scenario; they'd been brought to a complete stop in a deadly kill zone. And half his troops were blocked from joining the fight, including himself!

ᔕᕮᔔᑕᔕ᠕ᔕᕮᔔᑕᔕᑕᔕᔕᕮᔔᑕᔕ

"What's the story, Billy?"

"Five men, Captain. Seated around a table. Drinking whiskey and talking. I saw one pistol holster hanging on a hook, and a rifle propped against the wall. Couldn't see if there were others. No one watching the outside. One door in front next to the drive and one in back on the opposite side."

"Hmm ... all right, thanks."

The meeting Zac had arranged earlier in the day with the pro-Union side had been very positive and productive. The men who had attacked the pro-secessionist John Calvin confessed to the act, but swore Calvin had fired first, and Mrs. Calvin had been hit when she jumped in front of her husband, presumably trying to push him out of harm's way. One of the men even opened his shirt and showed where Calvin's bullet had grazed his chest.

Nathan was satisfied with the explanation, and announced there would be no charges filed from the event as long as the pro-Union side would provide him a list of names and addresses of the secessionists and allow Nathan and his men to take them into custody. They had enthusiastically agreed, and now Nathan stood outside the first of the homes on the secessionist list.

He turned and gave the men a serious look.

"Gentlemen, please remember, these aren't outlaws or soldiers, just common folks who've gotten themselves wound up in all the nonsense going on in the larger world. I'd prefer there be no bloodshed, if possible."

"Ah, Captain," Stan interrupted, "you are for spoiling the fun."

Nathan just scowled at him by way of answer. Stan answered the scowl with a broad grin.

"That being said ..." Nathan continued, "if there is going to be any bloodshed, I'd prefer it be *theirs* and not *ours*. So be careful and don't take any chances."

They all nodded their understanding.

"Georgie, you take front lookout; and Billy you watch the back. Jim, William, and Stan, go in by the back door when you hear my bird whistle. Tom, Jamie, and I will go in the front. Avoid the windows approaching the house. Though it's nearly dark, there's no sense taking chances on being seen. I'd prefer to just walk right in, and not have to shoot our way in. Let's move."

Five minutes later Nathan stood on the front stoep, pistol in hand. Tom was in front of him, his left hand clutching the doorknob and a revolver in his right, waiting for Nathan to give the signal. Jamie stood just outside the doorframe next to Tom, ready to step into the room as soon as Tom opened the door. Nathan said a quick prayer the men inside hadn't thought to lock the door. They would know soon enough, and he was prepared

113

to kick it in if Tom failed to open it. He was confident Stan would have no difficulty doing the same at the back door.

Nathan put his fingers to his mouth and made the sharp piercing *peeent* call of a common nighthawk. Almost immediately there was an answering call coming from around the house. He nodded to Tom, who slowly turned the doorknob and pushed the door open.

Tom and Jamie immediately rushed inside, pistols in hand. They were greeted by shocked looks, but fortunately nobody moved, and the men at the table all raised their hands in surrender.

A few seconds later Stan, William, and Jim stepped in the back entrance to the kitchen, also pointing pistols at the seated men. Though they'd entered the back door at almost the same moment as Tom and Jamie, they'd had to move down a short hallway to reach the kitchen.

Nobody spoke until Tom and Jamie parted to allow Nathan to step forward, Harry the Dog hard on his heels. Nathan had already holstered his pistol.

"My name is Chambers," he announced.

The man opposite him, seemed to relax somewhat. "Name's Walker. This is my home, Chambers. What makes you think you can just walk in here and point guns at me and my friends?"

But before Nathan could respond, Stan chuckled, "Is *stupid* question! He is not just *thinking* he can come in with guns, he is already *doing it!*"

Despite the tension in the room, several of Nathan's men couldn't help grinning. Stan was Stan, after all!

But Nathan resisted the urge to smile, and maintained a stern visage, "I am here from the office of Governor Pierpont of Virginia. Y'all are under arrest for sedition and armed insurrection against the government of this state and of the Union."

"But ... you can't prove we done nothin' wrong!"

"Oh ... so you deny supporting the secessionist, rebel government in Richmond? And are willing to swear loyalty to the Restored Government in Wheeling, as well as the Union of the

United States? And fight for said governments when called upon?"

"Well ... *no*. We don't believe in no so-called 'restored' government. And we don't believe what Lincoln and his abolitionists are doing is right. Virginia ought to be allowed to secede if it wants. And we ain't about to fight for no damned Yankee army; if anything, we'd fight for the other'n."

"Very well then ... as I said, you are all under arrest. And I don't have to prove you've done anything; you've just admitted to treason and sedition. Men, take their guns, and let's go."

As they made their way back to where they'd left their horses, Tom, walking next to Nathan said, "Well, that went more smoothly than I'd expected, sir."

"Yes ... once in a while, things *do* go according to plan," they shared a grin.

"Tom ... let's hit one more place on our list tonight, then the next one first thing in the morning, just before it gets light. If all goes well, that'll leave only one left, and then we can get back home."

"Sounds good, sir."

ဢ๛ඥ๗ဢ๛ඥ๗ဢ๛ඥ๗

Lieutenant Hawkins leapt from the saddle and looped his horse's reins over the back rail of the wagon ahead. He jerked his rifle from its scabbard and turned to the drivers behind him. The sounds of gunfire ahead had intensified, echoing noisily off the canyon walls. He was gratified to hear his men up front were now returning fire.

"Leave the wagon! Work your way to the front and join the fight. Collect the other drivers as you go and tell them I ordered them to do the same. We must extract ourselves from this canyon. Get the men out front moving toward the back if you can."

"All right. But where're *you* going, sir?"

His initial instinct had been to dash ahead, where the fighting was. But his next thought overruled the first: they must *not* become trapped in this canyon, at all cost!

"I must first go to the rear to organize the guard. They *must* hold open the way or we'll all be slaughtered! Now, *move!*"

"Yes, sir!" they shouted and jumped down from the wagon, moving toward the right canyon wall where the narrow stream bed gave them just enough room to squeeze past the wheels of the wagon in front.

Hawkins squeezed past the third wagon and saw the men in the second wagon standing, rifles in hand, gazing up at the canyon walls above them.

"Men, leave the wagon and come with me."

"But ... what about our men up front?"

"I will return for them momentarily, but we must ensure the way out is held open. Come!"

Without waiting for them to respond or comply, he hurried past. He gathered the last two drivers and then came out into the open at the end of the caravan. The six rear-guard privates were still mounted but had rifles in hand. They stared anxiously up the walls of the ravine above them. The horses fidgeted nervously, sensing their riders' anxiety.

"Lieutenant! Are we happy to see you! What's going on sir?"

He ignored the question and shouted, "Dismount immediately and get those horses between you and the canyon walls. Use them as a shield to protect yourselves!"

The men scrambled to obey this sensible command.

"The front of the caravan has been attacked, but I have not yet been there. It is vital you hold the narrow way to our rear. If we get cutoff from escape the enemy will have us in a death trap."

The men were all ears now, staring at their lieutenant like their lives depended on it—which was likely the case.

"You six, hurry back with your horses beside you to the opening of the canyon. Work your way outside ... carefully. If you're opposed, you must shoot your way out if possible. If not possible, come back and find me and I will send more men. If you make it outside, tie your horses and climb as high as you can up the hillside overlooking the entrance, half of you on each side. From there you must cover our escape. We will join you as quickly as we can. Shoot anyone you see not wearing a Union uniform!"

"Sir!"

"The rest of you men, with me."

He turned and ran back the way he'd come, while the dismounted privates moved out in the other direction.

As Hawkins neared the front, the constant gunfire grew louder until it was almost deafening, echoing off the rock walls surrounding them.

He realized he'd soon be unable to issue any verbal commands and would have to resort to hand signals. So he paused and turned to the men following and shouted, "When we break out into the open look up the hillside and target the puffs of smoke. If any of our men are wounded, drag them back under the first wagon. We must do what we can to extract our men from this trap!"

The men nodded their understanding, but their wide-eyed fearful looks didn't exude much confidence. For most of his men it would be their first action, so he couldn't expect much.

He turned and hurried along the wagons toward the front, his men following behind.

When they broke out into the open a scene of chaos greeted them. Gun smoke hung heavily in the still canyon air, while an uncoordinated melee of men shouted, reloaded rifles, and fired up toward the canyon walls above them. Bullets slammed into the hard gravel surface of the roadway, sending rocks and sand spinning in every direction.

Hawkins raised his rifle, targeted a fresh puff of smoke, aiming just under it; and fired. He laid the rifle at his feet, unholstered his Remington revolver, and raced forward, pistol raised overhead. He immediately targeted another smoke plume and fired. Then again, and again, and again, until all six cylinders were empty, and the hammer clicked ineffectively against the cylinder head.

He holstered the weapon and hurried toward a man who lay unmoving in the roadway, eyes closed. Soldiers knelt nearby, gazing up at the walls above them, firing at anything moving.

Grabbing the man under the arms he pulled with all his strength back toward the lead wagon. The man's inert form was a heavy burden and Hawkins could only drag it with aching slowness. A bullet flashed past his face so close he felt the breeze of it before he felt its impact against the ground near his right boot.

But then another man lent a hand, and together they pulled the wounded soldier to safety, shoving him up under the wagon.

Hawkins realized there were no animals up front beyond the lead wagon. His front guardsmen had wisely dismounted without being ordered, though they'd not had the presence of mind to retain their horses for cover. Apparently, the animals had all bolted away up the trail. But someone had had the sense to unhitch the mule team from the lead wagon so the structure could be used as a defensive redoubt without the fear of panicky animals pulling it away.

Hawkins shouted and gestured for his men to fall back to the wagon, while he swapped a pre-loaded cylinder into his Remington revolver in place of the empty one. He'd have to be more judicious in its use; he had only one more cylinder in his pocket.

"Here, Lieutenant," one of the men said, handing him back his rifle. He nodded his head in acknowledgement, and immediately set to work re-loading it. By now all his men had managed to scramble back to the relative safety of the wagon, though they wouldn't all fit underneath and several were still halfway exposed where they hunkered along its sides, including the Lieutenant himself.

Hawkins leaned down under the wagon and shouted, "Everyone reload your guns. You men closest to the back fall back to the next wagon and then start laying down covering fire. You two—carry the wounded man and go next." He looked at another man who'd been hit in the leg, and was clearly in great pain, though still managing to move. "Can you make it on your own?"

The man grimaced but nodded yes.

"Okay, as soon as that covering fire starts, you go too. The rest of us will pass by the wagon just behind and fall back to the next one and start covering fire. We'll leap-frog our way to the back of the caravan. *Move!*"

The men in the back of the wagon scrambled out from underneath and raced back to the wagon behind. The gunfire from above, which had eased somewhat once they'd all ducked under the wagon, now picked up again in earnest. The Union soldiers in the rear made it to the next wagon, then stood and began returning fire.

"Go!" Hawkins shouted to the men carrying the wounded man and to the private who'd been shot in the leg. The wounded man took off as quickly as he could, limping heavily, using his rifle for a crutch. The other two men dragged their burden from beneath the wagon. With a heave they lifted him from the ground, one man with his feet and the other up under his arms. They hustled him back to the next wagon before collapsing on the ground. The mule team of the wagon fidgeted nervously, but fortunately were wedged in so tightly they had nowhere to go.

"Come on!" Hawkins shouted and took off toward the rear. As he ran, he felt something bump hard against his right upper arm, like someone had punched him. He glanced down and saw his tunic had been torn and blood oozed from the gap.

Damn, I've been hit! No time for that now, he thought and kept running.

�৺ঌঌৠৼৠ঺ঌঌৼৠৼৠ঺ঌঌৼৠ঺

Though it had been a near thing, they all finally made it to the back end of the caravan. Miraculously, no one had been killed, and there had been no more major injuries since they had pulled back from the front. Fortunately, Hawkins' own wound proved minor; the bullet had torn through the tunic but only grazed the skin underneath, leaving a long, red, oozing furrow. One inch over, though, and he might've lost the arm due to a shattered humerus bone!

The enemy continued to target them, and incoming bullets impacted the wagon in front of them and the dirt of the roadway behind. But the enemy apparently hadn't thought to position any men this far back in the canyon. Only silence greeted them back toward the entrance, so Hawkins assumed the rear guard had met with no trouble and had secured the entrance as ordered.

He could envision the enemy realizing their mistake and even now struggling to work their way in his direction high up above

119

in the thick undergrowth and along the steep sides of the canyon. That would surely take some time—he hoped long enough for his men to make their escape.

They briefly debated trying to back the last wagon, at least, down to the entrance and salvage it. But Hawkins quickly decided it wasn't worth the risk. The drivers would be exposed for too long, and it was doubtful the nervous and balky mules would be up to the task.

"Come on, men. Time to go home," he said, to which he received grateful nods, and appreciative smiles.

ಬಿ೫ಿ೧ಕಿ೪ಕ೫ಿ೫ಿ೧ಕಿ೪ಕ೫ಿ೫ಿ೧ಕಿ೪ಕ

Before they were finished with the operation, Nathan and his men had raided four different farms and arrested fifteen men without serious incident. By the time they came to the last place, word had apparently gone around; two men greeted them on the porch with their hands in the air, and their bags already packed. They explained they knew this was coming and had no desire to risk getting shot by Nathan and his men.

Zac helped them arrange transportation for the prisoners so they could be sent to Wheeling for trial and incarceration. Nathan figured they'd work out the legal details once he got back and could talk with the governor about it. They'd have to put together some sort of ad-hoc trial to at least convict them of raising arms against the government. Then they'd have to figure out a prison. Perhaps the Union Army had something set up by now. It occurred to him this sort of thing was much better organized out in Texas, ironically, despite its lack of "civilization."

Nathan, Tom, and Jim sat at a table in the common room of the small inn in Fairmont where they'd been staying since their arrival. "What if we just said they was our baggage carriers?" Jim offered.

But Nathan scowled, "It'd be a stretch. I have a special pass for me and my 'military advisors.' I fear including the four freemen in that might be pushing our luck with the Army. They have a specific policy in place prohibiting taking slaves on the B&O, not

120

wanting to get bogged down in the event of a mass exodus triggered by the Confiscation Act, I suppose.

"I don't want to risk having to make other arrangements at the last minute. I'm already feeling anxious to get back to Wheeling and get to work training the Seventh Infantry."

"I agree with the Captain," Tom said. "Better to just arrange for a wagon and send our men along to escort them. Then we'll not have to worry about it. Besides, it'll do our guys some good and get them ... 'out of the house' ... for a few days. By the time they get back we'll be ready to use them in the training program. I think they've been suffering a bit of cabin fever being up at the farm back home with nothing to do while they know there's a war going on elsewhere."

"Hmm ... yes, I think you're right about that, Tom," Nathan said, looking thoughtful. "Have you heard any grumbling recently, Jim?"

"You mean about joining up and fighting? Nothing specific, but it's always there percolating, so to speak. But so far, the men've all said they want to wait and fight with *you*, sir ... assuming that don't take *too* long."

"Good. But still ... a long ride home wouldn't hurt them."

Jim grinned, "Hell, maybe if we're lucky they'll run into some bushwhackers or stray rebels on the way and can enjoy a good shootout."

Tom rolled his eyes and grinned, "One can only hope!"

They saw Zac Pierpont enter the room and gaze about. When he spotted them, he nodded and headed straight for their table.

They exchanged greetings and Zac handed Nathan a telegram. "It's from Frankie ... *er*, I should say, *Governor Pierpont.*"

"Oh? What's it about?"

"Mr. Chambers ... surely you don't think I'd read someone else's telegrams?"

Nathan just scowled.

"All right ... I may have had a peek. After all, it *is* from my brother."

"Let's have a look," Nathan said and opened the folded sheet of paper.

September 11, 1861. Dear Mr. Chambers. Have received word of another incident near you in Grafton. This time involving a Union convoy. Please investigate and take appropriate action prior to your return. Regards, F.H. Pierpont, Governor.

He handed the paper to Tom to read aloud for the others' benefit, after which he asked Zac, "How far is it to Grafton?"

"Oh, only twenty miles. It's the next stop on the B&O. You can be there in an hour by train."

Nathan was thoughtful for a moment, then said, "Zac, would you be willing to look after our new freemen friends while we're away? And perhaps secure us a wagon for their transport back to Wheeling upon our return?"

"Of course, Mr. Chambers. It'd be my pleasure, sir, and no trouble at all."

"Thank you kindly, Mr. Pierpont. Gentlemen ... looks like we're not going home just yet. Let's be on the first train east tomorrow morning. In the meantime, pass that bottle of whiskey, would you, Jim?"

ଧୀୟ୍ପ୍ୟରଖ୍ୟୀଧୀୟ୍ପ୍ୟରଖ୍ୟୀଧୀୟ୍ପ୍ୟରଖ୍ୟ

Lieutenant Hawkins applied his signature to another shipment manifest—goods being sent out to replace those he'd lost on his first, and likely *last* command. He wondered if the colonel had intentionally arranged it so he'd be responsible for re-equipping this new replacement caravan, just to rub more salt in the wound.

He sighed, blotted the signature, and set the paperwork in a neat pile to one side of his desk. There were four other similar piles and he was now out of desk space. *I hope the desk sergeant shows up soon to collect these, else I'll have to get up and take them myself,* he thought.

He turned his attention to the next set of logistical orders, let out a heavy sigh, and began to read. He was halfway down the page before he realized he hadn't absorbed a single word. He sat up and rubbed his brow, trying to discourage a headache that was starting to make its presence known.

How has my career gone so badly, so soon? he asked himself for the hundredth time. He knew it was just bad luck his caravan had been attacked; dozens had made it through with no troubles on that same route in the last few weeks. But the Colonel had been furious at the loss of the wagons and equipment, and had given Hawkins a good dressing down in front of the other officers and banished him to the quartermaster's office and desk duty.

He puzzled over it one more time, but still could come up with no answer as to what he could have done differently to improve the outcome, other than never going into that damned ravine in the first place.

The sound of someone clearing his throat brought him out of his reverie, and he looked up with a start. "Ah! Sergeant; good timing, I'm about out of desk space. Will you take away these orders, please?"

"Yes, sir. But first ... the Major asks you to come to his office, if you please."

"Now?"

"Yes, sir. The major said to ask you to come straightaway."

"All right," Hawkins said. He stood from the desk and straightened his tunic. He debated putting on his hat but decided against it; he was only going down the hall, and it wasn't required under the circumstances. *What now?* he wondered. *Is the major feeling inclined to add to my misery, as if the colonel hadn't done the job thoroughly enough?*

He entered the hallway and turned left. Passing three doors on each side, he turned at the last door on the left, stood to attention in the door frame, and tapped it gently to announce his presence. He saw the major seated behind his desk. For reasons he couldn't quite explain, he found it very satisfying to see his superior had an even taller stack of papers to deal with than he did!

A man in a fine, dark suit sat across from the major with his back to the door. Clearly a civilian. Hawkins was curious but had no guess what this might be about.

"Ah ... come in Hawkins."

123

"Sir!"

The gentleman stood and turned to face him as he entered. Now that he stood, Hawkins saw he was very tall, with dark hair and mustache and an intense, intimidating presence. He did *not* look like any normal civilian he'd ever seen. And adding to the strangeness of the situation, a huge dog lounged to one side, his tongue hanging out of a prodigious mouth.

"Lieutenant Hawkins, this is Mr. Chambers from the governor's office."

"Mr. Chambers. A pleasure, sir," Hawkins said, and reached out to firmly shake the man's extended hand.

"Lieutenant Hawkins ... the pleasure is all mine."

The major stood up as well, but to Hawkins' surprise, he grabbed his hat from a hook on the wall. "Mr. Chambers would like a word with you Hawkins. I will be ... out of the office for a bit. Good day to you, Mr. Chambers. It has been a pleasure, sir."

"Thank you major; likewise. I hope we may have occasion to meet again soon."

When the major departed, closing the office door behind him, Chambers moved around to the far side of the desk and sat in the Major's chair.

"Please, be at your ease and take a seat, Mr. Hawkins. As you can clearly see, I'm *not* a superior officer, so you've no need to be formal with me."

"Thank you, sir."

"And so you don't burst a button from curiosity, I'll get right to the point, Lieutenant," the man said, setting a stack of papers down on the desk in front of him.

He held up the first page so Hawkins could see it.

"Do you recognize this, Lieutenant?"

He gazed at it a moment and nodded, "Yes, sir. It's my post-engagement report concerning ... my recent command." Now he could feel his face turning red. *Great! Now the governor has heard about my failure! What next, the president?!*

Chambers reached into his pocket and took out a cigar. But he stuck it in his mouth without lighting it and chewed on it a

124

moment. He gazed at Hawkins, as if he were examining some strange animal.

"I've read your report, and have spoken with your colonel, and other of your superior officers, as well as several men who were under your command during the recent incident."

Hawkins nodded, but could think of nothing to say in response. This was likely going from bad to worse.

"My men and I have even ridden out to the site and have examined it in great detail. One of my men has ... some very *particular* skills in that regard. He can look at a given location, read the earth and tell what has happened there like you and I would read a book."

Hawkins again nodded but could feel a lump forming in his throat. Would the governor call for his court-martial? Or have him drummed out of the service entirely? He couldn't imagine the shame his father would feel, being an old soldier himself. He wanted to say something in his own defense, but under the intense scrutiny of this man's dark eyes he couldn't seem to come up with any words.

"Let me ask you a question, Lieutenant ... other than the obvious, *not going into that ravine in the first place*—what would you do differently if you were placed in the same situation again?"

Hawkins took a deep breath and thought about what he *should* say, what words might salvage his career and his family's reputation. Should he say what the colonel had told him, that he should've fought to save the wagons and equipment? Perhaps tried to attack the enemy up the steep canyon sides? Force the wagons forward under constant, withering crossfire?

But thinking these thoughts stirred something inside him, something defiant that just said, NO! *No, I did everything right! I saved my men. Isn't that the most important thing?*

"Sir ... I know what the colonel would say ..."

But the man surprised him by leaning across the table, removing the cigar from his mouth, and looking him hard in the eyes. "I don't give a *damn* what your colonel would say, Lieutenant! I want to know what *you* say."

125

Hawkins tried to swallow the lump in his throat, but it was uncooperative.

"Yes, sir. I'd ... I'd ... well, to tell the truth, sir, I wouldn't change anything. In my mind the most important thing was to extract my men safely from a deadly situation. First, by securing our escape route, and then by organizing a fighting retreat. And that's exactly what I did, sir. And I'm happy to say, though we ended with a handful of men in hospital, I didn't lose a single man."

"Hmm ... and what about the wagons, equipment, and animals lost?"

"Sir ... to me, those things can be easily replaced. That's just money. Men's lives are more important, especially men I'm responsible for—men under my *personal* command."

Chambers leaned back in his chair and chewed on his cigar.

"The only thing I wish I'd done differently, sir, is to not trust the reports I'd been given concerning the route and the activity of the enemy. I was told the way was secure and the enemy hundreds of miles away. Next time ... if there ever *is* a next time ... I will take responsibility for my *own* route, no matter what I'm told. Sending out scouts, securing potentially dangerous passages, pausing to reconnoiter narrow points where an ambush might be placed, and so forth. That's ... all I can think of I'd do differently, sir."

The gentleman nodded, but said nothing, continuing to chew on the cigar and stare at the ceiling. Hawkins still had no idea where this was going, or what the man was thinking.

"And ... what is your assessment of your antagonists, Mr. Hawkins—their makeup, numbers, command structure, etc.?"

"I've ... also given that a lot of thought since we've returned, sir. There were somewhere between twenty-five and thirty of them, by my estimate. And ... I'm convinced we were attacked by ... *irregulars*, sir, not Confederate soldiers at all."

"Oh? Why do you say that?"

"Several things added together, sir. First, they seemed ill-trained—they were poor shots, else we'd have fared much worse. And they seemed to take an inordinate time reloading between rounds. And though they did pick a good spot for an ambush, they'd done nothing to cut off our escape. I think even a halfway decent officer would've thought to pin us in so they might have their way with us. So it seemed like maybe just a disorganized gang of men, with rifles but no real leadership."

"Interesting ... but why didn't I see any of this in your report, Lieutenant?"

"It *was* in there ... originally. But the colonel made me remove it. He said it would not look good on our report back to HQ. That some rag-tag civilians had routed a Union army patrol and taken our wagons and supplies."

"I see ..." Chambers continued to gaze at the ceiling another moment. Then he suddenly sat up straight and looked back across the desk at Hawkins.

"Mr. Hawkins ... you might be interested to know my man Billy, who investigated the site, described the enemy almost exactly as you have. In fact, when I closed my eyes just now, I could almost hear his voice, 'around twenty-five men, amateurs, poor shots, sloppy at reloading leaving gun powder strewn everywhere, failing to position men to cutoff the retreat, then scrambling too late to correct their mistake.' You may also be pleased to know Billy found plenty of blood up on the hillside, indications the enemy had suffered multiple casualties from your stalwart resistance."

Hawkins eyes widened. This was not the news he'd expected.

"And ... it may ease your mind to know we have recovered your missing wagons."

"You have?!"

"Yes ... between the blood dripping from their dead and wounded, and the tracks left by heavily burdened wagons pulled by mule teams, it was not a particularly challenging task. They took the wagons to a nearby farm and hid them in a barn, along with the mule teams. Most of the supplies had not yet been unloaded, though it was clear there'd been some looting. Unfortunately, no sign of the missing horses or mules, sorry."

"But that's ... that's *great* news, Mr. Chambers!"

"We've also arrested the farmer and handed him over to your colonel, along with the wagons. I believe the man will give up his comrades in short order, if I correctly read your colonel's intentions concerning the interrogation."

"Yes ... I believe our commander has the appropriate ... *demeanor* ... for that sort of thing."

Chambers smiled and nodded. "Oh ... one more thing; do I assume correctly you were the only soldier present who fired a revolver, Mr. Hawkins?"

Hawkins nodded.

"Then you may be interested to know ... my man also found one dead body at the scene, though they'd clearly dragged away all the others. This fellow had fallen and become wedged in a crack such that they either hadn't been able to find him or had given up trying to retrieve the body as being too dangerous."

Hawkins raised an eyebrow at this, "Oh? Then I assume you found that he wore no uniform? Though ... that doesn't prove anything; many Confederate soldiers fight without uniforms, I've heard."

"True on both counts. But that wasn't what I was getting at, Mr. Hawkins. The thing my man found most interesting was— though it was more than seventy-five yards uphill from the roadway to where the man was hit—he'd died from a single gunshot wound to the throat ... from a pistol!"

The lieutenant was shocked, "You mean—"

"Yes ... that was one hell of a pistol shot, Mr. Hawkins! One of the best I've ever heard of under extreme duress. Congratulations, my good man."

"I ... uh ... thank you, sir." Hawkins shook his head in disbelief. But the joy of this good news was short-lived; it didn't change his present predicament. "Still ... I doubt it's enough to change the colonel's opinion of my conduct, even with the recovery of the wagons."

"Your colonel's a *fool*, Hawkins! It was all I could do to keep from telling him so to his face. It's idiots like him who ruin it for *good* officers like you."

He stood up from the desk and leaned across, extending his hand.

"I want to shake your hand again, Mr. Hawkins, this time to congratulate you on an *exceptional* performance on your recent mission. Not only did you do everything *right*, and correctly prioritized your men's lives over a pile of easily replaced equipment, but you were personally heroic in the process, selflessly risking your own life to save others. My God, sir, you ought to have received a medal for this action, not some *Goddamned* desk duty!"

"Thank you, sir," Hawkins said, smiling for the first time since entering the office.

Chambers nodded, sat back down, and continued to chew on his cigar.

"Don't take it wrong, Mr. Chambers, but ... though I appreciate your kind words of encouragement and support, still ... what can *you* do? Aren't you still only a civilian, as you say, even if you do have the backing of the governor? I doubt you'll change the colonel's mind about all this, no matter how hard you try."

But Chambers smiled broadly, the cigar clenched in his teeth. "The good news is, I don't *have* to change his mind, Mr. Hawkins. In fact, I don't *wish* to; it allows me to use his idiocy to my own advantage."

"What ...?"

"As you say, I *am* working for the governor of the new Restored Government of Virginia. And in that role, I am charged with recruiting, training, and equipping new regiments for the soon-to-be state of West Virginia. And my first task is, as you'd imagine, finding the best officers I can to fill the ranks and start training the troops.

"Now ... the other thing I've done is review your official Army record. Raised in Indiana, one year at Indiana University before enlisting and being commissioned a lieutenant, and ... most interestingly, your father was a veteran sergeant, wounded in the Mexican War. Do I assume correctly it was *he* who taught you how to be a proper officer?"

"Yes, sir. I've heard his tales about the war my whole life. And lately, with the war brewing he has sought to instruct me on many of the finer points so I'd ... well, 'come back in one piece' as he says."

"Excellent! He sounds like a good man."

"That he is, sir. And he's itching to fight again himself, only ... it's not possible on account of his wooden leg."

"Ah ... I see. Anyway, as I said, I intend to shamelessly use your colonel's *stupidity* against him. I wish to hire you away for the West Virginia regiments. I have even taken the liberty of drawing up your transfer orders and have already procured the colonel's signature on them."

"You have? I ... I don't know what to say, Mr. Chambers. Save maybe just ... thank you. *Thank you very kindly, sir!*"

"No ... thank *you*! Congratulations Lieutenant Hawkins and welcome to the West Virginia volunteer forces. Or rather, I should say ... *Captain* Hawkins!"

CHAPTER 5. VENGEANCE IS MINE

"Vengeance is mine;
I will repay,
saith the Lord."
– Romans 12:19

Thursday September 12, 1861 – Wheeling, Virginia:

"Damn ... I can't hardly believe it. I heard o' some terrible bad things before but ... *Lord Jesus* ... them little children," George said, his voice quavering with emotion and his eyes watering up.

The other men in the group gazed at him but said nothing. All were suffering the same shock from it.

Finally, Cobb said, "Well ... I ain't never heard o' Mr. Georgie telling a lie. So ..."

Big George looked up at him, "Didn't mean it *that* way. I know he don't lie. It's just ... too ..." he shook his head and couldn't finish the sentence.

"Well, that explains why all the white soldier-men done looked all gloomy when they came back that one time. Now we finally knows why," Tony said.

They sat in the classroom, which had become the unofficial meeting room for the group after their evening dinner, when not in use for the reading classes. They'd been in the room having their usual chat session when Georgie had happened by and stuck his head in to say hello. They'd invited him in to hear the latest on doings out in the wide world—with the war and whatnot. And Tony had finally asked the question he was curious about concerning that one day when all the old soldiers came riding back with the Captain and all looked downcast and angry. But no one had seemed inclined to talk about what had happened that day.

Now they knew.

"And ... what they done to that sweet young mother," Henry said, thinking of his own wife Lilly, and shuddering at the thought of anything bad like that ever happening to her. Or to Rosa, now that he thought about it some more.

They were quiet then for several moments, each alone with his own dark thoughts.

But then Ned surprised them by saying, "I reckon it was *them fellas* that done it."

"What's that, Ned?" Phinney asked. "What fellas?"

"Them that came over to burn this-here place down. You seen the way them fellas looked at our folks. Like they was ready to burn it down with our women and children still inside."

"Oh ... I don't know about *that* ..." George said. "I expect they was gonna shoo everyone outside first ... just wanting to scare folks, most likely."

"How'd you know, George?" Ned asked, getting heated. "Them kind would just as soon kill our folks as to look at us."

No one had an answer to this statement, so silence fell on the group again.

Finally, Tony said, "Well ... if it *was* them, the Captain ought to know ... he done ridden out there twice now to talk with them fellas, from what I heard. Maybe we should see what he says before we go to guessing on it."

"Yeah ... I agree with that," Ned responded, "but ... if it *was* them, then I wants to know what the Captain means to do about it. And if he won't deal with them ..." he left the sentence unfinished but gave the others a serious look that left little doubt what he had in mind.

☙♋☘☙♋☘☙♋☘

Nathan and his men were once again knee deep in paperwork in their regular office at the Customs House. Progress was painfully slow, but at least they now had additional help; young Captain Hawkins had joined them after arriving on the train the day before. His energy and enthusiasm had given them all a needed boost in this seemingly thankless and endless task.

Hawkins jumped in and helped wherever needed and quickly displayed to the others what Nathan already knew: he was extremely intelligent, hard-working, and likeable. And for someone still an "inexperienced kid" by most standards, he already possessed a good deal of military knowledge, thanks in large part to his father, the Mexican-American War veteran.

Nathan was so pleased with Hawkins he planned to place him in temporary command of the several hundred regimental recruits they'd gathered thus far, and to task him with their training starting the day after next. He figured to lend Hawkins his soldiers from Texas to help out, which would serve double duty as providing some well-needed expertise and experience, as well as giving the "old" veterans something useful to do. He smiled when he thought of the irony of *that*; none of his men from Texas were older than twenty-five years, even Jim! But to the new recruits they'd be the "old men" training them!

The other officers who'd accepted offers would be joining them in the coming days and weeks, and he'd have to work them into the training routine as appropriate to their rank. He wanted to spend some time talking to each before sending him out to the training ground to make sure he and they were of a like mind concerning how the regiment should be run. He meant for the new Seventh Infantry Regiment to be the model for all future West Virginia units, and didn't want anyone coming in with different ideas about it.

They'd been at their paperwork for several hours when Nathan noticed a movement in the doorway. He looked up to see the governor's personal assistant standing in the opening, patiently waiting for him to finish the paper he was reading.

"Hello, Mr. Reed ... what can we do for you?"

"Sorry to disturb you, Mr. Chambers, gentlemen. The governor sends his compliments and asks if you would come meet with him in his office, sir, whenever most convenient."

Nathan stood and stretched. "Well, based on my aching backside, I'd say *now* would be most convenient," he said with a grin, which Reed returned. "Lead the way, Mr. Reed."

After he was seated in the governor's office, and Reed had departed, Pierpont handed Nathan a piece of paper. The sheet contained a list of city and county names and dates, all within the last week.

"What's this, Francis?"

"It's a list of the latest *incidents*. The majority are acts against private citizens, though the attacks on Union assets are increasing."

Nathan frowned. "These are ... scattered all over the Union controlled territory in the western half of the state."

"Precisely."

Nathan sat back in his seat and gazed at the ceiling. "Despite all our efforts, the problem is getting worse. I feel like I'm trying to carry water in a sieve."

"Yes ... even as we work to keep things on track and try to reorganize the various county governments and their ability to enforce the law—ensuring those in charge are loyal to *our* side—this growing insurgency threatens to undermine all our efforts."

"Hmm ... the problem is ... we don't even know who our enemy is. It could be the neighbor next door who's ready to burn down your house, or it could be a whole group of semi-organized and fairly well-armed men ready to ambush a troop of Union soldiers."

"True ... and I think you have something there, Nathan. It's almost as if we have two sets of entirely different opponents operating at the same time. What I'd call 'bushwhackers' for lack of a better term; those who'd take advantage of the upheaval to get back at a neighbor they don't like, or to stir up mischief, or maybe just to engage in plain old thievery. And then there are men who, for whatever reason, want to fight for the Confederate cause but never enlisted. Perhaps because we drove the rebel forces out of this part of the state before they could do it."

"Yes, I think you have the right of it, Governor."

"I know I asked you to help enforce the law, but clearly you and your men aren't going to be sufficient to solve this problem, Nathan. Besides, I can't have you running all over the state while our recruitment and training efforts languish. At some point the federal government will give up and leave us to our own devices—the new state be damned—if we don't start providing our fair share of troops."

"Hmm ... I agree. But maybe in the meantime *they* can help us. Your honor, I think it's time you asked Washington for their help on this. It's time the Union Army stepped up and recognized this as a serious and growing problem. Assign some men and officers to this *specific* task until things are under control."

"Yes ... that seems reasonable. And necessary, at this point. We must at least be able to hold our election next month without fear of attacks on the polling stations. I will start making the necessary inquiries. I can ask John Carlile if he will meet with the secretary of war on it. There must be some good we can gain from having seated our *own* senators in Washington."

"Yes, that's a good idea, Francis. I'm sure John will do what he can on it. Maybe even speak with the president, if that's what it takes."

"I'll send him a telegram straight away, and another to the secretary of war."

"That would be good, and it'll help ease the burden on me and my men and allow us to make progress on training and equipping the new regiment. Thank you, your honor."

ಬುಡಿಲಿಕೋಸುಡಿಲಿಕೋಸುಡಿಲಿಕೋಸ

"So ... what the Captain say, Tony?" George asked.

It was the day after they'd first learned about the horrific atrocity against the young freemen family, and the same group of men were gathered in the classroom to hear what Tony had learned.

"He said ... he don't know who done it. May've been them fellas, led by a rascal named Ward, but he ain't sure. Says there ain't no 'proof' they done it. Though he never tried to convince me they ain't."

"You think the Captain *believes* they done it, even if he ain't got proof of it?" Cobb asked.

"He wouldn't say. But if I was reading his face rightly, I'd say he believes it to be so. And he's frustrated he can't do nothing about it. Says last time he rode out, Ward threatened to start shooting if he ever came back. Captain says if he tries to go there

135

again, he has to be prepared for war. Don't think he's gonna do that until he knows for sure."

After a long, thoughtful silence, no one was surprised when Ned said, "Then maybe it's time we freemen do something for ourselves. Maybe it ain't always the Captain's job to do *for* us. Maybe it's time *we* go to war."

ᏚᏍᎠᏣᏍᎦᏚᏍᎠᏍᏣᏍᎦᏚᏍᎠᏍᏣᏍᎦ

"What you mean, you ain't coming, Cobb? You yellow or something?" Ned asked, wrinkling up his brow.

Cobb frowned, and Tony could see his anger rising.

"Ned, stop that ... *now!* Ain't no need for such names. Cobb ain't no coward. Back when we was bustin' out from Mountain Meadows he done killed as many slavers as you or I. And he ain't never shirked a dangerous duty. Maybe we ought to just hear what the man has to say before shooting off our mouths."

Ned scowled, but closed his mouth.

"Thanks, Tony," Cobb responded. "As you say ... I ain't no coward. Ain't about bein' afraid. Since the Captain taught us to fight ... I don't feel afraid no more. It's just ..." he trailed off and stared down at his feet.

"Just what, Cobb?" George asked.

Cobb looked up and they could see a wateriness in his eyes, "The Captain ... he ... he done *right* by us all ... you know?!"

They all nodded agreement to this.

"And ... he ain't never lied to us, nor let us down. Hell, the man done risked his own life so's we all could be free. And gave up a whole pile of money that he could've had if'n he'd sold us off instead. So ... it just don't seem right to ... go behind his back. I was awake all last night worrying on it. And it keeps coming back to that; I just can't do it thinking it might go against his wishes. Like we's betraying his trust in us. That's ... all ..."

They were quiet after this speech, but Ned continued to frown. "Hey, where's Phinney, anyway?"

"He ain't coming neither. We done talked it over and he felt the same as me. Only ..." Cobb looked up and locked eyes with

Ned, "he had a pretty good idea what *you* was gonna say about it, and he didn't have the stomach for hearing it."

They were quiet again. No one seemed to know what to say. It was nearly dark, and they'd gathered in the barn this time, where there'd be no prying eyes. Tony, Henry, George, and Ned carried rifles. The Captain had let them keep them after the long trek north, as long as they never left the farm with them, which would still be against the old laws of Virginia.

Taking the rifles with them tonight would be another thing that would go against the Captain's wishes, this time explicit ones. They each also carried a small pack with extra ammunition and powder.

Henry, having joined the group after all the fighting was over, had never fired a weapon before arriving at Belle Meade Farm. But he'd now had several lessons from Big George and felt comfortable handling it, as long as he didn't have to hit a target too far away. And though he hadn't fought *with* them, they'd all heard the story by now of how he'd strangled a rebel guard in order to make good his escape. No one doubted his courage and fighting spirit.

And even though he'd never intended to go, Cobb had also brought a pack with him. He reached in and pulled out two gun holsters, each of which carried a loaded Colt revolver. They were the weapons he'd carried during the long road from Mountain Meadows for use whenever he'd ridden as a scout. The Captain had allowed him to keep them, under the same restrictions as the rifles. He reached out and handed one to George, and the other to Tony. "Here, take these with you. You may need them if things go badly and you don't have time to reload your rifles."

Tony gazed at him a moment, then nodded. "Thanks, Cobb."

George also thanked him, and immediately strapped on the gun belt.

Tony did the same, then looked over at Ned and Henry, "Well, may as well get on with it, if we's gonna."

⁞⁞⁞⁞⁞⁞⁞⁞

Though Tony didn't like "going behind the Captain's back" any better than Cobb did, he had a pretty strong feeling they were doing exactly what the Captain himself would do if he were in their position. There were some things a man just had to do, but the Captain couldn't do them just now, him being an important and well-known man. And the less he knew about what they were planning, the better it would be for him.

So they'd had to go about getting directions to Ward's farm surreptitiously. They'd recruited one of the young freeman boys to wheedle it out of Mr. Georgie. He'd been instructed to act curious about the neighbor who'd tried to burn down their classroom — what he looked like, why he acted like he did, what he'd said, where his farm was, what the farm looked like, what kind of crops he grew, and on and on. Mr. Georgie always seemed to like talking with the young boys, and never got tired of answering their endless questions.

When they were about halfway to Ward's place it occurred to Tony there was one question he should've had the boy ask Georgie: did the man keep any dogs? If Ward had dogs, their visit would likely be very brief. There'd be no way to sneak up on the house if there were dogs around.

Nothing he could do about that now. They'd just have to see when they got there. If a dog started barking, they'd have to give it up and run out of there as quick as they could. If dogs chased after them … well, they did have guns, after all.

When they reached the left-hand turnoff the boy had described, something about the Captain came to Tony's mind that he hadn't really appreciated before. He'd always admired how the Captain could lead men, speak to them to fire their spirits, ride a horse, shoot a gun, and was totally fearless. And all the other things that made a good soldier.

But he'd never before thought much about how the Captain always seemed to know what to do in any given situation. That he always had a *plan*. Thinking about it now, he realized those things went together, and it was one thing they'd neglected. They had no plan. The only thing they'd discussed was not shooting Ward and his men until they got them to admit to the murders.

138

But how they'd do that, they hadn't discussed. And Tony didn't trust Ned to not just start shooting first thing, then ask questions after.

So when they were a few feet off the main road, he raised his hand, the signal the Captain had taught them during their soldier training that meant to stop. He turned to the others, "Look ... if there's a dog, we gotta give it up and hot-foot it outta here, understood?"

The others nodded but said nothing. They were all breathing heavily from their long jog from Belle Meade. The twilight had nearly faded to darkness, but he could still make out the determined looks in their eyes.

"If we see anyone outside ... same thing, beat it out quick as quick. This here's only gonna work if we catch 'em by surprise, inside the house."

More nods.

"If we make it to the house ... I'll go in first, then Ned, Henry, and George last. Reckon you can see over our heads if need be, George."

George smiled, and nodded at this.

"Remember ... no shooting if we can help it, until we've had a chance to ask 'em if they was the ones as done them murders. It ain't gonna sit too well if we never get to know if it was them or not."

Ned answered, "All right, Tony. But then ... they still need killin' whether they done it or no; they was gonna burn our folks. That needs answering."

Tony looked at George and Henry. They both nodded their agreement.

"All right. Agreed. Let's move—quiet now!"

In a couple of minutes, the driveway rounded a corner and the farmhouse came into sight. They saw light streaming from two windows on the side of the house facing them. The house had a small front stoep on the left, facing the driveway and reached by two low steps. Tony gazed around, looking for any sign of men or animals moving in the near darkness. He feared seeing the telltale glow of a cigar on or around the porch. But there was nothing. And thankfully, no barking dogs.

He called another halt when they were still well outside the light cast by the windows, about thirty yards from the house. Turning to the others he signaled them to stay where they were. After handing his rifle to Ned, he left them crouched next to the ditch in the drive and crept up to the window nearest the front door, careful to keep low and out to the side of the stream of light. He slipped up to the wall next to the window and carefully leaned out for a look. But all he could see was an empty inside wall, painted a light green color. He slowly moved to see more of the room, but it was empty, just an entry room of some kind with hooks on the wall holding hats and jackets, and benches along the sides. A lantern in a nook up on the wall lit the room.

He looked back at his men, now invisible back in the darkness. He shook his head, letting them know he'd not seen anyone yet.

He ducked down and moved past the window, ducking under the ledge, to the one further back from the drive. He repeated the same careful movement next to this one. This time he saw the back of a man's head, leaning up against the glass. Across from him sat another man, who was talking and looking in another direction. So at least three men sat at the table.

Tony ducked down and hurried back to where he'd left the men.

"The left window is to a small entry room; nobody in there. The other'n has at least three men sitting at a table. Maybe more."

"Any guns?" George asked.

"Didn't see any. But I only saw heads."

They were all quiet for several moments and nobody moved. Their mission had suddenly become very real, and it was a sobering thought.

Finally, Tony took a deep breath and slowly let it out again. "We still gonna do this?" he asked in almost a whisper. Ned nodded immediately.

But George and Henry hesitated for a moment gazing back at Tony. They looked across at each other, then turned and nodded.

Tony knew if he waited any longer, he might freeze up and not be able to do it. So he turned and hurried toward the door. When he reached the front step, he looked back to make sure the others were right behind. Then he carefully stepped up to the door, reached out and turned the knob. The latch came back with a quiet click.

Tony pushed the door open and stepped inside. Six feet away a man stood in the doorway between the entry room and the room with the table. The man turned at the sound, and jumped, *"What the hell?!"*

The first man lurched back into the other room banging into a second man seated at the table there. *"Hey! Watch it! What the ... "* the man at the table started to complain. But he too looked back and saw Tony. He jumped up, spilling his chair backward.

The first man had ducked to the side, and now came back with something in his hands: a rifle! He pried back the hammer and leveled the weapon at Tony.

Boom! The gunshot rattled the windowpanes in the small room. Smoke curled up from Tony's gun, and the man slumped to the floor. The second man, who'd spilled his chair, also reached for something behind the wall. The other men were yelling, but it was just noise to Tony.

He dropped his rifle and reached down toward the pistol holster. But he was shoved hard in his left side. Tony stumbled to the floor, hitting hard on his knees. He looked up and saw Ned going through the open doorway into the other room. *Boom! Boom!* Two rifles fired at nearly the same time. Henry also moved past and pointed his rifle into the room. *Boom!*

George leaned into the other room, rifle held out front. But he lowered the weapon without firing. He came back into the room and offered Tony a hand up.

When Tony looked in it was all over. Four men were down; fortunately, none had been Tony's friends.

The first man Tony had shot lay crumpled back against the wall to the left. The man who'd spilled the chair was on the floor off to the right, but he might not be dead. He had a bloodied face, but no bullet hole in him that Tony could see. Ned had apparently hit him with the rifle butt after firing off his round at the man across the table, who'd been knocked backward to the floor, chair and all. Only the man on the far right was still seated at the table. A pool of blood oozed out from around his head where it rested face down on the tabletop. In his right fist he still clenched a pistol, though Tony couldn't tell if it had been fired.

"Sweet *Jesus!*" Tony said, finally finding some words. "Anybody hurt?"

"No," Ned answered. George and Henry just shook their heads.

Tony looked around once again at the dead men, wanting to make sure. He saw the man who'd been bashed by Ned start to move a bit.

"George ... Henry, get that one up in his chair. Least we still got one we can ask our questions."

George and Henry quickly moved to comply and yanked the man to his feet. Tony picked up the chair and they sat the man in it. He opened his eyes but seemed confused and unfocused. Blood streamed from a nose that had clearly been broken, and one eye was nearly swollen shut and turning a purplish color.

After a few minutes his good eye seemed to clear, and he looked around with it wide open. George hadn't fired his rifle yet, so stood back and aimed it at the man's chest to discourage him from going anywhere.

Finally, the man spoke, "So ... y'all reckoned on killin' some white folks, did you?" He coughed, and spit blood from his mouth. "Well, what're you waitin' on? Go ahead'n finish the job!" he glared at George.

But Tony stepped up in front of him and said, "We come to learn if y'all was who done in that young freemen couple and them little ones."

The man looked at him, and grinned, "Oh? Is that what it was? What if we didn't? Y'all was gonna just kill us anyhow? For sport?"

But Ned stepped up and punched him in the stomach with the butt of his rifle. The man doubled over, choking for breath.

"Yeah!" Ned answered, "Like the sport y'all was gonna have burnin' down our school!"

The man sat back up, and coughed again, "Ah ... should o' know'd ... Chambers' bunch of uppity coons. May as well go on ahead and kill me. Ain't gonna tell you nothin' anyhow."

Tony knew this wasn't going anywhere good and was starting to get anxious about getting out of there. This man would never tell them what they needed to know. He pulled out the pistol Cobb had lent him. He meant to finish this business, so they could get on home.

But as he held out the gun a sudden idea hit him. "You can at least tell me your name before I kill you," he said.

The man tilted his head as if thinking it over, "Sure ... why not. Name's Ward, and this is my place you done shot up. Or *was* ... I guess ... when I was still *alive*," he chuckled at his own grim humor.

"All right, Ward. Only got one more question for you. I want to know, how's it feel to die knowin' you and all your friends was killed by a bunch o' stupid blacks? And knowin' y'all ain't never even kilt *any* o' our kind?"

But Ward laughed, "Oh, you think not?" he laughed, and then started coughing, spitting more blood, reaching up and wiping it from his nose and mouth with his sleeve. "I'll tell you what, *Mr. Smarty Mouth*, we's killed plenty o' your kind! Includin' them squalin' brats. But sure enjoyed that young negress before we cut her up! Yep, she was sure a screamer! *Ha!*"

Bam! Tony fired the pistol into the man's stomach. Ward doubled over in pain. *Bam!* He fired again, this time hitting Ward in the leg. He pulled back the hammer again ...

Boom! Ward's head whipped backward, and the chair again tipped back onto the floor. A gaping hole in his forehead oozed a dark fluid. But Tony hadn't pulled the trigger this time. He looked back and saw smoke curling up from the end of George's rifle. Their eyes met and they nodded.

ജ്ഞാ൬ഇ൪ജ്ഞാ൬ഇ൪ജ്ഞാ൬ഇ൪

Nathan looked up from his paperwork and was surprised to see Governor Pierpont standing in the doorway. He immediately rose to his feet, as did the rest of the men in the room when they realized the nature of their visitor.

"Your honor," Nathan said, pushing his chair back and beginning to rise.

"Please gentlemen ... as you were, as you were. Mr. Chambers, a moment of your time, if you would ..." he said, and inclined his head indicating his desire for Nathan step into the hallway. He rose and followed the governor out.

"What is it, Francis?"

"Another incident, this one closer to home, I'm afraid."

"Oh? I thought you didn't want me dealing with any more of these."

"True, but I thought ... well, I thought you might want to look into *this* one."

Nathan raised an eyebrow.

"It ... involves your unpleasant neighbor Mr. Ward."

"Hmm ... not surprised. What's the scoundrel done this time?"

"Well ... this time he seems to have managed to get himself murdered."

"What?!"

"Yes, he was found shot dead this morning, inside his own home. And three of his close friends with him. Looks like it happened two or three days ago. I've instructed the Army to leave everything as is until you could come have a look. That is ..."

"What?"

"Well, considering the previous altercations you've had, and your suspicions of his involvement in other ... disreputable activities ... I wanted to make sure you hadn't ... *you know* ..."

"Oh. No, your honor. Much as I may have wanted to, it wasn't me nor my men who did him in."

"Good to hear."

"Come on, men. Let's go have a look at some more dead bodies."

Jim chuckled, "Sounds good, Captain. Serves to break up the monotony. Whose bodies is it this time?"

"Our favorite neighbor Ward and his buddies."

"Oh, well, so much the better, then; at least it's a happy occasion."

"Captain Hawkins, you're welcome to come along," Nathan said, seeing the young man looking around expectantly as the others prepared to depart. "A ride in the fresh air would do you good, no doubt."

"Thank you, sir. Don't mind if I do."

𝄃𝄃𝄃𝄃𝄃𝄃𝄃𝄃𝄃𝄃𝄃𝄃𝄃𝄃

On the ride out to Ward's farm, Nathan was thinking about how odd it was that investigating murder scenes had almost become part of the normal routine in the last few weeks. The only thing different about his one, seemingly, was that he knew the "victim." But that was mitigated by the fact he greatly despised the man, and knew he likely deserved whatever had happened to him.

Before they entered the house, he warned Hawkins not to touch anything, or step in any blood or on any objects on the floor. They'd all have a quick look and then move outside and let Billy do ... what Billy did best.

The scene was as he'd expected from the report he been given: four men shot dead around a table, with a couple of chairs tipped over. The men were in various poses as you'd expect. One was on the floor, slumped up against a wall, the other three had apparently been shot while still seated. Oddly, Ward himself had been shot three times: in the left thigh, in the lower abdomen, and the *coup de grace* in the center of the forehead knocking a large exit hole out the back of his head.

A half-empty bottle of whiskey sat in the middle of the table, along with four mostly empty glasses. A deck of cards lay next to the bottle—slumped over but not scattered. Apparently, they'd intended to play but hadn't yet started when they were interrupted.

Nathan saw nothing else of interest, so moved out to the entry room to give the other men room to lean in and have a look. He walked toward the window, thinking to gaze out at the fields, but when he stepped, something bumped against the toe of his boot. He bent down and picked up a small, brown-colored object. He gazed at it a moment and his eyes widened. He pocketed the object, and continued to the window, where he pulled out a cigar and proceeded to light it.

Tom stepped up next to him. "I saw you pick something up off the floor. Anything interesting?"

Nathan returned a serious look that startled Tom. And before answering, Nathan glanced around the room to see if anyone had heard Tom's inquiry. But no one was looking their way; most of the men had already gone back outside. "I'll tell you later ... back at the farm," Nathan whispered.

Tom raised an eyebrow but nodded his understanding.

"Tom ... I'll meet you outside in a moment. I ... wish to have a quick word with Billy before I join you."

Tom tilted his head and gave Nathan an inquisitive look but said nothing. He tipped his hat and turned for the door.

Nathan returned to the room with the table. Billy was bent over poking at Wade's body. He looked up at Nathan, "All were rifle shots ... except two of these. Only the head shot was a rifle. The other two ... .36 caliber pistol."

"Hmm ... have you found anything else of interest, Billy?"

Billy stood up and looked Nathan in the eye. "Yes, Captain. Outside ... before we entered the house. Like at the other farm, the one where the black family died ... I have found prints of men not wearing shoes ..."

Nathan took a deep breath and continued to lock eyes with Billy. "I see. Billy ... I think perhaps we should just keep this between you and I for now. Say nothing to anyone else about that, if you would."

Billy nodded, "I understand, Captain. I will ... say nothing that might ... hint at who may have done this. Until you ask me."

"Thanks, Billy. We'll speak on this matter again when we can be alone ... back at the farm."

"Yes, Captain."

❧❧❧❧❧❧❧❧❧❧❧❧

"Hey ... Tony, wait a minute ..."

Tony stopped, and turned toward the familiar voice.

"Hello, Rosa." She walked toward him between a row of beans where he'd been hoeing earlier. It was evening time, and he'd been heading back to the tents for some dinner. He couldn't help but admire the way she walked, and the fine look of her figure, and her lovely face.

"Tony ... can I walk with you back to the tents?"

"Sure ..."

They walked in silence, side by side for a while. Tony wondered what this was all about. She hadn't sought *him* out since ... well, *ever.*

"Tony ... I wanted to ask you something."

"Ask me what?"

"About a rumor going 'round. They says you, Ned, and some others done gone out last night ... with guns."

Tony looked at her, and shrugged, "Shouldn't believe rumors, Rosa. Just talk."

"Then it ain't true?"

Tony wondered where this was going. Why did she want to know, anyway? Was she trying to find something out so she could go tell the Captain? Trying to win his favor by bringing him news?

"Never said if it was or wasn't."

"C'mon Tony ... I's just curious, is all. I know you done all that fightin' before and know how to use a gun. Folks reckoned maybe y'all went after them as tried to burn up our school."

He stopped and turned toward her, "Look, Rosa ... why you want to be askin' them things anyhow? You wantin' to get me in trouble or something?"

She looked into his eyes, and suddenly looked sad and started to tear up, "I just ... I just ... wanted to tell you I *admired* what you done, is all ..." she said, then covered her teary eyes with her hand, and ran off toward the tents.

Tony stood where he was, staring after her, mouth hanging open. *Damn, Tony ... that was about as stupid as stupid gets!* he scolded himself, slowly shaking his head.

Tom and Nathan sat on the back porch of the Belle Meade farmhouse in what Nathan had taken to calling "the veranda," though the name was somewhat humorous and ironic. This sitting area was tiny compared to the expansive veranda of the Big House back at Mountain Meadows. It was really little more than an expanded back stairwell, only large enough for a single table and four chairs. It was such tight quarters that Harry the Dog had given up trying to wedge himself between Nathan and the porch railing and now took to laying on the lawn below.

The great veranda was one of the features Nathan missed most from Mountain Meadows; wide and spacious, roomy enough for dozens of tables, it wrapped around the entire house on all four sides, connecting the front and back entrances in one continuous wood-planked surface. It was covered in the front of the house and on its sides, so one could keep dry when it rained. But was open in back so one might enjoy the sun on a cool day, or a sunset after a hot day. He sighed a heavy sigh, thinking back on it fondly.

He leaned back and took another puff on his cigar. After a hot day, the evening was just beginning to cool, and a fresh breeze was blowing in off the river.

"So ... you were going to let me in on the mystery; what was it you found on the floor back at Ward's place?" Tom asked.

Nathan nodded, reached in his pocket and placed an item on the table. Tom leaned forward and stared at it a moment, then sat up wide-eyed.

"*Oh!* Is that ... what I think it is?"

"Yes. Now you understand my mysterious behavior back at the scene."

Tom leaned back in his chair and gazed at the sky, taking a puff of his cigar and slowly letting it out before leaning back toward Nathan.

"So ... what are you going to do about it?"

"Well, fortunately for you, you'll be able to sit right where you are and have your curiosity satisfied in the course of a few short minutes. Speaking of ... here comes Billy now. He's the first on our little 'guest list' for the evening."

Tom raised an eyebrow and gave Nathan an amused look.

"Hello, Billy! Come have a seat."

"Hello, Captain. Sergeant Clark. Thank you, Captain."

Billy sat in the chair closest the back stairs, which he'd just come up.

"Thanks for coming to talk with me, Billy."

Billy said nothing, just gave him a puzzled look; he never thought he needed to be thanked for doing anything the Captain asked him to do.

"Billy ... I think you have a pretty good idea who killed those men."

"Yes, Captain. I saw the barefoot prints leading up to the front door of the house, and then I noticed the thing now sitting on the table, before you put it in your pocket."

Nathan chuckled; there was no slipping anything past Billy.

"Billy ... I'm not inclined to let the rest of the world in on our little secret, other than Tom here. But I wanted to make sure you were feeling okay about that. I don't want you to feel I am asking you to do something ... dishonest, or dishonorable."

"Dishonest, Captain? I am not understanding ..."

"You know ... not telling anyone about who did the killing, even though you now know."

Billy tilted his head as if thinking over what Nathan had just said.

"No ... Captain ... I don't see how *not* telling a thing can be dishonest. Dishonest is when you tell a lie. And I haven't told anything, so how can it be a lie? No one can expect me to tell them a thing I don't wish to."

Nathan smiled, and took another puff on his cigar, nodding his head.

"And as for dishonorable ... Captain, I would have killed those men myself if you had asked me to. With no shame nor remorse. Same as many other times in the past."

Nathan reached over and patted him on the back. "I had a pretty good idea you'd say that, Billy. Good man! That was all I

149

wanted to speak with you about. Now, would you do me a favor and go fetch Tony; ask him to come see me straight away?"

"Yes, Captain."

After Billy departed, Nathan reached out and grabbed the item, putting it back in his pocket. Tom nodded.

Tom and Nathan enjoyed a glass of whiskey while awaiting Tony's arrival. When he arrived, he looked tense.

"Thanks for coming, Tony. Have a seat."

Tony nodded, and sat where Billy had been a few minutes earlier.

"We were out at Ward's farm today. Seems he and three of his friends have managed to get themselves shot."

"I ... don't think I know who that is, Captain."

"Sure you do ... you've even met him. He's one of the fellows who tried to burn down our schoolroom."

"Oh ... one of *them* fellas."

"Yep. Somebody went into his house yesterday and shot him dead."

Tony just stared at Nathan but said nothing.

Nathan reached into his pocket and brought something out, setting it on the table.

"Found this on the floor in Wade's house," Nathan said.

Tony looked at it, and his eyes widened. It was a well-worn, cut-off section of braided leather. About three inches long and an inch thick. Like the type of braided leather used in a ... bullwhip.

It was a piece of the famous bullwhip Nathan had chopped to bits the day he announced there'd be no more beatings on the farm. The pieces of bullwhip that many of the freemen now carried in their pockets wherever they went. The piece that Tony usually carried in his ...

Tony looked up and met eyes with Nathan.

Nathan took another drag on his cigar while gazing at Tony.

"I'm guessing this was about more than him trying to torch our classroom; am I correct?" Nathan finally asked.

"Yes, sir. It was on account o' that young freeman family that was murdered. With them little kids and all. That just didn't sit well with us."

"Didn't sit well with me either, I can assure you!"

"I know, sir."

"But ... after all we've been through together, you didn't trust me to deal with it?"

"Oh, *no*, sir! It ain't *that!* We trust you plenty. We trust you with our lives, Captain! It's just ... we reckoned ... you bein' an important man and all—workin' with the governor and whatnot ... we figured there was some things you just couldn't do, but maybe *we* could."

"I see. But you're wrong about me."

"What's that, sir?"

"I didn't hold back because I'm 'important,' or friends with the governor. I held back because I wasn't sure he'd done it. Though I didn't like the man, and he was a despicable scoundrel, I wouldn't kill him without knowing for sure he'd done it."

Then he leaned forward, and locked eyes with Tony.

"But believe me when I tell you ... if I would've known for *sure* he had done it, I'd have not waited a minute. I'd have ridden straight over there and shot him myself, governor or no!"

Tony nodded, "Yes, sir. I reckon so. And I felt the same ... about wantin' to be sure he done it and all. So we ... we went there thinkin' to make him tell the truth on it, make him admit he done it. *Then* we'd kill him. Only—"

"Only things didn't quite go as planned?"

"Yes, sir. Soon's we came in the house they grabbed their guns and woulda killed us all. So we killed them first."

Nathan breathed a deep sigh. "And now we'll never know for sure ..."

But Tony brightened up, "Oh ... but that ain't so, Captain, sir! The one named Ward, he weren't killed right away. Ned ... er ... I mean, *I* ... whacked him in the head with my rifle butt when all the shootin' was goin' on. When he come to, we sat him in a chair and had a talk. The man admitted to the whole thing."

"He did? You ... just shot him in the leg, and he started talking? How do you know he wasn't just saying it to get you to stop hurting him? That's the problem with interrogations involving severe pain; the subject will say anything they think you want to hear just to make it stop."

"Oh no, sir. It weren't like that. I done shot him *after* he confessed to it. Made me so mad I didn't want to kill him all at once. Wanted him to suffer a bit like them black folks had."

"Oh. He just admitted to it, with no coercion? That's surprising. The fellow was stubbornly tight-lipped with me."

Tony smiled for the first time, "I ... sort of tricked him into it, sir."

Nathan returned the smile and a curious look, "Go on ..."

"I asked him how he liked dying knowin' he was bein' kilt by a bunch o' stupid black men, with him never havin' kilt any o' *our* kind. He couldn't help but brag on how he'd killed them kids and that mother."

Nathan nodded, "Very clever, Tony. Very clever. Well done." He leaned back in his chair, gazed at the sky and smiled. Then he blew out another puff of cigar smoke.

"So ... what you gonna do now, Captain?"

"*Do?* I'm not going to *do* anything, Tony."

"But ... you know what we done. And we done it behind your back. Broke your rules."

"My dear fellow ... y'all are freemen now. It's not up to me to tell you what to do or what *not* to do. You must choose that for yourselves now. It's part of being a freeman; you make your own choices.

"Of course, you also suffer your own consequences. I only asked you not to take those guns off the farm simply to keep you out of legal trouble. But it's your choice. I gave you those guns because you'd earned the right to have them. You'd fought for that right. Some of your fellows even died for that right. What you choose to do with them is your business now, not mine."

"Then ... you ain't angry with us? You ain't gonna send us away?"

"Certainly *not!*" he grinned, and looked over at Tom, who was also smiling. "Tony, if I sent away every man who'd killed someone without my permission ... well, likely we'd have no white men left on this farm by now! And not too many black ones either, apparently!" he looked back at Tony and chuckled, before sticking the cigar back in his mouth.

"Now that we know Wade and his ilk actually did the evil deed, we know the killing was justified—righteously done. Hell, Tony, if we were still in the army, I'd pin a medal on your chest, not *punish* you."

"Thank you, sir. It's ... mighty relievin' to know you ain't angry."

"*I'm* not angry, but ... just don't tell *Stan* about it ..."

Tony looked confused by this, and even Tom raised a questioning eyebrow.

"Why? Why would Mr. Stan be angry?" Tony asked.

Nathan chuckled again, "Because ... I promised him *he* could kill whoever did those murders—'tear them apart piece by piece,' I believe he said. But now you've already killed them! He's going to be mighty put out about that!"

Tom laughed, but Tony just shook his head, and rolled his eyes. Then Nathan leaned forward, picked up the piece of whip and tossed it to Tony who snatched it out of the air.

"You might as well have this back ... if you still want it."

"Thanks, Captain. That I do ... that I surely do."

ಬಾಜ಼ಂಣಚಚ಼ಬಾಜ಼ಂಣಚಚ಼ಬಾಜ಼ಂಣಚ

Later that evening Tony and his usual group of men were meeting in the classroom, for their usual chat session. They were surprised when the Captain strode in and took a seat.

"Gentlemen."

"Hello, Captain."

"I'm sure Tony has told you all about our ... little talk earlier this evening."

They all nodded their heads, but nobody spoke. The mood had suddenly turned serious.

"I came here to say one thing. Well, two things maybe. The first is, to repeat what I told Tony; I'm *not* angry with you, nor disappointed. Y'all did as good men must sometimes do: take up arms and meet the enemy in battle. Thankfully y'all came out victorious ... *this time.*

"Which brings up the second thing I wanted to say. Y'all got very lucky; I hope you know that. I've seen a lot of these situations, enough to know when I see one that very nearly turned tragic. You're extremely fortunate one or even all of you weren't killed. Next time may not work out so well.

"So I'm asking you … as men I have a lot of respect for … to let *me* handle these things from now on, if you will.

"It's not just the wicked men like Ward you need to fear. Despite what Ward and those others had done, if you'd been caught killing white men, you can bet you'd have been hung, regardless of the righteousness of your cause. For no other reason than that y'all are black men and they were white.

"You and I may not like it or agree with it, but such is the world we now live in. One day it won't be so, but today it is. So … if someone needs killin', I'd rather have our white men do it, so there's likely lesser consequences. Do you understand me?"

They nodded but had somber faces.

"And I have one more thing to say, so I guess I lied, that was *three* things." He shared grins with them, happy to lighten the mood a bit.

"And that is, I know y'all are itching to get into this war and fight those that want to forever enslave your people. I don't blame you. But for now, it's not being allowed.

"I ask you to trust me on this as well; it's only a matter of time before that changes. A few months, most likely, rather than years. When I first got here, I was the only one saying it. But now I hear it from many different voices. The time is coming soon when the Army will be *begging* you to fight. Then you must remember the old saying, 'Be careful what you wish for, lest it come true!' When you're out marching all day through the mud, just to get shot at come night-time, you may wish you were back here, safe and sound on this farm.

"In the meantime, I really appreciate all you're doing to help get the crops in. Lord knows we can use a good harvest so we can all keep eating!"

They chuckled at this, and he reached out and shook hands and patted the men on their shoulders.

"Good night, gentlemen."

"Good night, Captain, sir."

Nathan sat in the small room that served as his library, slowly sipping a glass of whiskey and gazing at a newspaper, but too tired to get much out of it. He heard a soft knock on the door frame and looked up.

"Ah, William. Thanks for coming. Have a seat."

"Thank you, Captain."

Nathan shook his head, an amused look on his face.

"What is it, sir?" William asked, wondering what the Captain suddenly found amusing.

"On, nothing, William. I was just thinking this has been my day for having meetings with people, is all. Thankfully you're the last, because after this I believe I will need to get some shut eye."

William smiled. "What is it I can do for you, sir?"

"William, I'm going to jump right into it ... I've seen you together with Miss Margaret a lot lately ..."

William could feel his face turning red, "Well, sir ... we do have to ... discuss the reading lesson plans, and whatnot. And ... she seems to value my opinion on other topics. Like the new state constitution. And ... I suppose she enjoys listening to the violin ..."

Nathan waved his hand dismissively, "Yes, yes ... I understand all that. But that's not what I'm talking about."

William gazed at him with a confused look.

"William ... I'm a bit older than you and ... have a few more miles on me, I guess you could say. I've been around a lot of women, is what I'm getting at."

William continued to stare at him uncomprehendingly.

"William, I've seen how Margaret *looks* at you when you're together talking. And it's not about reading lessons, or the constitution. Do you take my meaning?"

"Oh! Yes, sir ... I mean, *no*, sir! I'm sure it's nothing like *that!*"

"William ... are you trying to say I don't know the look a woman gives a man when she's ... *interested* in him?" he smiled at William, enjoying his tease.

William blushed again, "No ... I didn't mean *that*, sir! I'm sure you've seen that look *many* times from *many* women. It's just ... *I've* never seen it ... directed at *me*."

Nathan smiled, "Perhaps you have, but you just haven't recognized it."

"But sir ... *me* ... and Miss Margaret? I ... I don't know about *that* ..."

"Why not? She's brilliant, kindly, and courageous. She's young and attractive. What's not to like about her?"

"Oh, it's not *that*, sir. I like her *very* much. But ... she's ... she's your *sister*, sir!"

Nathan was quiet for a moment but wore an amused look on his face. He took a sip of whiskey, and said, "William ... if you feel you need my permission to court my sister ... then consider it granted! You're one of the finest men I've ever known. And if someday I had the honor of calling you *brother*, I would consider myself extremely fortunate."

William was stunned. He looked down, removed his glasses, and wiped his eyes with his sleeve. "Thank you, sir. That means ..." but he could get no more out of a throat choked with emotion.

CHAPTER 6. THE SEVENTH (WEST) VIRGINIA

"The Bloody Seventh"
– *Regimental Nickname of the Seventh (West) Virginia Volunteer Infantry Regiment*

Tuesday September 17, 1861 – Wheeling, Virginia:

Nathan Chambers stood in front of a row of fifty young soldiers and one young lieutenant: fresh recruits in crisp blue uniforms with shiny brass buttons. The new uniforms were not, unfortunately, the rule yet in the Union army, as supplies and equipment continued to lag behind the more readily available human resources. Most new recruits in other units had to make do with a hodgepodge of clothing and equipment, usually whatever they had with them when they arrived. Many, being farm boys, even showed up without shoes.

But Nathan had called in a few favors from officers he knew in the War Department, so he'd been able to obtain a few hundred new uniforms with all the accouterments ... *this time*. His sources had warned him *not* to expect more of the same any time soon, as general shortages were pandemic for the foreseeable future.

The rifles were even more of an issue. With the enemy seizing and dismantling the federal armory at Harpers Ferry at the very beginning of Virginia's secession, military rifles were in high demand and very short supply. What was available was a very mixed bag of old flintlocks, smoothbore muskets dating from the War of 1812, hunting rifles, and various foreign-made rifles of odd calibers, including the cumbersome .69 monster. Nathan shook his head when he gazed down the barrel of one of these, imagining the horrific wound the weapon might inflict ... if it ever hit anything!

But such as they were, each soldier currently lined up in front of him had a rifle slung over his shoulder, and a full field pack on his back containing a percussion cap box, cartridge box, canteen, and other equipment. Plus, any personal effects.

Though it was nearly fall, the men sweated in their thick wool tunics under a bright sun in a clear blue sky. They stood in a recently cut hay field at the fairgrounds on Wheeling Island which had been taken over for Army recruitment and training. The facility, just north of the main road leading to Ohio on the west branch of the Ohio River, had been renamed "Camp Carlile" in honor of Nathan's friend John Carlile, now U.S. Senator representing the Restored Government of Virginia. The fairgrounds' exhibition halls and animal stalls were now being used for barracks, and its fields for training the new recruits.

Elsewhere around the several-hundred-acre fairgrounds, various groups of soldiers from the Seventh Regiment marched, drilled in the use of the bayonet, or practiced against targets with rifles; all under the watchful eyes of Nathan's veterans from Texas and the regiment's new officers.

And though Nathan wore the suit of a gentleman, and had no military insignia, there was never a doubt who was in command. They all knew he was the governor's right hand and also a well-known war veteran and Indian fighter from out West. And, they still didn't have a commanding officer for the regiment. So far, Nathan's efforts had been frustrated by a lack of quality officers and his resistance to the idea of a "political" officer.

"Gentlemen … you stand here before me today because you have distinguished yourselves in training the last few days," Nathan began. "Either your officers have recommended you, or my veterans from Texas … or Mr. Creek here," he gestured toward Billy, who stood a few feet to Nathan's right. Billy nodded in acknowledgment, but otherwise showed no expression.

"You have shown yourselves to be the quickest on your feet, the fastest learners, and the best with weapons, both bayonet and rifle. Y'all have undergone some valuable training already, but today your *real* training begins. You men will be the eyes and ears of the regiment, the skirmishers and scouts. You will be the first to find the enemy, the first to fight, and the last to leave in every battle. You must be the toughest, meanest, and most skilled fighters in order to do your job well—and to survive it."

He walked up and down the line, making eye contact with the men as he spoke.

"Your Lieutenant, Mr. Elliott here, is also the best of the young officers on this parade ground, so you will be well led. In the coming days and weeks, he will select from among you his sergeants and corporals to assist in command of the unit."

"So not only are you men the best of the best, with the best officer, but you also have the best trainer. Mr. Creek, as you may have noticed, is an Indian—a Tonkawa from out in Texas. But don't let his size and demeanor fool you; Mr. Creek is as deadly a man-killer as I have ever known, and that's saying a lot! And he was far and away the best scout in the U.S. Army before the war. If you men listen well, and learn what he has to teach you, you'll be the best skirmishers in the Army—and just might live to tell your grandchildren about it!"

He took out a cigar, lit it, and took several puffs before turning toward Billy, "Mr. Creek. The company is yours, sir."

"Thank you, Captain," Billy said, snapping a salute, which Nathan returned sharply.

But if the young recruits expected Billy to begin lecturing them or demonstrating his skills, they were soon disabused of the notion. Without a word, Billy walked to the very start of the line to his left. Lieutenant Elliott fell in next to him, following respectfully a yard to the side. Billy walked slowly down the line, gazing intently at each man; not at his eyes, but rather at his uniform and equipment. Sometimes he would reach out and gently touch an item or grasp something and give a quick shake. Then he'd tilt his head as if thinking about what he'd heard.

Nathan suppressed a very strong urge to grin or even chuckle as he watched the wide-eyed looks Billy elicited from the young men. Though he stood nearly a foot shorter than most of them, his stolid presence was intimidating. They'd all heard tales of Indians their whole lives but had never seen one in person.

Billy continued his unusual inspection tour until he reached the middle of the line. There he stopped and faced a young man who stood still, looking nervous at the sudden attention.

"Step forward," Billy said.

"Sir!" the private said, taking a step forward with his left foot and stomping his right next to it, as he'd been taught in the last two days.

Billy eyed him for another moment, then said, "Jump."

"*Sir?*" the young man asked, not sure he'd heard the command correctly.

"Jump ... you know, as high as you can, straight up," Billy said, and proceeded to demonstrate what he wanted, springing up about a foot off the ground and landing in the same spot. "Jump."

"Sir!" the private said and did as instructed, though with all the equipment he carried his feet barely cleared the ground.

Billy gazed at him a few seconds, then turned to the man next to him, "What did you hear when he jumped?"

"What's that, sir?"

"What sounds did he make when he jumped?"

The man looked puzzled, but shrugged and said, "Kind of a ... *whooshing* sound ... I guess. Then a sort of ... *thud* when he landed."

Billy frowned at him, "What *else?*"

The private thought a moment, then said, "Well, sir ... there was some ... *jingly* kind of sounds, and some clicking and rattling and what not. From things in his kit, I suppose."

"Yes! Exactly."

Billy turned back toward the man who'd jumped, "You are too noisy. It will get you killed."

He took another step back and addressed the whole unit, "All of you, jump."

The whole group did as ordered. Nathan wasn't surprised to see grins and some snickering among the young men.

Billy nodded his head, then turned back toward the unlucky young man who'd been singled out and still stood out in front of the line. Billy leaned in close and pointed to a bright brass button on the front of the private's tunic, "What's wrong with this button?" He turned toward the man he'd quizzed about the jumping noise.

"It ... it looks fine to me, sir. A nice shiny brass uniform button. Standard Army issue, I imagine."

"Too bright. Shiny brass reflects sunlight for a hundred yards. Or more. Even in thick brush."

Billy reached out and lifted the man's canteen up off over his head by the strap. He unscrewed the top and poured about half onto the ground. He handed the man back the canteen and took out his belt knife. Then he bent over and stirred the dirt where he'd dumped the water until it had turned into a thick, black mud. When satisfied, he reached down and scooped a dollop with his fingers. He straightened up and rubbed the mud against each button on the man's tunic.

"Mud is your friend. It can save your life; keeps shiny things from shining."

The man nodded his understanding.

He gazed up at the man's face, "You are too white."

"What's that, sir?"

"Your skin is too white. My skin is darker ... much better for hiding in the woods. Or at night. Hmm ... black men's skin is best—even better than mine. White skin is very pretty, maybe. But no good for scouting."

"Well, he can't very well change his skin color!" the man next to him said and rolled his eyes. Several others nodded their agreement.

But Billy didn't answer. Instead he bent down and scooped a handful of mud, then reached out and smeared it on the man's cheeks, chin, and nose. Several soldiers couldn't help snickering.

"Now skin isn't white. Mud is your friend."

Nathan bit down hard on his cigar and turned away to hide his grin and to keep from laughing at the humorous expression on the private's startled face.

But Billy wasn't finished yet.

"Give me your rifle."

161

The man pulled the rifle from his shoulder and presented it for inspection, as he'd been taught. Billy took it and gazed at it for only a moment before stating, "The fittings on this rifle are too shiny. What do you think we should do about that?"

But the young private was now catching on, and thought he knew the answer this time, "Use mud, sir!"

"No, wrong!" Billy couldn't help grinning this time, enjoying his little trick on the private. "Mud will foul the rifle and make it rust. Use axle grease. Nice and black but won't rust. Keeps rifle parts lubricated. Just don't get it where your hands go, or you'll drop your rifle. Never drop your rifle. Your rifle is your friend. And mud."

The man nodded his head, and smiled for the first time, catching on to Billy's subtle humor.

Then Billy addressed the whole company again, "A scout must travel light. You men have too much gear. Bring only what you will need. Nothing more."

Then he pointed at the man standing out front, and gestured to his left down the row, "Those of you to the left of this man, go back and fix these problems I have shown you. Use socks, rags, or other soft things to keep metal and wood parts from rattling. Cover shiny parts and faces with mud," then he grinned, "but no mud on rifles! Remember, axle grease!

"You other men, stay the same as you are now.

"When your Lieutenant dismisses you, do as I've asked. When you return in one hour, report to where you will see me standing. Over there across the field, next to those woods."

He turned and nodded at the Lieutenant, who barked out, "Company ... dismissed!"

❧❧❧❧❧❧❧❧❧❧❧

An hour later the company was again assembled, this time at the edge of the field next to a wooded area. Nathan sat at the edge of the woods on a tree stump, taking a little shade. Harry lounged next to him, also appreciating a break from the hot sun.

Nathan enjoyed a cigar while taking in the show Billy was orchestrating. When the troop members had begun arriving in

162

small groups, there had been a lot of good-natured teasing of the "mud-men" by the soldiers still in clean uniforms. And when he heard one of the clean soldiers say to another, "Let's show that redskin how white men can fight, with no need of his mud and trickery," Nathan just smiled and nodded knowingly, taking another long drag on his cigar.

The company was again lined up in the same order as before, only now the half on the left were covered in mud, on their faces and the fronts of their uniforms. Billy walked down the line, carefully inspecting each man. He carried a small bowl filled with mud and used it to correct any omissions he spotted. He also made each man jump and listened for any telltale noises. If he heard any, the man had to step out of line and re-pack his kit while Billy moved on to the next man. When he'd made his way to the end of the muddied men, he went back and re-inspected those who'd had to repack.

When he was finally satisfied, he stepped out in front of the whole company. "Now we are going to have a skirmish. The muddy men against the clean men. I will lead the muddy men and the Lieutenant will lead the clean. These woods are about ... hmm ... five acres and have a small stream down the middle. Open fields on three sides and the big river on the fourth.

"There are no rules in *real* war, only winning. But today we will have only *one* rule: both sides must stay inside the woods — no going out into the fields, or swimming in the river. Guns will be held as in battle but unloaded. And no bayonets today. The Captain would be unhappy with me if any of you children got killed." He smiled, and this time received many smiles in return.

"The mud men will enter the woods on the left end. The clean men on the right. You must find and capture the other men before they find and capture you."

He turned to the Lieutenant and nodded.

"Company ... move out!" the Lieutenant shouted.

ಶಾಶ್ರ್ಯಾಂ ಶಾಶ್ರ್ಯಾಂ ಶಾಶ್ರ್ಯಾಂ

Lieutenant Elliott figured his chances of outsmarting the Indian, Billy were slim, but he enjoyed the challenge and meant

163

to try his best to win. Still, each time he heard a clink or a jingle coming from the men behind him he cringed. And when he looked back into the gloom of the thick woods, he saw a whole row of white faces gazing back at him, along with shiny brass buttons twinkling whenever a stray beam of sunlight penetrated the canopy above. He breathed a heavy sigh. This wasn't going to be easy.

He'd decided to try a flanking maneuver, heading up the left side of the woods, near the edge. He figured he'd at least have a better than fifty percent chance the "enemy" would be guarding either the middle area or the other edge. He hoped to work his way around behind them and then take them from the rear.

After creeping along for about a half-hour, they came upon the small creek Billy had described earlier. It had carved a shallow ravine, about six feet below the rest of the woods, and about thirty feet across. It ran in the general direction he wanted to go, so he decided to have his men follow the stream bed. He figured getting below the surface might at least hide some of their faces and buttons, and the noise from the stream might help mask the noise of their passage.

He took his time and stopped regularly to take in his surroundings, looking for any sign of movement. The men behind him also gazed about steadily, ready to aim their rifles toward any sign of movement. But they saw nothing but trees and the occasional squirrel or bird flitting among the branches.

He'd been creeping along the streambed in this manner for more than a quarter hour when he caught a sudden movement to his left and in front. He looked and saw Billy Creek standing still in the woods, gazing in his direction and smiling.

Elliott raised his pistol and pointed it at Billy, "I guess I've caught you, Mr. Creek!"

But Billy just laughed, "Dead men can't catch the living, lieutenant!" He gestured back along Elliott's column of men. The lieutenant looked and saw a whole row of dark figures lining the top of the stream bank on both sides. They held rifles pointed at the men below, who'd not even noticed them until this moment.

The young lieutenant looked back at Billy, smiled, shook his head, and holstered his pistol.

"You win, Mr. Creek. And we are all dead men. A whole row of shiny, clean, dead men!"

"Cheer up, Lieutenant. You have done well, despite your shiny men. And tomorrow we won't have to get so dirty. Tomorrow we will learn how to scout an open area on horseback ... without looking like we are scouting ..."

⬥⬥⬥⬥⬥⬥⬥⬥⬥⬥⬥⬥

Ironically, in the great dining hall back at Mountain Meadows, with its massive table that could easily fit twenty dinner guests, the evening meals were typically served out for only three: Nathan, Miss Abbey, and Tom. Occasionally Jim might join them, or some out-of-town guest, but generally the room was nearly empty.

Yet here at Belle Meade, with its tiny kitchen table and no proper dining hall at all, the Chambers "family" had grown to *five* regulars, with the addition of Margaret and Megs. Miss Abbey had insisted Megs sit and have dinner with them now and no longer wait on them.

And after much fussing and arguing by Megs, Nathan had put a stop to it, ruling in Miss Abbey's favor. So Megs had relented and joined them at table.

Jeb, their gray-haired long-time head cook, still did most of the cooking, though the other two younger men would lend a hand, or substitute in from time to time. The long-time maids Sally, Cara, and Sarah took turns serving out the meals and doing other household chores.

The other former household slaves had been moved to farm duty, including Rosa, to Nathan's relief. He still worried she was harboring romantic feelings toward him and didn't know what to do about that. A safer distance was greatly appreciated.

The family dinners were a genial affair for the most part, with the cares of the day typically set aside in favor of comradery and good humor. And Margaret's easygoing demeanor had melded

165

so readily with the rest of the household it wasn't hard to imagine she really had been Nathan's sister since childhood.

"Nathan ... how is the training coming along on the new regiment?" Miss Abbey asked, just as Nathan had poked a large piece of ham into his mouth.

"Mmm ... hmm ..." he mumbled, busily chewing.

"Oh ... sorry, dear."

Nathan swallowed his bite and grinned, "That's all right, Momma ... it's going very well. The new recruits and officers are coming along nicely. And our men from Texas are thoroughly enjoying playing the 'experts.'" He chuckled, "You should have seen Billy today ... smearing mud all over the faces of his bewildered young scouts! It was all I could do to keep from bursting out laughing and spoiling the whole show!"

They shared a laugh as Nathan proceeded to describe Billy's amusing training regimen.

"So yes, I'd say the regiment is progressing well. The only issue I'm still worried about is finding a proper commanding officer."

"Oh? Aren't there any available?"

But Tom answered for him, "None that pass the 'Chambers Test.'" He smiled at Nathan, who rolled his eyes in response. "*Someone* ... not to name any names, mind ... is a bit ... *particular* about who should lead the new regiment," Tom added.

"Oh! Well, I guess I shouldn't be surprised," Miss Abbey said. "Not that you've ever had any strong opinions before, dear," she grinned.

"No, now ... that's not fair, Momma. It's not about being *particular* ... I just want everything to go well for the new regiment. You know ... set a good example for the others to follow. Too many officers I've spoken with are ... *inflexible* to new ideas. Think they already know more than they do. Aren't open to my ... *suggestions*."

"You mean they don't always agree with you?" Megs offered and gave Nathan a wry grin.

Nathan scowled, "Why do I feel like I'm outnumbered here? Margaret, feel free to jump in on *my* side! It appears I could use an ally."

She smiled, "Certainly *not!* I have no opinions whatsoever on military matters. It's one thing, thankfully, I know nothing about."

"Well, if nothing else, you could at least come to the defense of your brother when he's clearly outmanned, outmaneuvered, and outgunned," he said, grinning at her.

"Oh ... all right then, I can do *that*. Y'all ... stop picking on Nathan. You're like to hurt his *delicate* feelings!" then she laughed.

Nathan frowned at her, in mock anger. "You're no help at all. Okay ... maybe I am a *little* particular. But why not? Shouldn't we try for the best we can get when so many good men's lives are at stake? Not to mention the good of the state and the country."

"Yes, certainly," Tom answered, "but we can't wait until the war is over to decide on it. Perhaps you just need to select the one who'll do the least harm."

"Hmm ... it may come down to that, I'll admit. The good news is, I still have a little time to decide. But other than that, the regiment is coming along very nicely. I'm willing to bet it'll be one of the best regiments in the Army when all is said and done."

"That's wonderful, dear," Miss Abbey said. "And once the Seventh Regiment is out in the field ... what then?"

Nathan looked at Tom, then back at Miss Abbey, "Well ... it's my plan to train up the Eighth Regiment. Then ..."

"Then?" Megs asked.

"I intend to take command of the Eighth myself. Along with Tom and the rest of the men from Texas, of course. And maybe Zeke and Joe, if they wish to join us."

"You're going to ... go out and *fight*? In the *war?*" Miss Abbey asked.

"Of course, Momma. Did you imagine otherwise?"

"Well ... I was *hoping* ... you know. You served in the last war. And plenty of time out West after. I was just hoping ... this time maybe you could let *others* do the fighting. Maybe stay here and continue helping the governor with the new state?"

He frowned. "Momma, you know that's not going to happen."

"But ... why *not*, Nathan? You've already done your share of fighting! God knows I've spent twenty years already worrying about you. Isn't it time some other son's mother did the worrying?"

Nathan was quiet for a moment, gazing at Miss Abbey. He reached in his pocket, took out a cigar, stuck it in his mouth and began to chew on it, resisting the urge to light it up.

"We were both worried about you," Megs added. "Every day. All them years. Never knowing if you was alive or dead until we got the next letter ..."

"Momma ... Megs ... I'm truly sorry for all the pain and suffering I've caused you. I know there's no way to ever make it up to you. But you must know ... the man I am ... I could never sit back and watch other men go out and face the danger while I stayed behind in safety. It would ... it would ... *kill me* inside ..." he trailed off, almost in a whisper, looking down at his lap.

When he looked up there was a light in his eyes, "But ... there's more to it than just doing my duty, doing my *part*. It also feels like ... like it's my *destiny*, if you understand what I mean."

"Your destiny?" Miss Abbey asked. "To go out and get yourself killed in the war?"

"No, Momma, not to go get *killed*. I feel like ... like everything God has been teaching me ... training me to do since I was a small child has been to prepare me for *this one moment* in time. And I can't imagine *He* would've wasted all that time and effort on me just to have me ride out and get myself killed straightaway. I believe God intends for me to play a role ... perhaps even a *major* role ... in winning this war. So we can free *all* the slaves before the end. I have come to believe fighting to free the slaves is my purpose in life, the thing *He* has intended for me all along."

A thoughtful silence followed this statement.

Then Tom jumped in to fill the uncomfortable void, "It's really not far-fetched or immodest of him, Miss Abbey. Even now Mr. Lincoln has appointed George McClellan as commander of the Army of the Potomac, basically giving him control of all Union Armies in the East. But Nathan went to school with McClellan and fought beside him in the Mexican War. And I can tell you for certain Nathan is twice the officer McClellan could ever hope to be. How much better off would the Union be if Nathan Chambers were in command and not George McClellan?

"Since Colonel Lee opted to join the enemy, I believe Nathan is the best officer the Union has. And I'm not the only one who thinks so. General Rosecrans said much the same when we were up at Rich Mountain. And I've heard it since from other officers, as well."

Miss Abbey was stunned, mouth agape. "Nathan ... is it *true?* Are you really ... *that* important? I mean, to the country?"

Nathan was quiet and thoughtful for a moment, chewing on the cigar and gazing at his lap.

"Maybe, Momma ... could be. But there's only one way to know for sure, and that's to put myself out there."

The mood that had started out so jolly had suddenly turned dark and gloomy. An awkward silence fell over the room.

But at that moment the maid Sarah walked in with a steaming hot tray, filling the room with a pungent aroma.

"What is that ... *wonderful* smell?" Tom asked, happy to change the subject.

Megs looked up and smiled, "That there's a special treat me and Miss Abbey baked up this afternoon!"

"Oh, yes! With all the corn we just harvested, Megs and I were sitting here thinking on what we could fix with it that would be special. Then she remembered some of the ladies down at the general store talking about baking *corn* bread. So we decided to give it a try."

"It smells wonderful," Nathan said. "You made this yourselves? I've never known either of you to do any baking."

"Yes, dear. Megs and I did it together. Perhaps it's the start of something new!" she shared a smile with Megs. "Give it a try and tell us if we should continue our culinary efforts or give it up for a lost cause!"

Nathan grinned at them, reached out and snatched a square of the bread from the tray. He set it on his plate quickly, then stuck his fingers in his mouth and sucked on them. *"Hot!"* he said and shook his fingers.

"Here ... spread a little butter on it first," Miss Abbey said, handing the butter dish across the table to Nathan.

He applied the butter and took a bite, "Mmm ... very tasty. I vote you keep it up!"

Abbey and Megs looked at each other and shared a smile.

"Mmm ... yes, Miss Abbey, Megs. This is delicious," Tom added. "Perhaps growing corn will have its benefits after all! I can't imagine cotton ever tasting this good!"

Miss Abbey laughed, "Thank you, Tom. Oh, and Tom ... remember our little discussion earlier?"

"Discussion?"

"Yes ... no more formality at this table. This is the Chambers' family dinner table, and I'll have no more Miss *this* and Miss *that*. That goes for both me and Margaret."

"But ... Miss Abbey, though I appreciate being included, I'm *not* a member of the Chambers family like the rest of you."

"Tom ... how many times did you save Nathan's life on the trip back from Richmond?"

"Oh ... really only the once ..."

Nathan frowned at him.

"All right, perhaps twice ... okay ... maybe *several* times. But still ..."

"Tom, if not for your loyalty and heroic bravery our dear Nathan would not be sitting with us today enjoying this meal. He'd no longer be ... *among the living* ..." Abbey began to choke up and had to wipe her eyes with a handkerchief before continuing. "Anyway ... if that doesn't make you family, then I don't know what does! I promise I couldn't love you any more if you were my own son!"

It was Tom's turn to feel the emotions swelling, and he had to look down at his lap for a moment before answering. "Thank you, Miss Abbey."

"No, Tom! Not *Miss* Abbey anymore, for you. Call me just Abbey, or Abigail. Or even Momma as Nathan and Margaret do ... I won't mind. But no more *Miss!*"

"All right, all right. You win, Miss Ab ... er, *just Abbey*," he grinned brightly turning a little red as Nathan reached over and patted him on the back.

Tom laughed and said, "Well, now I know where you got your stubbornness, sir!"

But Miss Abbey answered, "Oh, no! He got that from his Daddy. He only got his pleasant, easygoing disposition from me!"

Nathan laughed, "You had the right of it, Tom. I really am doomed, having gotten a healthy dose of stubbornness from *both* sides!"

"Oh no, Nathan," Margaret jumped in, "Say not *stubborn*. It has such a negative connotation. You're not *stubborn* but rather *determined* ... and perhaps ... *resolute!*" She gave him a warm smile.

"Why, thank you, sister! Nice to have *someone* stand up for me at this table. And I take back what I said earlier about your being of no help. I knew there was a reason I liked you so well!"

They all shared a laugh and continued the remainder of the meal in a much lighter mood.

ꇙꇙꇙꇙꇙꇙꇙꇙ

When dinner was over, they filed out into the hallway where they found William sitting on a bench near the front entrance.

They all greeted him warmly, after which he turned to Margaret. "Miss Margaret ... may I have a word with you?"

"Why ... of course, William. What is it?"

William looked up at Nathan who nodded knowingly.

"William ... good to see you. Momma, Megs, Tom ... shall we retire to the veranda—such as it is—for a little evening libation before bed? These two may join us later if they wish, after they've ... had their discussion."

The three of them looked from Nathan to William, and quickly took his meaning.

"Yes, of course ... that's sounds just lovely," Abbey answered, taking hold of Megs' arm and heading for the back door, followed closely by the two men.

Once they were alone, William looked at Margaret and said, "Miss Margaret ... I have been thinking. Of a question ..."

She gazed up at him, waiting expectantly. William swallowed a large lump that was trying to form in his throat. He realized she really did have *very* pretty eyes ...

"Well, what I was thinking was ... there comes a time ... when a man, such as me ... and a woman, such as you ... Hmm ... well, they begin to contemplate pursuing the possibility of establishing bonds of mutual affection ..." he looked at her hopefully. But he saw he wasn't doing very well and might need to try a different approach.

She frowned, as if thinking over the meaning of what he'd just said.

He gazed at her hopefully for another moment, when suddenly her face lit up in a smile. She leaned up and kissed him on the cheek. "Yes," she whispered.

"*Yes?* You mean ..."

"Yes, William, you may court me. And then we'll see about those ... 'bonds of mutual affection'!" she giggled, and he thought it the loveliest sound he'd ever heard.

"Just come to the family dinner tomorrow night and we'll get started."

William nodded, suddenly speechless, his mouth wide open.

"Oh, and you might want to clean yourself up a little first."

He looked down at his filthy work clothes and realized for the first time that he had blood stains smeared across his shirt from training the new surgeons. They'd spent most of the day dissecting dead animals, mostly pigs.

"And perhaps a shave ..." she added and giggled again when he rubbed his hand across a chin covered in three days growth of stubble.

"Yes, ma'am," he said, and returned her smile, thinking maybe a bath would also be in order.

She flashed him another smile, then turned and practically skipped down the hall toward the back door.

William stood still where he was, gazing after her, smiling and slowly shaking his head in awe and wonder. Suddenly he felt a welling of excitement and joy such as he'd never imagined possible.

ಙಉ಼಼಼಼಼಼಼಼಼

In less than an hour, the three ladies excused themselves for the evening and headed indoors. So Tom and Nathan broke out cigars to complement their glasses of whiskey and leaned back to enjoy the little remaining daylight. Harry had assumed his usual spot, laying on the grass at the bottom of the stairs, his tongue hanging out to one side dripping a steady stream onto the lawn.

"Oh! I nearly forgot," Nathan reached into his pocket and pulled out a folded piece of paper. "The governor handed me this telegram just as we were leaving his office. It's from General Rosecrans. Have a look, Tom."

He handed the sheet across to Tom, who unfolded it and read:

> *September 16, 1861. The honorable Francis H. Pierpont, Governor of Virginia. Your honor, it is with great pleasure I inform you of a significant victory having taken place upon your soil yesterday. Rebel forces under the command of General R.E. Lee attempted a brazen assault upon our fortifications at the pass on Cheat Mountain. But said secessionists have been repulsed and thoroughly defeated by our brave garrison there stationed. Gen. Lee's army has thence been forced to retreat into the Kanawha River Valley. There he is joined by other rebel units under the command of Generals Floyd and Wise. We are vigorously pursuing the enemy with high hopes of smashing their formations and thereby expelling the foe from western Virginia for the duration of the war. Please convey my compliments to Mr. Chambers and kindly tell him I could very much use him in the field just now as one of my generals! Your loyal servant, Brig. General W.S. Rosecrans, U.S. Army, Dept. of W. Virginia*

"Well, that *is* good news, sir!"

"Yes ... my old mentor, Mr. Lee, is not faring so well thus far, it seems. But after Rich Mountain I was feeling confident

173

Rosecrans would make short work of the remaining rebels on this side of the mountains."

"Yes, I recall you telling the governor that very thing. Your words now appear most prophetic."

"So far ... but nothing is ever certain as long as the enemy still has armies in the field. Rosecrans admits he has yet to defeat Floyd and Wise."

"*Wise?* As in former Governor *Henry* Wise?"

"The same."

Tom scowled, "That's one person I dearly wish to put a bullet in. Preferably several, in extremely uncomfortable places! Hard to believe he's been rewarded for his illegal and despicable behavior by a general's commission!"

But Nathan was quiet a moment, and thoughtful, "I wonder ..."

"What do you mean, sir?"

"I wonder how much of a *reward* it truly is. If I am guessing right, our old nemesis Henry Wise is just now coming face-to-face with the realities of warfare. I wonder if it's all the honor and glory he'd imagined it to be."

"Hmm ... I'm guessing *not*, sir. And I'm hoping he's suffering terribly for it."

"You'll get no argument from me there, Tom," and he raised his glass of whiskey. Tom raised his and they clinked them together.

"To Mr. Henry Wise ... may he get everything he so richly deserves!" Nathan said.

"That and more!" Tom agreed.

After they'd downed a swallow, Nathan said, "Say ... speaking of rich desserts ... you said you had the final numbers on the harvest ready for me. How'd we do?"

"Surprising well, sir. Considering the ragged state the place was in when we arrived, we had a reasonably good harvest, thanks to Toby and the rest of the freemen, and all their hard work.

"And thanks to the war, and the Army buying practically everything in sight, the prices have been excellent. I'm now thinking we may actually make a slim profit on the year. Not counting the purchase of the farm itself, of course, which must be considered a long-term asset purchase and not an annual expense."

"That's excellent news, Tom!"

"Yes, I thought so too. Now we can afford to eat something besides corn the rest of the year!"

They laughed.

"Listen, Tom ... even if the final profit is slim, I'd still like to share it out among the freemen as we'd discussed."

"Already working on that, sir. Toby and I came up with a simple method of keeping track of each person's workdays, so we can pay it out according to each individual's contribution to the harvest. Not a daily wage, per se, but rather a proration of the available profit."

"That sounds good ... but what about those too old or young to work in the fields? And those that must watch the babies? And the house servants?"

"We talked about that and decided on giving them each a quarter-day or half-day credit for every available workday. But since that number is just a calculation, I can adjust it as needed, even at the last minute. We thought the important thing was to track the days of those doing the hard, dirty, hot work out in the fields. Give credit where credit is most due, as they say, rewarding those that've worked the hardest and longest with the most pay."

"That seems more than fair. Well done, Tom."

"Thank you, sir."

"And ... I'd like to start paying our white men again as well, since we haven't been able to pay them at all ever since we left Mountain Meadows."

"Oh, I wouldn't worry about that one too much, sir. The soldiers know you've been paying them twice what they could get working any other job, ever since we left Texas. In their minds they're still way ahead on it. And so far, there's been no grumbling. The original farmhands, however, would probably appreciate some back pay."

"Let's get them caught up when we pay the freemen."

"I'll take care of it, sir."

"Thank you, Tom. Well, with this good harvest, the good news from General Rosecrans, and the Seventh Infantry coming along so nicely, it feels like things are generally going our way at the moment."

"Yes ... all except ..."

"I know ... I know ... the damned guerrilla warfare. This insurrection is the one thorn in our side that just keeps festering. It almost feels like the better the news is on the battlefront, the worse the irregular situation grows. Almost as if they're trying to make up for the lack of success in the field by stirring up other mischief."

"Seems so, all right. Have you had any new ideas on it?"

"Nothing brilliant. My main concern just now is getting through the election without any major incidents at the polling places. But the governor and I have been leaning heavily on the War Department to provide troops to supervise the election. And I've been thinking ..."

"Yes?"

"I'm thinking we may soon be able to make use of a shiny new weapon at our disposal."

"And what would that be, Captain?"

"The Seventh Virginia Volunteer Infantry Regiment!" he said, then stuck his cigar between his teeth and grinned.

೫ಐಞಚಚ೫ಐ೫ಞಚಚ೫ಐ೫ಞಚಚ

"Rosa ... *please* ... wait," Tony pleaded at Rosa's back as she walked away. He'd tried to talk to her as she approached down the row of beans, but she'd purposely ignored him and strode on past.

Finally, she stopped and turned. It occurred to Tony this was almost the exact same spot where she'd stopped him a few days earlier. The day he'd hurt her feelings, which he'd felt badly about ever since. But every time he'd tried to talk to her about it, she seemed to avoid him, or to pull others into a conversation, making it impossible for him to discuss it with her.

"What is it, Tony?" she asked, with hands on her hips and a frown creasing her brow. Not a good sign, he decided.

"Look, Rosa ... the other day ... when you asked about me and the other fellas. You know, about the guns and all that. I ... I'm sorry for what I said. I shoulda knowed you wouldn't say nothing to get me in trouble. Lord knows you could've in the past, back at Mountain Meadows, but you never did."

She still looked stern, but he thought he detected a slight softening of her features. "Well ... never mind about that. It don't matter anyway," she answered.

"No ... it *does* matter. I ... I made you feel bad and ... I don't *ever* want to do that," he said. He decided to risk taking a few steps closer, so they wouldn't need to shout. He was encouraged when she stayed where she was rather than turning and walking away.

"Rosa ... I know things haven't always been ... *simple* between us. And I don't want to cause you no more problems nor worries. And I don't ever want to hurt your feelings."

She gazed at him another moment, and then her frown definitely softened. "Well ... I reckon I ain't always been so very easy to talk with either. Back at Mountain Meadows I was ... not always very nice to you. And you done deserved better from me."

He looked at her long and hard. It was the closest she'd ever come to admitting she'd hurt him or wronged him. It made him wonder if something had changed. But he didn't want to push his luck or get overly hopeful. It'd hurt too badly before, and he didn't ever want to feel that pain again.

"Well, past is past, I reckon. Anyway, I wanted to say, I'll tell you anything you want to know now, if you want to ask it again."

"Oh, no, but thanks, Tony. Henry already done told me the whole story. But don't worry, he only done it when I swore on my Momma's life not to tell another soul. And I ain't never gonna."

"Oh. All right. Guess we don't need to talk on it then ..."

"Well ... I don't have no more *questions*. But ..." she took a step closer, and gazed steadily into his eyes, "I never did get a chance to say how much I appreciate what y'all done—*righteously* done—killin' them wicked murdering devils. And ... how terribly *brave* I think *you* were, Tony."

She flashed him a quick smile, then turned and trotted off.

"Uh ... you're ... *welcome?*" he muttered under his breath as she moved out of earshot. He shook his head in confusion. *Now what did that mean?* he wondered.

₼₼₼₼₼₼₼₼₼₼

The next evening, William donned the nice white shirt, black tie, and gray slacks the Captain had bought the men when they were back at Mountain Meadows so they'd have something decent to wear to church. And William had recently acquired a gray suit jacket in town, so he was feeling fairly pleased with his attire, though the only clean hat he owned was the neat straw one also furnished by the Captain. He shrugged. It was better than nothing and didn't look too informal.

Of course, he'd had to endure a heavy dose of good-natured teasing from Stan and the others the entire time he was bathing, shaving, and getting dressed.

"Hey men ... better break out guns! There's some kind of *stranger* in house. Perhaps come to steal coins!" Stan said, when William stepped out all cleaned up and dressed.

"Oh, let him be," Jim answered, "he don't look *too* dangerous. More like a banker than a burglar!" he laughed.

But when William arrived for the "family dinner" he was greeted much more congenially; only Tom gently teased by complimenting him on how nicely he'd cleaned himself up.

William was surprised by Margaret's transformation as well. For starters, she had her hair pinned up on her head in a very stylish fashion with gold hairclips. He thought it very becoming on her, with the added benefit of exposing the soft smooth skin of her neck.

And the entire time he'd known her she'd worn only very conservative dresses, generally of a brown or gray color. But tonight, she wore a bright yellow dress, embroidered with white, orange, and yellow flowers around the neck, sleeves, and hemline. It even had a low front and revealed the slightest hint of her modest cleavage.

When she saw him gazing at her, Margaret smiled, "Do you like it?"

William nodded, but could think of nothing to say.

"It's Momma's. She let me borrow it."

"Yes," Abbey said, "and isn't it amazing how we are almost *exactly* the same size? It truly is as if you were always meant to be my daughter."

Margaret beamed, leaned across, and kissed Miss Abbey on the cheek.

സ്റോസ്റോസ്റോ

Though William started the meal feeling awkward, tense, and out of place, by the end of it he'd begun to relax and feel at home. He'd quickly realized he was entirely among friends, and everyone at the table was supportive of his budding relationship with Margaret.

After dinner, when the others headed out the back door to the veranda, William and Margaret excused themselves from the group and headed out the front door. Across the driveway to the right was a gravel path that gently wound through a sparsely wooded track down to the river's edge. At the end of the path was a clearing where the previous owners had erected a sturdy wooden bench, now well-worn and aged.

They sat down on the bench just as the sun was setting out across the wide Ohio River, making multi-colored ripples across the smooth, rolling water.

"It's a beautiful sight, isn't it?" Margaret asked.

But William was looking at her when he answered, "Yes ... very much so."

She looked up at him, and blushed, turning away again.

"I was speaking of the sunset, sir!"

"Oh ... *that!* Yes, it's beautiful as well."

She smiled.

They sat in silence for several minutes, gazing out at the brilliant display of colors painting the scattered clouds in the sky and the flowing water. Finally, William carefully reached out and clasped her left hand with his right. She gave him a gentle squeeze in response, looked up at him and smiled, a smile he readily returned.

After another moment of awkward silence, she said, "William ... I was just thinking ..."

"Yes?"

She blushed again and looked down at his hand holding hers. Then she looked up, and in a quavering voice said, "I was thinking you ought to kiss me, William."

His eyes widened. "I think ..." he started, then paused and smiled. "I think I should stop *thinking* so much ..." and he carefully leaned down and softly kissed her on the lips. When he pulled away, he saw she hadn't moved back, and her eyes were still closed as they'd been when their lips met.

"*Again ...*" she whispered, eyes still closed.

So he leaned down to kiss her again. But this time she reached up with her right hand and gently touched the side of his face, urging him to linger. This time her lips seemed softer, warmer, and more inviting than before. He felt a sudden desire to keep his lips pressed to hers as long as he could, for as long as she'd let him.

But after a few moments it was over, and they were sitting up straight again. She reached across and grasped his other hand, so they were now clasping both hands together as she leaned in against his shoulder. William thought it the most wonderful feeling he could ever recall.

They stayed like this for several more minutes, watching the sky's colors slowly fade from orange to red, and then to purple.

But into Margaret's happy thoughts, being with this wonderful man in this beautiful setting, a dark cloud suddenly passed—painful memories ... memories of being with another man ... an evil man.

Margaret turned toward William again and he saw she now had a serious expression, much different from what she'd shown all evening.

"William, before we go too much further with this ... *courtship* ... there is a serious matter I must discuss with you."

"Oh?"

"Yes ... I ... I want to be completely open and honest with each other, always."

"Yes, of course. I couldn't agree more. What is it that concerns you, Margaret?"

"William, I must make it clear from the start ... I *can't* marry you, at least not now."

"You can't?! Why do you say that?" William felt a sudden sinking feeling in his chest, like his bright and sunny world was about to come crashing down around him in thunder and lightning.

"Oh, it's not that I wouldn't *want* to, if things were to progress well between us. As I fully expect they will. It's just ..."

He had such a look of worry and concern she could hardly bear it and had to look away while she collected her thoughts.

"I was married once before, you know ..."

"Of course, Margaret. I know all about *that,* and it doesn't matter to me."

"Well, I appreciate that, William. But it *does* matter, you see ... I'm *still* married, under the law ... and in the eyes of God."

"Oh ... but not by *choice,* I'm sure. I've heard you tell the Captain you wanted to divorce ... *him.* Why not just follow through with it and be done?"

"Believe me, I would love nothing better."

Then she turned and looked William hard in the eye.

"William, if a woman goes to a judge asking for a divorce, he will not grant it without first informing the husband. And when he does that ..."

"Walters will know where you are!"

"Yes, though he probably already suspects it was Nathan who rescued me. And it is no secret Nathan is in Wheeling now. But I am still afraid of Walters, afraid to face him, afraid of what he'll do to me when he sees me again."

William frowned, "Well, *I'm* not afraid of the big bully. Margaret, I may not look like much, but out West I killed men much tougher and more frightening than him, I can assure you of that! I would protect you with my life. The degenerate villain!"

181

"Oh William, don't sell yourself short! You look a very strong and vigorous man to me! And I *know* how brave you truly are. Don't forget I have seen it with my own eyes the night those men tried to burn down our school.

"And, of course, Nathan has also promised to protect me, along with all his other men."

"Then it's settled, divorce him and be done. With all the men here guarding you, he'll dare not come within miles of this place. It's gone very badly for him in the past any time he's tried something against us."

But she didn't immediately respond and looked down at their still clasped hands.

"But William ... you aren't *always* going to be here, and neither is Nathan. You seem to forget there's a war on. Are you really going to stay home and guard *me*, while the rest of the world fights?

"You might be the most loyal, loving husband a woman could ask for, but in the end, you are also a fighting man, and a physician whose skills will be desperately needed to succor the wounded out on the battlefield.

"And is Nathan going to set aside his God-given destiny—a general leading great armies—just to sit home and guard his sister?"

She shook her head, "So who will protect me from Walters when you and your Captain and all his men ride out to meet the enemy in battle?"

William gazed at her wide-eyed and could feel his face turning red. "I ... I'm sorry, Margaret ... I guess I hadn't considered that."

She could see the pain the entire discussion was causing him, and her heart softened. "Don't worry over much, William ... there is always the possibility Walters may suffer his demise in the war. Doubtless many men will, especially on the rebel side, I believe."

He smiled and nodded, "One can always hope, I suppose."

"If not, then once the war is over, and all you men are safely back home again, perhaps I shall get up the courage to confront him and be done with it. Then maybe you and the Captain can persuade him to just ... give it up and leave me alone."

William snorted a derisive laugh, "Oh, you can be sure of *that!* Leaving me aside, the Captain is quite adept at *that* type of persuasion, I can promise you. And likely he'll wish to punctuate his arguments with a zero point four-four inch diameter lead sphere, delivered via nine-inch barrel at a velocity in excess of 900 feet per second by a thirty-grain explosive mixture of sulfur, charcoal, and potassium nitrate, ignited by a volatile charge of fulminate of mercury!"

She grinned, "Oh, William! I love it when you talk *scientific* like that!" and she giggled, suddenly lightening the mood.

He chuckled.

"Anyway, William, although we may have to postpone a possible wedding, we can certainly work on establishing those ... *'bonds of mutual affection'* you spoke of!" she giggled again and smiled brightly.

William rolled his eyes, "I suppose I shall never hear the end of *that!*"

"Certainly *not!* Even if I live to be a hundred, how shall I ever forget such a ... *romantic* turn of phrase?" she teased.

"Well, yes ... not the best possible choice of words, I now realize. But I figured if it was good enough for President Lincoln ..."

"Oh! *Yes* ... Mr. Lincoln, *of course!* I knew it sounded familiar. From his inaugural address ... *'Though passion may have strained it must not break our bonds of affection.'* Very good, William. Now I like it even better!"

They shared another quiet laugh. Then she leaned up and favored him with a long, tender kiss that made his heart flutter. And all concerns about the evil Elijah Walters quickly melted away like fog on a sunny spring day.

ಬಲೆ)ಲ೮ಚಚಬಲೆ)ಚ೮ಚಬಲೆ)ಲಚ೮ಚ

Captain Hawkins peeled off his thick wool socks, stiff from sweat, dirt, and hay chaff. He sat on the edge of his cot and stretched his legs out in front, wiggling his toes. It felt luxurious to have his feet out of his boots after a long, hot day in the sun running several companies of riflemen through their maneuvers.

He figured the men probably assumed officers were immune to the heat, dust, and fatigue of training; but unfortunately, such was not the case. All he wanted to do at the moment was lay back on his cot, close his eyes, and not open them again until morning. But even as he began to unbutton his shirt, he heard a knock on the doorframe of the cleaned-out horse stall that served as his room at Camp Carlile. He looked up and saw a familiar face looking at him over the stall door, illuminated by the light of an oil lamp hanging from a hook on the stable wall.

"Good evening, Captain Hawkins."

"Mr. Chambers! Good to see you, sir. Please ... come in," Hawkins said, rising to his feet.

"Thank you, but no, Mr. Hawkins. Please ... as you were. I don't wish to disturb your well-earned evening repose. I just came by to give you some news I think you'll appreciate."

"Oh?" Hawkins asked, sitting back down on the cot.

"Yes ... I've just come from a meeting with the governor and have stopped off at Lieutenant Colonel Kelley's tent before coming to see you."

"What's the good news, sir?"

Chambers smiled, and Hawkins thought it the type of smile the cat might show when contemplating the mouse.

"James ... how would you like a shot at those fellows who ambushed your wagon train outside Grafton?"

Hawkins leapt to his feet. "Do you mean it, sir? Oh, *would I ever, Mr. Chambers!*"

"We've just received good information on the perpetrators. They're led by a fellow named Zach Cochran, who was Sherriff of Taylor County before the secession. In addition to stealing your wagons, he's been forcibly collecting 'taxes' on behalf of the false government in Richmond, confiscating guns from pro-Union civilians, and generally carrying on like he owns the county. He and his band of secessionist guerrillas are headquartered at his house in the tiny village of Boothsville, about fifteen miles outside Grafton."

"Ah! So what's the plan, sir?"

"We're meeting tomorrow morning at first light in the governor's office: Lieutenant Colonel Kelley, Lieutenant Elliott of the scouts, and you. There we'll put together a plan of attack. I mean to take a couple of companies from the Seventh out there and put an end to his mischief. Are you with me, Hawkins?"

"Of course I am, sir; and with pleasure! And thank you very kindly, sir."

"The pleasure's all mine, Captain Hawkins. See you at first light tomorrow morning. Good night, James."

"Good night, Mr. Chambers."

James Hawkins leaned back on his cot but was now too excited to immediately fall asleep. He smiled thinking about getting a second chance to lead men into battle. And that it would be against the very same rebels who'd spoiled his first command made it all the sweeter. When he finally fell asleep, a smile still lit his face.

ಏಲನಲಞಲಏಲನಲಞಲಏಲನಲಞ

Saturday September 21, 1861 – Boothsville, Virginia:

The two hundred men and three officers from the Seventh Infantry gathered on the outskirts of Boothsville at 9:00 a.m. after a march from Grafton that had started at 2:00 in the morning, the unit having arrived in that city by train in the late afternoon the day before.

The unit was divided into two companies, each of a hundred men. Captain Hawkins commanded the infantry company, and Lieutenant Elliot the company of skirmishers and scouts who would serve as mounted cavalry for the operation.

Lieutenant Colonel John Kelley, currently the highest-ranking officer in the Seventh, was given overall command of the operation. Nathan had been highly skeptical of Kelley's appointment to the position at first, engaging in a heated exchange with the governor over it. But he did have to concede it was not strictly speaking a "political appointment" as the twenty-five-year-old did have previous military experience, though only a ninety-day enlistment as a corporal in the Nineteenth

185

Pennsylvania Regiment out of Philadelphia. But Kelley's father, Brigadier General Benjamin Franklin Kelley, had already proven his worth at the battle of Philippi, and was currently the commanding officer at Grafton, so at least Nathan knew he came from good stock. Nathan suspected the general had lobbied the governor hard on behalf of his son to secure the commission. But so far at the training back in Wheeling, Kelley had proven himself intelligent, competent, and an eager learner.

Nathan still had not selected a full colonel to take overall command of the Seventh, but in the meantime, he'd get a chance to see if young Kelley was capable of carrying off his first action.

Nathan, Tom, and the other veterans from Texas were truly only there to observe, so that they might later critique the action and address any deficiencies in future training sessions of the regiment—unless, of course, things went completely sideways. Nathan's men always traveled well-armed and prepared for any eventuality!

Nathan sat on Millie next to Colonel Kelley on his horse. Harry the Dog plopped down on the ground next to the horses, taking advantage of the brief respite after a long day and night of nearly non-stop travel. Kelley gazed through a brass spyglass at the town just ahead. It consisted of a few dozen houses, a church, and a general store which also served as the post office. Cochran's house was almost in the center, just a stone's throw south of the church.

Kelley lowered the glass and looked over at Nathan. Nathan said nothing, just nodded. The Lieutenant Colonel turned around on his horse to address his officers, sitting their mounts just behind.

"Lieutenant Elliot, circle your cavalry around the town to our right, cutting off any escape to the north. Captain Hawkins, march your men around to the left, cutting off any movement to the south. From there we'll slowly move forward, enclosing the enemy within our pincer, just as we planned—the goal being the capture of Cochran and his fellows. You're both confident of the location of his house from studying the maps, I assume?"

"Yes, sir!" they both answered.

"Good. All right, let's move out, gentlemen."

Nathan noted Kelley had correctly assigned the cavalry the objective farthest from their current location, as they could obviously move the quickest, with the infantry having a much shorter distance to travel before they'd be in place — the entire unit having arrived at Boothsville from the southeast.

Within a half-hour, the envelopment of the town was complete. As the soldiers moved forward, doors were opened, with force when necessary. All men in the town were forced out of doors to march with their hands in the air toward the center of town in front of the soldiers.

The town had been taken completely unawares, so there had been no time to organize any coordinated resistance. And the envelopment was so complete, the arms of the soldiers so clearly superior, none of the secessionists were inclined to resist on their own initiative.

Hawkins' company was the first to arrive at Zach Cochran's house outside his back door, which faced south. When they were within thirty yards, Hawkins called a halt. He saw Elliot's cavalry coming quickly down the street from the north and wanted to wait for them to be in position before confronting the rebel leader.

Hawkins thought he'd hail Cochran and see if he might surrender, before assaulting the house.

But apparently Lieutenant Elliot was thinking the same and beat him to it. As soon as the cavalry arrived at the north side of the house Hawkins heard Elliot call out, "Zach Cochran! Your house is surrounded by forces of the Union Army. Throw down your arms and come out with your hands in the air."

But no answer came from the house. Instead, the back door flew open, and a man came racing out carrying a rifle. He looked up and appeared shocked by the sight of Union soldiers standing in a row along the edge of his back yard.

Cochran stopped and raised his rifle, aiming at Captain Hawkins — the obvious target sitting up high on his horse. But two Union rifles fired almost simultaneously from the men standing closest to Hawkins, and Cochran fell without firing a shot.

A few minutes later, two more men came slowly out the back door. But these were unarmed, with hands held high in the air.

The nearly bloodless "Battle of Boothsville" was over. They'd captured approximately fifty assumed Confederate sympathizers and had killed their ringleader. Captain Hawkins holstered his sidearm, well satisfied the ambush of his wagon train was now officially avenged.

ജാധാരാജാധാരാജാധാരാ

"You did *what?!*" Nathan asked, angrily rising from his chair. Harry rose halfway up on his front legs and gazed expectantly at his master, tilting his head curiously at the unexpected outburst.

"Please, Nathan ... do sit down. And for God's sake, please lower your voice," Governor Pierpont pleaded. "I said I've offered James Evans command of the Seventh, with a colonel's commission."

"You've gone behind my back on it ... appointing a *political* commander. After we'd agreed not to do exactly *that!* And you did it while I was out of town supervising an action *you* requested!"

"Now, my dear sir ... *we* never agreed on it, *you* insisted on it and I relented under the assumption it wouldn't be necessary. But now it is. The decision had to be made, and I made it."

Nathan glared across the desk at the governor. But despite Nathan's rising anger, he was impressed Pierpont didn't look away, nor shrink back, but continued to meet his gaze steadily. He'd found over the years there were very few men who were willing and able to do that.

"Look, Chambers ... I'm sorry to surprise you like this. And you must believe me; it wasn't some nefarious plot on my part to do it while you were out of town ... at *my* request. But ... I really do think very highly of the man. I believe he will do a good job leading the regiment. And I just couldn't put him off any longer. He was all packed up and ready to ride to Ohio and offer his services there."

"Hmm ... then maybe you should've just let him go."

"Nathan ... you've admitted you haven't been able to find a capable leader who's willing to follow your lead concerning how the regiment ought to be trained and run — that the officers with field experience or West Point training are too headstrong or prideful to listen to reasonable suggestions."

"Yes ... true, but—"

"Well, perhaps it would be better to start with a man who's intelligent, capable, and a natural leader of men, but doesn't yet think he knows everything about warfare. Such a man might be more willing to listen to your ideas and take your suggestions to heart. Someone who'd be teachable, someone you could mentor and mold to your way of thinking on strategy and tactics."

Nathan relaxed back into his chair and let out a deep sigh. "And you think this James Evans is such a man? I spoke with him a few times at the Wheeling Convention and he seemed a reasonable fellow, but I don't really know him otherwise."

"Yes, I honestly believe he is. And he has already recruited nearly six hundred men—six companies—and is already training them up a Morgantown, which is twenty miles north of my old hometown of Fairmont. He's paid for their equipage out of his own pocket, which is not something to be taken lightly given the current shortage of resources on all fronts. If we don't take him on, we'll lose all those men to either Ohio or Pennsylvania."

Nathan nodded noncommittally, allowing Pierpont to continue.

"With the 300 men we've recruited here in Wheeling ... oh, and the company of Ohioans Captain Fisher brought over from Columbus last week ... the Seventh would be nearly up to full strength with Evan's recruits."

Nathan snorted, "Fisher's so-called 'Graysville Wildcats' only came across the border to us because they'd been rejected over in Columbus ... not exactly a stellar recommendation."

"True, but Fisher himself seems competent, a Mexican War veteran, from what I understand. And I'm confident you and your men will whip his 'Wildcats' into shape in short order."

Nathan looked down at his feet for a moment, then nodded again.

"And James Evans has already expressed great admiration for *you*, Nathan. He is most eager to learn anything you would be willing to teach him. In fact ... *dare I say it?* He told me he would immediately resign his commission if you didn't agree with it on your return. *There!* I've just given you veto power over the whole matter, to prove I haven't intentionally set out to bushwhack you!"

Nathan looked up at the ceiling while reaching into his pocket for a cigar. He stuck it into his mouth and chewed on it a moment before looking back at the governor.

"*Damn it*, Francis! I really do hate it when I end up sounding like the hot-headed, stubborn, set-in-his-ways curmudgeon, while you play the reasonable, cool-headed sage," he gave Pierpont a wry grin.

Pierpont chuckled. "Please ... just meet with him. Have a nice long chat and see what he has to say. See if you think he'll be a quick learner and willing to take direction from you. *Then* decide. If you do that, and give him an honest assessment, I will honor your decision, either way."

"All right. And ... thank you, Francis. Sorry for getting heated a moment ago. You deserve better from me ... You have a lot of things to worry over. I know you're just trying to do what's best."

"Never mention it, Nathan. We're all friends here. A little heated debate from time to time never harmed anyone."

"Thank you, your honor. Now ... where might I find ... *Colonel* Evans?"

"He's gone back to Morgantown to continue training his troops, there to await your final decision. Why not ride out there and inspect the troops? Speaking of ... if you approve of the setup there, I've been thinking ... perhaps we should move the rest of the Seventh over there and finish their training together, as a whole regiment. That will free up Camp Carlile to start building the Eighth, which you can supervise as soon as you're satisfied with Colonel Evans and Morgantown."

"Hmm ... it's a thought," Nathan agreed. He was warming to the idea of moving on to start recruiting the Eighth Regiment, and with it, if all went well, finally getting into the fight.

ᔕᕮᗞᑕᖇᏟᏗᔕᕮᗞᑕᖇᏟᏗᔕᕮᗞᑕᖇᏟᏗ

Oct. 4, 1861

Centreville, Virginia

Dear Evelyn,

Today the men have been brought to a very low state of sadness and remorse, but not for the usual reasons, the death of comrades from battle or disease. No, today the entire brigade is in mourning for the loss of our beloved leader General "Stonewall" Jackson due to his being promoted to Major General and being transferred over to the Shenandoah Valley to take command of all our forces in that district.

It is said our general is a man of few words, but today he rode his horse out in front of the entire brigade to wish us farewell, and to grace us with a rousing speech. It was the first time I had heard his voice in person, but it shall inspire me the rest of my days. We gave him a rousing cheer for a sendoff as he turned and rode away.

Otherwise I have very little news to report, as life has devolved into the seemingly endless drudgery of encampment, with no knowing when we will again receive orders to march.

Fortunately my immediate commanding officer, Captain Bob Hill, is a fine gentleman who takes special interest in the welfare of his men, so we are making the best of it. Also the weather has not turned too cold, and we are well provisioned, so I cannot in good conscience complain about my lot.

I would be remiss if I failed to thank you most profusely for your letter dated Sept. 15. Words cannot express how much it means to me to "hear" your words. And please do not be apologetic for having but little of interest to say or report as that is exactly the kind of thing I most like to hear about! I trust and pray you are well and in good spirits and will have the time to write me back when most convenient.

Your sincere friend,

Jubal Collins
2ⁿᵈ Lieutenant, 27th Virginia Volunteer Regiment
1ˢᵗ Virginia ("Stonewall") Brigade

Evelyn finished reading Jubal's letter, and set it down with a heavy sigh. Though she was always happy to know he was well, the arrival of his letters gave her a sense of anxiety on two fronts: first, she felt obligated to write him back within a few days, but she was having a very hard time thinking of things to say. At least when she was writing letters to Nathan, as tepid and uninteresting as they might seem to a stranger reading them, she enjoyed the challenge of surreptitiously infusing them with veiled meaning, innuendo, and emotion such that, hopefully, only he would understand.

But with Jubal there was no such underlying emotional or romantic attachment, and since she could hardly discuss her clandestine activities, that left very little to say.

The other more troubling aspect of his letters was the conflicting loyalties they fostered. She felt torn between the promise she'd made to herself never to betray him, and her commitment to the Hughes to provide any intelligence she learned—anything that might prove useful to the Union Army.

Damn it, Jubal! Why did you have to join up with what is turning out to be a key Confederate formation? Why couldn't you have been assigned to the commissary office or something? she groused for the hundredth time. *General Jackson promoted and transferred to the Shenandoah Valley? Hmm ... wonder if Jonathan and Angeline are already aware?*

She sighed again. She'd now have to play a dangerous game with Jonathan and Angeline, trying to determine what they knew about General Jackson without letting them know what she knew. And if it turned out they hadn't heard this news and weren't likely to anytime soon, then what? She'd have to figure out an excuse for how she'd heard about it without disclosing her ongoing correspondence with Jubal.

Well ... may as well get it over with, she decided. She stood, picked up a bonnet from the dresser, tied it in place as she glanced in the mirror, and headed for the door. *I'm overdue for a catchup meeting with Angeline anyway, so ... no time like the present, I suppose.*

Chapter 7. A Decision of the People

"Elections belong to the people. It's their decision.
If they decide to turn their back on the fire
and burn their behinds,
then they will just have to sit on their blisters."
– Abraham Lincoln

Thursday October 24, 1861 – Wheeling, Virginia:

Though Governor Pierpont had assured him Union troops would be guarding polling places in every western Virginia county currently under federal control, Nathan decided he couldn't just sit on his hands and await the result.

For one, almost all Union troops in the state were still exceedingly green, even their officers. He had no great faith in their ability to carry out their orders in anything more than a very literal fashion. He could easily envision the serious young men in uniform faithfully guarding the polling places, while gangs of pro-secession thugs roamed just outside preventing anyone from entering!

He also didn't trust the Union troops not to conspire with pro-Union civilians to prevent those inclined toward the "No" side from voting. For the United States government to accept the results and allow statehood to be carried forward, there had to at least be a reasonable appearance of fairness. That meant, ironically, a reasonable number of "No" votes.

So Nathan had split up his men into pairs and sent them off to towns where a strong secessionist element was expected. He'd armed each pair with a document stating their authority as government election officials, signed by the governor. They were to make sure the polling places were held open and accessible to all, and that the election was being run fairly and equitably.

He and Tom had selected the little town of Philippi, the seat of Barbour County. The town's claim to fame was as the site of the first land battle of the war—a rout of a surprised and unprepared regiment of Confederate soldiers by a much larger Union force. Because the rebel commander Colonel Porterfield had quickly recognized his untenable position and beat a hasty retreat, the Northern papers had derisively nicknamed it "The Philippi Races."

Ironically, Nathan and company had played a role in that Union victory at Philippi, though they'd never been there. Their attack on the rebel forces besieging Mountain Meadows and subsequent fighting retreat from Greenbrier county had devastated a freshly recruited Confederate militia force that had planned to join up with Porterfield near Grafton, but never had the chance.

So Tom and Nathan gazed around as they rode into the small town, imaging how the battle played out based on the accounts they'd read. It was a quaint little town in a tiny valley on the Tygart River surrounded by heavily wooded hills. The streets were neatly laid out, and as they neared the end of the main street they saw the courthouse ahead on their left.

Nathan thought this might have been a very pleasant break from their duties in Wheeling if it hadn't been for the steady drizzle, and a cool October wind, forcing them to keep their oiled overcoats pulled up tightly around their necks.

As they neared the courthouse, they noted it was as neat and picturesque as its setting; a perfect white picket fence lined the sidewalk in front, behind which sat the two-story red brick building. The building itself looked like a miniature version of the Capitol building in Richmond: a white columned portico holding up a triangular pediment, in the classical Greek and Roman style. Unlike its much grander cousin, this building featured a small, gold-colored cupula on top. Nathan was pleased to see the Stars and Stripes flying above the cupula. He'd read that a secessionist palmetto flag had flown on it prior to the Philippi Races.

But he was *not* pleased to see a large, unruly-looking crowd gathered in front of the courthouse and flowing out through the gate in the picket fence and onto the sidewalk. Sure enough, blue coated Union soldiers guarded the front doors, but it was obvious no one was going in to vote.

Nathan looked over at Tom and scowled. Tom grinned back, confident his captain would quickly straighten the situation out. And it would provide him sufficient entertainment to justify the damp three-hour ride from the Grafton train station.

When Nathan and Tom reached the edge of the crowd they continued forward on their horses, forcing the crowd to part. Tom pulled back his overcoat and pointedly rested his right hand on the handle of his holstered Colt revolver, scowling at anyone who looked his direction. And anyone too slow moving away from Nathan was graced with a threatening growl, and a show of large, sharp teeth from Harry. They continued right through the gate and only stopped when they reached the bottom of the shallow stairs up to the portico.

A Union sergeant stood in the midst of a row of six privates, all of whom held rifles with bayonets across their chests. He seemed startled when he saw Harry approaching and looked up at Nathan with a puzzled expression.

"Sergeant, my name is Chambers. I've come from the governor's office to inspect this polling station. Disperse this crowd immediately! Anyone resists, clap him in irons and make him sit out in the wet all day. That ought to cool him off."

"Yes, sir! With pleasure, sir! You heard that government official, men; disperse this crowd forthwith!"

The soldiers turned their rifles sideways, held them out from their bodies and began shoving, as the sergeant shouted, "Move away now. Move away! Clear this polling station! Clear away. Don't be causin' no trouble now ..."

The crowd began moving back, accompanied by shouts and curses, "Damned Yankees ... Traitors ..." and so on. But the soldiers took no notice and seemed unconcerned.

Nathan and Tom turned their horses and forced a way back out through the gate with Harry once again menacing any stragglers. Tom drew his pistol, but held it pointed upward. If anyone had an idea to do anything stupid, he was prepared to respond with deadly force if necessary.

But fortunately, nobody seemed inclined to put up a determined resistance. The town had been occupied by the Union

Army ever since the battle, so anyone pre-disposed to violence had presumably already been dealt with by now.

The crowd soon dispersed, leaving only a few stragglers — likely people who'd actually come to vote but had been prevented until now.

Nathan motioned the sergeant to come out to the road where he and Tom sat their horses, "Sergeant ..."

"Sir?"

"Make sure everyone who's peaceable and law-abiding is allowed to vote."

"Even those ... inclined to vote the *wrong* way, sir?"

"Yes, even those inclined toward the secession, sergeant. There's a reason they call it a democracy. We must allow even those who disagree with us to have their say."

"Yes, sir. If you say so, sir."

"One more thing, sergeant ... am I correct in assuming you currently have a *domicile* in this county?"

"A ... *what* .... sir?"

Tom chuckled, "He means, 'do you have a place to live?' ... a house, a barn, or even a tent?"

"Oh, yes sir. The company is bivouacked in a field across the way."

"Good," Nathan continued, "Then that makes y'all current residents of this county. Please do remind your men to cast their votes before the day's over," Nathan glanced over at Tom as he said this, and the two shared a serious look.

The sergeant thought about Nathan's instructions a moment, then lit up, grinning brightly. "Oh, yes *sir!* That I will. Thank you, sir!" and he snapped a salute, which Nathan returned instinctively without thinking, despite his lack of military uniform — a breach of proper military etiquette.

❧❧❧❧❧❧❧❧❧

An hour later, being satisfied the polling had returned to an orderly process, Nathan and Tom rode back along the road toward Grafton. This required crossing the Tygart River via the town's long, picturesque, covered bridge. The cool, drizzly weather obscured the far side of the river in a mist and made the ride under the bridge's roof a pleasant break. Harry took the opportunity to lighten his load by shaking a cloud of water from his coat, forcing Nathan and Tom to flinch and turn away lest they take a cold splash in the face.

Tom took advantage of their brief respite from the wetness to address the issue that'd been bothering him, as Nathan knew well from an earlier disagreement, "Do you really think it's right, allowing soldiers from other states to vote in the referendum to split Virginia? Like I said before, it just doesn't seem right, somehow. Like ... cheating, maybe?"

Nathan looked over and grinned, "Well, *you* voted, didn't you? And you're originally from Connecticut. And before you came to Virginia, you were a U.S. soldier stationed out in Texas."

Tom scowled, "Yes, but I've actually *lived* in Virginia this past year and more and have made it my new home. That's ... *different*, I think."

Nathan chuckled, "Yes, of course ... I'm just having my fun with you, on a serious question."

Tom nodded, and grinned, but kept his mouth shut, knowing Nathan well enough to understand a more serious response would be forthcoming.

"Tom, I don't believe we should cheat or lie in this election, and I do believe in letting everyone vote, including those we may disagree with ..."

"But?"

"But, firstly, Governor Pierpont and the new legislature have already approved it, so I am just implementing their orders."

Tom scowled at him; they both knew well if Nathan had disagreed with those "orders" he would never have enforced them.

Nathan nodded and smiled, conceding Tom's unspoken point. He continued, "Tom, these Union soldiers are here in this state, risking their very lives for our freedom and protection. God knows how long they'll be here—potentially long enough to establish legal residency, in many cases. Anyway, I think their sacrifice on behalf of loyal Virginians earns them the right to vote on the outcome of their potentially dangerous endeavors. Besides ... there's a war on, and in my view that negates some of the legal and political niceties that we might worry over in time of peace."

"But don't you think some may argue the whole election's illegal and therefore the new state isn't legitimate?"

"Yes, I'm sure they will. And they'll do it regardless of how we run this election, you can be sure of that! Especially those on the other side of these mountains. The very same people, I'd submit, who broke every law and rule of civility on the books to get their *secession* pushed through, regardless of what the people really wanted. Likely it's the worst offenders who will shout *'unfair'* the loudest!"

He turned and gave Tom a wry smile, which Tom returned with a nod.

"Tom, there's some things I *won't* do, even in a war, as you well know. I won't intentionally harm civilians nor destroy their means of survival if it can be helped. I won't tolerate forcing undue suffering or humiliation upon defeated soldiers once the battle is over. I'll not sacrifice my own men for no good purpose, and so forth. But otherwise, I'll do just about anything to win. As for politics and legalities?" he shrugged.

Tom nodded, "I agree with you there, sir. And likely whatever we do in this election, politicians and lawyers will gleefully argue over the outcome in legislative halls and courtrooms for years to come, well after the war is long over and forgotten."

"Maybe long over ... but I have a feeling this war may *never* be forgotten!"

ᏏᎦᏋᎧᏏᎦᏋᎧᎦᏋᎧᏏᎦᏋᎧ

Sunday October 27, 1861 – Wheeling, Virginia:

"Well, seems like good news all around, sir," Tom said, lowering the *Wheeling Intelligencer* newspaper and looking over at Nathan, as they sat on the veranda enjoying a sip of whiskey. "The election was a resounding success; the final tally being 17,627 *for* to 781 *against!*"

And then Tom couldn't resist adding, "Guess we didn't need those soldiers voting after all."

Nathan grinned at him, raised his glass to concede Tom the point, then took another swallow.

Tom went back to reading the paper, "And, it seems like our Seventh Regiment has also been successful in its first real action."

"Oh? I hadn't heard about *that*."

"Yes ... it says the battle occurred just yesterday." Tom read aloud:

> Union forces from Ohio, Pennsylvania, and our own Third, Fourth, and Seventh Infantry successfully recaptured Romney today, driving out a Confederate occupying force. We are happy to report our brave Union soldiers suffered only two killed and fifteen wounded in the action.

"And ... casualties on the enemy side?" Nathan asked.

"Hmm ... doesn't say. I'm guessing also very light. Perhaps they carried them away when they withdrew, so there was no way to make a count."

"Yes ... not much of a battle, sounds like. But a win is a win," Nathan said with a slight shrug.

"Almost always beats a loss!" Tom agreed.

"True. Both for the election and the battle!"

"Yes, sir. Though I'm sure our detractors will fixate on the low overall vote count. They're saying over fifty thousand on the west side of the mountains voted during the secession referendum back in May versus fewer than twenty thousand this time, even including the soldiers."

"Yes, but I also heard Governor Letcher just made-up vote counts from out of his head for several western Virginia counties whose ballots *mysteriously* went missing!" Nathan smirked. "I'm not too worried about that one, Tom. I've never yet heard an election thrown out because of low voter turnout. I think it just means a lot of people are confused and scared, and don't know what ought to be done. So I say it's a good thing they *didn't* vote!"

"You'll get no arguments from me!" Tom said and took another sip of whiskey. "So ... now the election is over, and the Seventh is successfully out in the field ... what's the plan, sir?"

"Plan?"

"You know, for enlisting. Are we going to train up the Eighth Infantry and then take it into action ourselves?"

Nathan stuck his cigar between his teeth and grinned, reaching out and slapping Tom on the back, "Yes, Mr. Clark, that *is* the plan!"

They raised their whiskey glasses and clinked them in agreement.

ಔಞಞೞಞಔಞೞೞೞಔಞಞೞ

That evening after dinner, as the happy company headed out toward the veranda, Nathan was surprised when Margaret took him by the arm and said, "Nathan, could I have a word with you ... perhaps in the library before we join the others on the veranda?"

Nathan returned a puzzled look, but said, "Of course, my dear."

Before they'd sat in the library, Nathan realized William had made no attempt to join them and had not asked her what she was doing. Instead he had proceeded out to the veranda with the others, clearly aware of what this was all about. The two had been nearly inseparable in the evenings since their courtship had begun a few weeks earlier, so it was highly unusual they'd split up after dinner like this.

"Is everything well with you and William, sister?" Nathan asked as they took their seats.

"Oh, yes. Very well, thank you, Nathan. It has been ... *wonderful* ... especially compared to my previous ..." she trailed off and a frown creased her brow. Nathan could well imagine the painful memories her previous marriage invoked.

"But what I wished to discuss with you does concern that, indirectly. Actually, I have two unrelated matters I wish to speak with you about. One is *business*, you might say, and the other more ... *personal*."

201

"Oh, all right. Which should we discuss first then?"

Margaret looked up at the ceiling a moment, then said, "Let's discuss business first. That will be ... *easiest*, I think."

He nodded in agreement and allowed her to continue.

"Nathan, I am becoming concerned about the new West Virginia state constitution. Though the meeting of the elected representatives to the constitutional convention isn't scheduled to start until late next month, I have already been engaged in informal discussions at the request of the governor. And I am becoming concerned about what's going to happen at the meeting."

"Oh? How so?"

"With everything happening in the country it never occurred to me that slavery would be an issue. Clearly if we were going to come in on the Union side of the conflict we would come in as a *free* state. It seemed so logical and obvious I never considered anything other.

"But apparently, I was mistaken. There's a strong belief among many of the elected delegates that slavery should be left alone. When first I heard it, I assumed it was an anomaly—that it was just a single delegate who was out of touch. But since then, I have learned that is *not* the case. It is a widely held opinion."

Nathan scowled, "Any idea what's driving that train of thought? I can't believe we just elected a bunch of pro-Slave-Power delegates in western Virginia!"

"No ... it's not that, I think. It seems more like ... they're worried about this growing internal strife within the proposed boundaries of our new state. That they don't want to add more fuel to that raging fire, perhaps. I believe they fear if we come out with a constitution abolishing slavery it will drive even more people into the rebel camp—that it will make the new government look weak, like we are just bowing to the wishes of Mr. Lincoln and his camp."

"Hmm ... yes, I can see that, though I don't agree with them on it. It seems to me those battle lines are already well drawn, and it's unlikely the slavery issue will push people one way or the other. There are relatively few slave owners in western Virginia, so it's unlikely to make any real difference."

"I agree, Nathan ... for what it's worth. But it galls me greatly to see everything we've worked for, and you've fought for, end in a *slave* state. And I'm certain the federal government will never agree to it. I can't imagine any scenario in which Mr. Lincoln would sign off on adding another slave state to the Union—he has enough troubles with them as it is!"

"And what of the governor? What does he say about all this?"

"He is supportive of me, of course. He too is personally opposed to slavery. But he is reluctant to take sides in the argument. He also fears being seen as too much a pawn of Mr. Lincoln, and feels he needs to stand 'above the fray,' as he says."

"Then what about John Carlile? He's now our Virginia U.S. Senator. He has the respect of everyone involved in the new government. They'll listen to him on it."

She paused before answering. "Nathan ... I know he's your good friend, but ..."

"Yes?"

"He, more than any other, has been the most surprising to me in this whole matter, and the most disappointing. Of course, after the governor refused me, I approached him next, thinking as you he was the man who could most sway opinion in our favor. I was shocked ... he is opposed to approving a constitution that bans slavery."

"*What?!*"

"It's true. Though he says he cares nothing for slavery, and is morally opposed to it, for him it's a matter of principle—that the new state must make a point of not bowing to the wishes of the presently elected administration. He believes bringing Lincoln a new state gives us leverage to exert our 'rights' as a state. And leaving slavery alone in the new state is the best way to enforce those rights."

"Damn it! I am sick to death of '*state's rights!*' I can't believe John of all people would hold with such nonsense."

"Unfortunately, he does, at least in this case. Of course, you can speak with him yourself, but I doubt you'll sway him. He can be ... a most *stubborn* man, from what I've seen."

Nathan thought about that a moment and had to agree. Once John made up his mind on something, he was fairly immovable. Fortunately, up until now, they'd been on the same side of nearly every argument.

"Clearly, you and I see eye to eye on this, Margaret, if no one else does. But I'm guessing you haven't come here just to vent your frustrations or to confirm I agree with you. How can I help?"

She gazed intently into his eyes for a long moment before looking down at her hands, resting in her lap.

"I ... hate to ask it of you—I know how much it means to you ..."

Nathan had a sudden sinking feeling about where this was headed, "Go on ..."

"Nathan ... other than John and the governor, you're the *one* man everyone in Wheeling looks up to and admires. You command their respect. And more than that ... you've been a slave owner in the past, so you know that aspect of it. And you're a military man who's been actively fighting against the insurrection. No one can deny you know of what you speak. Your voice would add incalculable weight to the abolitionist side of the argument. I want you to work with me at the convention—behind the scenes, of course—to convince the delegates to eliminate slavery.

"I also mean to push for public education for all children, including black freemen. Once again, the disadvantage of being a woman in this situation has raised its ugly head; many of the delegates simply refuse to speak with me, while I feel like others will oppose any idea I come up with simply because it's mine, rather than on its merits. I could really use your help and influence in all this."

Nathan was quiet for a moment, gazing at the floor. Then he looked up and said, "Do you understand what you're asking of me?"

"Yes, I do ... and as I said, it pains me to ask it. I know you're eager to join the fight. And William tells me you were planning on enlisting straight away now that the election's over—leading the next new West Virginia regiment into battle. Which is why I wished to speak with you now, before it's too late."

Nathan gazed at her for a long moment then nodded his head, "I will ... *think* on it." He stared at the floor for several minutes before looking back up at her. "And ... what then was the *personal* matter you wished to discuss?"

Margaret didn't immediately answer. Again, she stared at her hands. Nathan could see it was a difficult subject for her. When she finally looked up, he saw tears in her eyes. "It's that ... I am ... *afraid*," she said, in a voice quivering with emotion.

"Afraid? Afraid of what, my dear?"

"Of *him*. Of Walters."

Nathan scowled, "Oh, that. But don't you know you're perfectly safe here with me? I think he'll not dare come anywhere near after all the trouble I've caused him in the recent past. Not to mention you now have William keeping an eye on you, and he's much tougher than he looks, believe me!"

"Yes, yes ... of course I know all that. William said much the same thing. So I will repeat what I said to him: you won't always be here. What happens when you and William ride off to fight the war? What then?"

Nathan's eyes widened. He'd not considered *that* before. How *would* Margaret ever feel safe again, as long as Walters was still out there somewhere? He felt himself turning red in the face. He'd not given any thought to ensuring her safety once he was gone, and for that he felt ashamed. How could he fulfill his promise to protect her? And he knew it was no idle threat—he knew what Walters was capable of.

"I ... I don't know. But ... he has no way of knowing you're here. Perhaps he'll give it up for lack of knowing where you went ..."

"Walters may be odd and evil, but he's not stupid. And he's already suspicious of everything you do. Remember, I was captured trying to get to Mountain Meadows, and you can bet he knows about that. It's too much of a coincidence that I disappeared at the very same moment you made good your escape to the North. If I were in his shoes, knowing what he knows, I would assume you had fled to the North and taken me with you."

"Yes ... now that you put it that way ... it does seem logical."

"And ... I have noticed your name mentioned any number of times in the *Wheeling Intelligencer* recently, in connection with the recruitment and training of the new regiments and other service to the governor. So ... it's no secret where you currently reside ...

"I'm sorry to burden you with this, Nathan. You have already done more for me than anyone could rightly ask. But ... I have nowhere else to turn. You have been my savior in this, and my protector. I can't imagine what I'll do once you're gone."

"No ... no need to apologize, it's not your fault. And it's perfectly reasonable for you to be worried," he frowned, his concern for her evident in his expression.

"Nathan ... I have thought of a *possible* solution. That's really what I came to ask you about."

"Oh?"

"Yes. I was thinking, with the war ramping up, a man of his stature and wealth would likely be recruited for an officer in the new Southern army. If that were to happen, he would no longer be free to pursue me. He'd have to lead his men in the war, doing whatever tasks his superiors ordered of him. And with this part of the state swarming with Union soldiers, it's highly unlikely that would be anywhere near Wheeling. In that case I'd have nothing to fear, at least until the war is over."

"True ... *if* he is an officer. Hmm ... it's certainly worth looking into. I will ... make some inquiries. I still have a few friends in the War Department. And I'll ask the governor to do the same. Let's see if there is any mention in any of the dispatches concerning a Confederate officer named Elijah Walters. Ideally listed among the deceased," he grinned, but not in a pleasant way.

And though he didn't say it aloud, Nathan also started thinking about the mysterious, benevolent pro-Union agent known as "The Employer." It was almost certain he would either already know about Walters or have ways of finding out. And Evelyn clearly knew how to reach him ...

"That sounds like a good start, thank you, Nathan. Thank you very much."

"Don't thank me yet ... if he hasn't enlisted, or we can't find any word on him, then ... I don't know ..."

"Let's face that crossing when we come to it, dear. In the meantime, just knowing you're thinking about it and working on it has eased my mind."

She smiled at him and wiped back the remains of her tears. But now Nathan wondered how he could ever leave her unguarded if Walters could not be found, if he was still lurking *somewhere* out there ...

 ᏉᏕᎧᏒᏣᎧᏕᏉᏕᎧᏒᏣᎧᏕᏉᏕᎧᏒᏣᎧᏕ

"Ah, Tom ... I see you found the map I was asking for back at the Customs House."

"Yes, sir. And it's fairly recent with reasonably good detail. What was it exactly you were looking for?"

Nathan took the map and rolled it out on the kitchen table, setting a whiskey glass on each end to hold it open.

"I want to find an enemy-held town sizable enough to have a post office, and as close as possible to a B&O rail station."

"Oh! All right," Tom leaned over the map and gazed across it with Nathan. "Up until a few days ago I would've said Romney. But thanks in part to our own Seventh Infantry, *we* now control that one."

"Yes ... hmm ... what about this one?"

"Moorefield? Yes ... I believe the enemy still has the upper hand there. And definitely large enough for a post office. It looks like about ... thirty miles or so from a place called Paddy Town on the B&O line."

"Paddy Town? Oh, yes ... it's now called 'New Creek Station.' Map must be a little out of date."

"Yes, sir, likely so. Though not too badly ... the date on it says 1854. But why are you looking for a Confederate Post Office?" But as soon as the question came out of his mouth, Tom was pretty

207

sure he knew the answer. They hadn't received any mail from Evelyn or Adilida for several months now; clearly the route down the Mississippi was no longer tenable. "Oh ... sorry, stupid question. You're wanting to get a letter through to Evelyn, I presume?"

"Well, yes ... but not just for the usual reasons. This time it's for a specific purpose. Here, have a look." He handed Tom a folded sheet of paper.

Tom opened it and read:

Dear Miss Evelyn,

I hope and trust you and Miss Harriet are doing well. All is well with our household, and Momma says to send her love and best wishes. As always, I hope and pray these troubled times soon pass that our two families may be happily reunited once more.

In the meantime, I am hopeful you will find a way to reassure us of your continuing good health that we need not worry over much, despite the uncertainty of the times.

I was also wondering if you could do me a small favor. I understand you have an acquaintance whose Employer might be able to help me locate my old friend and neighbor E.W.—you remember the fellow? He dropped in unexpectedly at the last minute during the wedding we attended last year. I am thinking he might want to pay me another visit soon. I would like to be better prepared for his arrival this time that I might provide him a more welcoming reception, one more in keeping with what he so richly deserves.

It also seems likely he has volunteered his services with the gallant army of the South. Nothing would please me so greatly as to hear that was true. Of course, it would be an honor to know in which regiment he serves that we might keep tabs on his heroic service from afar.

I shall breathlessly await your timely response, if you can find it in your heart to do so.

Your family friend and obedient servant,

N.C.

And then Nathan added silently, *and P.S. Evelyn, dearest, I still love you ... God knows how I love you ... and miss you!*

Tom looked up from the letter with a smirk, "Well written, sir. I agree about giving Walters what he so richly deserves! That would be a real pleasure! I take it you're starting to have concerns regarding his whereabouts?"

"I wasn't ... until Margaret spoke with me last night. She was practically in tears for worry over it. At first, I thought it was just foolishness, what with all our soldiers guarding this place night and day. Not to mention the black men, who'd doubtless shoot the villain on sight!

"But then she pointed out it's only a matter of time before we all ride off to fight in the war—even the freemen eventually, if my assumptions are correct about that."

"Hmm ... true. And I'm sure Walters wouldn't stop with just Margaret. Miss Abbey, Megs, and anyone else you cared about would be in grave danger as well, should he show up here after we're gone."

"Agreed. Earlier today I fired off a few telegrams to people I know back in the War Department to see if Walters' name appears on any dispatches or lists of known Confederate officers. I've also asked the governor to keep an eye out for any mention of him in any reports."

"But ... you thought our old friend and benefactor 'the Employer' might have a better chance of tracking him down?"

"Yes, the thought occurred to me. And Evelyn is the only one I know who can contact him."

"Not the *only* one ... don't forget our friend and guide Joseph, who was instrumental in our escape from Richmond. He was also working for the Employer."

209

"Yes, I certainly hadn't forgotten about him! I shall never forget him and will be forever grateful. But I don't even know his last name. Nor even if *Joseph* is his real given name."

"It's *not*. But I *do* know his real, full name!"

"You *do?* Excellent, Tom! Well then, would you mind writing a similarly worded letter to him, in case for some reason my letter to Evelyn fails to get through? Though you'll need to be more explicit about Walters; Joseph likely wouldn't recognize him from just the initials nor would he know anything about the big wedding last year."

"Oh, that's easy. I'll just tell him to go speak to our mutual friend E.H. about him and give the exact same clues. And I'm sure the Employer will understand it in any case, after all the trouble we had with Walters right after the secession."

"Yes ... that makes sense. Thanks, Tom."

"Never mention it, sir. It'll give me a chance to send another letter to Adilida while I'm at it. But ... how shall they return an answer to us?"

"Not sure about Adilida. You'll have to figure out something on that. But as for Evelyn and Joseph ... I am confident the Employer will figure out a way to get in touch with us. He always does."

"Good point, sir. And ... who are you thinking of sending to the Confederate post office at Moorefield?"

"I had Georgie in mind. I was remembering how cleverly he played a simple farmer riding the mule when we were trying to escape Wise's thugs up in the mountains. A similar ruse would be in order this time, I believe."

"Good idea. But we should send Jamie with him as well. They can play a couple of farm boys looking to ride east to volunteer with the Confederate Army."

"Yes, that sounds good. And lest someone try to sign them up on the spot ... have them say they heard about my old West Point classmate, General Thomas Jackson, now called '*Stonewall*' and wanted to ride over to Richmond and fight for *him*."

Tom nodded and gazed at the map for a few more minutes before looking back up at Nathan. He now had a more serious look on his face.

"You don't intend to enlist until we find Walters, do you?" It was more of a statement than a question.

Nathan grimaced then nodded, "Sorry, Tom. I know it wasn't even two days ago I promised you we'd enlist straightaway and train up the Eighth as our own. But with Walters still out there somewhere ... I can't just leave with my family unprotected. And ... Margaret has also begged me to help steer the state constitutional convention. She fears it will result in a slave state, which the president will reject, spoiling everything we've worked for all these months. She thinks I can help sway it in the other direction. I ... think I should at least try."

"Never mind about *me*, sir. I trust you'll always do what's best. I'm happy to help in whatever capacity makes sense. If that's out shouldering a rifle, I'm content. But if that's here building a better state for our future home and to better aid the Union ... I'm okay with that as well."

"Thanks for being understanding, Tom."

"The *others*, however ..."

"Yes, yes, I know. I imagine Stan is fairly itching to kill someone by now ... not to mention Jim."

"Yes, likely so, sir."

"I'll have another talk with them."

"I think that would be prudent, sir."

"Margaret's concerns have started me thinking about the general security of this farm. I realized we've been leaving it vulnerable to attack while we've been out training the new regiments and off cleaning up after various violent incidents. Walters or just some pro-Confederate bushwhackers like our late neighbor Ward could take advantage of our absence."

"True. So what are you thinking on it?"

"I'm thinking we need to re-institute the Watch like we had at Mountain Meadows. Only this time our watchmen will have teeth!" he grinned at Tom.

"Yes, now the freemen are well trained and armed, they'd make quite a formidable security force," Tom agreed.

"My thinking precisely. And it'll give them something productive and useful to do during these winter months ... and perhaps help relieve the pressure to be out fighting in the war."

"Sounds good, sir. I'll talk to Jim and Billy about it, and we'll ask for volunteers straightaway, though I'm sure we'll have no shortage of men. They all hate Walters every bit as much as we do—maybe more."

"Thank you, Tom. That should help me sleep a little better at night."

ꝏꙮꙅꙅꝏꙮꙅꙅꝏꙮꙅꙅ

Evelyn shook her head in amazement at the coincidence as she strode briskly down the street on her way to the Hughes' house. After months of no word from Nathan and more than a month from the last letter she'd received from Jubal, she received a letter from each on the same day. And both included information she urgently needed to impart to Jonathan and Angeline, one way or the other.

Jubal's letter was brief, as he was hurriedly preparing to move out, and it invoked the usual mixed emotions in her: happiness for his continued good health and safety, worry over what to possibly say in a return letter, and anxiety over what to tell the Hughes.

Once again he had divulged information that might prove invaluable to the Union side: that the Stonewall Brigade was being transferred to the Shenandoah Valley to be reunited with their namesake general. Jubal was ecstatic, of course, but Evelyn feared it likely meant Jackson meant to go on the offensive soon, likely not waiting for spring as many had been predicting.

And, ironically, such an offensive could strike very close to where Nathan was actively trying to build the new state of West Virginia, not only threatening that effort, but quite possibly his very life. She would once again have to make sure Jonathan, a.k.a. the Employer, knew about this so he could pass it along to his Union contacts.

But the thrill she felt when she opened the other letter and realized it was from Nathan had quickly turned to cold fear as she digested its hidden meaning. Nathan had apparently received news that Walters was once again plotting against him and threatening his family. This time Nathan was specifically asking for her aid via the Employer to determine Walters' whereabouts. She stuffed the letters in a drawer and practically ran from the house, nearly forgetting her hat.

An hour later, Evelyn was feeling slightly more at ease, after Jonathan promised her he'd do all in his power to locate Walters on Nathan's behalf, saying, "Once again, let me assure you my dear, I am as committed to Mr. Chambers' well-being as you are ... though likely for slightly different reasons," he smiled.

She returned the smile and nodded.

"I still believe he is potentially one of the best officers the Union has, and anything I can do to remove obstacles in the way of his enlistment, I will gladly do."

And to put an exclamation point on this statement, he grabbed his coat and headed out the door that very moment to begin his inquiries into Walters' whereabouts.

After he'd departed, Angeline refilled their teacups, and said, "I'm happy you are here today, Evelyn. I was just going to send one of our men to fetch you."

"Oh? Why was that, Angeline?"

Angeline frowned. "We've been noticing a lot of activity in the Shenandoah Valley recently. First, General Jackson was transferred there and promoted to two stars. Now it is rumored his old brigade, also called Stonewall, has just been transferred there to rejoin him, along with several other formations, bringing him up to nearly division strength."

"Oh!" Evelyn responded, trying her best to pretend she didn't already know this information. "And ... what are you thinking it means?"

"I don't know ... but I suspect there is something afoot. Some sort of offensive is being planned, I'm almost certain. What I don't know is the direction of the attack—north across the Potomac into Maryland, west to threaten the new Virginia state government in

Wheeling, or east to Washington. And I also don't know the *when*. Will they launch a fall or winter offensive, going against normal practice in an attempt to catch the Union forces off guard, or wait until spring when the roads are better?"

"Yes ... I can see the concern. So, what are you thinking we can do to find the answers to these questions?" Evelyn asked, and immediately thought of Jubal, though it was unlikely a low-ranking officer such as him would be privy to such details.

But Angeline's answer surprised her, and at first seemed almost unrelated to the topic at hand, as if she had suddenly decided to change the subject.

"Evelyn ... do you know a lady named Varina Davis, who has recently arrived in Richmond?"

"Varina? No, I don't think so ... wait ... why does that name sound so familiar?"

Angeline smiled, "It sounds familiar, because Varina is the wife of the President of the Confederate States of America, Jefferson Davis!"

"Oh! Oh, my. And you want me to meet her? I would ask why, but given the conversation we've just been having, I can make a guess."

"And likely you would guess correctly, my dear," Angeline answered, smiling. "Oh, you are so very quick ... I do so love that about you."

Evelyn smiled, and nodded.

"I have a mind to pay Varina a visit at the so-called 'Confederate White House' over on Clay Street. And I want you to come with me. It's high time the two of you became acquainted."

"Oh, well, all right. That sounds fine. Are you thinking we can convince her to take in one of our ... *special* maids?"

"Perhaps, but not right away. She is very intelligent and thoughtful. I don't want to underestimate her and make her suspicious.

"Inserting a spy into her household would be such a major coup for our operations, we must move carefully—earn her trust ... make her believe we are her very best friends. Then introduce the idea, or ideally, she will hear of your services from others and will ask you for it herself."

"That makes sense. But then … if you are going to take a long-term approach to inserting a spy, how do you hope to learn of an impending offensive by General Jackson?"

Angeline didn't immediately answer, gazing intently at Evelyn with a serious look. "My dear, you have proven yourself brave and resourceful well beyond the norm. If it were not so, I would never ask what I am about to ask."

"Yes?" Evelyn asked, with a growing sense of dread and anxiety.

"When we go to visit her, I intend to do it when it is known her husband will be away … and then … I want you to search through Jefferson Davis's desk for the information."

സഗ്റോശ്രോസസഗ്റോശ്രോസസഗ്റോശ്ര

After several weeks of debating with himself, Tony had finally worked up the courage to press his luck with Rosa. The words she'd said to him after they'd killed those murderers, about admiring his bravery, were now burned into his brain. He'd replayed them over and over again in his mind, but still hadn't decided how far to let himself go with them.

Then for the thousandth time he pined for the loss of his best friend Johnny, killed during the battle to breakout of Mountain Meadows when the slavers had besieged the farm. Johnny had been the only person he could talk to about Rosa and hope to get some kind of advice—good, bad, or otherwise. He sighed a heavy sigh as the vision of shoveling dirt over the body of his best friend flashed unbidden into his mind.

Ned was a good friend, but he had no understanding of women and seemed entirely disinterested. No good going to him. Tony had also thought about speaking with Henry. But for some reason Tony couldn't comprehend, Henry seemed to have his own relationship with Rosa … not of the romantic kind, but more of a fatherly kind. He wasn't sure if it came down to it that Henry would side with him or with her.

And right now, he definitely needed someone on his side. He knew the Captain would be sympathetic—but he just couldn't envision going to the Captain for advice about a girl. Especially since he'd previously accused the Captain of having a romantic interest in her—falsely, it turned out.

No, he figured he was on his own this time. He'd just have to figure out Rosa all by himself. But it was a daunting task. He took a deep breath and walked over to her tent.

It was dark, but not yet bedtime, it being winter and the sun now going down even before dinner was served out. But there was still plenty of light in the area all around the tents, courtesy of oil lamps the Captain had provided.

Tony stepped up to the door of the tent and knocked on the wood frame. The door opened a moment later and Betsy looked out. She was a middle-aged black woman of large girth, who'd always treated Tony kindly.

"Hello, Betsy. I was wondering if I could speak with Rosa."

"Oh, hello, Tony. Rosa, come on out here, girl. Tony is here to speak with you."

A minute later Rosa appeared in the doorway. "Hello, Tony," she said, and he noticed she had a slight smile. He took that for a hopeful sign and returned her smile with one of his own.

"Hello, Rosa. I ... just come by to see how you was ... gettin' along."

"Oh, well ... I's gettin' along just fine," she said, and stepped out of the door, closing it behind her.

It was not yet terribly cold, despite the lateness of the evening, so he decided to press his luck a little. "Would you like to walk a bit?" he asked.

"All right."

She stepped down onto the grass and stood in front of him, looking up into his eyes.

He could see her face clearly in the light streaming from the surrounding tent windows, and once again he was reminded just how beautiful she was. The most beautiful girl, er ... *woman* ... on the farm by far. Though he'd never kissed a woman before, he suddenly felt a very strong urge to try it with her.

216

But he resisted that urge, fearing it might end badly. Instead, he turned and waited for her to step up beside him. But to his surprise, when they started walking, she reached over and took his hand. Her hand was small but felt firm and warm. He imagined his own hand felt cold and rough from working out in the fields. But then he realized she had also been working in the fields since they'd come north, so likely their hands were the same in that regard. So he relaxed a little.

He'd had a mind to walk down to the river if she was willing. There was a nice bench seat down there overlooking the water. But he realized it had gotten too dark to see and he hadn't brought any kind of candle or lamp. So instead he led her out across the pasture away from the tents, but still within the light from their lamps. There he stopped, and they turned around and gazed back at the farm in the darkness. The tents seemed to glow as the white canvas let just enough light through to give them an eerie, lifelike aura. The farmhouse loomed on the far side of the tents, its windows also streaming out light from many lamps and candles.

Tony was enjoying the feeling of Rosa's closeness and the touch of her hand, but now that he'd gotten her out here, he couldn't think of what to say. He longed to move their relationship to the next level, but the last time he'd tried that it had ended badly and she'd become angry with him. It'd taken months for things to feel better again. It made him hesitant and uncertain. But she had shown more interest in him lately, hadn't she?

But then she saved him from his indecision by saying, "Brrr ... it's getting cold out tonight, ain't it Tony?"

Now that she mentioned it, he could feel a sudden chill in the air that hadn't been there earlier. He'd been so focused on what to do and say with Rosa, he really hadn't paid much attention until now. They were both barefooted, and neither had on a jacket.

"You want to go back?" he asked.

She didn't immediately answer but turned and gazed up at him for a minute. "I think ... I'd be a bit warmer if you was to put your arm around me."

"Oh! All right. How's that?"

She leaned in against him, and he could feel the soft warmness of her body pressed up against his side as he wrapped one arm around her shoulders, gripping her upper arm on the other side. Cold or no, he decided it was a wonderful feeling, one he wished would never end.

"Mmm ... much better," she answered, and smiled.

He took this for a *very* hopeful sign! They stayed like that for several minutes, and though he was enjoying the feeling immensely, he still could find no words.

He was just starting to think about pushing his luck by leaning down to kiss her when she said, "*Oh!* Look, Tony ... it's snowing!"

He looked up at the sky, and sure enough, tiny flakes of snow could be seen coming down above the tents. Soon the flakes were settling on their hair and across their shoulders.

༄༅ⵣⵣ༄༅ⵣⵣ༄༅ⵣ

For the past several weeks Rosa had been thinking about Tony more and more. She'd always liked him growing up, and he was the one boy who hadn't ever picked on her or teased her. He'd always been kind and friendly. And now that he was grown into a man ... well, he was certainly handsome, strong, and brave — but still kindly like he'd been as a child. Being with him ... well, she could think of a lot worse things.

She'd also been dwelling on the things he'd said back at Mountain Meadows ... about them jumping the broom, becoming a family. About how being with the Captain would mean being only a mistress, never a bride. And even if she bore him children, he would never acknowledge them as his own, while she'd likely have to live with the knowledge he'd also have a white wife he took to bed. Then there was the shame she'd feel from the other blacks; they'd surely despise her and call her the white man's whore.

Her *mind* knew being with Tony was the right thing for her. She knew she'd be happy with him; he was a good man. But ... her *heart* still skipped a beat any time she even caught a glimpse of Nathaniel Chambers. And it always said to her ... *what if ...?*

But tonight, when Tony came to the door, she decided to take the next step with him ... to see where it might lead. So she stepped out into the darkness with him meaning to find out how it might feel to be ... *what?* Well, *more than friends* anyway, for starters. After that ... who knew?

Now as she leaned in close to him with his strong arm around her shoulders, she thought it felt mighty good, that she might be able to get used to this. And then she looked up at him, meaning to see if she might get him to kiss her, when she noticed it was suddenly snowing.

"*Oh!* Look, Tony ... it's snowing!"

He looked up and nodded. It was the first snowfall of the winter, and they watched the beautiful sight together in silence for several minutes.

It reminded her of last Christmas Eve, when the snow began falling early in the day, and hadn't stopped until early Christmas morning, leaving Mountain Meadows covered in a magical white Christmas blanket. She remembered the joyous evening, drinking Miss Abbey's brandy and singing Christmas carols around her piano with everyone in the house, both slaves and masters, including the Captain.

And she had a sudden image of the Captain's arm around her instead of Tony's, an image she could not will away. So she used the snow for an excuse.

"Tony ... with all this snow ... I think we ought to be gettin' back to the tents now. We ain't even got shoes on!"

He looked down at their feet, wiggled his toes, and smiled. "All right, Rosa. We'll go back."

ߖߪ߫߭ߖߪ߫߭ߖߪ߫߭

Abbey and Megs glared at each other across the room in the "library" of the farmhouse. Abbey couldn't understand how it had come to this.

"Megs, I don't understand why you are *so* mad."

Megs frowned, "I ain't ... *so* mad ... I'm just mad. There's a difference!"

"All right, then why are you ... *just mad?*"

"Well … I ain't really mad … more like *frustrated*."

"But why? What have I done to make you … *so* frustrated?"

"Not *so* frustrated … just frustrated!"

Abbey rolled her eyes in exasperation, "*Fine!* Just tell me what's wrong … *please!*"

"I want things to go back to the way they were."

"What?! Back to when you were a slave?"

"Yes! Well, no … not the *slave* part, but the other."

"The other? Whatever do you mean? I'm sorry, Megs, I just don't understand."

Megs sighed a heavy sigh and looked down at the floor for a long minute. Then she got up and came over to where Abbey sat and pulled up a chair next to her.

"Abbey … you know I love you as a sister."

Abbey nodded, but let Megs continue.

"But … sisters don't always get along. Not all day every day."

Abbey smiled and nodded.

"And … they can't always do everything together and in the same way."

"You … don't *like* doing things with me, Megs?"

"No, no … it ain't that. It's just … oh, Abbey, it ain't nothing *you're* doing wrong, it's all in *me!*

"Ever since I was a little girl, I've had this *need* … a need to *do* things … to get things done! I never was one could stand to be sitting still and doing nothing—like to drive me mad! I had to accomplish tasks set before me. And I had to do them *myself*, with my own two hands. Oh, I'm plenty good at bossing the other maids and the cooks to be sure, but that's 'cause they's just like … well, like having more hands to do things with, if you understand my meaning. Like I was still doing those things *myself*, but I had ten hands instead of just two, because them other slaves would do things just *exactly* the way I wanted them done or they'd be hell to pay! Am I making any sense, Abigail?"

"Yes … I think so."

"And … I really appreciate you wanting to help … to do your part, but …"

"But I'm *not* like another set of hands, am I?"

"No, you're certainly not, Abbey, God bless you! You have a mind of your own, your own ideas, about how things might be done better, more quickly, neater, cleaner, and so on.

"Oh, I appreciate you got a good, quick mind — don't mistake me. It just don't ... *work* for me. Oh ... I'm so sorry, Abbey. I ain't making no sense and just making you feel bad."

"No ... I think I understand, Megs. Before ... when you were my servant ... I'd tell you what I wanted done, and then you'd figure out how to do it, and would take care of it with little or no further direction from me. I would decide on the 'what,' and you would figure out the 'how,' one might say."

"Yes ... that's *right*. Now you understand me."

"Yes. But, Megs ... now you're free, it doesn't seem *fair* somehow, me telling you what to do all the time. Like you were still my slave or something."

Megs frowned and was quiet for a moment as if thinking of an answer to this argument. Suddenly her face lit up, "Think of it this way ... you'd agree Tom isn't Nathaniel's servant, nor is he any longer under the Captain's command in the Army? That Tom's free to leave at any time and go do whatever he pleases?"

"Well, yes ... of course."

"But, despite Tom being free to do as he wishes, the Captain still tells him what to do nearly every day, and he does it. Usually without another word of instruction from the Captain."

Abbey's mouth opened, and she gazed up at the ceiling. "I ... I see what you mean, Megs. You think we should be more like Nathan and Tom? Clearly, they are very good friends. Likely they're each the best friend the other has *ever* had, in fact, though they may not think of it that way. And yet ... Nathan clearly decides what will be done, and Tom then does it."

"Yes ... that's *it*. And it don't mean Tom is a lesser man, nor does it mean he's not as smart or capable. In fact, I'd be willing to say there are plenty of things Mr. Tom knows and is good at that Nathan doesn't and isn't."

"True ... and you think it would be better if *we* ... worked together like that? Like Tom and Nathan?"

"Yes, I think so, Abbey. I think that would work best. Like it used to be … you'd decide what needed doing, and I'd decide how to make it so. I'd like to try doing *that* again. And it don't mean I'm your *slave* … or you're better'n me. It's just … the way we two can best work together on things."

Abbey and Megs met eyes for a long moment. Abbey could see the earnestness and sincerity in Megs' eyes, and how much this meant to her. She smiled, "All right, Megs. We'll go back to doing things the *old* way."

Megs beamed and grasped Abbey's hands, "Thank you, Abbey, thank you! Hallelujah!"

🙰🙰🙰🙰🙰🙰🙰🙰🙰🙰

Friday November 15, 1861 – Thibodaux, Louisiana:

"Hello, Addie. I'm home," Edouard called out as he closed the front door, removed his hat and coat, and hung them in the closet just off the entryway.

"Hello, Uncle … we're in here," Adilida called back from down the hallway.

"Ah … there you are. How is our strong young boy today?" Edouard asked, sliding over a chair in front of the bed where Adilida sat, breastfeeding the baby.

"He is hungry, as you can see," she answered, smiling brightly.

"Good, good. He will grow strong and tall," Edouard responded, returning her smile.

"What news from the world, Uncle?"

"Of the war? Nothing new … the blockade continues—if anything, tighter than before. They are saying no ships dare run the gauntlet down the river now, even at night."

"And no sign of a Union attack? No hope of breaking this stalemate?"

"None so far. But I hear rumors of more action on the northern end of the river. Perhaps there will be a breakthrough from that direction one day soon."

Adilida nodded, and smiled, "You are not such a good liar, Uncle, but I do appreciate you trying to cheer me."

He snorted a quick laugh, then said, "But you have not asked if anything came in by the post."

"*Oh!* A letter, Uncle?! Oh, you shameless man. You insufferable tease ... hand it over," she said, slapping him playfully on the arm, causing the baby to squirm and grunt in annoyance at the sudden outburst and motion.

Edouard chuckled, and reached into his waistcoat pocket, handing across the letter.

Adilida snatched it and gazed at the front of the envelope. "Why ... it has been sent by the *Confederate* post ... from some place called Moorefield, Virginia."

"Yes, I saw that; so I stopped in at the library to borrow a map of Virginia, being the curious fellow I am. This little town is in western Virginia, but is apparently still held by the Southern side. Your Thomas has seemingly snuck across Confederate lines to mail this to you using the enemy's own postal service. Very clever, and very daring—just the thing I would expect from Thomas, I must say."

She nodded, then tore open the envelope. She read through it quickly before holding it up to her face and kissing it, sighing a heavy sigh. "All is well, and he is not yet in the fighting."

"Oh, thank God for that," Edouard said, crossing himself. She nodded and smiled, wiping tears from her face.

⁀⁀⁀⁀⁀⁀

Tuesday November 26, 1861 – Wheeling, Virginia:

The first day of the West Virginia Constitutional Convention held few surprises for Margaret. As expected, the first half of the day was spent electing a convention president and establishing the various necessary rules and procedures.

In the afternoon, the president opened the floor to anyone who wished to make a statement before formal proceedings commenced. Any elected representative was free to speak, of course; and several did. But so did any guest who petitioned to be heard. The president was free to accept or deny such requests at his discretion.

Margaret was not surprised when Nathan asked to speak first, to which the president readily assented. She knew he was itching to have his say before the convention became bogged down in the minutiae of legal proceedings.

Governor Pierpont had chosen *not* to attend, wanting to stay at a respectful distance since this was, after all, the constitution of the *new* state, West Virginia, and not the state he governed, Virginia proper. He did, however, ask Nathan to welcome and thank the elected delegates on his behalf. This made Nathan the *de facto* voice of the governor, which he was not averse to using to his advantage as much as possible—a fact Pierpont knew full well.

The meeting took place in the elegant Customs House courtroom, the very same place where the Wheeling Convention had been held, in which it was decided the west would split from the Virginia Commonwealth.

Nathan, Margaret, and Tom were seated in the guest area outside the U-shaped wood railing which delineated the large central area where the delegates were seated. Their seats were in the visitors' gallery to the left side of the room (if one were facing toward the front). Other guests were seated in the "jury box" on the far side of the room, or in back on each side of the room. The convention president and secretary sat up front in the tall judge's box and lower clerk's box.

Nathan took an aisle seat so Harry could sit next to him, though the dog was presently lying down happily on the highly polished hardwood floor, panting heavily.

When they'd first started coming to the Customs House during the Wheeling Convention, Nathan had felt self-conscious about bringing the dog inside. But he'd not known what else to do. He could hardly tie him outside where he was likely to howl all day, nor could he leave him loose to wander about the town frightening civilians. So inside Harry had come, to the shock and surprise of all concerned. But now, after all these months, his presence in every part of the Customs House was so common no one thought a thing of it any longer. Or if they did, they kept the thought to themselves for fear of the intimidating animal, and his equally intimidating master.

And Nathan was gratified to note the dog had also become accustomed to being inside the building and interacting with numerous strangers on a regular basis. He no longer bared his teeth and growled when approached, and even allowed people besides Nathan to pet him, though he always looked stiff and uncomfortable while they were doing it. But Nathan knew if he himself lost his temper at someone, the dog would react strongly, so he endeavored to keep such feelings in check, at least while inside the building.

So when it came time for him to speak, he had to stand and then step over the prone form of the dog, after which he smiled broadly and shrugged at the audience, causing a tittering of laughter across the room. He stepped up toward the judge's box and around the open end of the U railing to enter the central area of the room, where the prosecution and defense would sit during a trial. There he stood to address the elected delegates along with the guests seated throughout the room.

"Mr. President, Senator Carlile, honored delegates, gentlemen guests ... and most elegant *lady*," he said, nodding at Margaret, who was the only woman in attendance, though she, like Nathan was there as a guest. She returned the nod with a slight nod of her own and a demure smile.

"You delegates have been elected by your fellow citizens to undertake a momentous task, to participate in a most fateful and historic event. From now to the end of time, your names will forever be linked with a document expressing the supreme law of this new state; the law establishing the only state ever created by an act of sublime loyalty during a time of ultimate treason and betrayal. On behalf of Governor Pierpont of the *Restored* Commonwealth of Virginia, I would like to thank you for your service and congratulate you on your election to this most prestigious convention.

"This year I have stood on the battlefields of western Virginia, have witnessed the carnage and the courageous sacrifice of our fellow Americans on *your* behalf. Men from Indiana and Iowa, Ohio and Pennsylvania, New York, Massachusetts, and many other states. And yes, your brothers and neighbors from right here in western Virginia. These brave young men have spilled their blood to give *you* who sit here today the opportunity to take a stand. To stand against disloyalty, sedition, and self-serving treason. To stand up for the Union, for freedom, and for righteousness.

"History will judge how you repay the sacrifice of the sacred dead. Whether you build a foundation upon the rock of morality, as the Bible teaches us, or on the shifting sands of expedience and politics, as some would recommend. It is your choice how you will be remembered, what your new state will be known for, how this convention will be recorded for posterity.

"Gentlemen, I beseech you to do the *right* thing at this decisive moment in time, though it may not be the *easy* thing. The right path rarely is the easiest, and yet in the end it is worth the sweat and toil, for men who choose to take it will receive the laurels of history.

"Gentlemen, you all know of what I speak. Bring West Virginia into our beloved Union of the United States of America as a *free state!*

"Deny the Slave Power! Deny the aristocrats from eastern Virginia who have selfishly led our people into the dark abyss of civil war and self-murder to assuage their own greed and line their own pockets.

"Even now as we endeavor to break from them and create our own state, still they exert their noisome influence. They whisper of endless insurrection and guerrilla war if we displease them. They threaten and cajole and wheedle. They snivel and whine. They are tireless and shameless in the pursuit of their wants. And they care nothing for the wants of other men. They care nothing for the loyal free people of this new state and wish only to put them back under their domineering thumb.

"Do not fear them; their threats are toothless! Do not bow to them; their promises are empty!

"Do the right thing: refuse them! Make a brave and historic stand against their madness for freedom's sake. Bring the Union a *free* state!

"In the Book of Galatians, chapter five, verse one it says, '*Stand fast therefore in the liberty wherewith Christ hath made us free, and be not entangled again with the yoke of bondage.*'"

He turned and walked back toward his seat in the gallery. Many of those present, both delegates and guests, stood to their feet in enthusiastic applause. Several reached out to shake his hand or pat him on the back, smiling at him as he walked down the aisle.

Nathan was pleased and uplifted by their reception. It reminded him of the response to his speech at the Lewisburg Courthouse back before the secession. Lest he get too high, however, he reminded himself how those good feelings had not lasted. Those same people had later shunned him, though he himself had not changed.

When he returned to his seat on the bench next to Margaret, Tom reached across to give him a firm handshake and a hearty smile, whispering, "Well done, sir!"

Margaret leaned into him and gave his arm a squeeze by way of thanks and congratulations. Harry the Dog looked up at him a moment, then went back to gazing about the room, his tongue hanging out to one side, dripping a steady stream onto the beautiful hardwood floor.

John Carlile was the next to speak. As expected, after formal greetings, he launched into a "friendly" rebuttal of Nathan's speech:

"Gentlemen, I have the utmost respect for Nathan Chambers. He is one of the *truly* great men in our new state. Of that there can be no doubt. And I couldn't agree more concerning the Slave Power. I fear them not, and care nothing for their wants or needs. In fact, Mr. Chambers and I fought them together, tooth and nail, at the recent Secession Convention in Richmond, though we ultimately failed, as y'all know.

"Where I respectfully disagree with Mr. Chambers is concerning the whole free state, slave state issue. But you will never hear me argue in favor of slavery. I am morally opposed to it, and personally have no use for it. I would much rather see an emphasis on fair wages for good, honest labor. I would see slavery brought to its ultimate, inevitable end even as history demands.

"But what I *will* argue for, is West Virginia joining the Union on an equal footing with *every other state in the Union!* Ever since the Kansas-Nebraska Act, states have been free to choose their *own* path in this regard.

"I have heard it argued the federal government will never accept our statehood unless we come in as a free state. I say *nonsense!* No other state is required to outlaw slavery in their constitution. They may do so or *not* of their own free will. So why should we be *forced* to do so? Are we to be deemed a *lesser* state than the others? With fewer freedoms and rights?

"Even the United States Constitution does not outlaw slavery. Will we then agree to more restrictive rights than those enshrined in the supreme law of the land? What next? Will we be required to forfeit, *freedom of speech? Freedom of religion?*

"Gentlemen, if we specifically address slavery in our constitution, are we not simply bowing to the wishes of the administration presently holding power in Washington? What if Mr. Lincoln and his Republican Party fail to win the next election? Shall we then be forced to change our laws to suit the pleasure of the next executive, whomever that may be?

"Gentlemen, I submit to you … leaving the slavery issue out of our constitution does not mean bowing to the Slave Power, but rather it means *not* bowing to the power in Washington. It means allowing West Virginians, like the citizens of every other state, to choose their own course, in their own time. It means we will not be compelled to make our decisions by outside forces who may or may not have our best interests at heart.

"Like Mr. Chambers, I ask you to take a stand—a stand for the principle that West Virginians are the equals of any other citizens of the Union. That West Virginia shall have the very same rights and responsibilities as every other state in the Union, neither more nor less.

"Thank you for your thoughtful consideration of my arguments, and for your vital and selfless service to our new state."

As John turned and headed back to his seat, amid polite applause, he looked at Nathan, nodded his head, and smiled. Nathan returned the nod and the smile.

Margaret leaned in close and whispered, "Your speech was much better received."

"Maybe ... but his rebuttal was cleverly played. Deflecting my arguments rather than taking them on directly. I am a professional soldier, but he is a professional politician. I fear I am out of my depth in this arena."

She didn't argue but squeezed his arm once again to show where *her* loyalty and affections clearly lay.

಼ಞಬಞ಼ಞಬಞ಼ಞಬಞ

The speeches went on for several more hours, though there were no more guests who came forward to talk, only delegates. Some spoke in favor of Nathan's arguments, and others spoke up for John's. Still others talked about matters important to them, or just gave the kind of speech Nathan would sarcastically classify as "just wanting to hear themselves talk."

One of the delegates by name of Andrew Moore gave a speech that was written almost entirely by Margaret. The two of them had been conspiring about promoting public education for all children in general, and including free black children specifically. But Margaret declined to speak herself, fearing the opinion of a woman might not necessarily be well received among the company, and might even turn some men against whatever she was promoting on general principle.

Though that inclination galled her, it was more important to promote her *cause* than *herself*. So she'd asked Mr. Moore to speak, and he'd agreed if she would write the speech for him. When his speech was over, Nathan gave her arm a squeeze, returning the acknowledgment and congratulation she'd given him earlier.

During the speeches, Tom took copious notes on a small, portable desk he held in his lap. He recorded the opinions of the various delegates, particularly focused on the two main topics that were of interest to Nathan and Margaret: slavery and public education for all children. And he not only recorded the opinions of the speakers, but he also paid attention to the delegates, watching to gauge their reactions. This too he noted.

Tom would have liked to have had William's help on it, and they had discussed it at length. But William was also needed out with the new Eighth regiment training the surgeons, as he'd done with the Seventh. In the end they'd gone to Nathan to decide it. To Nathan the answer was simple; William *must* train the surgeons. The ultimate expertise and efficiency of those men would literally mean the difference between life and death for the soldiers in their care. All other considerations were secondary.

Tom, on the other hand, was no longer especially needed for the regimental training. Though he had extensive knowledge and expertise in all things military, he wasn't needed for his particular area of expertise. The logistics of running a quartermaster's office were already well documented, thanks to the weeks he'd spent upstairs in the military office down the hall from the governor, writing it all down. Now anyone who could read would have access to Tom's years of accumulated knowledge and expertise.

So it was decided Tom would serve as Margaret's *aide de camp* during the Constitutional Convention. He'd take notes, help her write speeches for delegates in agreement with her, run errands for her, and generally serve as her protector and escort during the proceedings.

Nathan would split time between the convention and the regimental training, going back and forth as needed. He'd speak with various delegates whenever Margaret thought it would be helpful, and he'd help strategize with her when needed, but it wasn't necessary for him to sit in on the convention all day every day.

When the speeches finally concluded, and the president brought down the gavel on the first day of the convention, everyone stood. John Carlile immediately walked up to Nathan, held out his hand and said, "No hard feelings, Nathan?"

Nathan took his hand and shook it firmly, "Certainly *not*, John! We've been through too much together to let a little difference of opinion spoil those positive feelings."

"Agreed. Thank you, Nathan. Miss Margaret ... a pleasure as always. Mr. Clark."

"Mr. Carlile."

With that he departed, seeking out whatever delegate he wished to speak to first as they passed out the doors of the room.

And though the handshake had been warm, and the words friendly, Margaret thought she detected a bit of coldness pass between the two men, like their friendship had been strained by their very public disagreement. She decided this convention was going to be a long, hard battle and was likely to test more than just the two men's relationship.

Chapter 8. Old Friends and New

"Old wood best to burn,
old wine to drink,
old friends to trust,
and old authors to read."

– Athenaeus

Tuesday November 26, 1861 – Wheeling, Virginia:

By the time they prepared to leave the Customs House and head for home, it was already dark outside. Fortunately, though it was cool, there was neither wind nor rain, so their ride back to the farm wouldn't be too unpleasant.

They walked down the broad front steps, Tom out front followed by Margaret holding tight to Nathan's arm. Harry padded along behind. Tom noticed a man sitting on the bottom step off to their right. *Odd*, he thought, *a very cool evening to be sitting out in the open on cold, stone steps.*

At the sound of their footfalls, the stranger turned toward them. "Good evening, masters and mistress. Might you spare a few coins for a poor fellow down on his luck?"

A common beggar, Tom decided. He could now see the man wore a shabby, torn coat and a dilapidated felt hat from which long unkempt locks of hair hung. *Likely it's a good place for him, despite the cold, with all the well-to-do gentlemen coming and going during the convention.* But though it was too dark to make out the man's face, something about him tickled the back of Tom's memory.

"Do I ... *know* you, sir?" he asked.

The man chuckled. "That depends ... are you a man who generally distrusts my kind ... until the man proves himself to be something *other* than what he appears?"

Tom smiled, "That would be a fair description of me. But let me ask *you*, sir ... are you the type of vagabond who's in the habit of saving people's lives by guiding them safely away from their enemies? Enemies who would otherwise rob them of life and liberty?"

Nathan and Margaret stood still, gazing from Tom to the stranger, their faces betraying confusion at this very odd conversation.

The man nodded his head, and said, "Yes ... I have been known to indulge in such behavior ... but only when *my employer* has put me up to it ..."

The man stood up and grinned. Tom stepped down to his level and immediately embraced him. "*Joseph!* My God, it's good to see you again, my friend!" he said, standing back and patting Joseph on the sides of his arms. "What a wonderful surprise!"

Nathan stepped down and held out his hand, "That goes doubly for me, Joseph, considering how you helped save my life when we were escaping from Richmond!" Joseph took the proffered hand and shook it firmly, a broad smile now lighting his features.

"Never mention it, Captain! That you are still alive and well is thanks enough for whatever small service I may have performed."

Margaret stepped up next to Nathan. She too now smiled brightly. "*The* Joseph? The man who helped save our beloved Nathan from Henry Wise and his hooligans? I've heard so much about you! Well, met sir, well met, indeed!"

"Joseph, may I introduce my *sister*, Margaret Chambers."

"Ah! Miss Margaret ... I have ... also heard somewhat of *your* circumstances as well. And may I say, I have greatly admired you from afar?"

"Oh, thank you, sir; most kind of you to say. And I am very gratified to finally meet you in person that I might thank you for everything you did on Nathan's behalf."

"You are most welcome, lady."

"But, Joseph," Tom interjected, "*why* are you here?"

"Oh ... isn't that obvious? I have come in answer to your letter on Mr. Chambers' behalf. I figured once I'd traveled far enough to put a response in a Union post office, I might as well go the 'extra mile' and meet y'all in person. So ... here I am!"

"Then welcome, welcome most sincerely, Joseph," Nathan answered. "But ... will you ride with us to our new home south of town? There is a chill in the air, and ... I'd not like to discuss our private matters in so public a place. We would be honored if you would come grace our home with your presence. I'm sure they'll be laying out a warm meal even as we arrive."

"Certainly, Mr. Chambers, I was hoping you'd ask. I most humbly accept your gracious offer of hospitality. I've not had a good, home-cooked meal since ... well, I can't remember when. And you may be pleased to know I still ride the wonderful gelding you gifted me when last we parted, sir. I have named him 'Captain' in your honor! Please ... lead the way, sir."

ᏧᎾᎿᎬᎾᏧᎾᎿᎬᎾᏧᎾᎿᎬᎾ

When they finally pushed their chairs back from their dinner, Joseph patted his stomach and said, "Miss Abbey ... Megs ... thank you most sincerely for that wonderful meal. As I was telling Mr. Chambers, I've been out traveling for such a long time now, I can hardly remember the last good meal I've had."

"Oh, Joseph! It's the very least we can do considering all you did for Nathan and our other men," Miss Abbey answered. Megs nodded her agreement.

He chuckled, "Well ... I'd have done it more happily if I'd known it would be so well rewarded!"

Once all the dishes were cleared away, and the whiskey and brandy were shared around, Nathan turned to Joseph and asked the thing foremost on his mind. "Please, Joseph ... if you would, tell us of the matter we asked you about in our letter."

He smiled, "Certainly, Captain."

Every eye was now on him, eager to hear what he might have discovered.

"I will begin at the beginning. When I received your letter from Tom, I immediately sought out the Employer. He was *not* surprised by its contents, however, informing me Miss Evelyn had already been to see him several days earlier with a similarly worded message. And he'd already been looking into the matter."

"You may speak plainly in this group, Joseph," Nathan said. "Everyone here knows of our concern about Walters, and what he may be up to." And silently he added, *and I shall speak with you later, alone, about Evelyn.*

"Ah ... very good, sir. That will make my story easier to tell. So the Employer had already begun inquiries with all his connections in Richmond and elsewhere, trying to track down Walters. He'd found mention of the name a few times in dispatches from a Colonel Burns stationed in Greenbrier County. Your name also appeared on those telegrams, Mr. Chambers, so you can imagine what they were concerning."

"Yes ... their attack on Mountain Meadows ... and after."

"Indeed. It was clear Walters was working in cooperation with the Colonel, up to the point of that officer's untimely and most fortuitous demise at your hands," he smiled at Nathan and nodded. Nathan returned the nod.

"After that ... we could find nothing. No word of him, and no sign he had enlisted or been commissioned."

"*Damn.* I feared it," Nathan said.

But Joseph raised his hand, "But, I did not give up the hunt there, Mr. Chambers ..."

"Oh? Sorry for interrupting. Pray, do continue, Joseph."

"Thank you. When the Employer reported his findings to me, I became determined to learn the answer for myself. So with his blessing, I rode out from Richmond to see what I might learn. I even went so far as to visit Walters Farm myself."

"Really? That was bold ... I can't imagine Walters being receptive to a man ... well, dressed as you normally are ... no offense, Joseph."

Joseph chuckled, "None taken, Mr. Chambers. As you well know, my present attire is only ... a *disguise* of sorts. But never fear, I have other disguises as well. Believe it or not, I rode up to Mr. Walters' house in a fine black suit and hat, and I had on me papers proving me to be a Confederate States government official—documents which were neatly forged, of course."

Tom shook his head, "I guess it shouldn't surprise me, Joseph, but ... once again you impress me with your cleverness."

Joseph nodded, but continued, "As I said, I rode up to Walters' house to see if I could lay the mystery to rest. And, you may be pleased to hear, Mr. Chambers, if I were to find him at home it was our plan and intention to try to recruit him into military service in my capacity as a representative of the Confederate government."

Nathan's mouth dropped open. "The Employer never ceases to amaze me with his resourcefulness and audacity. As much as I'd hoped Walters *was* enlisted, so he'd be forced to stay safely away from this farm, it had never occurred to me to try to *make* that happen!"

"Yes ... I must agree with you, Mr. Chambers. The Employer is ... a most clever and imaginative fellow. I find he often envisions solutions other men would never consider.

"Anyway, when I arrived, I found Walters not at home. Of course, I ... used my phony status to force my way into his home and interrogate the man he'd left in charge. A very disagreeable fellow who was tasked with keeping the farm running and the slaves in line while the master was away. And if I was to guess, the slaves are even less well off than when Walters is home — the hired man having little reason to care about their wellbeing. Suffice to say I have informed the proper authorities in the Underground Railroad that the place is ripe for an action. I'm hoping they'll be able to intervene to the benefit of all — except Walters, of course. But I digress ...

"The hired man begrudgingly told me what I wanted to know after much prodding and more than a little threatening. It seems Walters has been away from home for something around a month now, and the man does not know where he has gone. I pressed him hard on that point and am convinced he knows nothing. Nor does he know when to expect his master home. Walters gave him no indication of when he intended to return, but apparently said it could be only days, or it could be months. Knowing what we know of Walters, he likely doesn't trust the man, and wants to keep him in constant fear of his master's imminent arrival to keep him honest. But apparently the pay is good, and a large bonus has been promised on his master's return, so he has no intention of abandoning his post. He did believe, however, that Walters had traveled to the west, *not* toward Richmond."

Nathan frowned, "None of this bodes well for us ..."

"That's what I thought when I heard it. But ... well, I guess you know me well enough by now to know I wasn't satisfied with that little amount of information. So I set out to find him if I could. I left Walters Farm and headed west. I stayed in my guise of a Confederate official so I could interrogate citizens and soldiers as I went, searching for any sign of Walters' passing. Since he was well known in Lewisburg, it was simple enough to determine when he was last seen there and where he went after. Approximately a month ago, he purchased supplies from the general store, enough for a month or more of travel. The goods were loaded aboard a couple of pack horses. Oh ... did I mention he had three hired hands with him, all on horseback? And ... I'm sorry to say, they were well armed, and a generous amount of ammunition was included in his purchase."

Nathan sighed a heavy sigh and exchanged a hard look with Tom.

"The four of them departed Lewisburg heading west, that much I know for certain.

"After that the trail became more difficult. West of Lewisburg Walters is not well known, so I had to depend on less reliable accounts. 'I may have seen a fellow like that' ... 'yeah, I seen a fellow something of the sort, except he was taller and had darker hair,' and so on, and so forth. At the fork twenty-five miles west of town I had to choose between turning north and continuing west.

"I chose west, since that country was still held by the Confederacy, which would allow me to continue my present ruse. But despite very rigorous interrogations, including a nearly disastrous one of a Confederate colonel who became suspicious and nearly had me arrested — but that's another story for another day — I came up empty.

"So after a week or so, I backtracked to the fork in the road and headed north. I was immediately rewarded by the report of a recent sighting near Summersville. The man described Walters very precisely. But instead of three men, he was now accompanied by six, all mounted and well-armed.

"I took up the trail again, but … well, ironically, I was stymied by running out of enemy territory. I was forced to abandon my role as a Confederate for fear of encountering a Union patrol. I can only imagine my fate were they to find me riding around with papers identifying me as a Confederate official!

"So having no equivalent Union papers—a serious oversight on my part—I was forced to abandon my stylish clothing and return to my … more *usual* attire, such as I'm now wearing. And it nearly broke my heart to bury that beautiful suit and hat out in the woods along with my forged documents before continuing on my way." He sighed.

"It also made my job much more difficult. Easy enough to demand people answer your questions when they think you're someone of authority, but a vagabond? You're lucky if they will even look at you, much less talk with you. So I had to revert to stealthier and less straightforward inquiries. I picked up on a few likely rumors at Suttonsville, which eventually led me in a northeasterly direction all the way to Buckhannon. But from there the trail led up into the mountains to the east. You gentlemen know that area well, I believe?"

"Indeed, we do! Rich Mountain where we recently fought the battle is only a few miles from there," Nathan answered.

"Precisely. I wandered for a week and more around those mountains. Even had a word with the Hart family at their now famous farmhouse on the pass up Rich Mountain."

Nathan smiled and nodded, remembering the heroic part played by young David Hart, who led General Rosecrans up the backside of the mountain to launch his surprise attack against the enemy near the family's farmhouse.

"There were rumors of a new pro-Confederate guerrilla group operating in the area. Burning pro-Union houses, committing various acts of sabotage and murder against Union patrols and facilities, and whatnot. But nothing concrete or definitive that might prove it was Walters.

"But then ... I'm sorry to say the trail went cold. I could find out nothing more without actually joining up with one of the several rebel bands roaming the hills. And though I was tempted to make the attempt, I'd been poking around asking enough questions that I began to fear they might discover my true nature, and then ... well, let's just say if that were to happen I'd not be able to come here and give you my report."

He looked over at Margaret and said, "I'm very sorry, Miss Margaret, that I could not discover anything more definitive. And that I have not come here with better news. I can only imagine how ... *anxious* this must make you."

Though she had a serious, concerned look on her face, she smiled bravely and said, "Never mind that, Joseph ... I thank you for the heroic effort you put in on our behalf. That was ... well above the call of duty, sir. And for that I am extremely grateful."

William sitting next to her, also had a serious, concerned look on his face. He reached over and squeezed her hand under the table. She turned to him and smiled, but it was not a happy look.

"You're most welcome, Miss Margaret. Sorry I couldn't do more, but I thought it important to report to Mr. Chambers before searching further. Just in case ..."

"You did well, Joseph. I can't tell you how impressed I am once again, at your ingenuity and courage. And I thank you—and the Employer—most sincerely for your efforts on our behalf," Nathan said.

Joseph smiled, "Well, Mr. Chambers, I *do* have to say my employer's intentions and my efforts were not *strictly* altruistic concerning this matter."

"Oh? How so?"

"The Employer wishes to help eliminate any impediments to you donning a general's uniform and leading our troops into battle. He seems to hold a very high opinion of you in that regard."

Nathan exchanged a look with Miss Abbey and Megs, then said, "Thank you for saying so, Joseph."

Then Tom said, "If Walters is somewhere in the Rich Mountain area that's ... hmm ... just over a hundred miles from here. Not nearly far enough for comfort. What now, Captain?"

"For now ... we wait. And we watch," Nathan answered, and shared a serious look with Margaret.

ಐಐಖಜ಼ಐಐಖಜ಼ಐಐಖಜ಼ಐ

After Joseph was shown to his room, he heard a knock on the door. "Come," he answered. Nathan stepped in and closed the door behind him.

"Mr. Chambers."

"Joseph. Sorry to disturb you, but ... before you settle in for the night, I wanted to inquire of you about Miss Evelyn. How she is doing and so forth. I've had no message from her for several months, which I'm sure is not for lack of trying, on her part."

"Yes, the passing of mail between the two sides is rather sporadic and unreliable at this point. It was clever of you to send—*I am only assuming here*—to send one of your men across enemy lines to mail your letters."

"Yes, two men in fact."

"Ah. Anyway, that was well done. And to answer your question, Miss Evelyn seems to be doing well. She is certainly in good health and ... hmm ... of course, I don't know her as well as *you* do, but I have had occasion to see her from time to time in our ... *mutual* line of work. I'd say she seems happier than when I first met her. There's a ... *confidence* I think ... that wasn't there before. Like she is growing into her role. And I understand from the Employer she is becoming ever more vital to his plans and schemes, and continues to impress him with her abilities in every regard."

Nathan wasn't sure what those "plans and schemes" might be, and it worried him what Evelyn might be involved in, but he didn't think it was his place to ask specific details. "None of what you say surprises me, Joseph. Evelyn is ... *special*. In so many ways. I think ... I think she is capable of much more than she knows or believes. I'm beginning to understand that may have been the issue between us, that she believed she was a lesser being

240

for some reason. A belief I have *never* shared, by the way. In my opinion there is nothing *that* woman can't accomplish if she sets her mind to it."

"Agreed, Captain. She seems to me a very impressive and capable young woman ... nay, say rather, an impressive *human being*, be it man or woman."

He eyed Nathan curiously. "Was there something more, sir?"

"I ... was just curious ... did she happen to say anything ... you know ... *personal* ... concerning *me?*"

"Oh! Yes, of course, certainly! I'm so sorry, Mr. Chambers, with all my adventures trying to track down Walters it had fairly been driven from my mind, and the fact you would wish to know.

"First, I should tell you she was *most* distraught and concerned about the safety of you and your family with Walters still out there somewhere, threatening God knows what. She was most insistent the Employer do everything in his power to aid you."

Nathan nodded, but said nothing.

"And then ... she ... became quite emotional and volunteered to come with me to search for Walters, and after ... to report to you *in person* on the findings. But the Employer talked her out of it, convincing her it was too dangerous, and she had other more pressing duties in Richmond.

"I recall she responded, in almost a whisper, 'Sometimes I think I would risk *all*, even my very life, just to see *him* one more time.' And then she wiped a tear and departed the room saying no more. But ... I don't believe she was speaking of Walters when she said '*him*,' do you, sir?"

Nathan breathed a heavy sigh, "No ... I expect *not*. Thank you, Joseph, and good night."

"Good night, Captain."

But as Nathan reached out for the doorknob, Joseph said, "Oh, wait!" Nathan turned and saw Joseph slapping his forehead. "I nearly forgot and hadn't made the connection until just now ... I believe I may have something for you, sir."

Nathan raised an eyebrow, but waited for Joseph to explain, "Just as I was saddling my horse preparing to depart Richmond on my long journey, Miss Evelyn startled me by stepping up to me in the stall—a stall whose location I had believed was known only to me, by the way," he shook his head and had a thoughtful look.

"Yes, a very resourceful woman, as you've said … anyway, she reached out and slipped a small envelope into my pocket, saying, 'There is nothing incriminating in it, so if it falls into the wrong hands there is no harm. When the time comes you will know what to do with it.' Then she turned and strode away with no further explanation. I pulled it from my pocket and saw it was sealed and contained only a large letter *N* on the front. I pocketed it again, and have thought little further of it until just a moment ago. But now I am inclined to think 'N' may be for Nathan. What do you think, sir?"

Nathan nodded, "Yes … I think it likely and at any rate I am willing to risk being wrong." He extended his hand as Joseph picked up his knapsack from the floor and began rummaging through. In a moment he pulled out the envelope.

"Sorry, a little crumpled, but … still sealed at least. Here you are. If it turns out it isn't for you, I would be obliged if you'd return it that I might puzzle out its true purpose. And if it is for you … I pray it provides what you are looking for."

"Thank you, Joseph. Thank you very much, and goodnight once again."

"Goodnight, sir."

ಬಿಞಿಣಿಚಿಬಿಞಿಣಿಚಿಬಿಞಿಣಿಚಿ

Nathan sat on his bed, leaning over toward the night table to read the letter in the light of an oil lamp burning there:

Dearest N.,

I have felt a terrible dread since receiving your recent letter requesting our aid. Rest assured I have done all you've asked for and more to that end. I pray it will bear fruit as intended.

My days are filled with fervent prayer for the health and safety of your wonderful family, your stalwart men, and all those you have so graciously taken under your protective wing.

But my nights are filled with dreams of you, which is both a comfort and an aching emptiness all at once.

You may be pleased to know the matter that so mysteriously caused so much trouble and consternation back at M.M. is no more. I believe my actions since returning to R. have driven this vexing conundrum completely from my being, and I no longer fear its return.

Last, I pray for a swift end to this terrible conflict that you and I might pick back up where things were before I so abruptly failed you. Hoping you still may feel the same.

Your true friend … and more?
E.

Nathan flopped back onto the bed with a groan, still holding the letter in one hand and wiping his eyes with the other.

ಐಐೲೲಐಐೲೲಐಐೲೲ

"Varina, I would like you to meet a very dear friend of mine, Miss Evelyn Hanson," Angeline said, as Evelyn stepped up to where Varina Davis sat in the large living area that now served as a formal reception room in the Confederate Presidential Mansion, also known as the "Confederate White House." Evelyn had had to wait her turn for the formal introduction, as there had been a number of "higher ranking" ladies ahead of her.

Evelyn curtsied in the formal manner, but Varina, who was eight months pregnant with her fifth child, stayed seated, cooling herself with an elegant folding fan made of white lace. It was an unseasonably warm day in November for Richmond, sunny and almost cloudless, with very little breeze. Though the windows were open, Evelyn felt the room heating up, though it was only early afternoon. *And it probably doesn't help that the room is nearly overflowing with ladies,* she decided. Though there were a number of chairs spread about the room, most of the ladies were forced to stand as they sipped their tea and ate their small, sweet biscuits.

These ladies were the very *creme de la creme* of Richmond's upper crust, all elegantly dressed for a formal tea. Several of these ladies were already customers of Evelyn's business—that of supplying personal handmaids and butlers who were thoroughly trained in the traditional formal European manner, such as servants of royalty would be. And for those ladies whose husbands were important government officials or military officers, these highly skilled servants also worked as Evelyn's spies, surreptitiously collecting intelligence for her on behalf of the Union.

"Oh, yes ... I believe you have spoken of Miss Evelyn previously, Angeline," Varina answered. "Miss Evelyn ... a pleasure, my dear. And ... *oh my* ... Angeline, didn't you say Miss Evelyn was ... oh, I don't wish to be indelicate but ... *unattached?* Miss Evelyn ... surely it can't be true ... a lady of your exquisite charms, must simply be overrun with suitors. I can't believe you're not already married to the wealthiest and most handsome gentleman in Richmond, whoever that may be."

And though the line of questioning was borderline rude and definitely inappropriate for a first meeting, Varina spoke with such warmth and genuine sincerity that Evelyn had a hard time taking offense. And it was, after all, a compliment of sorts, though a bit of a back-handed one. Still, Evelyn felt herself blushing, feeling the eyes of all the ladies standing nearby beating down upon her.

"The pleasure is all mine, Miss Varina. And as for the other ... I was ... *very close* to someone for a time. But, I'm afraid it ended badly, and is not something I am fond of discussing. It has taken me ... some time to get over it, I'm afraid. And likely I've not given the ... how shall I say—*interested gentlemen?*—the attention they are no doubt deserving of."

"Oh ... perfectly understandable, my dear. When Jefferson and I were first engaged and a grand family wedding was at hand, we suffered a ... *disagreement* ... and canceled the whole affair. It wasn't until several months later we mended things and went ahead with a more modest nuptial.

"And I must apologize, my dear—where have my manners gone? That was a most unseemly line of inquiry. Come ... sit with me, will you please, that I might make amends. I am certain we shall become the very best of friends, if even half of the good things Angeline speaks of you are true."

"Thank you, Miss Varina. It would be a pleasure, though no apology is necessary," Evelyn answered, flashing her most dazzling smile.

Of course, Angeline had set the entire thing up. The formal reception at the president's mansion for the most important women in town was all a cover to introduce Evelyn to Varina Davis, and to get her into this house. Evelyn marveled at Angeline's ability to pull off such an event—basically inviting herself and all her upper-class acquaintances to a reception at another woman's house—and the presidential manor, no less!

And it was critical that Jefferson Davis should be out of town on government business at the time, so his office would be unoccupied and available for Evelyn's purposes. So far, Angeline had come through on all counts. But Evelyn knew the difficult and dangerous part was yet to come. She forced herself to remain calm and relaxed—chatting amiably with Varina—that she would not betray her growing anxiety over what she must do next.

☞☜☞☜☞☜☞☜☞☜

Prior to the formal reception for Varina, Jonathan and Angeline had left nothing to chance, preparing Evelyn for her mission in every conceivable way. First, Jonathan had acquired a blueprint of the presidential mansion. Then through his contacts he had learned which room served as Jefferson Davis's office, and how it was laid out. Fortunately for their purposes, the office was on the first floor, so there'd be no need for a risky trek up and down stairs. Jonathan had had Evelyn study the lower floor blueprint until she had it memorized, then he'd taken it away, provided her with a large sheet of parchment, pen, and inkwell, and had her draw it out from memory. If she missed any detail, he forced her to do it again until she felt she could do it in her sleep.

And since she'd be unable to take any documents away with her, and there'd not be time to write anything down, she'd be forced to memorize any important details she read: dates, places, names of officers, numbers of soldiers, formation designations, etc. All could be critical, and Davis's desk might be filled with dozens or even hundreds of such documents, likely mixed in with any number of innocuous and mundane ones.

Evelyn wondered if Davis's desk at his home might only contain personal items, since he presumably had an official government office elsewhere where he conducted his presidential duties. But Jonathan assured her he had it on good authority that Davis suffered from some sort of chronic, regular illness which caused him to prefer conducting business from his home. As a result, it seemed likely his home desk would have more critical information than his little-used official government one.

Jonathan was especially interested in her uncovering any references to General Jackson and the Shenandoah Valley District he commanded. So he had Evelyn memorize all the Confederate regiments known to be under Jackson's command, including Jubal Collins' Twenty-Seventh Virginia—but she already knew that one!

Once again, Jonathan had seemingly thought of everything. He had his men draw up dozens of official-looking but phony military and government reports and documents, along with many other innocuous ones: bills, personal letters, etc. He then set up a room in his house with a layout and furniture similar to that of President Davis's office, including even the very same model of desk; he'd acquired a copy from the same cabinet maker who'd built the one for Davis earlier in the year. This meant they not only knew about two secret, hidden compartments and the mechanism for opening them, they also had a key that would fit the three locking drawers.

Once the room was set up and the desk was in place facing the door, Jonathan positioned the fake documents in the room in the sort of semi-haphazard fashion that was typical of most people. The desk was filled with them, inside and on top, while others were scattered about the room in and on various pieces of furniture. Evelyn was then sent in to search through the office, find the important documents while ignoring the unimportant ones, and memorize any important details. All while being timed by Jonathan. Afterward she would sit and tell Jonathan what she had discovered, and he would critique her, telling her any details she got wrong, and any critical documents she missed, and where they'd been located.

Then he would replace all the documents with new ones and have her do it again. And then again.

They practiced for an entire day, until Evelyn was feeling exhausted, but completely confident. And they'd determined that seven minutes would be her limit; five was never quite enough, but ten seemed dangerously lengthy and generally unnecessary — anything not found in the first seven minutes was not worth the additional risk. Of course, she always searched the hidden compartments in the desk first; it stood to reason Davis would store the most critical and secret documents there.

So now, even as she sat sipping tea and discussing various innocuous subjects with Varina Davis, she reviewed the layout of the house in her mind and awaited Angeline's cue to begin the operation.

She hadn't long to wait, as one of the black maids stepped up to Varina, bowed, and said, "Missus, there's a gentleman here, says he has come on the request of Miss Angeline. The gentleman carries a violin in a case, Missus."

Varina looked over at Angeline and raised an eyebrow. Angeline smiled broadly, "Varina, dearest, I promised to keep you entertained in the discomfort of your last months of pregnancy, and I intend to keep my promise."

Varina smiled, and tilted her head curiously, turning back to the maid and saying, "Bring the gentleman in, if you please, Betsey."

"Very good, Missus," the maid answered, and retreated from the room.

Angeline stood, and crossed to the side of the room opposite where Varina and Evelyn continued to sit.

"Excuse me ladies … may I please have your attention," Angeline said in a loud, commanding voice. Evelyn admired how Angeline always seemed to be in control of any given situation. When she asked the other ladies to do something, they generally did it.

But this was also Evelyn's cue … she leaned over toward Varina and whispered, "If you will excuse me a moment, I must just visit your water closet."

"Oh, certainly, my dear. Shall I show you the way?"

"Oh, no … you must stay and see what Angeline has in store for you. I will ask one of the maids, you needn't trouble yourself."

"Very well, my dear. Just go down the hall in the back of the room to our left. There will be a maid down toward the back rooms who can direct you."

"Thank you, Miss Varina," she answered, and turned to slip away, even as Angeline began her announcement.

"Dear Ladies, in honor of our beloved First Lady, I have invited Richmond's preeminent musician, Max Sherman to join us today for a private performance. If you have not yet had the privilege of hearing Mr. Sherman perform, let me assure you, you are in for a beautiful treat …"

Angeline's voice faded into the background, along with the sound of applause as Evelyn walked down the hallway toward the water closet. Halfway down the hallway, she saw a young black maid making a bed in the bedroom to her left. The maid looked up at the sound of her footsteps.

"Can I help you, missus?" she asked, with a simple curtsy.

"Yes … would you be so kind as to direct me to the water closet, my dear?"

The maid smiled, "Oh yes, certainly missus. Please just follow me," she said, stepping out into the hallway and turning left in the direction Evelyn was already headed. Of course, Evelyn knew perfectly well where the water closet was, along with every other detail on the lower level of the house. But she had to pretend she knew nothing, since she'd never been in the house before.

When they reached the water closet, Evelyn turned to the maid and said, "I'm afraid I'm feeling a bit … indisposed, so likely I'll be in there a while. You needn't wait for me; I can easily find my way back to the gathering. Please do go back about your business."

"Yes, missus," the maid said, bowed, turned, and walked back the way they'd come.

Evelyn entered the water closet and closed the door. She waited a full minute, then quietly opened the door, stepped out into the hall, and reclosed the door, being careful to make as little sound as possible. Then she turned and continued down the hall toward Jefferson Davis's office.

When she reached the office, she found the door closed, but unlocked. She entered, closed the door behind her, and moved immediately to the desk, then moved around to the other side where Davis would sit. She reached around the left side to where one of the hidden compartments lay and opened it. But it was empty—*oops, that's not a good sign,* she thought, then moved to the second secret compartment and opened it. This one contained a letter; she quickly read it and returned it to the compartment. It was written by Davis himself addressed to his cabinet. In it he complained about General Joseph Johnston becoming snappish and insubordinate. Interesting, as Johnston and Davis were considered to be close friends and allies, but not immediately useful for her purposes. She presumed he'd kept it hidden as he'd not yet presented it to his cabinet and was probably debating whether or not he should.

She moved on, starting with the surface of the desk, mentally noting anything of a military nature. But she found little of interest.

She then started with the top left drawer—it was unlocked, which she also took as a bad sign. Either Davis was entirely trusting, which seemed unlikely of a man in his position, or the desk held nothing of importance. This drawer held only correspondence of a personal nature.

But the second drawer down *was* locked. *Good,* she thought, *maybe we're finally getting somewhere.* She pulled the key from the hidden pouch sewn inside her left sleeve and unlocked the drawer. She pulled out a stack of papers, placing them on the desk before going through them one by one. The first two were uninteresting, but the third contained a request from General Jackson for additional military equipment: food, fodder, clothing, and most of all ammunition—and lots of it! He was also asking for additional artillery, mainly four-pounders of the type easily transported ... as for ... an offensive? She went back through the numbers, memorizing the various quantities being requested. Further down the stack of papers she found a sheet signed by Confederate Secretary of War Judah Benjamin with orders moving additional regiments to Winchester, Jackson's headquarters in the Shenandoah Valley. *This is better,* she thought, and grinned. *If only I can find something telling me when he means to attack and in which direction ...*

But even as she leaned down to close the second drawer, a movement caught her eye and she looked up. The office door was opening!

Though they'd discussed various contingencies, including lies she might tell to explain her actions should she be caught during some part of the operation, this was the worst possible timing. She watched as the door came open, and a black man stepped in. He was a middle-aged man with graying hair at the sides, dressed in a formal black suit. Evelyn recognized him as the butler who had welcomed them in at the front door.

He had a frown on his face but said nothing as he quietly closed the door behind him and stepped up to the desk.

Despite everything she'd discussed and practiced with Jonathan, Evelyn felt suddenly frozen in place, and could think of nothing to say or do. She'd been caught red-handed, and she could think of no plausible, believable lie that would convince even a child of her innocence. So she said nothing, waiting to see what the butler might do.

He looked at her a moment, then said, "I'll not embarrass you, Missus, by asking what you're doing here and why ... if you'll not insult me by telling some kinda lie."

She met eyes with him for a moment, then said, "Very well. Then ... what now ... uh, Henry, wasn't it?"

"Yes, that's right, Henry ma'am, but most folks just call me Hank. And I recall you was introduced to the Missus as Miss Evelyn Hanson, so don't bother lying about that neither."

"I wouldn't dream of it, Hank."

"So ... when I saw you slip in here, I thought to myself, 'why would a white person want to sneak into Mr. Jefferson Davis's office?' And the only thing I could think of was to see if'n he kept any sort o' secrets in there amongst his papers. Now I for one, bein' uneducated in the areas o' readin' and writin', couldn't tell you for sure, but I'm guessin' it's so. What do you think, Missus?"

"Yes ... it's a reasonable theory, Hank."

"Course, I heard o' them sort of folks, what's called a 'spy,' but I done always pictured a man—sort o' small and sneaky like—but not never a lady, such as yourself."

Evelyn nodded, but said, "So again, I ask ... what now, Hank? Will you turn me over to your Missus and tell her I'm a spy? Because insulting or no, then I'll be forced to make up a story to try to convince her it isn't true."

"Well, Miss Evelyn, it also occurred to me the only folks that'd be interested in Mr. Davis's secrets would be them that wants the Union side—of Mr. Lincoln—to win the war. And me bein' a slave—though well treated, I'll grant you, but still a slave—it would seem I'd not want to discourage such behavior, don't you think?"

"Yes ... that would seem reasonable, Hank. One might suggest you and I are ... natural allies in the current troubles."

"It could be said, yes. But on the other hand ... Miss Varina treats me pretty good, for a slave, and she don't much care for the whole slavery thing, nor the Confederate government and such, even though her husband is ... well, what he is."

"And yet ... you are still her slave ..."

"Yes ... that is the heart of the matter."

"So ...?"

"So, I will make you a deal, Miss Evelyn. When the time comes I want to get away ... I mean *all* the way away ... up into the North, you is gonna help me. And for that I'm not gonna turn you over for a spy."

"You want me to help you escape from this house?"

"No, Missus. I can get my own self outta this here house, easy enough. It's after that I'm gonna have a hard time ... gettin' clean outta Virginia. And I reckon you wouldn't be doin' what I just seen you doin' if you didn't know people that could help me do that. Do I have it right, Miss Evelyn?"

Evelyn smiled, and extended her hand, "You have it right, Hank. And you have yourself a deal."

They shook hands, then Hank said, "Time to go, Miss Evelyn, 'fore someone else spots you."

She looked longingly at the next drawer down, the one that possibly held the answers to General Jackson's coming offensive. But she knew Hank was right, so she closed and locked the open drawer, then followed him to the door, and out into the hall.

There they parted ways with a smile and a nod, before she slipped back into the reception room and sat back down next to Varina, who was so enraptured with Mr. Sherman's performance that she never even noticed Evelyn's return.

ℰ𝒹ℰ𝒹ℭ𝒮ℭ𝒮ℰ𝒹ℰ𝒹ℭ𝒮ℭ𝒮ℰ𝒹ℰ𝒹ℭ𝒮ℭ𝒮

A few days after Joseph's departure, Nathan and Margaret talked quietly in the lower hallway of the Customs House at the end of a long day in the Constitutional Convention. They were waiting for Tom to return from checking in at the post office to see if they had any mail. When they finally saw him striding down the hall toward them they could see he had a smile on his face, and assumed it was some good news.

"Let me guess ... a letter from Adilida?" Nathan asked as Tom stepped up to them.

"No, but almost as good. It's from Captain Hawkins of the Seventh."

"Ah, excellent! Finally some news from him. We've heard nothing at all since they captured Romney. Funny ... though we no longer have any official association with the Seventh, still they somehow feel ... well, like our child, I guess."

"A rather noisy, unruly, and rambunctious child," Tom said with a chuckle. Nathan smiled and nodded, and Margaret giggled.

"Would you be so kind as to read Mr. Hawkins' letter to us, Tom, if you please?"

"Certainly, sir—with pleasure."

Nov. 20, 1861
Romney, Va.

Dear Mr. Chambers,

The Seventh is now well settled into camp at Romney after our capture of the town nearly a month ago. Speaking of, I have seen the reports in the papers to my great disappointment. Said reports make our action sound routine and little more than a skirmish, but nothing could be further from the truth. The Seventh performed admirably, and I like to think you would've been proud of us, sir.

As we approached the town the rebs, who were dug in on the far side of the South Fork, opened up on us with two cannon. Colonel Kelley ordered our artillery to answer, and for a time we had a duel across the river. What a noise! Sadly a shell landed in our midst, and the Seventh lost its first soldier in the war, Pvt. Jesse Taylor, a fine strong young man.

Then Col. Kelley gave the order to attack and our infantry jumped up with a great shout, raced down the hill and across the bridge, even as our cavalry splashed across the river. I now lead Company A, which was the first across the bridge. The rebs fired their guns but were overwhelmed, and soon broke and ran, our cavalry in hot pursuit as our infantry captured their two big guns. We killed somewhere between thirty and forty of the enemy, wounded several dozen more and captured fifty-some others.

*And despite what was said in the papers we only lost the
one man in the battle, with around twenty wounded. All
in all, a heady, lop-sided victory – officially the first action
of the regiment. We even received a telegram of
congratulations from the President and General Scott!*

*But now the camp has become dull and routine. It has
become very cold and many are falling sick. Hoping we'll
not be obliged to spend the winter here.*

*Give my best regards to your fine men, family, and the
governor should you deem it appropriate.*

*Your obedient servant and loyal friend,
Capt. J. Hawkins,
Company A, Seventh Loyal Virginia*

"Well, that's very gratifying to hear," Tom said.

Nathan nodded, but said, "Yes, it certainly sounds like our
training and organization has been to good effect so far. And Lt.
Colonel Kelley appears to be proving himself a competent leader,
as we'd hoped. But ... I fear Mr. Hawkins is mistaken about one
thing."

"What's that, sir?"

"Hmm ... though I'm sure it seemed a very great battle to him,
from what he describes this really was little more than a skirmish
after all."

Tom nodded, and added, "I have a feeling as the war wears on
he will discover that truth for himself, sir. Most likely the hard
way, sadly."

৪৩৫৩৫৪৩৫৪৩৫৪৩৫৪৩৫৪৩৫৪৩৫

Nathan sat by himself in the "War Room" in the Customs
House, a few doors down from the governor's humble office. He
was wading his way through a stack of papers containing lists of
officer candidates, including descriptions, letters of
recommendation, etc. for the new Eighth Infantry, and the Ninth,
which would be coming after. It was a dreary task made the more

so by his general opinion that all the candidates fell far short of the ideal.

Not for the first time, nor the last, he wished Tom was there to help him with it. But Tom was busy downstairs in the Constitutional Convention assisting Margaret.

He sighed a heavy sigh as he set down the latest missive — the man had actually included a letter of recommendation from *his own mother!* Nathan shook his head in disbelief and reached for the next sheet of paper.

But happily, he was saved from further tedium by the sound of voices coming from down the hall toward the governor's office. He heard Governor Pierpont's great booming voice, the tone of it betraying warmth and enthusiasm. Clearly, he was greeting someone who's arrival had been entirely unexpected, but much appreciated.

"Well! *My goodness, sir!* This is a great honor and privilege! I am so happy to finally meet you in person!"

"The honor is all mine, governor!" he heard a familiar voice answer back.

Nathan's eyes widened, and he leapt from his chair and strode out into the hallway. He was not surprised to see a man standing there in a dark blue Union officer's uniform — the gold star on each shoulder identified him as a brigadier general.

Nathan called out, "Well, your honor, it seems the standards of this gubernatorial office have diminished to a new low — apparently they'll let *anyone* in at the door these days!"

"Chambers!" General Rosecrans exclaimed, turning from the governor and striding down the hall to meet Nathan halfway. The two men shook hands warmly, patting each other on the shoulder with their free hands. "And hello there, Harry, my old friend," Rosecrans said, reaching down to scratch Harry on the top of his huge head. Nathan was surprised the dog seemed almost happy about the greeting. *Next thing you know he'll start wagging his tail and licking people, like a normal dog, and then where will we be?* He suppressed a chuckle at the image the thought invoked.

Governor Pierpont came and joined them, standing next to the general. Nathan noticed another Union officer following the governor, but hadn't seen his face, assuming he was a member of the general's staff.

"To what do we owe the pleasure, William?" Nathan asked, a broad smile lighting his features.

"I was just about to ask the same," Pierpont said.

"I've moved my headquarters to Wheeling for winter camp. Just arrived today, and thought I'd pay my respects to you two gentlemen."

"Winter camp? Well, then you'll be here for some time ... that's *excellent* news, sir. It is so good to see you again."

"Likewise, Nathan, likewise, though you may change your mind when you find out what I have in mind for you."

"Oh?"

He turned toward Pierpont, "With your permission, governor, I'd like to use Mr. Chambers' expertise to my advantage while I have him within easy spitting distance. I'll be working on my spring battle plans and am of a mind to shamelessly abuse his good humor and patience in helping me and my staff build out our strategy."

Nathan grinned, clearly *not* put off by the prospect.

"Yes, yes, certainly. I shall be happy to not hear his grumbling for a spell," Pierpont said. "He's become peevish lately — getting mighty tired of wading through training and recruitment paperwork, I expect. Perhaps we could make a small trade, general ... say, one of your staff officers to help us organize the new Eighth in exchange for Mr. Chambers working on your strategy?"

"*Sold*, your honor! I'll send a man over as soon as we get ourselves settled into our new HQ and winter camp. Perhaps, say ... toward the end of next week?"

"Excellent!"

Then General Rosecrans looked at Nathan and said, "I've brought along an old friend of yours, Nathan ... one of your classmates from West Point, I'm told." He stepped to the side and gestured to the officer who'd been quietly following behind.

Nathan saw the man clearly for the first time. He noted the Captain's bars on the uniform shoulders, then a familiar face. And though his dark hair was a bit thinner, leading to a higher forehead, and his face a bit rounder, Nathan recognized him immediately. "*Charles!* Charles Leib! I guess I should say, *Captain* Leib now! It's been ... hmm ... seventeen years, five months, and six days since we last saw each other at West Point."

"Exactly right, Nathan!" Captain Leib answered with a bright smile and a firm handshake. Though he hadn't a clue if Nathan was right or not about the time, he remembered Nathan's particular abilities in that regard well enough not to question him on it.

"My *God*, sir," Nathan said, "wherever have you been all these years? You left after the second year at West Point and I've never heard of you since ... except wild rumors, of course. Someone said you'd become a doctor, as I recall."

"Yes, that I did. Among several other things. Even got involved in politics ... helped Mr. Lincoln on his run for senate, and later for president. Made some bad enemies over that one ..."

He shook his head slowly and gazed at the floor for a few moments, as if recalling a distant memory. Then he looked back up and smiled, "Never could stand to stick with one thing or stay in one place very long."

Nathan turned toward the other men and said, "Charles was the very life of our West Point class the first two years. While McClellan was the boot licker, George Pickett the prankster, and Thomas Jackson — now 'Stonewall' Jackson, I suppose — the dour and all too serious killjoy, Charles was always the proverbial class clown. The one who had us in stiches. You always knew if there was raucous laughter coming from the boys in the barracks, Charles was somewhere in the middle of it."

"Good of you to say, Nathan. I was always fond of reciting a funny story or spouting out a witty line, true ... true."

"Well, then ... not much has changed I'd say," General Rosecrans said with a grin. "Except perhaps that Captain Leib has proven himself an extremely capable and reliable quartermaster. We're very happy to have him in the Western Virginia Department."

"Oh? Good for you Charles, good for you. An extremely difficult, challenging, and thankless task, to be sure. Well … I for one am appreciative, and I thank you for your service, sir."

"Thank you, Nathan. Most gracious of you. There are so very few who understand the demands of the position. I am almost constantly the subject of stern criticism and vehement animosity—everyone from the farmer who thinks I owe him for the pig taken by soldiers, to the colonel who wants me to buy him oats for his private horse. They all think I'm surely the most reprehensible scoundrel alive for telling them 'no!'"

"I shall have to introduce you to my man Tom Clark. He was my quartermaster out in Texas at Fort Davis. I've been forced to endure many such tales of woe from him as well. I'm sure the two of you will have much to commiserate about in that regard and will get along famously."

"Yes, certainly … it would be a great pleasure to make his acquaintance. I'm very much looking forward to it."

"I too can vouch for Captain Leib's good conduct," Pierpont added, "though until now I've only known him by reputation and results. Despite the inevitable grumblings from highly suspect sources, the good captain has proven himself the most honorable and capable of officers. Firm but fair, and the welfare of the brave soldiers at the front and the interests of the government always foremost."

"Thank you for saying so, your honor."

"Charles, are you also here for the winter months?" Nathan asked.

"Oh, no. Just for a few days to help the general get his winter camp in order—to make sure he has everything he'll need. Then it's back to Clarksburg for me. That's the main Union supply depot for the Department of Western Virginia, as you no doubt know. They seem fairly unable to get along without me these days, though I must say a few days away will be a great pleasure and respite."

"Well, then we must at least take advantage of you while you're here. General, I'm sure your staff will be busy getting your office set up this evening. Won't you and Captain Leib come out to the house and have dinner with my family tonight? I am eager to hear about your recent campaigns and to get caught up with Charles on all his doings since West Point. And Miss Abbey would love to finally meet you in person, sir, after hearing all my glowing reports. Of course, my men will be also be thrilled to see you again. They all have fond memories of our *little adventure* at Rich Mountain."

"Hmm ... let me ponder that long enough to give it due consideration, Nathan—*yes!* Thank, you sir. That would be splendid! I would be much obliged," Rosecrans answered with a broad grin.

Then he looked over at Captain Leib, who nodded emphatically, "Yes ... of course, certainly! I've never once been known to turn down a good home-cooked meal. And it will be a great pleasure to have the opportunity to get caught up with you, Nathan, after all these years. And to meet your infamous fellow quartermaster, Mr. Clark."

☙❧☙❧☙❧☙❧☙❧☙❧

It was a jovial gathering at the Belle Meade farmhouse kitchen table that evening. True to form, Captain Leib was the life of the party, trading humorous stories about the trials and tribulations of the quartermaster's duties with Tom Clark, who laughed so hard at one point Nathan thought he would choke.

Nathan found Leib's account of a claim presented by one farmer particularly entertaining, made especially so by Leib's humorous imitation of the man's comically crude use of the English language:

"As I sat at my desk one morning," Leib began, "a farmer entered the office. He was arrayed in all his glorious finery—holey and stained jeans, one pant leg tucked into the top of a boot, and a shirt whose buttons had been fastened offset by one, so the garment hung unevenly, the front tucked into the trousers, but the back hanging loose. An old slouched felt hat tipped back on his head topped off the look. He sauntered across the office, hands stuffed into his front pockets and a tremendous quid of tobacco stuffed into one cheek.

"'Is Cap'n Leib around?' And as he asks me this, a dark juice oozes out the corner of his mouth.

"'Yes, sir. I am Captain Leib. What can I do for you?'

"'Cap'n, I got a bill to settle with the Gov'ment.'

"'Oh,' I said, 'what is it concerning?'

"'Well, sir, it's on account o' a whole lot of things them Union soldiers done took from my farm, when General Rosey-My-Crans went off to Gauley Bridge.'"

General Rosecrans chuckled at the humorous butchering of his name.

Leib continued, "'Let me have a look at that bill.' He handed me a crumpled, torn off half-sheet of paper on which he'd scribbled a list in what could barely be described as English:

> 17 turkes tuck by solgers 20.00. Ditto 81 chicens 5.00.
> Ditto 1 caf kilt 5.00. Ditto 2 piggs 16.00. Total 46.00.

"So I tell him, 'I'm sorry, I can't pay that bill; I am not in charge of foodstuffs. If you'd brought me a bill for hay or oats, and I was satisfied the articles had been furnished I might pay for *that*.

"'You must go speak with the commissary officer, Lieutenant Allen. He *may* pay your bill, though I doubt it, given the lack of a receipt written out and signed by a commissioned officer.'

"'I were just over to Mr. Allen's office and already done axed for him, but he weren't in. So I reckoned I'd make out the bill to you, sir.'

"'I'm sorry, I can't pay it. But, let me ask you this, sir; are you a Union man?'

"'Well, yes I am; and there ain't many of us neither, where I come from.'

"'Where is that?'

"'Over to Braxton County way. Lookie here, Cap; if you'll see your way clear to pay this here bill, I'll give you two dollars and a half.'

"'Are you trying to insult me?' I asked, beginning to feel a bit heated.

"'No, sir; I ain't. I'm just offer'n to give you two dollars and a half if you'll pay this bill.'

"'I cannot pay it, sir!'

"'Well! Then all's I got to say is, if'n that's the way you're gonna act, then I ain't gonna be a Union man no longer!'

"'Please leave my office now, and good day to you, sir!' I said, and ushered him out the door.

"I'm sorry to say he is just one of many we've dealt with whose loyalty depends solely on what he can get out of the government."

Miss Abbey, who'd been giggling throughout this narrative, said, "My goodness, Captain! You are such a wit. And such a humorous storyteller, you really should write a book one day!"

He smiled, and nodded appreciatively, "Perhaps I shall, ma'am, perhaps I shall. Thank you for the compliment ... and for the excellent suggestion!"

General Rosecrans was also in good humor, though his own narratives, mostly prompted by Nathan, were of a more serious nature—giving a detailed description of his recent successful Kanawha River Valley campaign. While the others at the table listened respectfully, Nathan asked specific questions about various finer points of strategy and tactics throughout the narrative. It was clear to all present the two men were at a whole other level in that regard, and were also in close agreement concerning the general prosecution of the war.

But when his narrative was over, Rosecrans couldn't resist asking the question that was foremost on his mind, "So Nathan, when are you and your men planning to enlist? In time for the spring campaigns?"

Nathan didn't immediately respond but leaned back in his chair and gazed at the ceiling. He reached into his pocket, pulled out a cigar, and stuck it in his mouth, though he made no move to light it.

After a quick glance over at Margaret he answered, "I ... I'm not sure yet."

"What?! Why *not?* Surely, you're not going to just stay here and continue training up West Virginia's regiments? You're too valuable a man for such duty. I'd rather have the whole lot sent out with no training at all than suffer your loss in the field!"

"It's … not *that*. I agree with you, I have done enough here in that regard. The recruitment and training are now moving forward in a fairly efficient and workmanlike manner. No … there are … *other* considerations."

"Such as?" Rosecrans now sported a frown and was clearly *not* pleased with what he was hearing.

"Well, firstly, there's the Constitutional Convention for the new state. We're fearing it won't end well in several respects, and as a result may be rejected by the president, negating months of hard work. It feels like my presence is … *necessary* to keep the scales from tipping too far in the wrong direction."

Rosecrans raised an eyebrow at this, but then shook his head, "Well, that may well be, but that can't last forever. Likely it'll be settled by spring. What else?"

It was now Nathan's turn to frown. "It's this damned insurrection. The secessionist guerrilla bands and the disorganized bushwhackers and cutthroats. They just don't seem to go away, no matter what we throw at them. Again, I fear it will undermine our efforts to start up the new state. If it stays as it is now, it will be virtually impossible to organize county governments, for example. No way to actually govern the state, which could lead to even more guerrilla warfare and leave open the door to the enemy re-taking the state."

"Well, yes, it's a damned nuisance for certain. But still, not worth sacrificing one of our best officers to deal with! We have other men we can throw at the task. And though they may not be as competent as you, they should at least be able to keep a lid on the simmering pot, so to speak."

But despite Rosecrans' earnest appeal, Nathan still hesitated.

"There's … more to it than that, I'm afraid. It's become … *personal*."

"Personal? Whatever do you mean, Nathan?"

Nathan sat back in his seat and sighed, again looking over at Margaret. She met his gaze and nodded. She too had a serious look. William, sitting quietly next to her, also looked concerned.

"General, you may remember back at Rich Mountain when we were in the farmhouse and I described to you our adventures fighting our way out of my home in Greenbrier that we might relocate to Wheeling?"

"Yes, certainly I remember it. I've rarely heard a more heroic and daring tale. Why do you ask?"

"Well, do you recall me telling you the enemy was led by my erstwhile neighbor, by name of Walters, whose family had been feuding with mine for years prior?"

"Hmm ... that part sounds *vaguely* familiar ..."

"At any rate, Walters still holds a grudge against me, and has threatened harm to my family — Miss Abbey and Miss Margaret in particular."

"What?! What sort of fiend threatens fine, respectable, and entirely innocent ladies such as yourselves?" he asked, looking toward Miss Abbey and Margaret with a frown.

"The evil, murderous kind, General," Margaret answered, meeting his gaze steadily.

"It's true, I'm afraid," Nathan said. "And though I've done my best to put a bullet in him on several occasions, I have, unfortunately, failed to do so. I have even recently had a certain ... *man* I know ... investigating his whereabouts. To my dismay, it seems Walters has also come north and has apparently joined up with one or more of these secessionist guerrilla bands."

"And you fear if you leave home now ... your family will be in imminent danger? That he may try to harm them?"

"Yes ... in the past he has shown a cowardly inclination to attack my people when I am personally away. Either he is outright afraid of facing me, or he believes he will hurt me more by destroying my family — I'm not sure which and don't know that it matters. I just can't ... in good conscience ... ride off and leave my family helpless before his none-too-gentle mercies."

They were all quiet and thoughtful for a long moment, the jollity of the evening now turned to a somber, serious tone.

Surprisingly, it was Captain Leib who spoke up, "I'd suggest you see if Captain Baggs might run the scoundrel to ground."

"Baggs?" Nathan asked.

"Oh! You've not heard of Captain Baggs and his 'Snake Hunters'?"

"No. Is this another of your humorous tales, Charles?" Nathan asked.

"Well ... it's humorous, but it's no tall tale. The fellow is real. I should know, I have met him once in person."

"Go on ..."

"Well, as I understand it, when General McClellan first came to western Virginia, he was approached by a fellow named John Baggs who claimed to know every mule track and elk trail in eastern Ohio and western Virginia. He offered to raise a company of forty or so men to serve as scouts and irregular fighters for the Union cause. Apparently, the general recognized the potential usefulness of such a troop and mustered them into the service.

"They now function more or less independently, as I understand it — General Rosecrans can correct me if I'm wrong ... Anyway, Baggs' company have dubbed themselves the 'Snake Hunters' and spend their time roaming the hills and backwoods of western Virginia going after the secessionist bushwhackers. They have developed a reputation for tough fighting, neither giving nor asking for quarter from the enemy. From what I've heard, the secessionists have developed a healthy fear of them and have their own name for them: 'Baggs' Thieves.'

"From what I understand, the Captain and his men are fiercely loyal and devoted to just three things: each other, whiskey, and the government of the United States ... and don't ask me in which order!"

Leib proceeded to describe his meeting with the rustic, but capable Captain Baggs, when the latter came to him for some wagons. Leib had rejected the request, thinking Baggs hadn't the required paperwork, but had been impressed with Baggs' attitude, when he'd responded, "I really don't give a good Goddamn, Leib, if I get them wagons or no; whether we're ahorse, or have to walk it barefooted, we're fighting for the government either way."

But then Leib had discovered Baggs did, in fact, have a written order — from General McClellan himself — authorizing the wagons, so all was well.

Of course, Captain Leib told the story in his usual, witty manner, imitating the backwoods voice, mannerisms, and grammar of Baggs, to the amusement of the company.

Nathan smiled and laughed, but then became thoughtful. "You think this Baggs fellow is as good as he says he is?"

"That *is* my understanding, Nathan. General, have you heard anything different?"

"No ... I have likewise heard he has had some success, though he's only one man with one small company fighting against a vast unknown sea of enemies. What impact he may have in such a case is highly questionable."

"Well, maybe he'll have but little impact against the insurgents as a whole ... but perhaps he might successfully hunt down one *particularly* troublesome one ..." Nathan answered.

Rosecrans nodded, "Yes, could be so, Nathan ... could be."

ꝏꝏꝏꝏꝏꝏꝏꝏꝏ

As Stan sat on his bunk idly whittling down a stick of wood with his large hunting knife, Billy stepped up and tossed him something. Stan had to drop the stick to catch it. It was a long, narrow leather bag, with a long, curved stick protruding from the top, along with what were clearly arrows—feathers attached to the end of the shafts.

"What's this?" Stan asked.

Billy laughed, "As you are fond of saying, Stan ... it's a stupid question! You can clearly see it is a quiver of arrows and a bow."

"Yes ... I see that but ..." then Stan's eyes widened, and he pulled out the bow, gazing at it appreciatively. It looked very similar to the one he'd seen Billy use hundreds of times, except this one was bigger. Much bigger.

He looked over at Billy, "You ... you have made this? For me?"

"Yes."

Stan ran his hands along its length, feeling the smoothness of the highly varnished, yellow colored wood on one side, and a rougher surface on the other where the wood had been reinforced with a backing of animal sinew, glued to the surface of the wood.

"Billy ... it is ... *magnificent!* Thank you, thank you! I am never having such a gift before!"

He set the bow on the bed and leaned down, embracing Billy and kissing him on both cheeks, resisting the urge to lift him off his feet out of respect for his much-smaller comrade.

"You're welcome."

Then Stan said, "But ... when have you made this thing? It must take ... long time to do this, but I have never seen you working on it."

"When we arrived here in the North and suddenly had little to do, I began thinking ... now you've become a stealth fighter, you should have the right weapon.

"So I started looking for the right piece of wood. It takes many months to do this thing rightly. The wood must be cured and dried, carved to shape, then re-wetted and curved. Then adding the animal sinew, polishing, and more drying. After each step there is much waiting. I have worked on it ... on and off ... for many moons."

"Well ... it was very good thought, Billy. I have had much envy of your skill with bow. Is *very* good weapon—wonderful deadly and ... makes enemy shit britches and run screaming for momma!" he laughed.

Billy nodded and smiled.

"And arrows too ..." He pulled one of them out and could tell immediately these were also much larger than those Billy used himself—nearly as big around as a thumb, while Billy's were about the diameter of a little finger. And nearly a foot longer, with white goose feathers on one end and a wicked-looking, razor sharp steel arrowhead on the other. Stan tested the sharpness on his thumb and smiled when a thin stream of blood started oozing out. "You have used steel ... but don't your own arrows use shiny black stone?"

"Out west, yes ... the stone white men call flint. The flint is much sharper and makes a nastier cut when it enters flesh. But the stone arrowheads take long time to make and break easily if one hits something hard like a rock, or even a large bone. So I asked Georgie to make these steel ones for your arrows and for more of mine. They are good enough—reasonably sharp and have the right weight. And he can make dozens in the time it takes me to make one of the flint ones, not even counting the time searching for the black stones."

"Hmm ... was good thinking, Billy. These seem plenty sharp to me."

"Yes ... with that bow and those large arrows you could easily kill a buffalo or even a ...what is the great beast from Africa with nose like a snake?"

"Elephant."

"Yes ... you could even kill the elephant with this weapon. Except I don't think there are any here in Virginia."

"Yes ... is too bad," he shrugged, "Guess I must kill two-legged slaver-beast instead!" he flashed a wicked looking, killer grin.

Stan gazed at the arrow again, admiring its near perfect straightness. A glorious, thoroughly beautiful instrument of death! It was then he noticed Billy had painted the shaft a bright red, apparently having borrowed some of the paint used on the barns.

"Red? Why red? Is to frighten enemy?"

But Billy shook his head and grinned, "No ... it's so when you miss the target, we can find the arrows."

Stan puffed up, indignantly, "Humph! I am professional fighter Billy—skilled in all weapons. I will learn bow easy ... and will *not* miss target. There will be no searching."

Billy chuckled and headed for the door, shaking his head. Stan noticed Billy also carried his bow and a quiver of arrows over one shoulder. "Come, Stan ... show me your skill."

ಬಞಯಿಞಲಿ ಬಞಯಿಞಲಿ ಬಞಯಿಞಲಿ

An hour later, with the first three fingers on his right hand blistered and bleeding, Stan looked over at Billy and sighed. Billy grinned back at him. Stan had just shot the next to last arrow from his quiver and had missed. Again. This time about a foot high and several feet to the right of the target—a man-sized burlap bag filled with straw with a red circle painted in the middle, held up by a post pounded into the ground.

"Okay ... is not so easy as looks," Stan finally admitted with a sheepish grin. He had fired the full quiver of six arrows a dozen or more times and had not yet hit the target at fifty paces. Billy had suggested starting at twenty-five, but Stan had felt insulted and insisted on stepping out further—a decision he now regretted, having spent more time searching for spent arrows than actually shooting them.

Billy just laughed. Then he pointed at something out across the field back toward the farmhouse. Stan looked and saw the Captain striding out toward them, his large four-legged shadow ranging slightly behind and out to one side.

When the Captain reached them, he stopped and said, "There you are at last. I've been looking all over for you two. No one seemed to know where you'd gone."

"Hello, Captain. We've just been doing a little target practice with new toy Billy gave me," Stan held out the bow, and Nathan took it, examining it closely.

"Nice workmanship ... sinew backing, recurve design ... well balanced. Ash wood, isn't it?"

"Yes, Captain," Billy answered, after Stan looked over at him questioningly.

"I assume you made this, Billy? There's no one else around here could do it, I'm guessing."

"Yes, sir ... I thought Stan might find it ... useful."

Nathan nodded, continuing to gaze at the weapon. "But ... my goodness it's *big*! Must be a good," he set one end against the ground and the other reached his eyes, "six feet long! And the pull ... good *God*," he pulled back on the string, straining his muscles to bring it all the way back, after which he slowly let it down again, "what? Ninety ... or a hundred pounds?"

"That's correct, Captain ... it is over one hundred pounds. I measured it using some weights I'd found in one of the barns. But they were only a hundred pounds, and I didn't bother searching for more. I am guessing it's closer to one hundred and twenty. I have never made one so large or powerful before, but I thought Stan could handle it."

Nathan slowly shook his head and gazed up and down it admiringly.

"May I?" he asked, reaching for the last, red-shafted arrow from Stan's quiver.

Stan and Billy both nodded.

Nathan held the arrow up to his eyes and sighted along it, checking for straightness. He looked over at Billy and smiled, nodding appreciatively—he knew in some ways it was even more challenging to fashion perfectly straight arrows than it was to build a bow. Then he noticed the red color of the shaft, and looked over at Billy, "Red?"

Billy shrugged, but Stan said, "He was thinking the red would make arrows easier to find out in field when I … *overshot* target." He looked over at Billy and shrugged, "He was being right about that, of course, as he is with most things."

"Ah! Good thought." Nathan stood facing ninety degrees from the target and eyed it over his left shoulder. Then holding the bow horizontally, he laid the arrow across it, just above his left hand, nocking the arrow between the first two fingers of his right hand. He pulled back slightly, to give the arrow some tension, then held the bow vertically with his left arm extended while pulling back the bow string with his right until it just touched his right cheek, his muscles straining from the effort.

After taking a moment to align the target, he relaxed his fingers, releasing the bowstring. A second later the arrow *thunked* into the target, embedding itself nearly to the feathers. Not a perfect bullseye, but a respectable hit less than six inches off center at the edge of the red circle.

Nathan turned and shrugged, betraying a slight grin as he handed the bow back to Stan, who was wide eyed.

"Is *good* shooting, Captain! *Much* better than I am doing."

But Billy looked at Nathan knowingly, "When did you learn the bow, Captain?"

Nathan smiled. "It was just after the Mexican War when I received my orders to stay out in Texas and fight the Comanche and Apache. I thought it'd be a good idea to learn the enemy's weapons. So I asked one of the Tonkawa scouts to teach me."

He turned and patted Stan on the shoulder, "Don't feel bad, Stan ... it took me many long, painful months of practice to get anything close to good at it. And thank God my bow wasn't nearly as stiff as this one, or I'd never have done it! Good thing you're strong as a bull.

"Hmm ... is not the string pull that is bothering me, but my aim is ... seeming to *wobble* a bit ..."

"Like I said, you shouldn't feel bad. It's *so* much different from shooting a gun! There's simply no substitute for many long hours of practice. But if you are coming anywhere near the target on your first day, then I'd say you have a knack for it, and will become proficient much quicker than I did."

Billy nodded, "Stan is already getting it. He is a natural with any weapon, though he feels shamed he didn't hit the bull's eye on the first try," he snorted a laugh.

Stan laughed as well, shaking his head. Then he said, "But, Captain ... you were not looking for us just to be teaching humility ..."

"True. I came here to ask a favor of you. Both of you."

"Of course. We are your men, Captain. You are not needing to *ask*, just *tell* and we will do it ... whatever it is," Stan said, and Billy nodded his agreement.

"Thanks, Stan, Billy. You're good men. I know I can always count on you. I wish to send you on a little hunting trip."

"Hunting, Captain? What kind of animals you want us kill?"

Nathan didn't immediately answer, but took out a cigar, stuck it in his mouth and lit it. Finally he answered, "Snakes."

෩෨෪෨෪෩෨෪෨෪෩෨෪෨

The next morning Billy and Stan sat on their horses on the gravel driveway in front of the farmhouse. Most of the farm's inhabitants, black and white, men and women, gathered around to see them off. Word had spread they were riding out to track down Walters and kill him if they could. So their mission was suddenly the talk of the farm, and everyone wanted to wish them good luck and Godspeed.

Billy seemed overwhelmed and embarrassed by all the attention, gazing at his saddle horn or out at the horizon. But Stan beamed, chatting and joking with everyone who approached them.

They appeared well equipped and prepared for the task; each had four revolvers, two in holsters at their hips, and two more in holsters slung up under their shoulders. A large hunting knife in a leather sheath had been attached to a leather strap running across the chest and over one shoulder, it being about the only place left to carry it while riding. A rifle rode along in a sheath strapped to the side of each horse on one side, and their quiver of bow and arrows on the other. Stan led a spare horse and Billy the mule. Both animals were heavily laden with equipment and food, not all of which was intended for the two men; Nathan figured a little gift of some well-deserved sustenance and supplies might put them in good standing with Captain Baggs and his "Snake Hunters." And it might make them more agreeable to going along with Nathan's request that they track down Walters and his gang, wherever they may be lurking.

Nathan stepped up to them, followed by Tom, Jim, and the other white men. Jim called out, "Atten ... shun!," and all the men standing nearby, including all the black ones who'd fought in the recent escape from Mountain Meadows, snapped to attention and saluted the riders. Billy and Stan sat up straight and returned the acknowledgment smartly.

Then Nathan approached each of the riders and shook his hand, wishing him good luck.

"We will be for doing our best, Captain," Stan said. "But ... I am still not understanding why you and the rest of the men aren't joining us. Seems to me it will be much fun and good change from sitting around waiting to fight in big war."

Nathan frowned, and said, "Believe me, I considered it, and still badly wish to. But ... from all I've heard, Captain Baggs knows his business, although he is ... not exactly *regulation*, if you know what I mean. I fear if us regular army types showed up in a group, he might be put off by it, and feel like we were trying to take over his company. Or worse yet, he might defer to me and refuse to take the lead, even though he is clearly more qualified for this particular mission.

"No ... it seems to me from all our soldiers who came east from Texas, you two are the most likely to be comfortable with Baggs' ... *irregular* ... way of doing things. And the most likely to fit in with his company."

"Ah ... yes, I can see what you are meaning, Captain. Very good. Goodbye then. We will be bringing back Walters' head in sack, if we can find him," and to prove his point, Stan held up a small burlap bag with a drawstring he'd apparently procured for just that purpose.

Nathan grinned, "That would indeed be a lovely sight, Mr. Volkov!"

But Miss Abbey, standing a few feet away, listening in on the conversation, shuddered and said, "Ewww ... just don't show it to *me*, if you please!"

To which Megs responded, "Amen to that, Abigail! Though it'd be good to know for sure that he's dead." She turned and patted Margaret on the arm, who returned the gesture with a smile and a nod, though her face betrayed a worried expression.

When all their goodbyes had been said, Billy and Stan turned their horses and started up the drive. But after only a few paces Stan stopped Groz and turned the great stallion back toward the Captain. Billy turned his horse in response but had a puzzled look.

"Captain ... are you knowing ... hmm ... the proper Godly words for blessing our good fortune out hunting these 'serpents'?"

"Oh! My apologies, gentlemen ... I've been derelict in my duties this morning," Nathan answered, and though he smiled, his face betrayed a touch of embarrassment at the oversight.

"Hmm ... let me think ... Ah! I have just the thing, *'Behold, I give unto you power to tread on serpents and scorpions, and over all the power of the enemy: and nothing shall by any means hurt you.'* —Luke chapter ten, verse nineteen."

Stan grinned his broad, toothy grin and tipped his hat. Billy gave the Captain a serious look then nodded his head. They turned once again, and this time trotted their horses up the drive until they were out of sight down the road.

ᏸᏬᏒᏣᏣᏸᏬᏒᏣᏣᏸᏬᏒᏣᏣ

Two days later Jamie and Georgie returned from a mission of their own. On Tom's behalf they had retraced their earlier journey to the Confederate held town of Moorefield to its post office there. Though there was little fear of them being recognized after more than a month with young men their age coming and going through the town on a daily basis, they weren't taking any chances, and had spent considerable thought on changing their appearance from the previous journey, even foregoing shaving for the two weeks prior so they'd each have a healthy growth of beard.

As they approached the farmhouse, walking their horses up the drive, Tom noted their approach and strode out to meet them.

"Welcome home, gentlemen," he said when they met.

They tipped their hats and smiled down at him from their mounts, "Sergeant."

Tom gazed up at them expectantly, reluctant to ask the question that was burning in his mind.

But they sat silently gazing at him, with serious looks that made his heart sink, until Georgie could hold it no longer and burst into a broad grin, "It was there, Sarge! We got it for you."

"Oh! Thank you, Georgie … Jamie. I am much obliged; very much obliged indeed!"

"Never mention it, Sergeant," Jamie replied, and Georgie just tipped his hat and said, "It was our pleasure and honor, sir." He reached into his pocket and pulled out an envelope, handing it down to Tom.

Tom's heart leapt when he saw the Confederate mail postmark on the front: *Thibodaux, Louisiana.*

Chapter 9. Snake Hunting

"Behold, I give unto you power
to tread on serpents and scorpions,
and over all the power of the enemy:
and nothing shall by any means hurt you."
– Luke 10:19

Tuesday December 10, 1861 – Big Run Bridge, Virginia:

"So Billy ... how can we be knowing which side is which? I am itching to shoot somebody ... but who?" Stan asked. They crouched behind thick underbrush overlooking a narrow draw through which a swift river flowed with great vigor.

They'd heard gunfire a few minutes earlier, so had left the road, dismounted, and headed into the woods intending to reconnoiter. After tying their horses, they'd crept to the edge of the little valley, clutching their rifles. Now, looking down on the scene, they could see the bridge across the river had been broken in the middle. Though the wooden structure still stood thirty feet or more above the rushing water, it was missing about ten feet of the decking in the center, making it impossible to cross.

A group of fifty or more armed men were spread along the near bank, taking cover against incoming rifle fire from a dozen or more men in the woods across the river. From what Billy and Stan could see through the trees, neither side wore any sort of uniform, and both sides were a dirty, scruffy looking bunch of men.

Clearly the men on the near bank had wanted to cross over the bridge, but upon finding it out of service had tried to ford the stream. Instead they had come under heavy gunfire. At least one man had been killed already; his body lay sprawled across some rocks at the edge of the stream. They could see a half-dozen or so horses tied back in the woods, but the rest of the men had obviously come to the place on foot.

Billy didn't immediately answer but continued to gaze down at the battle scene below. Finally, he turned to Stan and said, "There is a man back in the woods guarding the horses. Looks like he is alone."

Stan grinned, "Ah! And you are thinking we go ask him ... *'nicely and politely,'* as Captain would say?"

"Yes, nicely and politely ... with a knife at this throat," Billy answered, and snorted a quick laugh, "as *Sergeant Jim* would say!"

A quarter of an hour and a brief scramble down the hillside through the heavy undergrowth found them behind some trees looking out at where the strangers' horses were secured. As Billy had reported, a single man with a rifle stood next to the animals, gazing out toward the raging gun battle a few dozen yards farther down the hill.

With the almost constant noise of gunfire coming from below, it was child's play for Billy and Stan to creep up behind the man. And soon he was held securely in Stan's iron grip, as Billy held a finger to his mouth to indicate silence while holding a razor-sharp hunting knife in his other fist.

The man's eyes were wide with fear, but to his credit, he resisted the urge to scream or call out.

"Now ... we are needing to know which side is of Union ... and which side is of Confederate in gunfight," Stan said leaning forward and speaking into the man's ear, so he'd not have to yell over the sounds of the battle.

"I ... I ..." the man stuttered, clearly afraid to say the wrong thing, knowing he had a fifty-fifty chance of answering in a way that would likely get his throat slit.

"Do not be worrying ... just give truth. I am promising will not kill you either way. If you are on *wrong* side, will just tie up and leave you here. We want join gunfight but don't want to shoot our friends. So ... are you Union fellow or rebel fellow, huh?"

"Uh ... me an' the boys are all for the government. You know ... the one in Washington."

"Oh ho! Is *good!* So are we of Washington Government!" Stan responded, but did not yet relax his grip, though the man seemed relieved his assailants appeared to be friendlies.

"Who is your leader?" Billy asked.

"Well, that'd be the Captain, I reckon."

"Captain? What is Captain's name?" Stan asked.

"Well ... Captain Baggs, of course."

"Oh! Is even better. We are looking for Captain Baggs and for you ... hmm ... 'Serpent Hunters' for most of week. We are come from Union government of Wheeling."

"*Snake* Hunters," the man corrected him. "And who might you be, and why are you looking for the Captain?"

"Our own Captain sent us. I am called Billy Creek, and this is Stan."

"Private Stanislav Volkov," Stan said, finally releasing the man's arms so he could shake his hand with great vigor.

"Wilbert Potter. Good to meet you, and damned happy I am to hear we're on the same side. You fellas look like you'd be none too friendly in a fight. And, seein's how we's pinned down and can't seem to pass this river, I reckon we could use your help. How many others you done brought with you?"

"None ... just us," Billy answered.

"But ... what about your Captain you spoke of? Where's his regiment?"

Stan answered, "Oh ... he does not have regiment. Captain Chambers is ... hmm ... how you say? With having only his own men ...?"

"*Independent?* Like us here?"

"Yes ... *independent* ... I think this is right word. He is not yet with Army but works for governor of Wheeling."

"Governor Pierpont? He sent you to find us? Reckon it's none o' my business to ask the why of it, but we sure could use that regiment about now."

But Stan gave him a broad grin, "Not for worrying, Potter! We two are being enough. We will get you across river. Just go tell your Captain of us so your men will not be shooting us. Tell him we will clear away enemy on other side in ..." he looked at Billy and shrugged, "about one hour, maybe ... more or less."

Billy nodded, but returned the shrug.

Potter gazed from one to the other, eyes wide and mouth open. "Well, I reckon you know your business. And you surely look like you could take on a whole army. Am I correct you're a real Indian … from out West?"

Billy nodded, but said nothing.

"And you," the man continued, looking at Stan, "you ain't from around here neither …"

"You are correct, Potter. I am … from *Texas!*" Stan said, and chuckled at his own humor.

ഇയ്ക്രരുഇയ്ക്രരു

A half-hour later, Stan and Billy had made their way to a likely crossing point a mile or so to the left and upstream of where they'd first gazed upon the gun battle. They'd found a spot with no large rocks where the stream was relatively flat and wide. Here the current would be less vigorous, and the water less deep. Even so, the river rushed along with a great tumbling roar. With its tremendous speed and force even Stan, with his great size and strength, would be hard-pressed to make it across without being swept off his feet. For Billy, crossing this stream unaided would be impossible.

But fortunately, they'd planned for this; they carried with them a simple but effective solution. After leaving Potter they'd returned to the horses and collected their arrow quivers and two coils of light, strong rope, along with the burlap bag Stan had brought along for transporting Walters' head, though he had a different purpose for it at the moment. They left the rifles behind, but still carried their pistols.

Billy tied the end of one rope around a tree trunk near the water, and the other end to the back of an arrow. He drew back his bow and let fly. The arrow embedded itself deeply into a tree on the far bank about twenty-five yards away.

He returned to the tree where the rope had been tied and re-tied it to take out the slack. Next, he handed Stan his bow and quiver, and unbuckled his four pistol holsters, placing them in the small burlap bag.

He tied one end of the second rope to his belt, and Stan held the other end. Then he turned and waded out into the stream, holding tight to the rope stretched tautly across the stream.

Billy made good progress at first. With the water just up to his knees he had not yet required the rope for assistance. But when he was nearly to the middle the water had come up over his waist and he'd have been swept away without the extra support.

Finally, the flow was just too great, and he gave up trying to keep his feet on the bottom. Instead, he allowed his body to float to the top, and pulled himself along the rest of the way, hand over hand, until he was back in shallower water and could stand once again.

Though he felt stiff from his dousing in the icy-cold water, he resisted the urge to curl up into a ball and shiver. Ignoring his chattering teeth, he moved quickly to where his arrow was embedded in the tree. He pulled out his hunting knife and dug the arrow out. After a quick inspection of the arrowhead, he untied the rope and looked back over at Stan, who was now standing next to the tree on the other side.

Billy gave a nod. Stan waved, then turned and untied the rope on his side, slowly letting out enough slack so Billy could re-tie his end securely around the trunk of the tree. He'd been willing to trust the arrow would hold under his own slight weight, but he had no delusions it would withstand Stan's great bulk. Likely the arrow itself would simply shatter, despite the wood's great strength and flexibility. Once Billy had re-secured the rope around the tree, he waved at Stan, who pulled the rope taut, and then re-tied his end.

But rather than immediately moving out into the water, Stan tied the burlap sack with Billy's pistols to the second rope Billy had attached to his waist. Billy untied his end and looped it over a tree branch. When Stan was ready, he gave the signal, and stretched the rope tight. Billy slowly pulled the rope across the branch, and watched as the burlap sack, with its precious cargo, slowly made its bouncy, dangling way safely across the stream above the water.

Once the sack had reached Billy, he opened it, and removed the pistols, laying them on the ground near the tree. Then he waved to Stan, who pulled the rope back across. They repeated this maneuver three more times; once for Stan's pistols, and once each for the quivers holding their bows and arrows.

Finally, Stan himself came across. Unlike Billy, he never had to give up on keeping his feet on the stream bottom. But he did struggle mightily as the river neared his waist. And without the rope to steady him, even he would have never made it across.

When he was safely on dry land, he grinned at Billy, who was still shivering in his wet clothing, "Well, that was fun. How you say ...? *Invigorating?*"

Billy said nothing, just rolled his eyes and scowled as he strapped his pistol holsters back on. Stan did likewise, and then proceeded to string his great bow, which required a herculean feat of strength to accomplish. When he finished, he looked at Billy, who'd already strung his, and they exchanged a nod. Without another word, they headed off into the woods, and up the hillside, Billy in the lead.

ഇരുഇരുഇരുഇരുഇരുഇരു

Wilbert Potter was feeling anxious and twitchy, sitting as he was next to Captain Baggs behind a large, fallen log. The Captain was none too happy with him and glowered every time he glanced his way. Bad enough he'd abandoned his post guarding the horses without orders. But to make matters worse, the Captain assumed he'd made up the fanciful story of being captured by a giant and an Indian to excuse his dereliction. He'd even smelled his breath after accusing him of breaking into the whiskey while on duty. And though Potter loved his Captain with the fierce kind of loyalty known only among fighting men, he was still intimidated by him. Though often smiling and jolly, Baggs was a fierce-looking, burly man with dark eyes and even darker beard who looked like he could wrestle a bear and come out on the winning side. Not a man to be trifled with, but one you wanted on your side in a fight.

But Baggs' stern looks had softened somewhat when the gunfire from the opposite bank had slackened, and they'd heard strange sounds: shouting, cursing, and even what sounded like ... *screaming* ... though that seemed incongruous; their enemies, whatever else they might be, were determined fighters, not inclined to cowardice.

Now there'd been no gunfire for at least ten minutes, and no sign of the enemy. Baggs looked back at Potter questioningly. "You said the strangers told you an hour, Wilby. Reckon it's been an hour and a quarter since you left your post."

"Yes, sir. But they said ... *wait!* Listen, Cap!" he pointed out across the river. Baggs turned and listened.

"Hello! Hey ... hello, you Union fellows over the river!" someone shouted out from the far side of the river, though they could not see where the sound was coming from. The voice was booming, loud enough to be heard above the sounds of the rushing water. And it had a strange, foreign accent which none there save Potter had ever heard before.

Baggs shouted back, "We're here. Show yourselves!"

"We come now. We are friends; not for the shooting! We have driven off enemies and bring prisoners."

"Then come on out so's we can get a look at you. And just keep your hands in the air," the Captain shouted back.

But the large voice laughed, "Is stupid idea! Prisoners will run if we raise hands. But not for worrying, Baggs ... rebel *bezobraznik* bushwhackers will come with hands in air, or we will be killing them!" the voice laughed again, a boisterous, jolly kind of laugh that made Baggs grin, despite the tension in the air.

The Captain stood, holstered his pistol, and shouted out "Hold your fire, men. Seems these odd fellows are on *our* side!" He too had a strong, projecting voice; a kind that expected to be obeyed without question.

Potter felt great satisfaction and relief when the giant and the Indian stepped out from behind the trees with pistols in their fists. Three glum looking prisoners with hands held high shuffled along in front of them. Baggs glanced over at Potter, grinned, and nodded his head. Potter returned the grin; happy to be back in good standing with his Captain, at last.

"Come on over now," the giant called out. "The water is … *invigorating!*" he laughed again.

A half-hour later, Baggs and his fifty-some Snake Hunters were safely across the river. Like Stan and Billy, they'd used ropes to help the men cross, though they had no need of arrows; their horses were able to wade and swim across, despite the strong current.

The Captain had dispatched a dozen or more men to see to repairing the bridge so they could get their supply wagons across. The sounds of axes chopping trees could already be heard up the ridge.

While that was going on, Billy and Stan went back up into the woods to retrieve their precious spent arrows, most of which had found their marks. Stan was pleased with his improvement; of the five arrows he'd fired, two had felled their men. And thanks to Billy's red paint, he was able to find the ones that'd missed.

They dragged five bodies back to the river's edge and laid them out, side by side. Baggs came over and examined the faces one by one.

"Goddamn it! This'n here we done caught two or three months back. Now here he be again, like a spate o' bad luck!" he scowled, turning to spit a dark glob from the chewing tobacco he had in his cheek.

He continued down the row. When he noticed one had a red-shafted arrow sticking from his chest he looked up at Stan and Billy in surprise, "Arrows? You fellows killed them with arrows? Well, I'll be damned if that ain't … well … I don't even know how to properly say it. *Poetic,* maybe? Killed these-here Goddamned 'Moccasin Rangers' with arrows. I'll be a three-eyed toad if that ain't poetic! Don't that seem poetic, Wilby?"

"Yes sir … I reckon so. Though I don't rightly know nothin' about no poetry. But that there's some sweet justice anyway, that is."

"Moccasin Rangers?" Billy asked.

Baggs looked at him with a grin, "It's the name they done give themselves. Tryin' to be *cute* I reckon. Like they was some kind o' real life savages, sneakin' around in the woods … or some such. Oh … meaning no offense to *you*, sir!"

Billy just shrugged.

Baggs laughed, "In fact, it's why we took to calling ourselves 'Snake Hunters' … on account o' there's a kind of Goddamned, verminous viper called 'Moccasin' that lives in pools and streams. Likely we came up with the idea one night when we'd busted out a keg o' whiskey and was all a bit looped. Don't recall who done come up with it first, do you, Wilby?"

"No, Cap. We all just woke in the morning and someone said, "Let's go kill them damned Moccasins, *Snake Hunters!* And we been sayin' it ever since."

"Yep … reckon that's how it was, all right."

While they were talking, Stan stepped up to the body with the arrow, planted a boot on the man's chest, grasped the shaft and yanked. The arrow came out with a crunching, sucking sound followed by an eruption of fluid that covered the front of the man's shirt in blood. Potter's eyes widened but Stan leaned down and casually wiped the blood off the arrow on the man's shirtsleeves.

Baggs now sported a broad grin on his face. "Seems like you boys'll fit right in!" Then he laughed, and turned, heading over to inspect the progress on the bridge repairs.

Billy and Stan crossed back over to fetch their horses from where they'd left them tied back in the woods. Then they had re-crossed the river, this time in the more comfortable and less sodden position atop a horse.

A few hours later, as the bridge repairs were nearing completion, Baggs sat with the two strange newcomers on large rocks at the river's edge.

"So, Volkov, Potter tells me the Gov'ner over to Wheeling sent you. What's it all about?" Baggs asked.

Stan looked up and grinned, "Our Captain … name of Chambers … sent us to ask your help."

"My help? Help with what?"

"The Captain is understanding you are having good fortune in woods, hunting these … *Moccasin Snakes*."

Baggs grinned and nodded, "Yep, me'n the boys've been out here for months crawlin' through the woods, living on nothin' but huckleberries and birch bark … killing these *Goddamned, bushwhacking, rebel snakes* wherever we find them. What of it?"

"My Captain wants to kill one *special* Goddamned, bushwhacking, rebel snake."

"Oh? And why should I want to do *that*? As you can well see, I've got no end of the fucking secesh varmints as it is—tryin' their best to blow my head clean off ever' damned chance they get! Why would I want to go out of my way to look for this *one* particular rebel for your Captain?"

"Hmm … well, he *did* send two barrels good whiskey with us …"

"Whiskey!" Baggs grinned broadly. "Well … why didn't you say so in the first place, Volkov?!"

😌😈Čč😌😈Čč😌😈Čč

While his men were busily finishing up the bridge repairs, hammers banging noisily above them, the Captain ordered the guards to bring the three prisoners over to where Stan and Billy had laid out the bodies. Baggs pulled out a pencil and a small, folded piece of paper from his pocket, and asked the prisoners to identify each man, which he wrote down on the paper.

Then he proceeded to record the prisoners' names, after which he put the pencil and paper back in his pocket.

Then he stepped in front of the prisoners and glowered at them. "Well now … you boys got anything to say for yourselves? Bushwhacking sons of bitches, *pah*! Sneakin' around like no good vermin out in these-here woods? Robbing and murderin' good, honest Union folk, like you got no sense o' shame, nor any honor!"

The men seemed embarrassed by this haranguing, looking down at their ragged shoes. None would meet his eye for several minutes, until the one on the right glanced up and said, "Well, sir … we ain't done none o' them things."

"Oh? Then why was you out in these woods, armed for war, and shootin' at us'ns as was just tryin' to cross this-here river-run?"

"Oh! We wasn't shootin' at y'all, no sir! We was just … out huntin' squirrels is all. Ain't that right, boys?"

The other two nodded their heads emphatically, and the one on the left said, "Yessir … just squirrels. We weren't never trying to kill any o' your kind as was crossin' yonder creek."

"Oh! So I suppose you … just *mistook* my man Hopkins lyin' dead over there … for a … *really* large squirrel … is that it?" he asked, grinning and nodding his head emphatically, mimicking the prisoners.

The one in the middle started nodding along with him before recognizing the sarcasm and switching to shaking his head, "Oh, *no* sir … musta been … a accident … I reckon …" he trailed off lamely.

Baggs folded his arms and scowled, then spit dark tobacco juice to the side. He turned toward Billy and Stan, who were watching the interrogation with curiosity. "What you gonna do with such as these, I ask you? You seen that dead fella down there … we done caught him already once … not long ago and sent him off a prisoner. But the army don't know what to do with 'em; they don't reckon them soldiers, so can't think o' nothin' better'n makin' 'em swear an oath o' loyalty, giving them a clean shirt, and sending them on their way. Then they's right back out here, shootin' at us-kind like nothin' ever happened. No, sir. That just ain't workin', and it ain't how it's gonna be from here on."

He gave them a hard look for a moment, then turned back toward the prisoners, unholstered his pistol, and shot the middle one in the center of his chest. Before the other two could react, two rifle shots rang out, almost simultaneously—the two guards taking their cue from their Captain. When the smoke cleared, all three prisoners lay dead on the ground.

Baggs holstered his pistol and turned back toward Billy and Stan, still scowling, "Any objections?"

Stan just shrugged, then turned to Billy and said, "Seems squirrel hunting is … *dangerous* business."

Baggs laughed.

Billy nodded his agreement but resisted the urge to grin. He didn't generally agree with shooting prisoners, but Stan's grim humor *was* hard to resist.

Baggs ordered his men to dig a pit and bury the bodies. He wasn't religious about doing so if they were in a hurry, but right now they couldn't go anywhere until the bridge was ready. And it'd give a few of his men something useful to do while they were waiting.

Stan pulled out one of the maps Captain Chambers had given him, intending to confer with Baggs on Walters' possible whereabouts. He spread the map out on the ground and put a small rock on each corner to hold it flat.

"We started from small town called Ripley ... here, just after daybreak ... and headed east," Stan began, pointing to the place on the map.

"Yep, same's us, only we got a jump on you. Headed out o' there yesterday and camped out in the woods last night," Baggs answered. "We were headed for Spencer, just over ... here. That's twenty-five mile—give or take—between the two, so figured to get in after noon. We'd heard they was some snakes up around Spencer, and several more farther on toward Arnoldsburg. Reckon they got wind o' our doin's and thought to hinder us by breakin' this-here bridge. That puts us now ... right here, at Big Run where the road crosses by the bridge. With this delay we'll be lucky to reach Spencer before nightfall.

"Guess I ought to be sore about it, but ... well, hell; these things happen." He grinned then spat more tobacco juice, not seeming particularly upset.

"So where you figure this fella you're hunting ... what was his name again?"

"Walters."

"So where you figure this *Walters* might be?"

"Before we left Wheeling, we only heard of him ... here, at Buckhannon. But first night after a day riding train we visited old friend of Captain Chambers, name of Captain Leib."

"Cap Leib, the quartermaster up to Clarksburg? The fellow secured us a couple o' fine wagons. Seems a decent enough sort; got no complaints on him, despite his polished buttons."

"Yes ... is same fellow. He was telling us where *you* might be found—south of town called Parkersburg. He is also confirming report we had of fellow like Walters leading bushwhacking snake gang out east. Where we were doing fighting in Rich Mountain battle."

"Oh ... you boys were in that one, were you? Good piece o' work that was ... Anyway, Rich Mountain's a tiresome long hike from here—a hunert miles or more, like as not. Good news is, we're headed in that direction anyhow. You two join us, I expect we'll find more snakes to kill along the way. Once we've finished rousting out the bunch o' vermin 'round these parts, we can talk about headin' out to wrangle your man. Sound fair?"

Stan would have preferred a firmer commitment, but there was not much he could do about it for the moment. Probably best to save his *particular* powers of persuasion for later when the time came for that talk.

So he shrugged, "Is fair. We will help kill bushwhacking snakes along the way."

"Good! Seems you boys know the killin' business, so we're happy to have you. Welcome to the Snake Hunters."

"Thank you," was all Billy could think to say, but Stan just shrugged.

⁀❦⁀❦⁀❦⁀❦⁀❦⁀❦

As Baggs had predicted, the sun was setting by the time they finally neared Spencer. What he hadn't predicted was the dramatic change in the weather that'd hit them shortly after they left the newly repaired bridge at Big Run.

A cold front rolled in, with thick, low, scudding clouds covering the sun and dropping the temperature like a stone. The front brought with it a frigid, biting wind that cut to the bone. The only good part was it hadn't yet rained ... or snowed, but that was still a possibility.

Billy and Stan broke out their long, oiled overcoats and anything else they could wrap themselves in that was warm. But many of the Snake Hunters had only the clothes they were wearing, and some of these hadn't completely dried from the river crossing before the cold front hit.

The Snake Hunters did not suffer their ill fortune in silence, however. Baggs was forced to endure a non-stop stream of complaints and curses from his tired, cold, ragged company. Early on he'd given up his horse and sent it off with the forward scouts, so whatever his men suffered, he suffered as well.

Billy and Stan had taken his cue and dismounted as well, now leading their horses rather than riding.

To his credit, Baggs kept up a steady flow of encouragement and good humor, walking up and down the line as the men marched. "C'mon Martin … buck up Cooper … we're almost there, then we'll get ourselves warm. We'll build a big ol' fire when we get to town; I promise ye men; never fear. Keep movin' Cole … one foot after t'other, Wheeler. A nice hot meal when we gets to Spencer, boys … I've a mind to break out the whiskey when we get there," and on, and on, nearly non-stop.

Stan was impressed with the man and his company. They'd grumbled and complained; and ragged and undisciplined they seemed, yet still they obeyed and kept at it. Not a single man gave up or slipped away, as would be normal under such circumstances in many other irregular units.

As they approached the town, about a mile out, a man stepped from his hiding place behind a tree and walked out into the middle of the road. He stopped and wrapped his arms around his own shoulders, hopping up and down to keep warm, looking as miserable as Baggs' own men.

Baggs held up his hand for a halt and greeted the man as if he'd been expecting him, "Baldwin."

"Cap Baggs."

"What's the story, Baldwin? Are the snakes still in camp out north o' town?"

"No, sir. Though this God-awful cold snap has made your march a misery, no doubt, it *is* your great good luck."

"Good luck? How d'you figure, Baldwin?"

"Good luck on account o' them snakes done got froze solid out in their tents and come into town for to get theyselves warm. And it don't seem like they was expecting you today. As you can see, they ain't even set no guards out. I done sent our folk out to north and south to make sure no one's about, but I reckon they'll confirm all's quiet.

"We heard rumors they'd ruint the bridge over to Big Run, so I reckon they all figured you'd be hung up down there 'til sometime tomorrow at the least. But I know you better, sir. So I stayed out here ... freezing off my manly parts ... thank ye kindly for askin'. I reckoned you'd show up sooner rather than later."

"You figured right, Baldwin! There's a good fellow. So ... where's the bastards holed up, then? They done fortified a church or some such?"

"No, sir ... though it's what you'd o' done in their place, I reckon. But like I says, they don't appear to be expecting you to be paying 'em a visit this evenin'." He grinned, an evil looking leer, "Cap ... these sorry sons o' bitches have done gone right back to their own homes and hearths. Scattered theyselves all about town, the fools."

Baggs' face lit up and he beamed, "You don't say?! Damn ... that *is* good luck."

He turned back toward his men, "Good news, men! We're not only going to put a whuppin' on a whole passle o' snakes this eve, we're goin' to warm our frozen backsides in the process!"

Stan and Billy exchanged a look and a shrug. They couldn't reckon what he meant by it, but figured they'd find out soon enough.

An hour later they knew. With the help of Baldwin and several other Union sympathizers from Spencer, they'd quickly located the homes of the individual snakes they'd been after.

Stan stood with his arms crossed and a scowl on his face. He wasn't sure where Billy had got to in all the commotion, but figured he'd turn up later. He always did.

Stan watched as three of Baggs' men kicked in the door of a house and entered. Shots rang out, accompanied by a woman's scream. Moments later two men came out dragging a man's body by the legs before dumping it in the middle of the street. The third man came out escorting a woman by the arm. She was punching at him ineffectually with her free hand, which only made him laugh. He shoved her out into the street, where she immediately fell to her knees and started weeping over her dead husband.

Five more of Baggs' men entered the house, two carrying torches. In less than ten minutes they came streaming back out, their arms loaded down with foodstuffs, and one carrying a rifle he hadn't entered with.

Stan noticed they no longer carried torches. A few minutes later he saw bright orange lights flickering through the windows and the open doorway. Flames licked up the walls and quickly engulfed the house.

A man approached Baggs at a trot and stopped to make his report, "Cap Baggs ... Mr. Parker says to tell you we done finished up with all the Snakes' houses up the north side and asks, 'what next?'"

Baggs scratched at his beard as if contemplating the question, but before he could answer, the woman looked up from where she knelt and screamed, "Baggs! Your men ain't nothing but murderers and thieves!"

He gave her a serious look and nodded, "Yep ... I reckon so, ma'am. I reckon so, from where you sit. I ain't gonna deny the truth o' your words. But this here's war ... and such is how war is."

"Y'all calls *these* men snakes ... but they's all good men. It's y'all that's snakes ... no-good, Godless, snakes! Looters, butchers, and rapers of women ..."

"No, ma'am! There's where I must take exception ... I'll gamely bear your insults long as they's true. But I dare any man to swear my men ever done laid an unwelcome hand on any woman, nor bruised any child. There's the line we don't cross, ma'am. I'd skin my own men for doin' such a thing and they know it well.

"But as for your husband ... he was a bushwhackin' *snake* and got what was comin' to him. Good day to you, ma'am." He tipped his hat to her, turned and strode out to meet with Mr. Parker somewhere off to the north, his men following in his wake.

It was the fifth house Stan had watched them burn so far this evening. And he knew there'd been many others; he'd seen the glow of fire coming from various points around town in the distance.

But to Baggs' credit, his men were well disciplined; they'd not molested the women nor harmed the children, just as Baggs had claimed. Nor had they damaged any property or looted any houses other than those belonging to the rebels.

And before they torched each place, they'd warned the surrounding neighbors so they could be prepared to flee should the fires spread. Fortunately, none had, probably due to the frigid temperatures, and the surrounding vegetation and rooftops being cold and damp from the December weather. Also, the houses of the town were spaced well apart, helping to prevent the fires from crossing from one building to the next.

But Stan decided he did *not* like this method of warfare. He didn't care for the idea of bringing the war to men's own homes, putting their women and children out into the cold in the middle of winter. But he had to admit it would likely discourage others from joining the bushwhackers. And ... the house fires had allowed them all to finally "warm their backsides" even as Baggs had promised.

ᔪᔦᑕᔧᑖᔪᔦᑕᔧᑖᔪᔦᑕᔧᑖ

Nathan and Harry slipped into the hall of the convention, trying to be quiet and inconspicuous so as not to interrupt the current speaker. But it was a difficult task, considering both man and dog were large and imposing individuals. Nathan sat next to Tom and quickly shook his hand, then leaned across and grasped Margaret's two hands as well. She graced him with a squeeze and a quick smile. Harry plopped down on the hardwood floor with a heavy sigh, prompting a round of sniggers and chuckles throughout the room, and a scowl of reproach from the convention president. Harry seemed unconcerned, hanging his tongue out in the usual manner.

Nathan slipped a piece of paper into Tom's hand. He quickly read it, smiled at Nathan, then handed it on to Margaret. She read the brief telegram to herself, then looked back at Nathan and nodded.

> *Dec. 9, 1861, Clarksburg, Va. Nathan, have hosted your men Volkov & Creek this eve. Had word of Baggs at Parkersburg and sent them there wishing them good hunting. Will send any news.*
>
> *Best,*
>
> *Capt. C. Leib, Quartermaster, US Army Dept. of W.V.*

૨⟩ଽ⟩ભଓଽ⟩ଽ⟩ભଓଽ⟩ଽ⟩ભଓ

Despite a late night of drinking and feasting, the Snake Hunters were already up and moving before first light. The previous evening, Baggs had announced he'd received word of more snakes up around Arnoldsburg, another fourteen miles farther east. It'd take a full day on foot if they were to get there before dark.

Stan hadn't seen Billy the previous evening but wasn't especially concerned about it. Billy rarely slept under a roof, at least not with other men. Stan figured he'd had no interest in bedding down with dozens of men he didn't know in a barn Baggs had requisitioned and fortified for a bunkhouse.

And when Stan stepped out of the barn to relieve himself, just before sunup, he wasn't at all surprised to find Billy there, chatting with the off-duty sentries warming their hands around a glowing fire. He looked well rested and refreshed.

Stan assumed he himself did not look half so good. His pounding head gave mute testament to a night spent indulging in a bit more celebration than was good for him. He decided Billy was fortunate in his ambivalence toward whiskey and other strong liquor.

But Stan had always had a hard time resisting the jovial comradery of a group of fighting men, and drinking always seemed to go with it. Especially when in high spirits following a victory, such as it was.

"Good morning, Billy," Stan grumbled.

"Good morning, Stan. You look like something the Captain's dog got tired of chewing on," Billy smirked.

"Da ... and am feeling of same. Like most women I've known, whiskey is being not so friendly the morning after ... hmm ... after too much *indulgences*."

Billy laughed, and the two sentries chuckled and shook their heads knowingly. Stan grinned, but it was more of a grimace than a smile.

"And where have you been, Billy, while I was in barn last night punishing myself with too much whiskey?"

"Scouting. Same as I always do," Billy answered, resisting the urge to use Stan's favorite line on him: *is stupid question*.

Stan gazed at him dully, then nodded, "Da, da ... of course you were. I am being too thick-headed for thinking on it."

He was tempted to walk over to the well and dump a bucket of water over his own head, but the freezing temperatures and biting wind discouraged the idea. So he settled for a wipe-down with a wet rag he dipped into a nearby water bucket.

"You eat something, Billy?"

"Yes. I have eaten. Some jerky and hardtack from my pack. But I have seen they are cooking a breakfast with some food they stole yesterday. Over that way, around the barn. There may still be some left."

So Stan headed off in the direction Billy had pointed. His stomach growled at the thought, doing its best to override his pounding head.

☙ℰℭℛℭℬℰℰℭℛℭℬℰℰℭℛℭℬ

That day was nearly a repeat of the day before, sans the damaged bridge crossing; a long, cold march along the road, followed by an evening spent burning the homes of rebel snakes, this time in Arnoldsburg.

A key difference, however, was the lack of any actual rebels in town. Apparently, word of Baggs' impending approach had spread, and the snakes had opted for a retreat to their camp somewhere out in the woods, despite the continuing frigid weather; lowering clouds now carried the threat of snow.

But that hadn't stopped Baggs from rousting out the women and children and burning the homes of any men identified as rebel guerrillas. Fortunately for him there were several Union sympathizers in town who were only too happy to turn on their secessionist neighbors. One was even able to provide Baggs with the location of the rebel camp, some five miles to the north at a place where a stream called Sinking Spring Run emptied into the West Fork of the Little Kanawha River.

There had been little celebrating that evening, as the men knew the morning would likely find them in pitched battle with their enemies. Enemies who'd had a chance to dig in, and knew they were coming—never a welcome prospect, even for veterans like Billy and Stan. It made for a much more sober gathering, with men more apt to clean a rifle or sharpen a knife than down a drink.

The next morning, a three-hour march that started just before sunrise found Stan and Billy crouched next to Baggs and three of his senior men, gazing out at the rebel camp. Billy, already recognized as a scout par excellence by the Snake Hunters, was preparing to give Baggs his report.

Billy had left in the middle of the night after Baggs told him the expected location of the rebel camp. He'd spent the pre-dawn hours reconnoitering it while waiting for the arrival of Baggs and his men. Stan had wanted to go with him, but Billy said no; he would only scout, not attack, so Stan would only slow him down. Stan was a little peeved by this rebuff, though he knew it was likely true. But Billy was always brutally honest, a trait Stan could find little fault in, so he didn't argue the point.

"The enemy has dug in on that knoll," Billy began. "It is a good place for defense; two sides back up to where the small stream joins the larger."

"That'd be Sinking Spring Run coming in from the north, joining the West Fork as it bends to the west," Baggs said, and nodded.

"He has around forty men," Billy continued, "all have rifles and a few with pistols. They seem to have plenty of food, or at least they ate well to break this morning's fast. Though most slept in tents or on the ground, they have a dug in place with a low roof toward the back of their camp. Maybe a place for storing food and other supplies, but could be for their commander, if they have one."

"Ha. If they do, he'll not be in command for long," Baggs snorted.

"They have dug trenches on the sides away from the river and laid logs in front, so they will have good cover. As you can see, they have cleared the brush and trees for a few dozen yards all around. And they must be attacked up hill, or by men trying to cross the rivers."

Baggs scowled, "Any other *wonderful* news for me, scout?"

Billy looked puzzled, not understanding what Baggs found wonderful about the present situation. So he just shrugged.

Baggs turned to his men, "Piss-poor spot for a fight from where we sit."

They nodded, and the one named Fisher added, "And it sounds like we can't wait them out neither; they got plenty of supplies and easy access to water."

"True ... all true, curse the foul luck. Guess I should o' asked General McClellan for a cannon or two instead o' them wagons, though they'd be a nuisance to lug around in the woods."

The men nodded but had nothing useful to add.

"Damn. Damn it all to hell," Baggs said, then looked up at the sky, wrapped his arms around himself and shivered, "and this weather ain't ezacly to my liking neither."

"No, sir. And no damned snakes' houses to burn out here for to keep our precious bums warm," Fisher said with a wry grin.

Baggs looked at Stan and raised a questioning eyebrow. But Stan could think of nothing useful either, so he shrugged. "Sometimes there is nothing to do but pull up britches and fight. Hmm ... a few men of us will be killed, of course. But *is* war ... not whoring. These things will happen."

Baggs nodded but seemed unconvinced. Stan realized this was not Baggs' usual way. He was much more comfortable sneaking up on his enemy or ambushing him; a hard-fought frontal assault was not much to his liking, nor his expertise.

But Baggs' dilemma was resolved before he was forced to make a hard decision. While they crouched, gazing up at the enemy's fortified camp, Wilbert Potter crept up behind Baggs and tapped him on the shoulder.

Stan noticed two men he'd brought with him, men who were *not* of the Snake Hunters; they wore the uniform of Union soldiers!

Baggs turned around and nearly jumped when he saw the soldiers. Though they crouched down, recognizing the danger of the situation, they both saluted Baggs.

"Captain Baggs?" the one in front asked. He wore a sergeant's yellow stripes on his dark blue tunic sleeve. The other was a private.

"Yes, I'm Baggs. Who're you men, and where'd you come from?"

"I'm Sergeant Perry, and this here's Private Stone. We're with the Eleventh Virginia ... the *loyal* Virginia, of course."

"But ... how the devil did you get way out here in these woods?"

"Oh, our Major ... uh, Major Trimble that is ... sent us out ahead to reconnoiter the river on account o' he's got some boats coming to ferry a company of us back up to the North."

"I was standing there, doin' my duty watching the horses again, as usual," Potter added, "when next thing I know I'm staring down two rifle barrels. Happy I was to see 'em wearin' the blue, I can tell you that!"

"Yep, and when he told us his commander was Captain Baggs, who was out scouting an enemy position, we came straightaway. What's the situation, sir, if you don't mind my asking?"

"Not good sergeant, not good—look for yourself. Rebs have got themselves a good defensible redoubt over yonder. Like as not several o' my boys'll get themselves kilt if we try rushing 'em."

The sergeant crept up next to Baggs to have a look. "How many you reckon, sir?"

"Oh ... at least forty we figure. All well-armed, with plenty of ammo and stocks."

"Hmm ... forty you say? Well, Major Trimble's got a whole company with him ... just over a hundred officers and men. You reckon they might be of assistance to you, sir? No offense, Captain ... not meanin' to imply you *need* any help, sir. I'd not want to insult you nor your men."

"No offense taken, sergeant," Baggs answered, then turned and continued to gaze off at the enemy's camp.

"Take me to your major, sergeant. I'd have a word with him, if I may."

"Yes, sir. He's just a couple miles back, over to the east from here where we made camp last night. Lucky we didn't press on to the river and blunder right into these yahoos."

Though he wasn't invited, Stan decided he wanted to come along and hear what this major had to say. And since Baggs didn't object, he figured that was permission enough. Fisher also went with them. Billy stayed behind to continue observing the enemy.

When they arrived at the Union camp, Sergeant Perry led them straight to Major Trimble. Trimble was presently sitting on a chair wearing blue pants with a red stripe down the side tucked into well-worn riding boots. His suspenders dangled down at his sides and he only wore a gray, long-sleeved undershirt. He had a bucket of water in front of him, his face was lathered with soap, and he held a razor in his hand. He looked up with curiosity as the men stepped up to him. He glanced from Baggs to Stan, who seemed to startle him, likely from his great size.

The sergeant and private snapped to attention and saluted, as did the three men who'd followed them, Stan included, though they wore no uniforms.

"Major, this here's Captain Baggs of the Virginia Homeguard Independent Scouts ... also called 'Snake Hunters,'" the sergeant announced.

"Ah! Baggs. I've heard of you and your men, of course, though I haven't yet had the pleasure. I'm Trimble, Eleventh Virginia. I'd salute, but as you can see ..."

The Major spoke with a crisp, British accent, which surprised the newcomers.

"No need for that, Major," Baggs responded, lowering his hand and grinning, "stay as you were, sir. And the pleasure is all mine, Major; happy to be makin' your acquaintance. But I'm thinkin' ... on account o' your fine speech and all ... you ain't from around here, sir?"

Trimble smiled, "Well, I could give my usual flippant, response ... 'No, I'm from Philadelphia!'," he chuckled. "But as you surmise, sir, I am a recent transplant from Her Majesty's own United Kingdom of Great Britain and Ireland. Served in the Crimea under General Scarlett. Fought in the big brew-up at Balaclava."

Trimble looked at Baggs expectantly but received only a blank look.

"You know ... *Charge of the Light Brigade* and so on? No?"

Baggs looked over at Stan who just shrugged, and then at Fisher who did likewise. He turned back to Trimble, "Sorry, Major ... ain't had much formal schoolin'. Never heard of any such battles ... though I'm sure you done your duty as was called for, sir."

Trimble frowned, but then sighed and seemed to relax, "Ah, well ... At any rate, when I enlisted and informed them of my previous military experience, they made me a major straight away, though I'd been no better than a ranker in Scarlett's army." He waved the hand, still holding the razor, dismissively.

"Sorry ... I digress, gentlemen. You're not here to hear my long, sad soliloquy; of that I'm certain. Baggs ... last I'd heard you were operating over by the Ohio ... somewhere south of Parkersburg, as I recall. Didn't expect to find you in this section of woods."

"Oh, we *was* over there, sir. But found it to be slim pickin's. Too many blue coats and brass buttons marching around ... no offense, sir. Then a man I know sent word of a group o' snakes

297

operating 'round these parts, so we packed up and come over to have a little look-see."

"Ah. And … have you found your quarry, sir?" the major asked.

"Oh, yes, sir! You could say we done a good bit o' business over to Spencer town, and then a bit more back at Arnoldsburg."

"Ah, happy to hear it! You've fared well then, I take it? Taken many casualties?"

"Only one kilt, over to Big Run where the rebs done broke a bridge and then bushwhacked us trying to wade the creek. Otherwise, nothing to speak of."

"Good, good! We've also had an easy go of it, thank the luck, though there's been little enough action. Our regimental base is at Parkersburg, but I was sent with a company some months back to patrol the roads north of Charleston. Doing much the same business as you, no doubt … trying to track down these elusive 'snakes,' as you call them. Not an easy job, I find. I'll hand it to you if you've had any success at all. We heard of some activity out east of here, so set out to have a look. But never found more than a few sorry-looking sots. Claimed to be hunting squirrels, if you can believe it?!"

Baggs smirked and gave Stan a look. Stan rolled his eyes and shook his head, "Yep," Baggs said, "We seen our share o' them squirrel hunters ourselves, Major."

"Yes, I'm sure you have. Anyway, since our tour was about up, and with this God-forsaken, miserable weather setting in, I arranged for HQ to send down a small fleet of boats to ferry us up the Little Kanawha back to Parkersburg. Save us the long hike. Sent the sergeant here over to the river to see if there was yet any sign of them. Guess he found you instead."

"Yessir, that he did. And it was a timely meeting, I'm thinking."

"Oh? How so?"

"We've tracked a group of snakes over to the river. They've built themselves a bit of a fort on a rise hard by the river where Sinking Spring Run empties in.

"Ah. How many rebs?"

"Forty or so, we reckon. Well-armed and supplied. We figure they got wind of us coming, and now are well dug-in; clearly expecting our visit."

"And *your* numbers?"

"Fifty-three officers and men. Oh ... make that fifty-five ... forgot about our most recent recruits." He glanced over at Stan and grinned. Stan nodded.

"Hmm ... bit of a tough nut to crack then, sounds like."

"Yes, sir. That's what we was thinkin'."

"Well, I've got no artillery, more's the pity, but I do have a hundred good officers and men, itching for a fight. Lord knows they're bored to distraction and could use the action."

"Well, I can't say I would mind your help, sir. But ..." Baggs was suddenly thoughtful.

"But what, Baggs? What's troubling you, sir?"

"Well, it's just that me and the boys've been hunting down these rascals for months now. Crawlin' on our bellies through the woods, wadin' the streams, eatin' bugs and tree bark when we could get no better. And now we've finally run a good bunch of the varmints to ground. I don't much like the thought of your boys steppin' in at the last minute and grabbin' all the credit."

Stan was surprised. He cared nothing for such considerations and hadn't taken Baggs for someone who did either. But apparently such was the case.

"Ah ... yes, I understand your concern, Captain," the Major answered, not seeming at all put out by it. He reached down and scooped several handfuls of water, rinsing the soap from his face before toweling it dry. Then he stood and pulled up his suspenders.

"Tell you what, Baggs. When we get back to civilization, we'll tell the papers it was a joint operation between Captain Baggs and his Snake Hunters, and Major Trimble with a company of the Eleventh Virginia Volunteer Infantry Regiment."

But Baggs didn't immediately agree, and still had an anxious look on his face. Stan realized it wasn't necessarily Baggs himself who wanted credit; he was worried his men would feel betrayed if the regular army got the credit for their all their hard, dangerous work.

Major Trimble sensed Baggs' hesitation, so decided to sweeten his offer, "Listen, Baggs ... once we wrap up these scoundrels, I'll give you enough boats to transport the prisoners back to Atheneum Prison in Wheeling. We'll still say it was a joint operation, but us men of the Eleventh will debark at our HQ in Parkersburg. Then you can take the prisoners the rest of the way up the Ohio yourselves. You'll be the ones who deliver them to the proper government authorities at Wheeling and you'll be the darlings of the newspapers up North when you do."

This brought a smile to Baggs' face. He held out his hand, "You've got a deal, Major."

Trimble took the proffered hand and shook it firmly, "Good. Then let's sit down and make a plan. Sergeant, go fetch the Lieutenant over to my tent, if you please. And do just come join us yourself. There's a good fellow."

"Yes, sir!" the sergeant saluted, then turned and trotted off to find the Lieutenant.

ಬಡೆಂಞಬಡೆಂಞಬಡೆಂಞಬಡೆಂಞ

Peter Sourburn glanced at his pocket watch in the light of the small fire they'd built behind a berm on top of the rise that currently served as a fort for the local Moccasin Rangers. This fire pit was the one place men could come to get warm in safety; they dare not light any fires out by the forward lines for fear the enemy would target men in the glow.

He noted it was nearly seven o'clock and already pitch black out. He felt able to relax a little for the first time since mid-morning when the forward pickets had been forced inside the log perimeter by the arrival of Baggs and his so-called Snake Hunters.

Sourburn uttered a curse under his breath. *Baggs!* The man was a *devil*. He seemed to be everywhere you didn't want him, but never anywhere you did. He was the one man every Ranger most wanted to kill, and the one man they couldn't seem to ever get at.

Sourburn had ordered the men to keep a close watch on the enemy, and only every-other man would be allowed to sleep in shifts throughout the night. Even then, they'd sleep in the trenches with their rifles hard-by and loaded so they'd be ready the instant there was trouble.

But most likely there wouldn't be. Even Baggs with all his tricks was unlikely to try an attack on an unknown fortification at night. It would give every advantage to the defenders, who knew their ground even with no light to see. And the open slope in front of them would show dim silhouettes of any advancing enemies, even in near total darkness. So there was little fear of being taken by surprise. Baggs was unlikely to risk it.

No, the most likely time for an attack would be just as the sun was rising in the morning, trying to catch them still napping. But they'd be ready; Sourburn was determined he'd see to that!

He leaned forward to get a bit more of the fire's heat, pulling his uniform coat up tight around his neck in an attempt to staunch the flow of cold air creeping down his back. He reflected on how he was the only man in camp wearing a uniform, such as it was. Not a real *army* uniform, but rather the uniform he'd worn in his role as Deputy Sheriff of Roane County before the troubles. Before the secession.

He sighed a heavy sigh. *Back when things were normal.* Not for the first time he pined for those days of light duty and little danger. *And regular meals with a warm bed at night,* he reminded himself. It had been such a dull posting, in fact, he'd also taken a job as Postmaster just to fill the time.

Then he grinned at the thought of the uniform he wore; how that fact alone had singled him out as the *de facto* leader of the group. Multiple disparate groups of men from different counties had been drawn together by their common desire to resist the Yankee sympathizers and the Union army's occupation of the western half of Virginia. And because he wore a uniform, and nobody else did, men just naturally looked to him to take charge. So he had; simple as that, though he'd never claimed to be an officer.

Now he wasn't so sure it'd been a good thing. He felt responsible for the lives of these men and inadequate in his knowledge and abilities. They looked to him for guidance and leadership, but more often than not he had no idea what they should do, and just went with his gut instincts. He'd seen the knoll backed up against the confluence of the two streams and knew enough to understand it was a good defensive position, needing only the clearing away of underbrush and erection of a low fortification to make it a good redoubt against Baggs and his men.

He'd have preferred to run away, leading Baggs on a fruitless chase through the woods until he gave it up out of pure frustration or boredom. But the nasty winter weather that'd hit in the last few days made that option untenable. To ask men to live out in the woods for weeks on end in the cold of winter, with little shelter and dwindling food stocks was not a pleasant prospect. Better to dig in and try to fight off Baggs right here, still only some five miles from town.

He knew their numbers were roughly equal, and he'd never heard of Baggs carrying artillery, so he liked their chances. Besides, they didn't have to actually beat the enemy, just keep from being overrun. Eventually Baggs must tire of the sport. And likely he'd run out of food stocks before they did. Then he'd have no choice but to leave them in peace. They might even have a chance to turn the tables on him, and then the hunter could become the hunted. Sourburn liked that prospect, and it brought another grin to his face.

His reverie was suddenly interrupted by a shout. He looked up and something caught his eye. A strange, streak of light moving across the sky. His first thought was a shooting star, but then he remembered the heavy cloud cover. He watched the light as it arced high above the camp and then began its descent. It was entirely baffling; a phenomenon entirely out of his reckoning. He watched, open-mouthed, as the object sped to earth, hitting with a *thunk* on top of the thatched roof over their dugout storage bin. Sparks scattered from the object, immediately catching the roof's matted grass and branches afire. Flames leapt up.

Sourburn sprang to his feet. The storage bin held among other things, their kegs of gunpowder! "Fire! Fire!" he shouted, and then realized his men might be confused and think he meant for them to use their rifles. "The storage bin is on fire!" he shouted. "Quick, fetch buckets and run to the river!"

And then he remembered the enemy, and added "Men on the woods side, stay at your posts. Watch for the enemy!" but even before he finished the command, he saw another fiery missile hit one of the tents, ripping through the fabric, scattering sparks as it impacted. In seconds the tent was also ablaze. And before he could think what to do or say, another tent was hit. It, too, quickly ignited.

A dozen men had jumped over the logs and were already racing down to the water's edge at the smaller of the two streams, buckets in hand. A thunderous eruption of rifle fire with multiple fiery flashes came from directly across the river. Three men fell. The others dropped their buckets and scrambled back up the hill. Sourburn watched in horror as several dozen men with rifles jumped into the stream and began wading across.

"Prepare to fire!" he shouted, unholstering his pistol and gazing down at the approaching enemy, many of whom had already reached the near shore. Then his eyes widened in shock when the growing firelight revealed the enemy's rifles held bayonets! And then he noticed a gold sparkle on the front of the enemies' jackets, twinkling in the dark from ... brass buttons ... on uniforms! *Regular Union soldiers! Damn! Where'd they come from?*

But even as he strove to digest this dire news, he heard a great shout behind him, and the sounds of many rifles fired off randomly, in chaotic fashion. Though the raging fires made it difficult to see the other line out toward the woods, he could see men fighting hand-to-hand *inside* the camp.

"Fire at will!" he shouted at the men hunkered down behind logs, facing the river. The rifles of his men quickly answered. He turned and sprinted across the open ground toward the other line.

He had to circle wide around the still burning storage bin, praying to God the powder didn't go off as he was passing near. His eyes were momentarily dazzled by the raging fires.

When he arrived at the front lines all was in chaos. Men wrestled on the ground, trying to bash one another with rifle butts, or skewer each other with knives. None of these men wore uniforms, so at first glance it was impossible to tell his men from the enemy.

And then his eye was caught by a gigantic man grasping a rifle by the barrel in one huge hand, wielding it like a club, knocking men aside or to the ground with the buttstock.

Sourburn raised his pistol, aimed it at the man's broad back, cocked the hammer and ... Something hit him hard in the center of his chest, a blow of stunning force that knocked the breath from him and staggered him back a step. He gazed down and in the center of his tunic saw a neat hole, oozing red around the edges.

He could not catch his breath. His sight dimmed. The pistol fell from his lifeless grasp. He glanced up and saw a man gazing straight at him, holding out a pistol. Gun smoke swirled up around the man's face—the face of a living nightmare, *an actual Indian!*

What an odd ending, he thought, before all went dark.

ഇഇൠ൮ഇഇൠ൮ഇഇൠ൮

Stan had a feeling the remainder of the evening would've looked a lot different if Baggs and his men had been completely in charge. He had a vision of a raucous and undisciplined camp of drunken revelers celebrating their victory, such as he'd seen that first night back in Spencer after burning the snakes' houses.

But Major Trimble was a different sort of officer altogether. Though pleasant and affable to speak with, he believed in running a tight ship. He'd clearly been trained in a rigid, professional, soldierly fashion, and expected the same of his men.

So though there were happy feelings of success and comradery between the two disparate groups of men, the celebration was subdued. And the Major had posted sentries and continued to send out regular patrols, though it was likely they'd captured or killed most of their enemies for miles around.

As soon as the fires had been put out and the prisoners secured, Trimble had ordered his camp relocated to the enemy's redoubt, it being more defensible and closer to the river. His men accomplished this with efficiency and in short order, to Stan's way of thinking.

But though Trimble didn't believe in letting down the regiment's guard, he wasn't personally opposed to celebrating a victory. He'd invited Baggs' officers and his own to his new command tent, set up next to the burned-out rebel supply bin. Fortunately, the Union troops were able to throw enough water on it to put the fire out before the gunpowder went off, though Baggs had been disappointed the powder had been soaked and was no longer useable, being fused solid.

And though he wasn't technically an officer, Stan invited himself, not expecting anyone to object. And when he'd approached, the Major had waved him over to sit beside him. Baggs sat on the other side of Trimble. Though the Major had brought along a camp chair, it was the only one they had, so all sat on the ground in a circle around the campfire—the very same the Confederate leader Sourburn had used to warm his hands just before the battle.

Baggs had broken out one of the whiskey kegs Stan had given him, and shared it out, for which the Major was grateful. His company had run out of decent liquor several weeks back, and though some men weren't opposed to drinking the local, home-distilled spirits when they could get them, Trimble found the stuff entirely unpalatable.

Trimble raised his metal canteen cup, "Gentlemen. Here's to a finely executed battle," he looked over at Baggs and nodded, "and to the Snake Hunters, may they have continued success against the rebels. Cheers!"

They all took a drink, then Trimble turned to Stan, "And much thanks to you, Mr. Volkov. Your idea for the Indian to shoot fire arrows was the key to our victory, I have no doubt."

"Billy." Stan said.

"What's that?"

"His name is Billy. Billy Creek. Billy shot fire arrows."

"Ah. Sorry, I stand corrected. At any rate, I am most grateful to Mr. Creek for the timely exercise of his archery skills."

When Stan looked confused, Trimble clarified, "uh ... his skills with bow and arrow, I should say."

"Oh, yes. He is very skilled. With bow ... with knife, rifle, pistol ... even bare hands. He is *true* man killer." Then he grinned, "I am wanting to be like *him* when grow up!" then he laughed.

"God help us if you grow any more!" Trimble said, looking up at the younger man who towered over him by nearly a foot. "Anyway, your plan was the key to a successful operation. Rarely have I seen one come off so smoothly. Like clockwork, wouldn't you say?"

"Da, da. Was good. Very good. But ... those of us from Texas are used to such, fighting for Captain Chambers. Our Captain expects to win every battle and kill every enemy. And ... we of his men *like* to give Captain what he wants."

"Captain *Chambers* you say? Sounds like my kind of officer. What regiment is he with?"

Stan shrugged, "None yet. He is working with governor ... training new Virginia regiments. Seventh, and now Eighth. Though I am thinking maybe he will take charge of Eighth when ready. Oh ... this is reminding me of question ... have been wondering ... how can *your* regiment be Eleventh Virginia, when Eighth is still in training? To say nothing of Ninth and Tenth."

"Ah! Good question, Volkov. My understanding is they handed out the regimental numbers some time ago, and it can take months to fill out the numbers, commission the officers, acquire equipment, train the ranks, and so forth. The truth is our Eleventh is also still in training, officially, and not yet listed for active service. We've not yet come up to our required numbers, you see. But those of us in *this* company were among the first to sign on. We'd been enlisted, trained and equipped for many months, and getting bored sitting around camp. So I pleaded with our Colonel to let me take a company of men out for a little training exercise, to which he consented. So here we are."

"Oh! Now this is making sense. Well, I am happy we Snake Hunters helped in training!"

Trimble shared a smile with him and nodded. They raised their metal cups and clinked them before taking another drink.

Chapter 10. Into the Lion's Den

*"When you go into the lion's den, you don't tippy toe in.
You carry a spear, you go in screaming like a banshee.
You kick doors in and say, 'Where's the son of a bitch!?'
If you go in any other way you're going to lose."*
– Brian Billick

Friday December 13, 1861 – Sinking Springs Run, Virginia:

Thanks to Trimble's more constrained celebration, Stan felt clear headed and refreshed in the morning, for which he was grateful. He'd sought out Billy first thing, finding him out past the edge of camp, keeping an eye on the surrounding woods.

Now that they'd crushed the bushwhackers in the local area, Stan wanted to talk with Baggs about going after Walters. This time he meant to get a firm commitment on it.

They walked together back to the middle of the camp near Trimble's command tent. There they found Baggs, pencil in hand walking down the row of laid-out dead men, recording their names. Surprisingly only five rebels had been killed and none on the Union side, with very few wounded. The attack had been such a complete surprise with such overwhelming force there'd been little time to fight. Most rebels had surrendered before ever firing a shot.

In the lead up to the battle, Baggs and his Snake Hunters, with Stan at the fore, had quietly crawled up the hill on their bellies. So by the time Billy's arrows were launched they were within a few yards of the enemy's lines, unobserved by the enemy. As planned, as soon as they heard the sound of Trimble's guns on the far side of the river, they scrambled to their feet, and launched their assault.

The rebel prisoners sat cross-legged on the ground next to the bodies of their men, their hands bound in front with a length of thick rope. Baggs quizzed them on the names of the dead men as he went along. When he came to the last body, he noticed the man wore a uniform.

"And ... who's this dandy with the brass buttons?" he asked.

"That there's our leader ... or was," one of them said, "he was deputy sheriff in this-here county before the fighting. Name's Peter Sourburn."

"Hmm ... all right," Baggs said, scratching the last name with his pencil on the small, folded piece of paper he held cupped in his left hand.

Fisher, who'd been watching him as he wrote down the names, said, "No, Cap. Not *Lower*burn ... the man said *Sour*burn ... with an 'S'!"

"Oh ... shit! I'll fix it ... ah ... dang it! Pencil broke again. Damned thing keeps breaking on me. Must o' crushed it when I was crawling up the hill in the dark last night. Hell, I'll fix it up later when I fetch a new pencil out o' my bag."

Stan stepped up to him, and surveyed the prisoners, thirty-four in all, "What about these prisoners? You will be shooting them now?" He noticed several bound men winced and involuntarily ducked their heads when they heard this.

But Baggs just scowled. "No, Volkov. I ain't gonna shoot them."

"Oh? Why not? You are now going soft?"

"Well, for one, I ain't gonna do such a thing in front o' the Major and his men. Regular soldiers can be ... *squeamish* ... on it. Likely I'd have to endure an earful of nonsense after, and I'm in too good a humor this morning for such bellyaching. And for another, it's gonna look mighty fine leadin' such a passel o' snakes into that prison in Wheeling with them newspaper writers hard by writing the whole thing down."

"Hmph. I will never understand why man cares about such. But what will you do with prisoners while you are hunting more snakes? I want to make plans for killing the stinking villain our Captain wants."

"I won't have to do nothing with them prisoners. The Major's gonna supply us with enough boats to ferry them and all my men back to Wheeling. He says the boats should be here in a few days. When they get here, I intend to board and head upriver."

"But ... then ... when will you be returning?"

"Well, I do like the thought o' spending Christmas in a real bed. And drinking good whiskey with a roof overhead. With this foul weather settin' in ... I'm starting to think we may wait 'til it warms up. Say ... more toward spring, around end o' February or more likely March."

"March?! *Blyad!* What about fellow we hunt? You said you'd help us if we helped you kill snakes. We have killed snakes ... and captured more; and much of this is being thanks to Billy's fiery arrows."

"Now, lookie here, Volkov; I never *promised* nothin'. I said when the time done come we'd *talk* about it. Well ... we ARE talking about it. But I'm decidin' the answer is 'no.' At least for now. You want to consider takin' up the varmint's trail again come spring, we can talk on it then."

Stan suddenly had a dark look, "*No!* I am *done* talking ... I am about to start cracking someone's thick skull!" he growled, balling up his right fist.

Baggs' eyes widened, and Fisher took a step back in alarm. The three men standing guard over the prisoners turned their rifles toward Stan. They looked nervous and uncertain about what was happening.

But Stan felt a sharp pain on the back of his left arm. He glanced down and saw Billy had reached out and pinched him to get his attention. His friend held a serious expression when their eyes met. For a long moment there was silence as the two men stared at each other. No one else moved.

"It is of no matter, Stan," Billy finally said. "Never mind him. We will find Walters and kill him ourselves. We don't need them."

Stan said nothing but continued to stare at Billy. Finally, he nodded, let out his breath in a great sigh, and relaxed his fist. He looked back toward Baggs and his men and could see they had also relaxed. The guards had returned to pointing their rifles at the prisoners, and Baggs was grinning. "No hard feelings, Volkov?" he offered, extending his hand.

Stan scowled at him, then turned and stalked off. Billy gave Baggs a similar withering look, then followed after.

Billy had to go at a fast trot to catch up with Stan's broad strides, finally reaching him about halfway across the camp. "Stan, wait ... I have thought of a plan."

Stan stopped and turned, "Plan? What is plan?"

"I was thinking just now ... we have all these snakes for prisoners. And from what Baggs says, they are coming from counties all around the state. Maybe one of them has seen Walters or knows where he is."

"Hmm ... is good thought, Billy. Could be. But ... soldiers may not like us poking prisoners with knives for answers. They may be ... how is it Baggs was saying ... *squeamish?* Yes, I think that is right word. Anyway, how you think we get them to talk, to give away one of their own ... without the *bruising* of a few?"

Billy scratched his chin for a moment, gazing down at his feet. When he looked up, he was grinning, "Well ... we *do* still have some of the Captain's whiskey."

Stan smiled and nodded his head, "Is good thinking, Billy."

💩💩💩💩💩💩💩💩

An hour and a quarter later, they'd interrogated more than half the men with no success. It was a slow, time-consuming process as they had to take each man away from the group one at a time to ask their questions, knowing no one would talk in front of his fellows, whiskey or no.

But after each had been quizzed about Walters they couldn't just be put back into the group of other prisoners; they'd likely spread the word about the questions being asked, which could encourage someone to make up a story just to get a shot or two of the whiskey. They decided they'd have to move the prisoners to a new spot with new guards after the interrogation.

So Stan had talked with Major Trimble to get his assent to the plan. He was agreeable, as long as they promised there'd be no torture of the prisoners, to which Stan agreed. Trimble even offered up his command tent for the project, so they'd have privacy when quizzing the captives.

It had seemed a good plan, but now Stan was beginning to have his doubts, and was starting to re-think his promise of going soft on the prisoners as one of Trimble's privates brought in the latest captive and sat him down on the floor of the tent.

"What is name ... and where from?" Stan asked, already bored of the routine. This part was just to get them talking and relaxed a little. Stan knew it was always easier to get someone to open up if you used their name. And he knew Baggs had already written down all their names with his pencil, so they had no reason not to tell him.

"I'm Jeremiah Crane ... from Upshur County way," the man answered, looking back and forth between Stan and Billy anxiously. He was lean, with long, ill-kempt hair and only a thin, wispy beard. Not much more than a boy.

"Upshur? What town you from, Crane?" Stan asked. They had a map of the area rolled out on Trimble's camp table and were taking turns between asking questions and marking points on the map where men were from and where they had been recently.

"Oh, well I reckon the biggest town there 'bouts would be Buckhannon. My folks own a small spread 'bout thirteen miles east o' there."

At the mention of Buckhannon, Stan's interest perked up; Buckhannon was the place of the last known sighting of Walters.

"Is good, Crane—we are looking for man ... maybe a rebel like yourself ... was said to be somewhere near Buckhannon."

"Uh ... why you lookin' for this man?"

"Oh, well ... we have certain *business* with him."

"Well, I ain't gonna tell you nothin'. You's on the side o' them Yankee invaders. Ain't gonna help you catch a fellow reb. No, sir," and though his words were bold, he said them in a quavering voice that betrayed his fear of these men. He knew he was at their mercy, and even if he hadn't been bound, likely there'd be little he could do against them. The one was clearly a real, savage Indian from out west ... likely the one who'd attacked their camp with fire arrows the night before. And the other was the most frightening man he'd ever seen; huge, strong, and fierce looking. Not men to be crossed lightly.

And his fears seemed to be realized when the big man pulled out a large, wicked looking knife and held it up in front of Crane's face. He flinched, and tried to move back, but the man grabbed his bound hands and stretched them forward. Then with a sudden movement he sliced through the cords binding Crane's hands.

"Uh ... thanks," Crane said, and rubbed his wrists where the rope had chafed them.

But Stan just smiled, shook his head, and returned the knife to its sheath. "Do not be worrying so much, Crane. We are not wanting to hurt you. We are wanting to be helping you, no?" he turned toward Billy, who nodded, and smiled.

"Uh ... how will you be helping me?"

"Well ... let me ask you, Crane ... are you liking to be drinking the whiskey? Yes? Ah, is *good*! We have some *fine* whiskey; is from Kentucky ... is very good! And if you are telling us what we want to know, nobody is getting hurt, and you are getting good whiskey. And no one of your friends will be knowing nothing about it. Yes? There's a good fellow.

"So ... this fellow we seek ... he is from down to Greenbrier County. He has very large farm there. Many slaves. This fellow is ... hmm ... maybe forty years, more or less. But strong, not feeble. Not too tall, with chest like beer barrel. Is said he has men with him he bosses. Eight, ten ... maybe more? Are you knowing man like this, Crane?"

Billy had pulled out the whiskey bottle from his pack and set a tin cup on the Major's camp table. He now eyed Crane expectantly, waiting for the right response before filling the cup.

"Uh ... could be," Crane said, eyeing the whiskey bottle eagerly. "What was his name, anyway?"

But Stan shook his head and waggled his finger in front of Crane's face, "Oh no, Crane. I may be big fellow, and not speaking like am from around here, but don't mistake me for fool. *You* must be telling us man's name to get whiskey."

"Oh. O' course ... sorry. Wasn't thinkin' o' that. But ... can you tell me anything more? The Greenbrier County thing would help, 'cept I don't rightly know where most men I meet come from, and some ain't too talkative on it. Likely for fear o' gettin' their home folks in trouble. Seem to recall seeing several men who might look like that."

"Hmm ... I will tell you *one* more thing. This fellow is cold and mean as *real* snake, not like you normal fellows Baggs calls snakes. Does not look at man when he talks ... and never laughs, never smiles. Very strange man. And would rather kill than shake hands ... enjoys beating black men with whip until dead," Stan scowled darkly at the thought.

But Crane perked up at this description, "Oh! Yeah ... I know'd a fellow like that. Gave me the chills, he did. Couldn't get away from him fast enough. Had this odd way of looking at you ... like you was no more'n a dead thing layin' on the ground and not a man at all. No smile, nor frown, nor scowl, just ... *nothing*. Spooky it was."

Stan exchanged a look with Billy, then said, "And ... the name?"

"Uh ... yeah. It was ... hmm ... what was it? It's been a month or more, and I only spent a few days with his gang before sneakin' away."

Stan realized he was holding his breath in hopeful anticipation, silently willing Crane to remember the name.

"W ... something. Wilson? Wilkins? No, that ain't right. Walker, maybe? Yes, that seems like that may be it. Walker ... I think."

"Are you sure?" Stan looked him hard in the eyes, as if trying to read the truth in them.

Crane looked down anxiously. "No ... sorry, just can't seem to recall. But I think that's close ... something like ..."

"Walters?" Billy asked, gazing intently into Crane's eyes as he said it.

"Oh! Yep! That's it. Walters. Yes, I'm sure of it."

Stan looked at Billy, who nodded and said, "He tells it true."

"Is good!" Stan said, patting Crane firmly on the back and smiling. "Now you are having drink of good whiskey."

Billy pulled the cork from the bottle and poured a small amount into the tin cup on the table, then handed it across to Crane.

"Just *one* drink? I thought you was gonna give me the whole bottle."

"Is not so fast, Crane. You get drink for answers. We are only starting. Now we need know everything you are recalling of Walters. Where he was when you saw him, how many men he has and what weapons they carry, where he was going, and so on. Everything you heard him saying. Every time he took piss or shit in woods. This we want know. Each time you answer question, we give another drink. Is good?"

"Yeah ... okay. And don't worry, as I said, I wasn't much liking this Walters, rebel or no. I'll not mind if you put an end to a fellow like that. Then I'll never have to see him again."

Then Stan smiled his wicked, predatory grin. "Oh, do not be worrying, Crane. When we are finally catching Walters, we will be killing him until he is *completely* dead this time."

෨෪෬෬෨෪෬෬෨෪෬෬

"I am sorry to hear your son David is not at home," Billy said, taking another sip of hot coffee at the Harts' kitchen table. Stan nodded his agreement. The last time they'd been in the Harts' house it was just after the Battle of Rich Mountain. At that time, wounded soldiers filled every room and the walls were pock-marked with bullet holes from the battle.

"He was a brave man and guided us well. Without him our attack would not have succeeded," Billy concluded.

"Thank you for saying so, Mr. Creek," Joseph Hart said. Mr. Hart looked old, and haggard, to Billy's eyes. A man who'd seen a lot of years and raised many children. His wife, Susan, likewise looked careworn, gray-haired and bent with age.

"Seems he took a liking to young Captain Brantley during the fighting here," Mr. Hart continued, "Left with the intent to sign on with the Tenth Indiana. Though they was mustered out from their initial three-month enlistment while still up at Beverly, they was re-formed out in Indianapolis a few months back. Now they's

314

part o' General Thomas's division, Department of Ohio from what I understand. We done got a letter from David a few months back. He was out in Kentucky at the time, though Lord knows where he may be now. They made him Commissary Sergeant, though I know he was hoping for a lieutenant's commission on account o' his service to General Rosecrans. He didn't say what happened on that, so we can only guess."

Stan nodded, "Well, he was fine fellow, as Billy says. And we are thanking you for hospitality. Warm coffee is very good for cold bones. We have had ... long, icy ride before getting here."

"I should think so!" Mrs. Hart said, "all the puddles is frosted over, and smells like it's gonna snow. Brrr ..." she wrapped her arms around herself and shivered. "How long y'all been out ridin' in this God-forsaken coldness?"

Stan looked over at Billy and shrugged, "Today is only coming from town of Buckhannon, so ... hmm ... five, six hours maybe. But before is two long cold days from place where Sinking Springs Run joins big river."

"Well, no more traveling for you men today," she declared emphatically, brooking no argument. "We'll fetch you a warm meal and a warm bedroom after. It's the least we can do for good Union men, and friends of David's."

"Thank you kindly, ma'am," Billy answered. "We are much obliged to you."

"Is true," Stan nodded, "will be good to be out of cold wind for the day."

"Mr. Creek," Mrs. Hart said, "I have to say ... you seem a proper gentleman to me. And put a lie to all the stories we've been told of Indians being savages."

But Billy just shrugged, "Thank you, Mrs. Hart. It is ... kind of you to say. I have lived with the white soldiers most of my life, so have learned their ways. But," he grinned at her, "underneath I am still a savage, ma'am."

Stan grinned and nodded, "Oh, dah! Is true. Billy is great fighter and man-killer. Have seen none better ... and have seen *many!*"

Mrs. Hart looked shocked, but Joseph Hart chuckled and shook his head, "Well, then we can be grateful y'all are on *our* side! Lord knows we can use all the hard-fighting men we can get in this-here war. We're happy to have you both on the government side, sirs!"

Stan and Billy nodded and grinned in agreement.

ଔଈଔଈଔଈଔଈଔଈଔଈ

"Billy ... are you finding any tracks? I am now regretting leaving horses back at Hart's farm. How many days have we climbed these hills?"

"It is six suns since we left the farm," Billy answered matter-of-factly. Stan was not usually one to complain, but this long, fruitless search was beginning to wear on his patience. And Stan's thinning patience was beginning to wear on Billy.

"Suns!" Stan spat back derisively, "have not seen any suns since we left Baggs and Snake Hunters back at river. Nothing but clouds, rain, and wind. Luckily no snow ... *yet*. I am missing hot Texas sun for first time ever."

"Yes ... me too. And, answering your first question, 'no'—I am not seeing any tracks. As for the horses, you know as well as I, it would not be possible for them to pass the places we've been. Are you forgetting walking over that deep gorge with only a rope for a bridge two days ago?" Billy chuckled, "I am laughing at the thought of your stallion Groz walking that rope!"

Stan laughed, "Yes, is funny thought. Sorry, Billy—is not the cold and tiredness ... is lack of *action*! Am wanting squeeze Walters' poxy neck ... but there is nothing but dripping trees. *Blyad* ... it is tiresome!"

Billy nodded, but didn't reply. He'd suddenly paused, gazing intently at the ground in front of him. Stan also stopped and leaned over his back to look. But Stan saw nothing but the usual dripping, soggy undergrowth and moss.

"What is it?"

"A man was here. He was wearing soft shoes ... the kind Indians wear."

"One of so-called 'Moccasin Rangers' you think?"

"Maybe ... though I've not seen any wearing them, despite the name."

"Hmm ... maybe this one has heard of the great Billy Creek and wants to be *real* Indian," he smiled.

"Well ... if you haven't noticed, even I rarely wear them. White man's boots last longer and protect feet better in rough country. And they hold better to stirrups when riding."

"True ... what then?"

"I ... don't know, but I will follow this track. We've seen nothing better in days."

"Is good, Billy. Let's go."

ಶಂಲ)ಡಲ(ಡುಖ)ಡಲ(ಡುಖ)ಲ(ಡ

Two hours later they crouched behind a bush gazing out at a narrow pathway through the woods. Even Stan could make out hoof marks and boot tracks along the muddy path from his vantage point a few yards away. Not only that, they could hear voices and the sounds of a busy camp up the trail to their left. From the sounds of it, likely only a few dozen yards off. Too close for comfort. If the camp had put out sentries Stan and Billy were likely already inside their perimeter. This meant they were in serious danger of blundering into an armed enemy at any moment and were very lucky they hadn't already.

They'd followed the moccasin trail for several miles in a relatively straight line before it was finally lost, trampled over by boot tracks that led directly to the forest path they were now gazing at.

Billy turned and signaled off to the left, away from the trail. Stan nodded, understanding he meant to sneak through the woods to get a view of the camp without being seen; obviously they couldn't just walk down the pathway. If not Walters, it was at least a safe bet these were rebel bushwhackers. Union men would have no reason to be out here, unless they were a group like Baggs' Snake Hunters.

They'd heard no rumors of any Union men active up in the woods, but plenty of secessionists. The Harts had proven a wealth of information and rumors. After the Battle of Rich Mountain,

Joseph Hart had begun using the farmhouse as a kind of inn or alehouse for travelers. He'd suffered a good deal of property damage, lost crops and livestock during the battle, and had several empty rooms since most of his children had long since grown up and moved out on their own. So opening up the place to travelers and locals, of the pro-Union persuasion of course, had been the obvious and sensible thing to do. As a result, the Harts were well conversant with all the news and rumors circulating in the area.

And to Stan and Billy's satisfaction, several rumors described a man fitting Walters' description. So they'd left the farmhouse nearly a week ago feeling confident they'd quickly track down their quarry. Such had not turned out to be the case. But now, finally, they'd apparently enjoyed a stroke of good fortune.

They stashed their packs in a relatively dry spot under a bush and then crept through the thick woods, as slowly and quietly as their experience and skills would allow. As they moved, the camp noises grew louder. They heard a crackling campfire and smelled its smoke. They heard individual voices and snorting horses. Peeking through the dense underbrush they saw a large campfire surrounded by a half-dozen tents of various fabrics and colors.

Stan was trying to make a count of the men — something like a dozen — and was mentally tallying their weapons when he felt Billy tap him on the arm. He turned and saw Billy pointing at something in the camp. Stan returned a questioning look. Billy put his fingers at the sides of his head pointing up like ... horns? Like a cow, or a ... a devil! *Walters!* Stan grinned and nodded. He turned and looked where Billy pointed. And there he was! After all the searching, their quarry was at last in sight. Walters sat in a folding camp chair; his riding boots propped up on a section of log. It was the only chair in sight; the other men sat on stumps, rocks, or on the bare ground.

Typical of Walters, Stan thought with disdain, *the man cares nothing for others, even his own men.* Stan slowly slipped his rifle from his shoulder where he'd carried it by a leather strap. Billy did likewise. Fortunately, the day had been mostly dry, so Stan had reasonable confidence the powder in the loaded guns hadn't fouled.

He also unstrapped the safety strap on his two pistols at his hips and made sure they were loose. Though he didn't look, Stan was confident Billy had done the same. Fortunately, they'd had plenty of time during their long rides and hikes to discuss various plans covering differing scenarios they might encounter when they finally found Walters. And this was one of the more likely ones, so had received quite a bit of attention. There'd be no need to stop and discuss what to do next.

They'd decided one of them would take out Walters first with a rifle shot, and the other would target any man who went for a weapon or seemed to notice their direction. They'd then abandon the rifles as reloading would take too long. They'd open fire with two pistols each while charging forward with a shout. The shock and overwhelming firepower would hopefully scatter the enemy in panic, as they'd assume they were being attacked by a much larger force. Once the enemy was out of the way, Stan would remove Walters' head with his great knife, stick it in the bag, and they'd be on their way.

Stan liked the plan for its simplicity, audacity, and opportunity for ferocious offensive action, designed to shock and defeat an opponent of much greater numbers. But if Sergeant Jim had been there, he might've reminded Stan that most such plans "turn to shit as soon as the shooting starts."

Stan tapped Billy's shoulder, made the devil horns sign, and pointed to his own chest. Billy nodded. Stan got down on one knee and stretched the rifle out in front of him, slowly threading it through the branches of the bush, careful not to jiggle any branches. He lined up Walters in his sights, cocked the hammer, took a deep breath and ...

A rifle shot rang out. But Stan hadn't squeezed the trigger and neither had Billy. The sound had come from behind them, back in the woods. Stan had forgotten about the possible sentries!

He glanced quickly to his left and suffered a terrible shock. Billy lay slumped forward to the ground on top of his rifle. His hat had fallen off. Blood poured from his scalp.

Stan yanked his rifle from the bush and swung it around. He immediately fired into the woods where a small puff of smoke was rising. He'd hurried the shot and hadn't bothered aiming; he was certain he hadn't hit anything. But he'd only meant to force the man's head down to buy himself a moment to move without being seen.

He dropped his rifle and rolled Billy over. The left side of Billy's head was bloody mess and his eyes stared up lifelessly. *Damn! Damn! Damn! No, Billy, no!* he thought. But even as he did, his instincts took over; he scooped up his rifle and headed off into the woods even as two more gunshots rang out, this time coming from the camp.

Stan didn't bother returning fire; he wouldn't hit anything anyway, moving quickly through the woods as he was. And the smoke from his own gunshots would only give his position away. Better to head off into the woods and hide until his enemies gave up the chase. He was confident he could move through woods quicker than they and would soon lose them. Likely they were all farm boys or even raised in a town or city and had little woods craft.

He had guns and plenty of ammo. And he still had his bow and arrows strapped across his back. That gave him a definite advantage; he could kill from a distance without giving away his location.

An hour later, after leading his enemies on a long, twisting path, he rested in a hollow under a gigantic fallen tree. He breathed heavily from his exertions; he rubbed thighs, aching from the effort of moving quickly while crouched over or crawling along the ground.

And as he sat, and finally had time to think, tears began streaming down his face unbidden. *Damn it, Billy! Damn it to hell!*

◧◐◑◨◧◐◑◨◧◐◑◨

"Sorry, Mr. Walters. The fellow's a giant all right; biggest fellow I ever did see! But he moves fast and he's crafty. We'd catch sight of him off through the brush, and then we'd lose him. Then we'd see him again somewheres else. And I'll be dad-gummed if we don't up and lose him again. He led us a twisty path all hither and yon 'til we was pert-near out o' breath. Finally lost him altogether. Searched and searched, and never another sign o' him. Reckon he done got clean away, finally," Hiram Snyder explained, nervously clutching at his hat while avoiding all eye contact.

Walters scowled. He was unconvinced. The large stranger wasn't nearly as clever as they were making him out to be. More likely they were exaggerating his abilities to cover their own ineptitude and incompetence.

"But at least we bagged this one, sir," Snyder added, prodding the body with his foot.

Walters snorted. He'd seen them drag the fellow in shortly after the brief exchange of gunfire an hour earlier, but he'd not yet had time to examine the body closely; only a quick glance to confirm, to his relief, the man wasn't wearing a blue uniform.

He'd been more concerned with organizing a defense in case these were only scouts from a larger raiding party. But no others had appeared, so he was now inclined to believe the strangers had been here alone. Maybe just locals who were curious about their camp. They might have even offered to join up if Walters' sentries hadn't fired on them, though the sentry claimed the strangers were aiming rifles at the camp.

"But ... ain't it strange, sir?" Snyder continued.

"Isn't *what* strange?" Walters asked in his usual disinterested tone.

"Well ... it's just ... though he's dressed like a regular fella, this'n here appears to be a real, honest-to-God savage. Like out o' them picture books from the West."

"What?!" Walters felt a cold chill run down his spine. He'd heard nearly those identical words more than a year ago, back on his own farm from one of the farmhands. *An Indian?! No ... it can't be!* he thought and stepped up to have a look.

Walters looked down at the body. Sure enough, the man had the dark skin and unmistakable facial features of an Indian. Walters' mind was reeling ... though he was not good at remembering faces, he was convinced it *had* to be! It was just too great a coincidence. A giant and an Indian together—aiming rifles right at his camp ... straight at *him?!*

"Chambers!" he said aloud and scowled again.

"What's that, sir?"

Walters gazed at the man, and with an effort of will resumed his preferred bland expression.

"Nothing. This incident just reminds me of ... of an old *friend* of mine. Snyder, I want another search party put together. Take six ... no, eight men this time. And take the best hunter or woodsman we've got ... Carter, maybe ...?"

"Uh ... I think that'd be Riley, most likely, sir."

"What? Oh ... all right ... Riley then. Go with them and scour these woods until you track that man down. I want him found, and I want him alive! You can hurt him all you want, and be sure to bind him tightly, but I want him able to talk when I get my hands on him. I need to know why he's here and ... and *who* sent him."

"Yes, sir, it'll be done as you say."

Walters turned and strode toward his tent, snatching up his camp chair on the way. He entered the tent, closed the flap and sat.

Chambers! Damn the man ... he has a long reach if he can find me way out here in the mountains. Very nearly killed me, too, if the sentries are telling it true!

For the first time in over a year, Walters felt the icy chill of fear—the first time since Chambers had slipped away to the North with all his household; since the night his Indian had murdered all the sentries in their camp. Well, at least now that damned Indian was finally dead.

But the more he thought about it the more the fear turned to anger and rekindled the fires of his old hatred. *It's been too long since I thought about you, Chambers; too long. I'd nearly forgotten.*

Visions of the fighting, the killing, raiding, and the blood— rivers of blood—flashed through his mind. All that he'd seen and done since the last time he'd worried about Nathan Chambers at all.

But suddenly the old feelings came flooding back in. The defeat. The humiliation. The burning hatred. Forced to give up the chase. Helpless to avenge the loss of a dozen slaves—slaves Chambers had helped to escape. The raging anger knowing the man had stolen away Margaret. *Stolen my own wife!* he scowled, *how dare he?!*

You think you're so smug. So safe. Up in the North, where no one can find you. Where no one can reach you. Ha! But I know where you are, Chambers! I know where you live! You could've gone anywhere ... could've hidden where I'd never find you. But your bloated ego wouldn't let you. You had to play the hero ... making your grand speeches! Fool. I read about you in the papers ... had a debate with John Carlile about the new state. And the paper said you were assisting the pretender governor ... assisting him to build a new false government ... in Wheeling!

By God, Chambers, if I have to walk all that way, I swear I will find you and I will strangle you with my bare hands. Then I'll gut that whoring slut Margaret with my knife after I cut out her lying tongue! And that uppity bitch, Miss Abbey—I'll give her a reminder of what a real man does to a harlot! Then I'll make her squeal like a pig and beg for death before I finish her!

He'd worked himself up into a fiery rage and was now pacing back and forth in the tent, though he could not recall getting up from the chair.

Two hours later he'd finally resumed his seat, the anger reduced to a low simmer. Now his active mind happily worked over the details of various potential schemes and plans for revenge.

A sudden, loud noise from just outside interrupted his reverie, and thoughts of Chambers were swept away ... for the moment.

ༀༀༀༀༀༀༀༀༀༀༀༀ

The sentries had been increased on the off chance the two strangers were part of a larger assault force. And the well-supplied search force had been sent out after the giant. Otherwise, the camp had settled back into its normal routine.

Those not needed for specific duties tended to congregate around the large campfire in the center of camp, not far from Walters' command tent. A dozen or more men were now gathered there, attempting to stave off the worst of the chilly weather.

Occasionally there'd be light-hearted banter, but the gathering was typically subdued, a reflection of their commander's demeanor. No one wanted to be on the receiving end of his ire, and loud, raucous behavior was a good way to get there.

Hiram Barnes had just finished a low-toned but humorous account of their earlier search for the giant, including a comical description of his large, closely cropped scalp, which he described as looking much like a pumpkin. Barnes was small and lean, so his attempts to mime the giant were just the right touch of absurdity to tickle Silas Carter's fancy.

Carter, standing directly across the fire from Barnes, chuckled softly cupping his hand over his mouth, straining to suppress an unwanted outburst. He glanced down and absently toed a partially burned and smoldering branch back into the fire. He looked up to ask Barnes a question about the giant.

But when they met eyes, the question escaped him; Barnes' eyes were wide, and his face had changed in an instant from humor to wide-eyed shock. For a moment Carter couldn't figure what had affected Barnes so strongly. Then he noticed something sticking out from Barnes' chest. It was the pointed steel head of what looked like a small spear with a red shaft. Thick red liquid dripped from the point. No one spoke. The popping of the fire was the only sound.

Barnes sank to his knees. He slowly tilted forward, his face falling toward the fire. Carter snapped out of his malaise and shouted, "Hey!" stepping forward, meaning to catch Barnes before he fell into the flames.

But the world erupted in a tremendous cacophony, from a peaceful crackling campfire to a chaotic maelstrom of noise. First, a rifle shot rang out, and the man to Carter's left crumpled to the ground.

Seconds later a heavy splash of water hit the campfire, scattering sparks in every direction and raising a great puff of steam and smoke. A white cloud swirled up around the stunned men as a sound like a roaring lion assaulted Carter's ears.

Through the smoke and mist he saw a huge, hulking form and something long and thick like a pole hurtling toward him. Before he could raise a hand or duck it hit him hard across the face, knocking him backward onto the ground.

Gunshots rang out—pistol shots, cutting through the fog inside Carter's own head. Though his vision swam from the blow, he saw the shadowy figure was doing the shooting; flashes came from his silhouette with each hammering noise.

This giant man was also the source of the roaring noise. A non-stop, deep-throated snarling shout rang out from the huge mouth. And Carter heard words in the thunderous bellowing, "Death! Death! I will kill you all! Kill all you fuckers! Kill! Kill! *Arrrrrghh!*"

Men scattered in every direction, yelling, screaming, and scrambling to arm themselves with rifles, still neatly stacked yards back from the fire.

Though dazed, Carter wasn't totally out of the fight, and unlike most of the men, he carried a loaded pistol in a holster on his hip. He unholstered it, cocked the hammer, and tried to steady his aim. He felt weak and wobbly, and the shadowy figure was moving around in the swirling smoke when he fired. But to his surprise, the figure stopped mid-stride. A hit!

But victory turned to deadly defeat. The form turned toward him. A bright flash illuminated a nightmare visage; great head closely shaved, glaring eyes bright as flame, and wide-open mouth full of teeth. A great growling shout continued from that dark maw. A burning hard pain tore through Carter's chest, and he couldn't breathe. The world went black and all noise ceased.

ॐॐୠ୦ଔ୦ॐॐୠ୦ଔ୦ଔॐॐୠ୦ଔ୦ଔ

Though Stan had led his pursuers on a twisted, bewildering path through the woods, he'd never intended to run away. Not without his friend. Not without Billy.

Though Billy was dead, he'd not leave his friend's body behind. They'd been through too much together. He'd not allow their enemies to desecrate or make sport of it. Not now. Not ever.

He fought down a growing urge to sob, to break down and release his grief. A grief that threatened to overwhelm all conscious thought. Not yet. No time now. He focused instead on his building anger ... on making them *pay!*

Once he was sure his pursuers had tired of the chase and returned to camp, Stan slowly worked back in that direction, this time taking extra care to avoid being seen by sentries. He hoped to perhaps catch one or two unawares and strangle them. But he eventually made it back near the camp without encountering any enemies.

He found a good hiding spot where he could observe the camp while contemplating his plan of attack.

He was gratified to see they'd left Billy's body where they'd dragged it earlier, a few feet back from the campfire, still in plain sight. Good! That would save him the trouble of searching for it.

He watched as the enemy put together another search party. Nine men, well-armed and well-provisioned, carrying canteens. Clearly, they did not intend to return to camp without finding him. But he had other ideas.

He waited a good hour after the searchers departed to make his move. He wanted them to be well off into the woods so even if they heard something they'd be too far off to intervene.

It was now nearly dusk, which was the other part of his plan; the men by the fire would have a hard time seeing him, and afterward, as he made his way back out into the woods, darkness would fall, aiding his escape.

He stood slowly from behind the bushes and leaned his rifle against a tree. Then he pulled out his bow and one of the red-shafted arrows. He liked the idea of initiating his attack with the very weapon Billy had given him—had made for him with great skill over months of hard labor with his own hands. The thing suddenly had new importance and meaning. And it would initiate Stan's vengeance for Billy's death.

He nocked an arrow in the string but didn't yet pull it back. Though he was now more confident in his aim, having practiced religiously every day since receiving the bow, he wanted to be closer when he launched his attack. He meant to charge the camp and create as much confusion and havoc as he could so he'd be able to retrieve Billy's body. And that meant he'd need to be nearly on them before he opened fire.

So he crept within a few yards of the fire, keeping low and being careful not to bump into any bushes or low branches, even as Billy had taught him. When he was in position, he made a quick count of the men around the campfire. Fourteen he could see. Probably others nearby in the tents or beyond.

But the good news was they seemed to have relaxed and were not nearly as attentive as they'd been earlier. They'd even stacked their rifles a few yards back from the fire. *Confident fools! So sure there is no more danger. But you are ... oh so wrong!*

He picked out a fellow who was talking animatedly with his back turned. Then he noticed a large bucket of water right behind the man, and it gave him another idea.

He grinned.

Stan pulled back on the great bow, aimed, and let fly. He slung the bow over his shoulder, and snatched up the rifle, aimed and fired, even as the first man was still slumping to the ground.

He dropped the rifle and rushed forward, jumping over a stump and stooping to scoop up the water bucket. As he ran, he yelled; a great roaring battle challenge to his enemies, venting rage built up in a dark place deep inside.

He pulled up just short of the first dead man and tossed the water, bucket and all onto the fire. It erupted in sparks, steam, and smoke, creating a thick, swirling cloud. Even as the bucket was hurling through the air Stan picked up a log laying by the fire and threw it at a man standing on the opposite side of the fire. He'd noticed the man had a pistol holster and had reacted quickly to the attack. He only wanted to make the man duck. But the log hit hard, and the man went down.

He pulled both pistols from their holsters and fired at a man to his right, and then at another. Both men went down.

A flash of light to his left caught the corner of his eye. A shot rang out even as he felt the wind from a bullet streak past his left ear. He turned and fired at the point of the flash.

Over to the left, three men had reached the stack of rifles and were already turning to target him. He opened up on them with both pistols; *bam, bam, bam, bam, bam!* All three fell. Only one still twitched. But none rose.

Directly across the fire Stan saw a man aiming a rifle. He swiveled his pistols toward the man who flinched and ducked his head in response. Stan pulled the trigger on his right pistol; *click!* He pulled the left; *click!* The man looked up in surprise.

Stan rushed at the fire and leapt over, holstering his pistols in mid-air. As he landed, he pulled his knife. The rebel's rifle flashed and popped, and Stan felt something hit his left upper arm like a hammer. He ignored the blow and continued his rush. The man stepped back, attempting to shield himself with the rifle.

Stan grabbed the man's rifle, jerked it from his grasp, and stabbed him in the chest in one motion. He pivoted to his right and swung the rifle with his left arm at another man standing there, knocking him to the ground.

Stan pulled the other two pistols from their holsters tucked up under his shoulders, and continued firing. He knew in battle that to stand still was to die, especially for a man as big as he. So he moved, fought, moved, fought, and moved again.

The campfire area was soon clear of living men, but others were moving out from the tents or coming in from further back in the camp. A rifle shot rang out from across the camp with a flash and puff of smoke. But Stan ignored it. It was a miss, and the shooter would take a half minute to reload.

He aimed his pistols at anyone else with a rifle and fired. But from this distance he knew a hit was unlikely. He just wanted to force their heads down so he could grab Billy and run for it. He hadn't enough ammunition to kill them all. It was time to go.

He turned and sprinted back toward where Billy lay next to the smoldering fire. But then another gunshot rang out. This one caught his attention—a pistol. This man was a danger if he got close; he'd have multiple shots. Stan looked back, spotted the man, and fired. The man returned fire. In the gun flash he clearly saw the face of the shooter: *Walters!*

Stan scowled. He stopped and turned to face the hated enemy. Levelling his pistols at Walters, he fired both weapons until each was empty. And still he pulled the hammers and squeezed the triggers, *click, click, click, click, click!*

As the gun smoke swirled away, he saw Walters, back by the tents, still standing, but no longer holding his pistol. He leaned hard against a tree trunk, clutching his left arm.

"Damn you, Walters! Why won't die?! Why won't die, you bastard!" he shouted, and threw his empty pistols down in disgust.

He turned away and ran, jumping over a dead body, and then another. As he neared the fire he reached down and snatched a loaded pistol from the grasp of the man he'd whacked earlier with a log. He resisted the urge to turn and take another shot at Walters; he knew it was too late.

Another rifle shot rang out, slamming hard into a stump a few feet to Stan's left with a loud *whack!* And then another rang out, and another. Dirt kicked up between him and the fire.

Time to go, Stanislav! he scolded himself as he reached Billy's inert form where it lay on the ground near the fire. With a heave he slung Billy up over his right shoulder, glanced back and fired two more shots left-handed in the general direction of the tents. Then he raced into the darkening woods. More rifle shots rang out behind him and bullets ripped through the underbrush as he ran.

ঌৎৣৎৣৎৣৎৣৎৣৎৣৎৣৎ

"Yes ... it's bad, sir. Sorry, Mr. Walters. The bullet smashed up the bones in the wrist and cut the veins. The tourniquet has kept you from bleedin' out, but you ain't like to keep the hand. Good news is, you'll still have the arm."

"Hmph! What good is an arm with no hand?" Walters scowled, gazing up at the man from where he sat on the chair in his tent. He'd have preferred to present his bland expression, but he was in too much pain to pull it off. So he settled for an angry frown and a grimace.

Never in life had he felt such horrific pain nor felt such devastating fear. Fear of Chambers' terrifying giant, fear of the death he'd narrowly avoided, and fear for the looming prospect of some unskilled fool with a saw taking off his mangled left hand. Thank God it wasn't the right one—at least he could still fire a pistol and hold a pen. And swing a bull whip.

But he'd rather die than let the others see his fear. So he focused on channeling the pain and terror into anger. Focused all his thought on Chambers and his men. The men who'd caused him so much mental anguish in the recent past and who'd now made it physical. Focused on all the ways he'd repay them in kind, repay them three-fold. An eye for an eye ... and then some!

He reached over and grabbed the whiskey bottle off the camp table. But he realized he had no other hand with which to pull the cork.

The man who'd been tending him leaned forward and said, "Uh ... shall I ..."

But Walters shook his head and glared at the man, who straightened up and stepped back. Walters put the top of the bottle to his mouth and pulled the cork with his teeth. He spat it on the ground, then took three long swallows. It burned his throat and nearly made him cough. But the fire of it was a welcome respite from the searing, throbbing pain in his hand.

"Go fetch a competent surgeon, if we have such a thing. And a saw. Let's get this over with!"

The man nodded and left.

As the tent flaps settled back in place, Walters leaned back in the chair and closed his eyes. *Chambers ... you will rue this day with all your soul. This I swear on my life ... and my dead left hand.*

CHAPTER 11. IN FROM THE COLD

"A cold coming we had of it,
just the worst time of the year for a journey,
and such a long journey:
the ways deep and the weather sharp,
the very dead of winter."
– T.S. Eliot

Saturday December 21, 1861 – Rich Mountain, Virginia:

After more than an hour and several miles of twisting, turning scramble through the dark woods, Stan paused to catch his breath. It came out in great steaming gasps, barely visible in the fading light. The temperature had dropped precipitously once the sun had set, more so than in recent days.

And Billy's weight over his shoulder, which seemed so light at first, had become a tiresome burden. But a burden he would never relinquish. Not as long as there was life in his breast.

And though the frosty air felt good at the moment, cooling the heat of his exertions, Stan knew it would be a long, bitter night. Especially as he'd been forced to leave their packs behind in his hurry to avoid getting shot in the back. He had no food, no water, and no blankets or extra clothing with which to cover himself.

He shrugged. He'd suffered many other such nights; one more probably wouldn't kill him.

He was now confident his enemies had given up the chase for the night with complete darkness coming on swiftly. *If* they'd had the courage to follow at all after the devastation he'd wreaked in their camp. He'd seen no sign of them since he'd plunged into the bushes, dodging rifle fire.

And for the first mile or so he'd feared running into one of their sentries. But for some reason he couldn't understand, he hadn't seen any. And now he no longer feared encountering them.

They'd never have positioned a sentry this far out from camp—too exposed and isolated to serve any purpose.

Tomorrow they'd likely be back out in force. And somewhere out there was the search party they'd sent out earlier in the day. He'd have to move cautiously tomorrow if he hoped to avoid them.

But tonight, the biggest danger would be freezing to death, as he dare not light a fire. So when he started moving again, he went more slowly, gazing about for any sign of shelter. A hollowed-out stump, fallen log, or cave—anything that might help stave off the frosty weather that would likely turn deathly cold well before the dawn.

He'd not walked another ten steps when he felt something touch him on the back. He pulled the one loaded pistol from his belt and spun around, cocking the hammer as he did.

And he saw … nothing. There was nothing there. Just the empty woods.

And then he felt it again, this time stronger, like a fist pounding against his back. He spun around again. But again, no one was there. He stood still, mouth agape, at a complete loss as to what had just happened.

Then he heard a sound he had not expected, someone speaking in a quiet, rasping voice. And the uncanny voice was quietly calling his name, "Stan … Stan …" His eyes went wide, and for the first time since becoming a grown man, he felt the chill of superstitious terror.

But then with a force of will he shook his head and shuddered to clear away such foolish thoughts. He lowered the hammer on the pistol and stuck it back in his belt. Then he slowly lowered Billy's body until its feet touched the ground. He held the body upright and gazed at it. And to his shock, Billy's eyes were open and alert. The hairs on the back of Stan's head stood up and a shiver ran down his spine.

"*Billy …?*"

"Hello, Stan."

"Are … are you *alive?!*"

"Yes ... I think so. Or else we are both dead and this is hell. But ... I think it's too cold to be hell ..."

Stan saw it was true; this was not some evil shade of Billy, but the real living, breathing man.

He reached out and embraced his friend, lifting him from the ground and kissing him on both cheeks before setting him back down.

"Billy ... Billy! You were ... you were *dead!* I saw you die myself. They shot you in head and dragged your body away covered in blood."

"I ... I don't remember any of that. I remember you and I finding their camp ... and sneaking up on it and then ... nothing."

Stan bent down and for the first time examined Billy's head wound. Though he could see little in the fading light, he carefully felt with his fingers. Blood covered the entire right side of Billy's head and had run down across his face. It had completely matted down his dark hair on that side. But when Stan felt of the wound, he could tell it was a long gouge and not a neat hole as he had assumed.

"Oh! Was only glancing blow to side of head. Bullet did not go into head. Hmm ... no broken bones I am thinking, or you would not still be living.

"But is *much* blood. I was believing half your head was gone; me and enemies. But ... must be *very hard* head, Billy!"

"I recall my mother saying the same, sometimes," Billy answered and smiled a thin, pained smile. But then he wobbled, and Stan reached out to steady him. Billy might be alive, but he was far from well.

"Since you are no longer dead, I would like to keep you this way," Stan said and smiled. "We must find shelter or will freeze, and both be dead; this time for real. Shall I carry you further?"

"No ... I believe I can walk. It will help me stay warm, and I can help look for a place."

"All right. You go first so I can catch if you ... wobble."

Billy scowled at him but nodded. He turned and led the way, moving slowly and unsteadily. Stan followed closely behind like a nervous mother hen, ready to catch Billy at any moment should he stumble. But in less than half an hour Billy stopped and pointed off into the woods, "There."

"There *what?*"

"There ... there is a darker patch of darkness. Whatever it is will help keep off the chill."

Moments later they were dug down under a monstrous tree that had fallen across another downed forest giant eons ago. Both were moldering with age, but their tremendous girth still held the topmost log several feet off the ground. Stan piled branches and leaves on top of them and all around them. Then he wrapped his arms around Billy and lay next to him to share body heat and keep them both warm.

"Thank you, Stan. For warming me and for ... fetching me back from the enemy. That could not have been easy. I see you have been wounded — your left arm is covered in blood."

"Is nothing. Only scratch — like your head. Bullet passed through flesh but missed bone. Is good. William will enjoy burning with whiskey ... then torturing with needle!" he chuckled. Billy snorted a short laugh, knowing he'd likely be receiving similarly gentle treatment from William. *If* they ever made it that far.

They lay quietly for several minutes, but as Billy was feeling himself drift off to sleep, he suddenly remembered a strange dream he'd had after he was shot.

"Stan ... how does a person know if a dream is ... just a dream or is something more real?"

"Real? Dream is just dream, not real ... why are you asking stupid question, Billy?"

Billy didn't immediately answer, and Stan was starting to think he'd fallen asleep, when he finally said, "I will tell you of the dream I had after the bullet hit my head. Then you will tell me if it was only a dream, or something different."

"All right; what was this dream?"

"I was in a strange place where I could see nothing ... nothing at all, though it wasn't dark like night. Nor was it light, it was ... something else."

"Hmm ... like fog ... like grayness?"

"Yes ... maybe ... but with no form. And I could see nothing at all, not even my own body. I was there ... and *not* there. But I knew someone else was there with me though I couldn't see him. Somehow, I knew it was Grandfather. He greeted me and we talked long and long, such as we have not done since he died many years ago."

"Is good, Billy. Your grandfather was fine fellow, from stories you tell."

"Yes ... he is the best man I've known. Wise as an ancient tree, strong and hard as a stone mountain. But also, warm and soft as a well-worn fur coat. It was a great pleasure to be with him again, and it warmed my heart. So I said, 'I am happy to be with you again, Grandfather, shall we now be together always?' and he didn't answer for a long time. And it seemed ... somehow ... he was gazing far away ... perhaps seeing things that are and things that were. Or maybe ... things that may yet be. Long time he was silent, and I was silent with him. Then finally he said, 'No Grandson, now we must part. It is time to go.'

"I suddenly felt a great sadness at our parting, and asked, 'But ... where are you going, Grandfather?'

"And he answered, 'It is not *me* who is going, it is *you*. You must return to the Sun's World. It is not your time to come to the Spirit World.'

"'Is that what this place is, Grandfather? The Spirit World?'

"'No, Grandson ... this is ... a *between* place. Where the veil is thin and if one is wise, he may see things on the other side. It is a kind of meeting place, maybe. Not of the Spirit World, nor of the Sun's World. But one may see both from here.'

"'But I see nothing, Grandfather. Not even you.'

"'It is not easy for those of the Sun's World to see far here. You are used to the light and the Spirit World is too dark, and this place too has no light.

"'And even for me ... I do not see things in the Sun's World as you do. The light is too bright ... it dazzles my seeing. Only the brightest spirits shine through it, but I do not see them as the fragile bodies we have in that world. The spirits of those in the Sun's World shine as bright lights to those on this side who have a strong bond to them. So when I am in this place and you are in the Sun's World, I see you as a strong burning—glowing warm and bright as the Sun itself. And now you are here, I can also see those you are bound to back in the Sun's World.'

"'Who do you see, Grandfather? And what are they doing?' I asked.

"'There is one who is ... a mighty war chieftain. He is your leader ... the one you fight for.'

"'The Captain.'

"'Yes. The one you call Captain. I see him as a dazzling white star ... his spirit shines so brightly, so intensely it is almost hurtful to my sight. I see ... he will have great need of you in the years to come and without your help his star may fade from the world.'

"I was troubled to hear this, but asked, 'Who else do you see, Grandfather?'

"'There is one other who burns very brightly. And there are others I can see, but more dimly, like far away stars. Those are ones with whom you have a lesser bond. Comrades in arms, friends, and such.'

"'And who is this brightly burning one, and what is he doing?'

"'This one is to my sight as a great, raging fire—like a forest all ablaze. And yet from this dangerous spirit comes warmth and caring.'

"'Stan,' I said.

"'Yes, it is the one you call Stan. And I am seeing this one is in great need of you, Grandson. Even now he is in grave danger. I have seen ... if you do not return his fires will be quenched even before another sun.'

"'Then you are right, Grandfather; I must go. But ... I do not know the way.'

"'It is not so easy to return to the Sun's World from the Spirit World. One must have a guide or a strong bond to a spirit from the Sun's World to point the way.'

"'Like the Captain's great hound?'

"'Hmm ... yes ... I can see it in your mind. This is likely such a bond. Anyway, lucky for you I was here to meet you and speak with you else you might have wandered into the Spirit World and never returned.

"'But from *this* place, this *between* place, it is simple to return and requires no guide. You must only wish to go and focus on a single strong bond from the Sun World, and you will return.'

"So I bid farewell to Grandfather, and thought myself back here with you. And then ... I was dangling over your shoulder, bouncing along. So I started tapping you on the back."

Stan shook his head, "Hmm ... maybe was more than just dream ... seems to me Tonkawa folk have some strange magic ... unlike us Russians—we only have silly kind for to amuse the small children. So ... maybe was something more. Anyway, I am happy you have returned, Billy."

"And I am happy to help you live another day," Billy answered.

Stan chuckled, "As Captain would say, 'amen to that,' Billy. Amen to that!"

⍟⍟⍟⍟⍟⍟⍟⍟⍟⍟⍟⍟

"Come, Billy. Sun is nearly up. Time to go," Stan said, gently shaking his sleeping friend.

Billy sat up and rubbed his eyes. "Okay."

Stan had been up for a half-hour already and was anxious to get moving. He knelt next to Billy, their log ceiling too low for him to stand.

"How you feeling today?"

"Uh ... like I got shot in the head?"

Stan laughed, "*Da, da.* But you are still living, yes?"

"Yes. Today I am still alive, I am sure."

"Is good. Sorry to say I have no food or water for you. But many streams in these hills, so will not die of thirst today."

Billy shrugged. It wasn't the first time he'd gone without food and water, and certainly wouldn't be the last.

"Billy, I am thinking ... we must get down from these hills. And soon. Not just get away from enemies, but today there is snow in air. Already little white flakes swirling through the trees."

337

Billy looked out and saw it was true. Though there was not yet any snow on the ground, the sky had a pale look, and tiny white flakes floated on the breeze.

"Yes ... we must go back. We need supplies. Back to the Harts' farm maybe."

"Billy ... there is thing I did not tell yesterday for wanting you to rest. When I came to get you out of camp, I saw Walters again. He shot pistol at me and I shot back. I gave all my bullets, but still I could not kill. Damn him! He is demon and just won't die. How many times has the Captain tried to kill him? And Sergeant Jim? And now me. And yet still he lives."

Billy saw Stan was upset and even shamed for failing to kill Walters. He reached up and patted him on the arm, careful to avoid the one with blood on the sleeve. "There is no man who can't be killed. It is just bad luck, Stan."

Stan nodded, but then his frown turned to a grin, "But ... did wing him. After fight he was leaning against tree holding left arm."

"Oh! Maybe he has bled out then. Even a bullet to the arm can kill a man."

"*Nyet!* Not Walters ... he is too mean to let a little thing like that kill him," he laughed.

Billy was pleased he had lightened the mood.

"Well, nothing more to do about him now. Let's get going, Stan. What weapons do we have?"

"No rifles, but three pistols. I have reloaded, but now we only have lead to reload one more time. And I still have knife ... oh, and I see you still have yours," he patted Billy's chest, where his knife still hung, secured in its sheath.

"No rifles? Not good," Billy answered, slowly shaking his head.

"Oh! But we still have bows. I have grabbed your quiver when I lifted your dead body. And you still have all arrows, though I am down by one."

Billy gave him a curious look, "And ... did you put that *one* to good use?"

Stan beamed, "Oh, *da, da! Very* good use!"

Billy returned the smile, "All is well then. With our bows we will give them much to fear. Maybe even more than with rifles."

"Is true ... is true. For some reason men here in East are more afraid of arrows than bullets. Is not sense to me but have seen it with own eyes."

"Yes. I think they have forgotten how to fight Indians, and it makes them afraid."

"Hmm ... could be, could be. But ... seems to me they are right to be afraid of *you*, Billy!" Billy smiled, but shrugged his shoulders.

"Anyway, bows are ready," Stan continued, "I have already strung them thinking ... hmm ... might have *use* today," he grinned.

He handed Billy the pistol he'd taken from the enemy. Billy examined it for a moment, looking at both sides. A .44 caliber Remington, reasonably new and relatively clean. He half-cocked the hammer and spun the cylinder, verifying Stan had reloaded it. Finally, he leaned out into the daylight and gazed down the barrel for several minutes. Satisfied, he nodded, lowered the hammer, and slipped the weapon into the holster on his right hip.

"Let's go," he said.

℠℠℠℠℠℠℠℠℠

Though it'd been a week since they'd left the Harts' farm, they figured they could get back to it in two days hard hiking if they weren't delayed overmuch by the enemy. Not only was it mostly downhill this time, but heading out they had taken a zigzagging, circuitous route in an attempt to find the enemy's camp or intercept a clear track or trail to it. This time they knew the direction in which their destination lay and could move straight toward it. Or at least as straight as the terrain would allow.

So at midday they stood at the edge of the ravine they had crossed three days earlier via an improvised rope bridge some seventy feet across and a hundred feet above a boulder-strewn, raging stream. The bridge consisted of two ropes, one roughly four feet above the other, stretched tightly across the chasm and tied off to sturdy tree trunks on either side. They'd left the bridge in place thinking they might have use of it again going back down the hill, which now proved to be prophetic.

Billy carefully inspected the ropes to ensure they'd not been tampered with or damaged by animals, including the two-legged kind. Satisfied, he moved over to a fallen log and sat down heavily with a sigh.

"How is head?" Stan asked.

"Pounds like Georgie's hammer on his anvil," Billy answered with a grimace. "But I will live."

"Is good. I prefer you living—you make much better company that way. And I don't have to carry," Stan chuckled.

Billy grinned, but was in too much pain to fully appreciate Stan's attempt at humor. He now understood what the Captain likely had gone through after getting pistol-whipped in the head over in Richmond, though he was certain his injury was not nearly as serious as the Captain's had been. He was already feeling better than the day before and could not imagine a scenario where his condition would now worsen. So he shrugged off the pain and focused on relaxing and resting his muscles for a few minutes before they attempted the river crossing. Stan sat down next to him to give himself a rest as well. It would've been a good time to eat if they'd had anything. And it was galling to be so close to so much water with no way to reach it. Still, they had slaked their thirst an hour earlier at a tiny stream they'd crossed, so they weren't desperate. Unfortunately, they'd left their canteens behind in their packs, so they had nothing with which to carry the water.

After a few minutes' respite, Stan stood, stretched, and shouldered his quiver and bow. "I will go first," he announced, and immediately moved toward the rope crossing.

Billy stood, and also slung his quiver over his shoulder. But he kept the bow in hand and pulled out an arrow. He nocked the arrow and moved off a little way into the woods to keep a watch while Stan made the crossing.

If Stan had any fear of the passage, he didn't betray it, stepping out onto the rope with no hesitation.

For a man of his size and weight, it was a challenging balancing act despite the supporting rope at shoulder height. It would be easy to become over-balanced in either direction and end up hanging upside down, gripping one or the other rope for dear life. But Stan worked his way across steadily and confidently, never wavering.

Billy resisted the urge to watch Stan's progress, instead focusing on any movement out in the woods. All seemed well when a slight movement caught the corner of his eye off to the left. He turned and saw a flash of light followed by a *boom!* He jumped up and raced in the direction of the rising puff of smoke.

The shot had come from fifty or sixty yards away. For his weapons to be effective he had to close the distance. As he ran, he prayed Stan had not been hit.

Another shot rang out and another puff of gun smoke drifted up. This shot had come from the same area as the first. *Good*, Billy thought, *they are not spread out.* He continued moving quickly through the woods, careful never to expose himself to his enemies.

When he'd closed the distance by half he slowed, watching carefully for any sight of the enemy. He stopped, pulled back the bow, and released. There was a scream. *Damn, not a kill!* he thought and moved again, this time to his left rather than forward. He nocked another arrow as he moved, stopped, aimed, and released again. This time no scream but rather shouting. He could not make out the words but could imagine the gist. He continued to move.

Another shot rang out and a bullet impacted in the tree next to him as he stood to fire another arrow. He let fly and moved again. Two more shots rang out. A bullet ripped through his shirt and he felt a burning across his abdomen.

Time to go, Billy, he thought and turned back toward the rope bridge. Once again, he prayed Stan had not been hit and that he'd bought him enough time to get safely across.

Three more shots rang out as Billy raced through the woods. But this time he was not hit. He shouldered the bow as he ran and without hesitation sprinted toward the rope and leapt out onto it, grasping the shoulder-height rope as he landed on the lower one. Another shot rang out as he strove to steady his balance and keep moving forward. He felt the breeze of a bullet pass close by his right ear.

Then a quick series of pistol shots rang out in rapid succession, *bam, bam, bam, bam, bam!* But these shots did not come from behind him, rather from the opposite side of the river in front.

Billy glanced up and saw Stan striding toward the edge of the ravine. He stood fully upright, a pistol in each fist and a furious scowl on his face, firing as rapidly as he could cock the hammers. He made no attempt to conceal himself or take cover, as if baiting his enemies to shoot at him. Which was exactly what he was doing, Billy realized—risking his life to give Billy the chance to make it safely across.

Billy redoubled his efforts and nearly fell. But he caught himself and swayed dangerously before rebalancing and scrambling to safety. He immediately stopped, unholstered his pistol, turned and fired at the enemy position on the other side.

"I am safe, Stan ... we must fly!" he shouted even as he moved around behind the tree and cut loose the ropes with his knife. If the enemy had had the courage to attempt the dangerous crossing, they no longer had the means.

But the fury of battle was on Stan, and he could not easily be swayed from trying to murder his enemies. When he'd fired off all his rounds and the pistol hammers clicked, he holstered the guns and drew his bow. He nocked a large, red-shafted arrow but could find no easy target. He was unwilling to waste the precious arrow, so he hesitated. Another rifle shot rang out and dirt kicked up near Stan's feet.

"Stan ... come ... now!" Billy shouted.

Stan turned, nodded, and sprinted back into the trees where Billy waited. Two more rifle shots rang out before they were well behind cover in the thick woods. They continued for several hundred more yards before pausing to rest.

With the ravine between them and their enemies, they were safe for now. Having previously scouted the stream, they knew there were no other reasonable crossing points for several miles in either direction. They'd chosen this spot for their bridge because it was the narrowest point, not because it was easy.

"Billy, you are hit again. Pull up shirt and let's have look."

Billy did as he was bid. The lower half of his abdomen was covered in blood and Stan felt the chill of fear again. But fortunately, Billy had been turned with his side toward the enemy when the bullet struck. So it had torn a long furrow across his midsection a few inches above the belly button but had not penetrated deeply. Blood seeped slowly from the wound.

"Hmm ... will be more fun for William when we get home," Stan said and grinned.

Billy nodded, then shrugged and lowered his shirt, resisting the urge to say, "I'll live" once again. He was starting to think that might be tempting the gods a little too much.

ಐ೫⊃೮೩೮ಐ೫⊃೮೩೮ಐ೫೦೮೩೮

Billy awoke early the next morning feeling more wretched than he could ever recall. His day started shortly after Stan got up from their makeshift bed of leaves and branches. The sudden loss of his large, warm body left Billy shivering from a biting cold that immediately went to the bone. And when he went to sit up, a sharp, stinging pain in his midsection shocked him into sudden, full consciousness. When he sat still long enough for that pain to relent, his head began to pound mercilessly.

He gritted his teeth, and forced himself to his feet, where he stood unsteadily for several minutes while his vision swam before his eyes, a swirling whiteness that was impossible to put into focus. At first, he thought his head injury must have affected his eyesight. But then he realized the white, fuzziness he was seeing was snow. A blizzard had struck during the night, covering everything in white. Now a fitful, gusting wind swirled the snow in a blinding, frigid cloud so thick Billy couldn't tell if it was coming from the sky or being blown off the ground. Or both.

Stan stepped up in front of him and leaned down, looking hard into his face. "You are looking like shit," he said, and for once he wasn't smiling.

343

"C ... c ... c ... c ... cold shit," Billy answered, trying to keep his teeth from chattering. "And h ... h ... hungry ..." he added, noticing for the first time his stomach had decided to add to his general misery, threatening to cramp up for lack of food.

"Yes ... me too. But food and warm will not come to us here ... we must go," Stan answered, shouldering his quiver and bow, while handing Billy his quiver and pistol belt.

Billy took the offered burden and grunted; even that small weight seemed immense. He strapped on the pistol, shouldered the quiver, and gazed out across the snow-covered terrain. He tried to remember which way they'd been traveling last night before he'd collapsed from exhaustion. He noticed Stan staring at him, looking concerned.

"We must go this way, Billy," he said, waving his hand off to their right. Billy met eyes with him for a long moment, then nodded. They both knew without speaking of it, that Billy could no longer lead the way. His injuries were too great, the cold too terrible for his lean frame, and his energy nearly spent. Stan turned, and strode off through the swirling snow. Billy gritted his teeth and followed.

The good news was they'd seen no sign of the enemy after crossing the gorge the previous day. But that had been little consolation as the temperature continued to drop and a cold breeze kicked up. The weather, combined with no food and multiple wounds, had made the remainder of the day a long, nightmarish slog for Billy. And his sleep during the night had been fitful; a never-ending nightmare of stabbing pain and shivering, biting cold, despite Stan's best efforts to warm him with his own body and strong arms.

But Billy was determined not to hold his friend up, nor to get him killed. So he trudged on, focusing on placing one foot in front of the other. It galled and shamed him not to be doing his part, not to be doing his usual scouting. He'd always been the one keeping watch over the others, keeping them safe from unseen dangers.

But now it was all he could do just to keep moving, knowing if he faltered Stan would try to carry him, and then likely they'd both die out in the cold, swirling snow. *Not that ... never that ... never that ... never that,* he said to himself, repeating it over and over as he watched Stan's feet moving ahead of him. By sheer determination he continued to put one foot in front of the other ... one foot in front of the other for what seemed like hours, or days, or ... forever.

ഇൗഇൟഭൟൟഇൟഭൟഇൟഇൟ

"Billy! Billy!"

He looked up into Stan's face. They had stopped, and Stan looked down at him.

"You are asleep walking," Stan said, shaking his head in disbelief.

"No ... I ... I was ..." Billy tried to answer but couldn't think of the words to say. His head felt thick and fuzzy.

"Look, Billy—snow has stopped. And wind. We can now see a bit."

Billy looked around, and saw it was true. He could now see far off into the tall dark trees. Though all was white under them, there was no longer any snow in the air. The sky even seemed lighter, as if the clouds had thinned somewhat and the sun was trying to poke through.

"And ... other good news, is snow has never been too deep," Stan continued, pointing down at their feet.

Billy saw the snow barely covered his ankles—only three or four inches deep, likely.

"Must've just been blowing around and not coming down," Billy answered in a voice that seemed faraway and weak to his own ears. His throat felt raspy and dry, and he realized they hadn't crossed any streams since the beginning of day.

"Is much good. Now we can make better time ... if you are up to it," Stan said. Billy noticed Stan still had the same concerned look he'd had when they got up in the morning.

Do I look that bad? he wondered, and decided he probably did. "Yes ... I am up to it," he lied.

Stan frowned at him another moment, then shrugged, turned, and continued in the direction they'd been going. Billy immediately felt the strain of Stan's increased pace and wondered how he could possibly keep up. But then he remembered what Grandfather had said about him being needed by his friends and especially the Captain. He redoubled his efforts, angry with himself for indulging in weakness and self-pity. With renewed determination he resolved to keep up with Stan for as long as it took, until his last breath, if necessary. He would only quit when he dropped dead and his heart no longer pumped blood through his body. *Thank you, Grandfather,* he whispered to the vision of warmth sitting cross-legged in the back of his mind.

ಬಿಐಐಐಐಬಿಬಿಐಐಐಬಿಬಿಐಐ

At midday, what would have been lunchtime if there'd been anything to eat, Stan called a stop. He could feel his own weariness heavily, so he knew Billy must be near the very limits of his endurance. And Stan's left arm ached and stung mercilessly from the shallow bullet wound he'd received in the battle. He could only imagine how Billy must be feeling from his much more serious wounds.

A few hours earlier they had stumbled upon a logging trail, or at least he assumed that was its purpose based on the stumps all along it. He vaguely remembered seeing it on their way uphill, now nearly a week ago. Billy would remember for sure, if he were of his right mind.

And that was now Stan's greatest concern, aside from Billy's health: his current state of mind. They sat resting a few feet apart on low stumps that Stan had cleared of snow with a swipe of his strong right arm. He gazed at Billy, trying to divine how much his friend had left to give. He had a sinking feeling it was not much more. Then ... well, then he'd just have to carry Billy, as he had before when he thought he was dead. His friend would object, of course, if he were still conscious. But what else could they do? He would never leave Billy behind. He would die first.

But now Billy did not even seem to be aware of where they were, or what they were doing. The last several times Stan had spoken, Billy had said nothing, staring back with a blank look. Could a man lose his mind, even before his body gave out? Stan had heard of such things happening to men in wars or under other extreme conditions, but he'd never seen it himself. When they'd stopped this time, Stan had to take Billy's arm, lead him to the stump, and push him down on it to sit. There'd been no recognition or acknowledgment when Stan spoke.

He could at least relieve Billy of all his burdens. Clearly in his present condition he had no need of weapons. It was hard to imagine he would even recognize an enemy if he saw one, let alone have the strength to fight.

They'd rested for a quarter of an hour when Billy seemed to revive a bit, and he looked up. He gazed across at Stan but seemed not to focus on his face. Stan smiled reassuringly, but Billy did not respond in kind. Instead he suddenly looked serious, and concerned; much different from the lethargic, drained look he'd had most of the day. He sat up, and his expression turned dark and deadly.

"No! You'll not get me without a fight!" he shouted out, rising to his feet.

"Billy ... it's me ... Stan ... I will not harm you. Sit ... rest. You are tired and wounded."

"No! No, get away!" Billy shouted, pulling out his bow and nocking an arrow. He pulled back the bow and aimed it straight at Stan's face.

"Billy ... don't do it," Stan said, holding up his hands, "it's your friend, Stan. You are not needing that ..."

But Billy ignored his pleading and let fly.

Stan flinched, but the arrow missed his head, passing just inches from his left ear. He heard the arrow impact behind him, and he heard a grunt. He spun around and saw a man with a rifle, not fifty feet away, Billy's arrow embedded in the center of his chest. The man's eyes glazed over as he slumped down into the snow, the rifle falling from lifeless hands.

Stan dropped onto his knees behind the stump he'd been sitting on, pistols already in his fists. He spotted another rifleman next to a tree a few yards beyond the first and opened fire. But he had to duck before he saw the result as a rifle bullet impacted on the top of the stump and ricocheted just over his head. He popped up and fired again, this time toward a puff of smoke rising further back in the woods.

Then he heard a pistol shot behind him, and Billy shouting, "Watch your back, they are also behind us!"

Stan immediately lay flat on his belly in the snow, and none too soon; a bullet impacted the stump again, only on his side this time. The shot had come from behind, even as Billy had warned.

"Damn it to hell!" Stan shouted, and rolled onto his back. He fired another chamber back toward where that shot had come from. He saw Billy lying prone behind his stump looking out the other direction, firing a shot at someone back that direction.

"Can't stay here, Billy! They will slaughter us like pigs in pen!"

"You lead, I will follow!" Billy shouted back.

Stan began to rise but suffered a sudden evil premonition; if he charged off into the woods to attack their enemies, Billy would *not* follow. He would spend his life to guard Stan's back. And Stan would never see his friend again in this world.

"No, Billy. This time *you* lead," he answered. Billy turned his head and their eyes locked briefly.

Billy nodded, "Okay. Let's go!" He was on his feet with a shout, firing his pistol, racing forward into the woods toward their enemies.

Stan leapt up behind him, and he too let out a great shout. He resisted the urge to look behind him and fire off a few parting shots; he knew from his army training it would be wasted effort and ammunition. Those behind must be ignored. When surrounded, one must move boldly, attacking a single point in the enemy line with all the firepower and aggression you could muster in the hope of punching through. You could only pray those behind would not react quickly enough to take you in the back.

As he raced through the trees, he squeezed off pistol rounds at any target he saw. He was surprised Billy was also moving quickly. He seemed to have revived somewhat and was fighting with renewed vigor. Stan noticed Billy holster his pistol, likely now empty, and smoothly draw out the bow once again. As quick as thinking he launched another arrow even as he ran.

A man stepped out to Stan's left, about thirty yards away, pointing a rifle. Stan aimed his left pistol and fired. The man dropped to the ground. Another appeared a little to the right. Stan aimed the pistol and *click:* empty!

"Damn it!" he spat, dodging to the side as a rifle bullet impacted the tree trunk next to him. He remembered the Captain trying to teach him the trick of counting his shots even in the thick of a fight. But he could never learn to do it, always too fired up to think on it until it was too late.

He saw another man and tried the left pistol, but it too was now empty. *"Damn, and damn,"* he cursed and holstered his pistols even as he ducked under a low tree branch. He reached up over his shoulder to grab the bow when a man stepped out from behind a tree trunk and aimed a rifle at him from only twenty yards away, Stan dove to the ground, taking a face full of snow as he did. But there was no shot, and he feared the man was now targeting him where he lay on the ground, unfortunately with no tree or stump to hide behind.

But when he looked up the man had dropped his rifle, unfired. He clutched at an arrow shaft sticking out from his belly before collapsing into the snow.

Thank you, Billy, he thought and jumped back to his feet, rushing forward.

He ran toward where the man had fallen, and Billy met him there.

"This one was the last," Billy said, dropping behind a fallen log next to the dead man and turning back to look in the direction from which they'd come. "All the others are now behind us."

Stan slid in next to him and looked back as well. He now held his bow and had nocked an arrow, though he had to admit he still felt more confident with a pistol or rifle. "Just hand me dead fellow's rifle, Billy," he said, "and thank you for feathering bastard for me. I was dead for sure this time."

But Billy returned a startled look, "What? I didn't kill him … I thought you did."

"Nyet. Have not yet loosed any arrows. You have killed so many you are forgetting."

But Billy slid over to where the dead man lay, keeping on his belly the whole way. He dug the fallen rifle from the snow, then the man's ammunition pouch and powder horn. Finally, he reached across and yanked the arrow from the man's belly. It came out with a gush of thick, dark red fluid that burned a hole in the snow.

After he'd handed Stan the rifle and ammunition, Billy examined the arrow.

He held it up to Stan, "Look, Stan ... not one of mine. See the feathers ... these are of some wild bird ... turkey maybe. Mine are all from the geese on the Captain's farm."

"Well, is not mine," Stan answered, shaking his head, and wondering if Billy was still not thinking clearly, "is not big enough, and besides, shaft is not red like mine."

But Billy continued to shake his head as he examined the arrow. Then he had a sudden thought and rubbed the blood off the arrowhead in the snow. When it was clean, he held it up, "Look! It is made of the black glass-stone! Like we Indians use out West. Mine are now all of steel from Georgie's forge."

Stan looked, and his eyes went wide; it was true!

"What in seven hells ...?" Stan said.

But just then another rifle bullet impacted on the fallen log.

Billy slipped the mystery arrow into his quiver, and said, "Time to go, Stan."

"Agreed," he answered.

They scrambled back on all fours until they were behind some covering bushes, then stood and raced off through the woods.

ಬಿಎಂಬಿಎಂಬಿ

Susan Hart carried a well-worn wooden tray loaded with four metal mugs, filled to overflowing with beer. It was an awkward and heavy burden, and she could feel the weariness in her bones. Next year she'd turn fifty, and today, like many other days, she was feeling her age. She wondered how many more years she had in her.

The house was filled with travelers this evening, not surprisingly. The weather had turned bitterly cold and icy, so

350

anyone intending to head down the mountain to visit relatives for the holiday was forced to make other arrangements. For several, that meant her house, now converted to a makeshift inn, of sorts. It was a lot of extra work, which she didn't care for, but it helped bring in extra money, which she did.

Tonight, however, the burden had been pleasantly eased by the arrival of two of her sons, Ben and Oliver, from up in Pennsylvania. She smiled at the memory of her joyful surprise when they'd showed up earlier in the day unannounced at the door. She also decided those two strong young men could carry beer mugs for the remainder of the evening and give her a rest! She smiled at the thought.

Just as she was passing the front door on the way to the sitting room, now serving as a dining hall, she heard a loud pounding on the door. Not a polite knock, but the kind of pounding that shook the door frame and made the wood creak. More like someone kicking at the door with a boot!

"Keep your britches on!" she shouted, "No need to kick the door in. I won't be a moment." She set the tray down on the small entryway table and pulled the door open.

She gasped, startled by the vision that met her. A man stood in the doorway, or rather filled it with his immense size. He was covered with frost and snow from head to toe, with tiny icicles hanging from his scruffy beard and mustache. He held something large and heavy in his arms, which had forced him to kick the door instead of knocking. At first, she couldn't tell what the thing was that he held, but then she realized it was another man, though much smaller.

"Hello, Mrs. Hart," the large man said. His voice was deep but sounded much weaker than the last time she'd heard it nearly a fortnight ago.

"Mr. Volkov! You look a fright! And is this Mr. Creek? Is he … is he …?"

"Yes, it is Billy, and no … he is *not* dead … yet. May we come in, ma'am?"

"Oh, my goodness, of course, of course! Come, there is a fire and I have a nice beef stew bubbling in the pot."

"Mmm ... stew ... yes. Food would be *most* welcome. It has been ... hmm ... many days since we have eaten."

"Oh, you poor dears," she cooed, as she ushered him into the entryway, brushing snow from his back and sleeves. She noticed the blood stain on his torn left sleeve. "My goodness, are you injured?"

"It is nothing. We are both ... hmm ... how you say? Worse for wear? Yes, we are both suffering some wear, Mrs. Hart."

"Well, there's a doctor of sorts over to Beverly. I'll send one of my sons in the morning to fetch him," she answered, frowning with concern.

"We are obliged," Stan said, while walking with her into the dining hall. As he entered the room, he nodded to Mr. Hart where he sat sipping on a beer at a long table next to several other men. Two young men standing near the fire stepped aside to let Stan through. He gently lowered Billy to the hardwood floor and laid him out next to the brick fireplace where a fire was burning brightly. The sudden, intense heat of it after days of bitter cold was almost painful.

Mrs. Hart left the room but returned a moment later with a small wool blanket, which she laid over top of Billy, and a feather pillow for under his head.

"Thank you, Mrs. Hart," Stan said, holding his frozen hands out over the fire as the ice on his beard began to melt and drip on the floor. "Now ... if you don't mind ... I was just thinking about that stew ..."

Chapter 12. Of Friendship, Love, and Enmity

"'Tis death to me to be at enmity;
I hate it, and desire all good men's love."
– William Shakespeare, Richard III

Tuesday December 24, 1861 – Rich Mountain, Virginia:

After exchanging brief introductions with the guests, Stan dove into the large, steaming bowl of stew Mrs. Hart set before him, washing it down with a mug of cold beer. He'd been at this happy task for several minutes when Joseph Hart, sitting across from him at the table smoking a cigar, surprised him by saying, "Oh ... I forgot to say it after the surprise at your arrival earlier, Volkov, but ... Happy Christmas to you!"

"Christmas?" Stan answered, looking up from his bowl.

"Why, yes ... didn't you know? Today is December twenty-fourth ... tomorrow is Christmas morning."

"Oh! I had ... lost track of days out in woods," Stan set down his spoon and sighed a heavy sigh, looking thoughtful.

"What's the matter, Volkov? You don't like Christmas?" Hart asked.

"No, I like it plenty good. It's just ... back home at farm we have been making toys for the little ones. On Christmas morning the Captain dresses in furs as Saint Nick and gives them out to children on farm," he grinned, "and I am one of his *little* helpers." He sighed again. "I am sorry I will be missing it this year."

"Ah. That does sound a right pleasant duty, all right. I can recall the excitement around here in the old days when our children were just tots. The look of joy in their bright little eyes warmed the heart, that's for certain."

"Yes ... is true," Stan said, "there is nothing like." He smiled wistfully at the thought.

Then he was surprised again when someone sat down to the right of him at the table and he looked over to see Billy wide awake, gazing up at him.

"Billy! You are alive ... again!"

"Yes ... I was lying there ... thinking about going to be with Grandfather, when I smelled that food. I think it brought me all the way back from the dead!"

Stan laughed, and pushed his bowl over in front of Billy. "Here, have mine. I have already eaten full bowl and will wait for Mrs. Hart to fetch another."

"Thanks," Billy answered, and then said no more for several minutes, busily spooning the hot meal into his eager mouth.

When Billy had finished his bowl and Stan was halfway through his second, he said, "Billy, do you think we should rest up and then try going after Walters again?"

Billy was thoughtful for a moment before answering. "No ... we have come close, but we have missed. It is our duty to return to our officers and report our failure, though I know it will gall you. Walters will move his camp. Maybe even to a different county now that he now knows the Captain is trying to kill him."

"The Captain? How will he know? Oh ... Not too many men look like you and me, I suppose. Hmm ... yes, Walters will know."

He scowled, "Yes, it galls me to return without Walters' head in sack. But you are right, Billy. We must go home and tell Captain what happened." He sighed another heavy sigh, then shrugged his broad shoulders and scooped another spoonful of stew.

ಬಿಎಂಡಿಎಂಡಿಎಂಡಿಎಂಡಿಎಂಡಿಎಂ

At noon on Christmas day Nathan received the gift he'd been praying for. A telegram was delivered to Belle Meade Farm by a rider, sent by Governor Pierpont. The envelope was addressed to "Captain Chambers, Customs House, Wheeling, Va." He immediately opened it and read:

> *Captain, found serpent but not kill. We are worse for wear but is not too bad. Staying with Harts on mountain. Will rest then come. Stan.*

Though terse and troubling, it did prove Stan and Billy were alive and safe, something the whole farm had been worried over ever since the news spread through Wheeling four days earlier of

Captain Baggs' arrival at Atheneum Prison with a boatload of secessionist prisoners, but no sign of Stan or Billy.

Nathan had grabbed his hat and hurried to the prison, but Baggs and his Snake Hunters had already deposited the prisoners and left. Nathan learned Baggs had gone with Archibald Campbell, the popular and likable editor of the *Wheeling Intelligencer*, to tell his story of the Snake Hunters' capture of the rebel bushwhackers.

By the time Nathan arrived at the newspaper office he had worked himself into a state of great agitation, and had to pause and calm himself with a force of will before speaking with Baggs.

But the tale Baggs told had turned Nathan's anxiety to wrath at the former's admission he'd refused to aid Stan and Billy even after they'd fought for him on several occasions.

Baggs, though not one to be intimidated, accepted Nathan's angry chastisement with humility, if little shame. "Look, Chambers, I get your ire. If it'd been two o' my boys I'd be lathered into a froth as well. But I had my own men to consider; the weather had taken a bad, cruel turn and the fellas was pert-near worn to the bone. And we was damned near out o' supplies and ammunition. In need o' rest and refittin', as they say. Did offer to help your boys hunt the jasper down come spring, but they wasn't buyin' what I was sellin'. So, I fear they headed out on their own to track down the varmint. Heard they was headin' east over to Buckhannon way, but after that ...?" he shrugged.

The worry over Stan and Billy had put a damper on the Christmas Eve celebration, with Nathan refusing Miss Abbey's half-hearted offer to sing Christmas carols despite their lack of a piano. Instead, he'd turned in early, even forgoing his usual glass—or two—of whiskey. Between growing anxiety over his missing men, and the holiday bringing his aching longing for Evelyn to the fore, he'd ended the day in a foul mood.

On Christmas morning it had been all he could do to perform the task that'd been so happy and joyful just a year earlier: dressing in furs as St. Nick and handing out handmade gifts to the little children on the farm. The whole time he was doing it, he couldn't help thinking about Stan's booming, joyful laughter and beaming smile at the sight of the little children's wide-eyed pleasure. The fear of never hearing that sound again triggered a painful knot in his stomach.

Now that he'd read the telegram, confirming his men were alive, he felt like he could finally breathe again. But he still worried about their condition. If the indomitable Stan admitted that they were "worse for wear," it was likely they were in pretty bad shape. Nathan immediately dispatched William, with all his medical gear, to the rail station to catch the first train out of town headed to Rich Mountain.

He sent Georgie and Jamie with William to assist and escort as needed. Nathan was itching to go himself, enduring a great measure of guilt for sending Billy and Stan off on their own to — presumably — nearly get themselves killed. But Nathan had already made a commitment to accompany General Rosecrans and his staff to Washington City the day after Christmas to sell their spring campaign plans to General McClellan — a meeting Nathan was *not* looking forward to.

 ₧⚭₧⚭₧⚭₧⚭₧⚭₧⚭

As William hurriedly packed his gear, preparing to depart for the train station, he heard a soft knock on the doorframe of the small apartment that served as the bunkhouse for the soldiers on the new farm. He looked up and immediately stood, as Margaret entered the room.

"Margaret! I was just going to come see you and wish you goodbye once I'd packed all my gear. I assume you've heard the good news about Billy and Stan?"

"Yes ..." she replied, but her face didn't reflect the joy that was currently surging through William's veins. He was puzzled at first, and then it hit him; in the telegram Stan had admitted their failure to kill Walters. In his joy at the news of his friends' survival, he'd not given much thought to the negative side of the story and how it might affect Margaret.

He stepped up to her, placed his hands on her shoulders and looked into her eyes. "I ... I'm sorry, my dear ... that they weren't successful ..." he faltered, struggling for something to say.

356

She nodded and offered up a wan smile before tearing up. He returned the smile hesitantly, feeling sheepish and inadequate, wracking his brain for what words might ease her suffering. But she stepped up and leaned into him, wrapping her arms around his chest. She buried her head against him and sobbed. He held her gently and decided there was really no need for words after all.

ᴤᴑᴤᴑᴄᴙᴄᴤᴤᴑᴤᴑᴄᴙᴄᴤᴤᴑᴤᴑᴄᴙᴄᴤ

But aside from continued concern over Walters, the good news about Stan and Billy gave Belle Meade Farm a sudden burst of joy and good feelings that'd been sorely lacking even the night before.

Miss Abbey sat in the library sipping tea when Megs entered, smiling brightly. Abbey readily returned the smile assuming Megs, like her, was now finally able to relax and belatedly enjoy the holiday. In addition to the general anxiety and uneasiness of the situation, the two women's relationship had felt somehow strained and odd lately, ever since Megs had asked for things to be more like they'd been before her freedom. It had put Abbey in an uncomfortable position that she'd still not completely reconciled.

But Megs surprised her by handing her an envelope.

"What's this?" Abbey asked.

"It's my Happy Christmas gift to you, Abbey," Megs answered, continuing to beam.

"Oh! Megs, how thoughtful, though I've not gotten you a gift ... nor anyone else for that matter. What with all the worrying over the men ..."

"Don't you fret 'bout that none, dear. I ain't bought you nothin' either. It's just something I've been thinkin' on, and ... well, after the good news today it just seemed like a good occasion to put the idea to paper and make a gift of it."

"Well, now you have me curious," Abbey said, and pulled the letter from its envelope.

Dear Abbey,

My Christmas gift to you is a new flower garden, here at Belle Meade Farm. Though maybe not so grand nor glorious as yours was back at M M, it may serve.

This one will not be built of slave labor, but the labor of love. And if you are willing, you and I will plan this garden together, and then plant it, along with any other of the women on the farm who wish to help of their free will.

Your loving friend and sister of the heart,

Megs

Miss Abbey wiped tears from her eyes, then leaned over and embraced her lifelong friend, whispering, "Thank you, dear. Thank you ever so much. This is the nicest gift anyone has ever given me."

"You're welcome. I was ... trying to think of something we could do together ... as equals, but with you knowing so much more of the flowers and such that it will feel ... I don't know ... *natural* I guess, for you to take the lead on it, and me to happily do the work."

Abbey smiled at her as the tears flowed again, "I knew there was a reason I have always loved you so ..."

And once again they embraced.

☙ℰℐℭଔ☙ℰℐℭଔ☙ℰℐℭଔ

Tony and his normal group of friends were in the classroom having their usual chat when the news of the telegram from Stan reached them; one of the young boys slipped his head in at the door and shouted it out at them in great excitement.

Tony was a little surprised at their spontaneous reaction when he thought on it after. They'd all leapt to their feet, shaking hands, embracing, and generally behaving as if they'd just received a miraculous and unexpected Christmas gift, which in fact they had.

He'd not really thought until that moment, about how attached he'd become to the men the Captain had brought from

Texas. He no longer thought of them as "white men," likely because they never treated him as a "black man." It had been a subtle change that'd occurred over time, to where he now thought of them all as fellow workers and soldiers: *the Captain's men.*

By their joyful reaction, he assumed Big George, Henry, Cobb, Phinney—and even Ned—were feeling the same.

In the midst of their celebration, he saw Rosa standing at the door, looking in. She smiled when he saw her.

"Hello, Rosa. Come on in," he said, returning her smile.

"Hello, Tony ... fellas. Just wanted to make sure you'd heard the good news. From the looks on your faces, I'd say 'yes.'"

"Yeah, one o' the boys just told us."

Henry looked from Rosa's face to Tony's and smiled. He turned to the others, "Come on, fellas. Let's leave these two to talk while's we go see what the Captain hisself has to say about Mr. Stan's telegram." The others looked at Henry, then over at Tony and Rosa, and got his gist. They all headed out the door, still laughing and chatting animatedly.

"It's wonderful news, ain't it, Tony? Mr. Stan is always such a happy, jolly man—the thought of him bein' hurt or worse ... it was just awful to think on. And even Billy, odd as he is ... grows on you after a time, once you get used to his ways and see he really is a kindly man underneath."

"Yep ... I was feelin' the same. It's surprising how much them being gone was bringin' the whole farm low. But now ..."

"Now ..." she gazed into his eyes with an odd, unreadable look.

He returned her gaze, with a curious expression.

Then she suddenly flashed him a smile, leaned up and kissed him on the lips.

His eyes went wide, and she must have thought his expression comical, as she laughed then said, "Happy Christmas, Tony," then turned and strolled away.

He stood where he was, mouth agape. He slowly reached up and touched his lips where she had just kissed him, and he whispered, "Happy Christmas, Rosa."

Tuesday December 31, 1861 – Thibodaux, Louisiana:

Adilida and Edouard sat on the veranda looking out over the vast yard of his house, overhung with great trees, their long Spanish moss beards swaying gently in the soft breeze. Though it was New Year's Eve, the weather was mild and warm. Adilida had already put the baby to bed, and was now enjoying relaxing with a splash of warmed cognac as Edouard sipped his whiskey.

As she set her glass down, she sighed.

"What is it, my dear?" he asked.

"Oh, nothing, Uncle. I was just thinking tonight means the end of a whole year in which I have been parted from my love. It is a very melancholy thought, and puts a damper on any celebrating."

"Yes, I can see that, my dear. But think of it not as the end of an unhappy year but rather as the start of a *new* year which may see you two reunited."

She smiled, "Yes … I hadn't thought of it that way. Thank you, Uncle. That *is* a much happier thought."

"You're welcome. And besides … this past year was not *all* bad … even as we two sit outside on this veranda, inside this house lives and breathes a true miracle … a fine strong boy such as we never would have imagined possible only a short time ago."

She gazed up and him and smiled. Reaching out she grasped his arm, leaned into him, and squeezed as tears rolled down her cheeks.

Tuesday December 31, 1861 – Richmond, Virginia:

Evelyn poked at the logs on the fire, then settled back into her chair. She picked up her glass of brandy and took another sip. She'd started the evening with a warmed glass, but after the first one was empty, she hadn't bothered with those that had followed. And now she couldn't remember if she'd refilled the glass three times or four. She was feeling a bit tipsy and feared her head would punish her in the morning, but at the moment she didn't care.

She had begged off the numerous invitations to celebrate, including one from Angeline Hughes, which likely would've been extravagant and elegant well beyond the norm. But she just couldn't bring herself to celebrate the way she was feeling tonight. New Year's Eve meant a whole year of being separated from Nathan; a year in which she'd seen him but one time, and that under extremely uncomfortable circumstances.

She took another sip. Ironically, the more confident and self-assured she felt in her new, clandestine role, the more she missed Nathan, knowing the thing that had initially kept them apart, her lack of self-esteem and confidence, was now all but gone. It had been months since she'd heard that odd little voice in her head asking, *Who am I?* Now she no longer had to ponder that question. Now, only the war and her responsibilities in it were keeping her away from Nathan.

And ... oh, how I love him! How can I continue living without him? How can I possibly endure another year like this one? Or even another day?

But if we were together right now ... what then? The war would still rage. We'd both feel compelled to fight, each in our own way. Is our bond to each other strong enough to resist such a powerful, terrible force drawing us apart? I ... just don't know.

But in the back-and-forth battle between her head and her heart, the heart was not yet ready to concede the fight. As she leaned back in her chair and closed her eyes, Nathan's face appeared to her mind's eye, clear and sharp. His dark, intense eyes, his lean handsome face, the power and strength in him seemed to almost illuminate his features ... and yet there was also a kindness and gentleness there, a soft, warm, emotional side that was not afraid to cry at a happy thought or a sad tale. She leaned forward to kiss his lips, and jerked awake, spilling her drink. She wiped ineffectually at the spill on her dress, then leaned back and indulged in a good, long cry until she drifted off into a dreamless sleep.

Tuesday December 31, 1861 – Washington, D.C.:

"So ... earlier you were saying that General McClellan has finally scheduled a meeting for tomorrow with General Rosecrans and his staff?" Tom asked. "I assume you are still planning on attending ..."

"Yes, and yes—though I still think it's a bad idea. McClellan and I don't see eye to eye—never have, as you well know. I have a bad feeling about this ... like it could easily backfire and work against Rosecrans, and I've told him so—several times. But he won't hear of it, and insists I attend. I think he's nervous about the meeting and wants my support."

"Surely you don't think McClellan would turn down the plan just to spite you?"

Nathan leaned back in his chair, pulled out a cigar, stuck it in his mouth and chewed on it a moment before responding.

"Tom ... my old friend, Stonewall Jackson, has proven himself a formidable foe ... my mentor General Lee is still a force to be reckoned with ... and we dare not discount our old nemesis Henry Wise. But in my opinion the general who poses the biggest threat to the Union Army right now is ... *Major General George B. McClellan!*"

Tom laughed and nodded, taking another sip of his whiskey.

They were sitting at a small table watching couples dance on the other side of the room. A string quartet played accompaniment from the far end of the hall, which was one reason Nathan had chosen this table, it being a bit quieter, allowing he and Tom to converse.

General Rosecrans had invited them to this event knowing they would otherwise likely spend New Year's Eve alone in their boarding house, as they knew very few people in Washington City. A number of mid-ranking government officials, Army officers, their spouses, and young adult daughters were in attendance. Conspicuous in their absence were any eligible young men; those not already off fighting or training with the regiments would've been ashamed to make an appearance for fear of being labeled cowards or shirkers.

General Rosecrans and his staff had attended as well, and for several hours Nathan and Tom had enjoyed their company, especially the ever-entertaining Captain Leib. But the officers had excused themselves and retired an hour earlier, leaving the duo to fend for themselves.

Nathan and Tom were still feeling the afterglow of the good news about Stan and Billy, bolstered by regular updates on their condition—which was steadily improving—via telegrams from William. William had confirmed that their wounds, though serious, were not life-threatening, and that they should soon be on the mend. They were expected to be well enough to travel within the next few days, which would make for a very joyous homecoming.

As they sat, Tom noticed Nathan had a thoughtful, faraway look, and decided he'd risk broaching the subject foremost on his mind, "This is reminding me of the event we attended back in Richmond, sir."

"Yes ... I was just thinking the same," Nathan answered, then sighed. "But I believe I'll be better able to keep my temper in check this time." He offered up a wan smile.

Tom nodded and raised his glass, before taking another sip. Then he found his own mind wandering, contemplating what Adilida might be doing at this very moment ... wondering if she was also thinking of him. He chose to believe so, and silently wished her all his love and best compliments for the New Year. And he prayed it would be the last one they ever spent apart.

Nathan's mind was wandering down similar paths, wondering which of the many lavish Richmond New Year's balls Evelyn might be attending. But he suspected wherever she was, and whomever she was with, she would be spending at least a portion of the time thinking of him and ... missing him.

"Tom ... I'm choosing to think this coming year will bring good things. That somehow, some way, in the midst of all this war and chaos, we will find a way to reunite with our beloved ladies."

Tom nodded, raised his glass and said, "To Evelyn and Adilida ... may God bless them and keep them safe ... and bring them swiftly back into our arms."

Nathan raised his glass in answer, "Amen, Tom. Amen to that. To Adilida and Evelyn."

They clinked glasses and had another swallow.

\<End of Book 5\>

If you enjoyed *Insurrection,*
please post a review.

PREVIEW:

INVASION
ROAD TO THE BREAKING BOOK 6

The impromptu train-car meeting was winding down when the door on the back end of the car suddenly burst open, and a thin, baby-faced lieutenant stepped in, immediately coming to attention and snapping a salute at General Lander. "Pardon the intrusion general!" he said, between gasps for breath.

"Never mind that, Lieutenant; what is it?" Lander answered, returning the salute, but remaining seated.

"Sir, a scout has just arrived at the gallop from Bath. He reports the rebels have reached the town, and the remnants of our garrison are engaging them as ordered. But they are vastly outnumbered, and Lieutenant Adams, who was left in command, sends you a message that he means to attempt a fighting retreat to slow the enemy's advance, but he expects the enemy to flank him and likely he'll soon be cut off from escape."

Lander nodded his head, then gazed down toward the floor and sighed. For a moment no one spoke. Then Lander sprang to his feet. Nathan could see a look of fire and determination in the young general's eyes.

"Then we shall not forget their sacrifice, and shall strive to ensure that it has not been in vain. Lieutenant, spread the word among our officers; there is no time to lose. We must be across the Potomac and our bridge dismantled before Jackson and his rebels arrive, and they are now less than five miles away."

"Sir!" the lieutenant snapped another salute, then turned and raced out the door.

Then Lander turned to Nathan and Rosecrans and said, "Though my exodus is now all the more urgent, I fear you gentlemen may be in grave peril; the rail line heads south from here and passes within two miles or so of Bath. It is only a matter of time before Jackson destroys the tracks in the entire area. If he thinks to do it before completing his conquest of Bath and of

Hancock, you may be cut off and at his mercy. Perhaps you should debark, along with all the companies on this train and join us in crossing over the river to Hancock. You are certainly welcome, and I would find your presence a great comfort and a blessing in this hour of need."

Rosecrans and Nathan met eyes for a moment, then Rosecrans turned to Lander and said, "Thank you General ... that is most gracious of you. But my place now is back at Wheeling organizing what's left of my department to defend that city. Should Jackson continue west, we must do all in our power to stop him from reaching Wheeling, or I fear the new state will be doomed."

Then Nathan said, "I too have urgent obligations back at Wheeling. We will take our chances with the train, General. Hopefully our friend Stonewall will be focused on the fight and won't give thought to the railroad until after."

Lander nodded his head, then reached out to shake hands with Rosecrans, and then Nathan. "I pray you're right, Mr. Chambers. General ... it has been a pleasure, sir, but I must now urge you to tarry no longer. And Mr. Chambers ... I look forward to seeing you in uniform when next we meet, ideally with a couple of gold stars on each of your shoulders," Nathan smiled and nodded, but could think of nothing to say in response to that; there wasn't time for a lengthy explanation, and anything abrupt would seem disingenuous. So he just said, "Thank you General, and good luck to you."

"Godspeed, gentlemen," Lander said, then turned and strode out the door, his staff officers fast on his heels.

Even as Lander was exiting the back door, Captain Hartsuff was heading for the front. As he reached for the door, he turned back to General Rosecrans and said, "Already on it, sir. Train will be moving again post haste."

"Good. And pass the word throughout the train—all soldiers, and all other able-bodied men, are to arm themselves, load their weapons, and prepare for battle."

Acknowledgments

I'd like to thank Gay Petersen and Leslie Johns for assisting in the writing and editing of *Insurrection*, including reading the beta version and providing invaluable feedback.

And special thanks to my editor, Ericka McIntyre, who keeps me honest and on track, and my proofreader Travis Tynan, who makes sure everything is done correctly!

And, last but not least (at all!), the experts at New Shelves Books; my trusted advisor on all things "bookish," Keri-Rae Barnum, and the guru Amy Collins!

Recommended Reading

Apparently, **Captain Charles Leib**, who like his commander General Rosecrans was a real, non-fictional person, took Miss Abbey's advice in chapter eight to heart and decided to write a book about his experiences as a quartermaster in the Union Army during the war. His book title reflects a humorous jab at his political enemies who managed to get him removed from his posting after accusing him of embezzling a million dollars from the government. Like his dinnertime stories in *Insurrection* (some of which are borrowed straight from his book) his narrative is highly entertaining and gives one a good flavor of the chaos and difficulty of the job. See *Nine Months in the Quartermaster's Department; or The Chances of Making a Million,* by Charles Leib, late Captain and Assistant Quartermaster, US Army, copyright 1862.

The Seventh (West) Virginia was one of the foremost regiments in the Union army by the end of the war. Although I have added fictional characters and have used some degree of literary license in the description and timing of certain activities, the war record of the regiment is factual. For an excellent nonfiction narrative detailing the creation, men, and war action of the actual **Seventh (West) Virginia Volunteer Infantry Regiment**, see *The Seventh West Virginia Infantry – An Embattled Union Regiment from the Civil War's Most Divided State*, by David W. Mellot and Mark A. Snell.

GET EXCLUSIVE FREE CONTENT

The most enjoyable part of writing books is talking about them with readers like you. In my case that means all things related to *Road to the Breaking*—the story and characters, themes, and concepts. And of course, Civil War history in general, and West Virginia history in particular.

If you sign up for my mailing list, you'll receive some free bonus material I think you'll enjoy:

- A fully illustrated **Road to the Breaking Fact vs. Fiction Quiz.** Test your knowledge of history with this short quiz on the people, places, and things in the book (did they really exist in 1860, or are they purely fictional?)

- **Cut scenes from** *Road to the Breaking.* One of the hazards of writing a novel is word and page count. At some point you realize you need to trim it back to give the reader a faster-paced, more engaging experience. However, now you've finished reading the book, wouldn't you like to know a little more detail about some of your favorite characters? Here's your chance to take a peek behind the curtain!

- I'll occasionally put out a **newsletter with information about the Road to the Breaking Series**—new book releases, news and information about the author, etc. I promise not to inundate you with spam (it's one of my personal pet peeves, so why would I propagate it?)

To sign up, visit my website:
http://www.ChrisABennett.com

ROAD TO THE BREAKING SERIES: